SWIPE *Me*

Ana Shay

Cover Illustrations by Elen Bushe

Cover Design by Regan Kindrick

Editing by My Brother's Editor

Copyright © 2024 by Ana Shay

All rights reserved.

To all the Tinder dates I never had.

ONE

Devin

"Here we go again." I sighed, parking outside my house. I could already hear the music blaring, and I couldn't believe that we were still throwing parties to celebrate our win over a month later.

Rose Bowl Champions.

You'd think we'd won the national championship the way this team was celebrating. Yes, the win had thrust us straight into the sights of draft scouts, but if we wanted to get to the NFL or be taken seriously as contenders for next year, we needed to keep focused.

I dusted off my worn-out jeans and rested my head against the back seat as I stared at the house. The lights were on, and I could see the shadows of my teammates in the windows. No doubt, they were pulling beers and smoking cigars, and the idea of going in there made me sick.

Alcohol made me sick. The mere scent of it was just a reminder of everything I'd left at home.

Closing my eyes, I tried to center myself with the techniques that yoga teacher tried to teach us, but it was useless. No amount of ocean breathing, or whatever she called it, would help. My brain was relentless and kept going back to the last time I saw my sister, Chloe. Her doe eyes were highlighted by the stains of mascara running down her cheeks as she begged my mother to let her stay, who was too pissed off to even look at her daughter.

Suddenly, all the tension I felt that day came rushing back to me, like it was seeping into my veins, and questions I'd asked myself were playing on repeat.

Why couldn't my life be simple like Aiden's? Why couldn't my family be perfect like Adam's? Why couldn't I just let all the memories of my family go for one night? Why? Why? Why?

"Damn it!" I yelled, banging my hand against the steering wheel in frustration.

BANG! BANG! BANG!

Pain ricocheted through my arm, and finally, my brain stopped. Too focused on the searing agony I caused myself. Red lumps flamed across my wrist, and I had no doubts it would bruise.

"Stupid," I chastised myself, rubbing the injury like it would do anything. Having the most sacks won't be of any use if I can't play again. I couldn't hurt myself. Not now. If I did, I'd have no chance of making it into the NFL, and then I'd have no chance of saving them.

Four more months.

That's all it was. Four more months until the NFL draft. Since I was a junior, I was eligible, and I'd already informed Coach that I was putting myself forward. He was supportive when I told him and thought I was good enough to get drafted now; if not, at least I'd still have another shot next year. All that mattered to me was getting that rookie contract as soon as possible because then I'd have enough money to move my mom and sister to whichever state I ended up in, and we could start fresh. My sister would have a new life, away from all her grief and those bad influences.

Cheers echoed down the street from inside the house. I sighed, thinking about the smile I've got to plaster on my face tonight. If Aiden's dad didn't own this place and the rent wasn't so cheap, I would never have considered staying in a house with a bunch of my teammates. Now that it's the offseason, it's party central most weekends, and I'm just not that guy. I need to stay focused because this could be my one and only shot at getting into the NFL. Playing another year of college ball meant risking another injury, which was a serious possibility since I'm a defensive end. I couldn't blow this.

I walked to the front door with my pearly-white teeth on display. The team thought I was out studying. Hell, they might have even believed that I was out banging some chick. I didn't care. I let them think what they wanted to because I didn't want any of them to know what was really going on back home. I didn't want to be pitied. I'd come too far and worked too hard for that.

As I opened the door, the team cheered my entrance. There were at least twenty players sprawled out throughout the open-plan kitchen and living room. Some were on the sectional, others were lounging on the kitchen counter, and a few were playing pool. Even though it was a tight squeeze, this was a regular weekend for us.

"Hey guys," I said to no one in particular, hoping I could sneak into my room with no one noticing.

A beer was shoved into my face, and the hand holding it was connected to my best friend, Adam. The cold glass tickled my palm as I pretended to take a large swig, wiping my mouth as I pulled the bottle away. If I didn't drink, there would be more questions. Ones that I didn't want to answer. The bitter taste of the beer sat on my lips as a reminder of what I needed to do. Stay focused.

"Devin! Just who we've been waiting for." Aiden, the owner of the house and our sophomore starting quarterback, smirked. His hand slid through his jet-black hair, and his voice commanded the room when he spoke. He was the very definition of a leader without having to try hard. Draping his arm around me, he leaned in. "We were about to start another competition, but we obviously had to wait for you."

He was met with a crescendo of grunts, scoffs, and coughs as I rolled my eyes. For a guy who was the face of our team, he had way too much time on his hands. He was also a child in an adult's body, still mildly obsessed with bets and pranks. Every Saturday, he had a new bet going, which usually involved the female student body in some form or another. Tonight was no different, and I could only imagine what he had planned.

His giant paw smacked my shoulder. "These ball sacks think they can get more pussy than me on Covey Connections." He barked out a laugh as he looked around the team with disgust. "So, that means we're going to play a little game to prove them wrong."

He had this crazy look in his eyes. The only other time I'd seen it was when he came up with a "brilliant" prank to pull on our next-door neighbors. He wanted us to hide in their closets while they were in class and then jump out while they slept. It was creepy and criminal. To this day, I'm still not sure who he ended up convincing to do that prank with him. Personally, I think it was just an excuse to see our neighbor, Lyss, in bed. The guy had a serious hard-on for her; he just seemed too chicken shit to admit it.

Every member of the team was holding their phone, which was nothing unusual. What *was* unusual were the bored expressions they were throwing Aiden's way. If he wasn't captain, I swore none of us would entertain his antics.

"You're going to need to create a profile with a new name and no reference to the football team on it," Matty, one of my other roommates, explained. He had the same bored expression as everyone else with his phone in hand; only his surprised me. He'd been dating this psycho, Olana, for over a year. If she caught wind of this, she'd bite his balls off and feed them to her pet ferret, Fred. Yes, she was a college student with a ferret, and it was one of the main reasons we hardly saw her. Aiden didn't allow pets. A rule he made the day he saw her sauntering into the kitchen, wearing the thing around her neck like a scarf.

"Chop, chop. Get your phone out." Aiden clapped, looking at me pointedly.

Digging into my jeans, I followed his orders. Aiden watched over me as I spent the next ten minutes creating an account and a profile for myself. I put the least amount of effort possible into it and picked a picture of me working out, holding a set of dumbbells with my shirt off for the main profile. When I originally posted it, it got a lot of likes, so it had to be a good one. Since I didn't have time to write up a whole new personality, I just put Cole Walker as the name, leaving my first name out.

Aiden looked around the room, satisfied, and shouted, "Alright, ladies, you've got ten minutes to make as much of an impression as you can with as many pussies as possible." His vile words were ignored by everyone, I assumed, because they all just wanted to get this over and done with as quickly as possible. "Go."

I took my time leisurely swiping through the girls. Everyone else was frantically moving their thumbs across the screen, hoping to win. What were they trying to win? I didn't know, but since Aiden declared it, we had to go with it. I was left asking myself why I couldn't be so carefree again. I had no desire to even try to win this game. I'd swiped a few times without looking, but as I glanced back down at my phone, a face appeared that made me stop in my tracks.

Her big brown eyes looked like chocolate peanut butter cups, and her pink lips were luscious and plump like cushions against her glowing caramel skin. I liked everything I saw.

Who is this girl?

Going entirely against strategy, I checked out her bio to see if I could find out more. There wasn't much on there. Just her name, Reign, and a statement. *"Not looking for a Prince, just a one Knight stand."* That was more forward and cornier than my grandma's cornbread, but I didn't hate it. It wasn't like I was looking for anything serious, either.

Thumbing through her photos, she had the usual dating app pictures. The first one was of her on the beach showing off her toned, hot body. The girl looked tiny but perfectly proportioned. The next one made me smile. She was sitting with a dog, snuggled by a fire, looking so cozy that I wanted to jump right in and join her. Another swipe and there was the generic duck selfie photo all girls do, but hers was different. She was the first girl to ever make it look hot. Plump, pouty, and kissable lips filled my screen, and I needed to know more.

Frowning when I got to the final picture, I thumbed up and down the profile to see if I'd missed anything. There was barely enough information on her to get an accurate picture, but I had this nagging need in the pit of my stomach that I knew wouldn't go away until I met her.

Did I just think that?

Shaking my head, I stopped that thought. For the last two and a half years, I'd had one cardinal rule to live by: no girlfriends. It's worked perfectly. Half the time, girls didn't want to get to know me; they just wanted to come to our house parties or say they'd screwed a football player. I couldn't lie; I'd taken advantage of it before. It wasn't like I had time to wine and dine a chick, what with trying to keep my scholarship and family intact, all the while playing good enough football to be considered for the draft.

"Dude." Adam elbowed me. "Who are you looking at? You've got this dazed look on your face," he joked, peering over, trying to get a better look at my phone.

Snatching it away, I turned my screen off and glared back, hoping he didn't see her. I wanted to keep this little diamond to myself. Who was I kidding? A little ball of anger radiated in my chest as I looked around the room at all the other guys. She probably came up in all of their searches. They could have matched with her too. I dropped my eyes, skittering my gaze between their phones, watching the rapid pace of their thumbs. My only potential saving grace was that they'd all been swiping so fast; they hopefully didn't stop to take notes on the brunette goddess with the molten eyes.

"Nothing. just got a text from my sister," I lied, shoving my phone into my jeans.

"Time's up, gentlemen! Stop your thumbs." Aiden looked around the room, glaring at us until all the phones were out of our hands. "We will meet back here in twenty-four hours to see who has the most matches," he called as everyone relaxed back into their own conversations, forgetting about his game.

It was stupid anyway. How was he going to monitor everyone once they left this room? Someone could go home and swipe until they have no fingerprints, and he wouldn't know. But we all knew that Aiden wasn't the smartest crayon in the box; he was just good at keeping them color-coordinated.

Settling down on one of the barstools in the kitchen, I watched the second half of the basketball game with the guys and my lukewarm beer. It was a good game, but not good enough to stop my mind from wandering back to that girl with the plump lips and chocolate eyes. I wanted another look, just to make sure I remembered her face correctly. I'd have to wait until later to check, though, since I didn't want anyone to find out. Unfortunately, that didn't stop the itching in my fingers.

I brought the beer to my lips, pretending to take another swig, and a tiny amount of the liquid seeped through. My gut churned, and I worked extra hard to hide my reaction. As much as I wanted to sneak away, I knew it wasn't the right time. The game only just started, and I knew my teammates. They would stay until the end.

This was going to be a long night.

A few hours after the game had finished, players had broken off into groups, which gave me the perfect opportunity to excuse myself.

Climbing the stairs to freedom, I opened the door to my small but perfectly proportioned room. No one else wanted it, but I liked it. It wasn't like I needed much, just a place to sleep and study. Thankfully, Aiden cut me a deal with the rent since it was half the size of the others, and I was grateful for that, because the less debt I had on my credit card, the better.

I collapsed down onto my black bedsheets and looked around my empty room. No one could see what I was doing; I was alone in here, but I still waited for the hall to go quiet before pulling my phone out and going straight to the Covey Connections app. My fingers tingled with anticipation, hoping she was still on my screen and I hadn't accidentally swiped her away. The last time I was this excited was Christmas when I was nine and my dad got me my first football. It was pathetic but thrilling all at the same time.

My face beamed when I saw her dark eyes on my screen. Deep and intense. I studied her face a while longer, looking for any imperfections. Something that would make her seem more real and less perfect. Her skin was smooth, but I could see the texture, which meant she hadn't edited the photo. Her smile was straight, white, and perfectly proportioned to the rest of her face. Nope. I couldn't find it. This girl was absolutely perfect in my eyes, and the fact that I couldn't find out any more information about her only made me more determined.

I nearly jumped out of my bed when I heard rustling outside my door, worried that someone would find me obsessing over this girl like Gollum and the ring. Swiping right, I quickly closed the app and tossed my phone onto the comforter next to me. If anyone opened that door right now, they'd just see me staring at my ceiling, not drooling over someone I'd never met.

When the feet passed my room without a knock, I slowly let my breath out, feeling ridiculous that I was sneaking around on a dating app. Something I'd never admit to anyone.

Lying there, listening to the rumblings of my roommates, I considered opening the app again, just to look at her face one more time to make sure I pictured it correctly. But that would be creepy, right? Besides, I guessed that since I swiped right, she wouldn't show up unless she matched with me.

God, I hope she matched with me.

It was pathetic how much a couple of pictures had riled up something inside me that no girl in the flesh had since I started here at Covey U. With every chime of my phone, I felt my teeth clench and fingers tap, hoping it was her. Each time, I was mildly disappointed when it was someone else.

I didn't let it dampen my hope. Patience was one of my key attributes, or so the draft scouts would have you believe. I knew when to wait and when to strike. I may not be interested in a girlfriend, but there was something about this girl that I knew made her worth the hit.

Two

Reign

My hands fidgeted. My body moved from side to side, squeaking against the plastic seat covers. Why was I so nervous? It was just a date. I snorted and then looked around the bar, hoping no one heard that. *Could this really be classified as a date?* Did one night of agreeing to bump uglies count?

I rolled my eyes, wondering what my mother would think about this. She was probably rolling in her grave right now, looking down on me with disappointment. This kind of thing was beyond her Southern comforts and certainly not something she'd believe her sweet daughter would do, but it wasn't like I had a choice at this point.

It'd been months, and I had *needs*. Needs that were too hard to fix on my own.

I glanced around the tables, frowning as I watched friends laugh and lovers kiss. They all looked so happy and carefree. I remembered when I used to feel those emotions. When I used to wake up so happy that it felt like bubbles were popping in my stomach, and I couldn't wait to start the day. Now, I was lucky if I could haul myself out of bed in the morning. I'd been so devoid of energy and emotion these last few months that I'd almost forgotten what it felt like to have them at all. I'd been trying to get my lust for life back for four years now, and I thought I finally had it with Clay. Too bad that ended worse than a fart in a spacesuit.

He was the sole reason I was here in the first place. I needed to start fresh, and that meant leaving Louisiana and coming back to California, my home state. It all sounded idyllic at first. Come back, see old friends, start a new life. Unfortunately for me, all my friends had moved on to colleges out of state, and I was stuck at Covey U without a friend or a decent living situation.

I was in a funk. That much was obvious, but I needed to get out of it. Life was too short for wallowing in my own self-pity, after all. So, I thought about what I could do that would liven things up. Meet a guy, but *don't* date him. That sounded novel and not something I'd usually do, but I wanted to be daring, and if Cole really looked like his picture, well, then I was in for a treat. I mean, honestly, I have never seen rippling biceps and washboard abs close up before. I couldn't stop thinking about that one photo on his profile where the veins in his arms were bulging out because he was lifting a weight heavier than a truck.

Yeah, Cole was exactly what I needed.

I'd gotten bored with all those fake romantic dates on *The Bachelor*. Don't get me wrong, I still loved the show, but all those sickeningly sweet, daringly romantic moments that I watched alone in my room had me craving something more authentic. More carnal. More *Cole*. Animalistic, brawny sex with a guy who I'd never see again.

Something that felt a bit like excitement trickled down my spine, and I wanted to see it through because maybe this would finally be the night I got my itch well and truly scratched.

After checking the time on my phone, I was starting to get nervous. He was ten minutes late. Ten minutes. Who arrives late for guaranteed sex? My mind couldn't help but wonder if this was all one big troll and Cole didn't exist. He did look way too hot to be real. But then I thought about something even worse. What if he had walked in, saw me, and turned straight around? I would be mortified if he canceled on me.

My heels and toes tapped against the concrete floor as I desperately tried to force all of that nervous energy to the ground.

Fifteen minutes went by.

Right.

I couldn't sit any longer. I needed to get some air before I screamed. I pushed out the barstool, and just as the tips of my heels hit the floor, a deep Southern accent stopped me in my tracks.

"Hey, darlin'."

His voice was much thicker than Clay's and not what I was expecting in our Northern California college. It was commanding and masculine and already had me melting into a puddle of goo at his feet.

Hot *and* Southern? I didn't know if I could handle this.

Taking a chance, I let my eyes travel from his well-worn Timberlands to his faded, ripped jeans. He was already perfect, and I hadn't gotten past his belt buckle. My mouth went dry as I took in the tight black shirt that stretched across his broad chest.

Was there drool coming out of my mouth? Because I felt something trickling down my face. Maybe it was sweat. I didn't know what was worse.

When I'd finally garnered enough courage to look at his face, I choked back a nervous laugh. His chiseled bone structure was striking, and his hazel eyes were everything. Why on earth was this guy on a dating app? Surely, he had girls lining up to climb him like a tree. What was the catch?

"Hey," I drawled out, trying not to fumble my words. "It's Cole, right?" I said as casually as I could, pretending I hadn't stared at that gym selfie of him last night like it was my newest reality show binge. I still couldn't believe he was here for a hookup with me. *DATE.* I meant *date.* Although, that really sounded unbelievable looking at him now. He clearly didn't date. Just slept around.

Cole gave me a slow nod, and my goodness, he could literally breathe, and I would find it sexy. "Yeah, and you're Reign," he stated, shoving his hands in the pockets of his jeans, leaning forward on his heels. I shook my head a little too vigorously and gave him an overeager smile, but he returned it, nonetheless.

Then it got bad.

The awkward silence grew louder and louder until it was thrumming in my head to say something.

What was I supposed to say, though?

We'd both agreed this would be a one-night stand, so should we just go to my place, or do we have drinks first? There was no way I could leave here without a drink. I was going to need alcohol in my system to have the confidence to get naked and mount this hot piece of man meat. Unlike him, I did not wear small clothes to emphasize my abs or lack thereof.

"Can I take a seat?" He motioned toward the booth, and I made some embarrassing grumbles, shuffling to make space for him.

As he relaxed in the booth, I took in his intoxicating scent. It was a mix of fresh laundry and pine, a sign he showered before coming here. That was more than I could ever say for Clay, who thought showering twice a week would mess with his vibe.

I shook my head. I needed to stop bringing that noodle dick up. He was an ass of epic proportions, and he didn't deserve any space in my head. Especially when someone like Cole was sitting in front of me.

Widening my eyes, I focused entirely on Cole. He clasped his hands together as though he was stopping himself from touching me. They looked like mitts, and I had a feeling he could probably crush my head if he were so inclined. His shirt was freshly ironed, and his pants looked clean. Yeah, he was definitely *not* Clay. I guessed a guy like him showered at least once a day, maybe even twice after training, because there was no doubt in my mind that Cole was an athlete of some kind. The way he filled his clothes and moved with such ease screamed it.

As he tucked himself farther into the booth, our arms and thighs touched, sending so much electricity through me that I jumped and let out a little yelp. Besides his smirk, he pretended not to notice. A gentleman too.

While he got comfortable, I maneuvered my body so I could lean against the wall and look at him straight on. My knees knocked his thighs in this position, but that was better than his whole body pressed against mine. This damn booth just wasn't made for someone of Cole's girth. *Cole's girth…stop it, Reign!* Stop thinking about Cole and his girthiness. As I tried to adjust, my eyes wandered down to his corded arms. *Those biceps couldn't be real!* But, if they were anything to go by, there was no noodle dick in sight with him.

A sharp pain coursed down my back, and it was only after I tasted blood that I realized I was biting down on my lip. Hard. Cole's eyes narrowed, intently watching me release my lip like he was about to pounce. My cheeks flushed. My body heated. I couldn't stop the thought of his lips against mine, his hands gripping at my waist while he kissed me ferociously. That was when I knew I was done for. He hadn't even touched me, and I was already having the tiniest buildup of an orgasm. How the hell was I going to survive the night if I was already like this?!

He looked at me.

I looked at him.

Could he hear my thoughts?

The silence swallowed any calm, replacing it with thick tension and making it hard to breathe. I racked my brain, trying to think of a question. Anything to move the conversation forward and away from his bow lips. When I'd finally come up with something and I'd mustered up the courage to ask, the waitress was hovering by our table, waiting to take our drink order.

As I looked up to smile at her, she raised her brow in question. I knew what the question was. She was wondering how the hell I snagged a guy like Cole. Believe me, it was the same question running through my head.

"What can I get you?"

"Can I have a gin and tonic?" I smiled, hoping that would calm my nerves.

"Water, please."

As the waitress left, I took Cole in. "You're not drinking?"

He looked a little uneasy before he said, "Yeah, I'm not much of a drinker. You go ahead, though."

Well, this is awkward. The only way I was going to be able to climb this mountain of a man was with alcohol, and yet he would be completely sober.

"Makes sense." I nodded, but it didn't. It didn't make any sense at all. He looked like a playboy, but he was acting almost shy. "Don't want it to ruin your workout routine." I slapped his thigh, and his head whipped to where I'd hit him.

What have I done?

I started scratching my neck because my skin was itchy. I was coming up in a rash because I was embarrassing myself by the second. How long would I have to make idle conversation with this guy? We both knew that wasn't why we were here and the more I talked, the more opportunity I gave him to back out of the deal.

When we accidentally caught each other's eyes, I swore I saw fear and uncertainty lacing his. He couldn't be nervous, could he? The thought made me laugh. Not one of those cute, girly giggles. No. One of those hardy, deep chuckles that would be awkward enough if I could stop it. I couldn't, though. It just kept coming out, but strangely, he joined in.

"Sorry!" I blurted. "I'm not laughing at you. I've never done this before, and it's just…well, you know…awkward," I said, assuming that my eyes roaming across his body were enough of an explanation that he was rendering me speechless.

"Don't worry." He flashed a reassuring smile. "It's fine. I get it. This is my first time." He paused. That couldn't be the end of his sentence, right? The intensity of his glare as he watched my reaction was unnerving.

There we had it.

The reason why this guy needed a dating app for hookups was because he'd *never* actually hooked up with anyone. How did this happen? What did I do to deserve the honor of deflowering him?

"I meant on Covey Connections, or any dating app, for that matter," he clarified, because my eyes must have been running wild. *God Reign, focus!* Of course, this guy wasn't a virgin.

"But why were you on there anyway? You clearly don't need it," I sputtered out, immediately regretting it. He wasn't fazed by my outburst, and I noticed the muscles in his arms flexed under my scrutiny. Mhmm, I wonder what they would look like flexing over me.

"I could ask you the same thing." He smiled smoothly, interrupting my train of thought.

I rolled my eyes, groaning at his response. There I was, asking him a genuine question, and he thought I was fishing for compliments.

That was when it hit me. A wry smile formed across my lips, and I narrowed my eyes. "You have a girlfriend, don't you?" That had to be the only explanation, because once a girl got a guy like this, they'd never let him go. But then I gasped, and my eyes widened. "Oh, no. You're married, aren't you? I'm going to be on that reality show *Cheaters,* aren't I?"

"No." He chuckled. "I'm neither of those things." He leaned back in the booth, looking around at the other patrons. I could only look at him. "I've just found myself around the same sort of girls throughout college, and I wanted to see if there was something different out there." With his lips flattened, he looked stoic, and his eyes roamed my face as though he was memorizing every inch. It was a little unnerving at first because I'd never really had anyone look at me so closely.

I wrinkled my nose. "So, you picked me?" I wasn't sure whether to be complimented or insulted. I knew I wasn't the typical jersey chaser, but I wouldn't say I was *that* different from other college girls.

He nodded and squirmed in his seat, a surprising gesture for such a bulky guy. "Yeah." There was caution in his voice as he waited for my reaction. "You're beautiful…and you seem different," he answered honestly, using that word again, albeit positively. I wanted to think he was just laying on the charm to prepare me for getting naked, but there was a vulnerability behind his eyes, and I couldn't help but smile at his genuineness.

"Why am I different?" Yes, *now* I was fishing for compliments because it wasn't every day a guy who looked like a model said something like that to me. This could be my only opportunity, so I was taking advantage.

"Well, for starters, you're wearing more clothes than any girl I've dated since I enrolled here." He gestured to my black skinny jeans and matching lace top. It wasn't horrendously revealing because I kind of thought he would see the goodies anyway. Might as well keep something a surprise until it happens.

"That says more about you than them," I pointed out, and he chuckled, looking back at me with the kind of heat I'd never felt before. When the waitress came and dropped our drinks, I took a sip as I eased into the conversation.

This wasn't so bad. Talking to Cole was easy. He was easygoing and a little flirty. There was no need for any false pretenses with him.

"You're right, but the biggest turn-on for me is confidence." He winked, his eyes twinkling back at me. Sea greens and browns mixed together, making the most beautiful hazel eyes I'd ever seen. "And I liked your no-bullshit approach to this date."

"Yeah, well, on that point…this isn't really a date, is it?" I cocked my eyebrow, looking at him questioningly. I know, I know. I spent the better part of an hour trying to convince myself it was a date, but I needed to be honest with myself before I got hurt. "A guy like you wants a hookup. I *need* a hookup, so that's all it's going to be."

His eyes widened, and I could see the shock registering across his face. Maybe that was a little more confident than he was expecting. "Wow." He chuckled hesitantly but pointed his thumb over his shoulder. "Should we just leave now and get down to business, then? We're wasting valuable time." Cole's mouth split into a grin, and I couldn't help but laugh.

I shook my head dramatically, flagging the waitress down to order another round. "Oh no. If I'm going to do this, I'm going to need a few more drinks," I replied, polishing off my first gin and tonic while Cole watched me intently as he drank his water.

"Am I really that bad that you need to be sloppy drunk to even consider having sex with me?"

I nearly shriveled into nothing when he said the word "sex." It sounded dirty and raw and everything I wanted to feel inside. If only I dared to point out his striking resemblance to that guy in *Magic Mike*. Instead, I whacked him gently on the chest, almost hurting my wrist in the process. That confirmed it. He was definitely an athlete with a body that hard.

"Oh, you know that's not it. When we were texting on the app and you were so keen to meet, I kind of thought I was being catfished. I was expecting a forty-year-old man to show up. Not all this." I waved my hand flagrantly in his direction with a snarl of disgust on my face as I took another sip.

Eyes hooded, he leaned in and asked, "Would you have still gone through with it if I was forty?"

"Irrelevant," I quipped with a cocked brow. "I think the real question is, am I going to go through with it *now*?"

His lips curved on one side in a smirk. "I already know the answer to that."

"Oh, you do?"

"Yup. I saw you wipe away the drool when I said your name, Reign."

My legs quivered, and I gulped just to hide my reaction.

"You're a sucker for a Southerner…or at least I hope you're a sucker."

My jaw dropped open in shock.

"Oh, look, you're already getting ready." He chuckled, and I immediately shut my mouth before smacking him on the arm again.

My face flushed in embarrassment. What have I gotten myself into? This guy was way more than I could handle.

"You've rendered me speechless. That doesn't happen often," I admitted, placing the glass down.

"Good, as what we agreed to do doesn't involve much talking, anyway." The glint in his eyes and the playful smirk on his lips was making my chest hurt. Anxious fluttering affected my breathing, and a hot, tingly sensation coursed through my body.

I was getting hot for Cole, and he hadn't even touched me. All he'd done was wink and give me a smile. It had been a while, but I didn't think it had been *that* long.

I brought my next drink up to tip with his. "That's why I need this."

The clink of the glasses was like an iron-clad agreement. This was going to happen, and I swallowed the hot liquid, hoping it was a good decision.

"How about we play a little drinking game to loosen us up?" he suggested. Drawing closer to me, his mere presence was making me feel weak.

He was so close, his chin was nearly resting on my shoulder, and my lips were mere inches away from his. There was something about his playful expression and easy demeanor that had me playing along.

"Oh yeah? Like what?" I questioned, surveying the crowd. "It's not like we can play strip poker in here."

He took a sharp breath, and I smiled, hoping I was affecting him the way he was affecting me. "I was thinking more along the lines of Truth or Dare with a twist, but I like the way you think. So, let's save that for later." He finished with a wink.

"What's the twist?"

"If you choose dare, it's always a kiss between us." My eyes dropped to his full lips, and an overwhelming ache radiated through my body. How I wanted them to be against mine. "But it can't be on the lips."

"Not the lips?"

My heart rate increased because I started to think about all the places I could leave a kiss in a public place. His cheek, his wrist…his neck. Even though I wanted to be daring, this felt a little out of my comfort zone. "I'm not sure."

He looked down at my body, then back up to my eyes with a wolfish grin. "Well, if we go ahead with what we have planned, we'll be kissing more than what's on show here." Cocking his eyebrow, he challenged me.

Grabbing my drink, I took another long sip and nodded my head. It was all the encouragement he needed. "Alright, let's do it."

"Truth or dare?" he asked.

"Truth."

"Okay, easy one. Where are you from?"

"Are we really going to play the get-to-know-you game? This is supposed to only be a one-night thing."

Chuckling a deep, husky chuckle, he nodded. "You're right. I'll make it harder for you. Have you ever had multiple orgasms?" Looking at him, shocked, he shrugged. "New rule: since you didn't answer the first one, you have to answer both." As if on purpose, he swiped his tongue out, licking his pillowy lips, readying himself for the inevitable. My body tingled at the thought of the places his tongue could be tonight.

"I'm originally from California, but I've lived in Louisiana for the last four years," I answered quickly.

"I knew you loved Southern boys."

Gosh, that smile of his could light up a room.

"Not anymore."

"Bad ex?"

I shook my head. "It doesn't matter." There was no point in talking about it now. It'd happened, and I was here to get over it. "Truth or dare?" I asked him.

"I believe you need to answer the second question, darlin'."

Urgh. I was hoping he'd forgotten.

"No," I quipped. That was all the detail I was willing to give, and he seemed satisfied.

"Well, we'll just have to deal with that tonight, then." He contemplated. What I wouldn't give to know what he was thinking about right now. I was hot just looking at his pensive stare.

I leaned forward, getting into his personal space and liking the intake of breath he took. We were already so close I was practically on his lap. "Truth or dare?" I asked, swiping my lips with my tongue, watching his reaction.

"Dare." His rough hands cupped my cheeks, and he leaned in. I held my breath, fully expecting him to kiss my lips, but he didn't. Instead, he rested his forehead against mine, searching my eyes, and gently dipped his lips down, planting the lightest of kisses on the corner of my mouth. If I hadn't seen him do it, I would question if it happened. He lingered there, letting me bask in the minty scent as he pulled away. That move alone had my body heaving for breath.

Cole relaxed back onto the barstool, taking a swig of his water, and looked around the bar as though he hadn't noticed how flustered I was. "Truth or dare, Reign?" He smiled when he finally looked back at me. That was when I realized he knew exactly what kind of torture he was inflicting.

"Truth," I pushed out, and he looked back, bored. I couldn't kiss him, not just yet.

"Are you a freshman? I've never seen you around campus."

"I thought we already put an end to all these get-to-know-you questions."

He held his big paws up, and I bet one of his palms could wrap around the entirety of my neck. "Hey, you asked for truth, but since you've questioned it again, you have to answer this too. When was the last time you had sex?"

Why on earth did he want to know that? "Fine. I'm a sophomore; I transferred from SLU last semester. Honestly, I don't want to think about the last time I had sex, but it was over six months ago, and that's all you're getting."

"Hey, you gave more than enough in that answer," he replied, and that was when the buzz started to kick in. Four gins down, and I was loosening up in the best way possible.

"Truth or dare, Cole."

"Dare." This time, he lifted my wrist up to his lips and kept his eyes on me as he slowly and sensually kissed the sensitive skin there. It immediately sent tingles through my body, straight down to my panties. I was not expecting that. I felt his smile against my wrist as he kissed deeper, watching the shock on my face.

The way his tongue flicked out and tickled my skin ignited a burning need in my belly. I wanted Cole. More than I'd wanted anything or anyone before. "Truth or dare?" he asked, still holding my wrist hostage.

Still flicking, licking, and biting.

I didn't want him to let go.

"Dare." I'd finally built up the courage to kiss him. His eyes darkened as he watched me put one of my hands on his thigh so I could inch closer to him. When our lips were barely a whisper apart, I let our breath mingle before dragging my cheek across his and gently kissing the skin just behind his ear. Cole's hands instinctively gripped my hips, biting into my flesh as I nipped his earlobe.

"Truth or dare?" I whispered in his ear.

He growled, forcing me fully onto his lap, and I didn't hear his response; I just felt his face nuzzling into my neck, biting and kissing the sensitive skin, burning every part of me he touched. I moaned, grabbing the collar of his shirt, and leaned my head back for easier access. I closed my eyes, wanting to feel his lips everywhere.

Cole looked up at me, his lips only inches from mine. He glanced down at my mouth, then back up to my eyes, leaning closer in. I knew what he wanted. He was asking permission with his eyes, and I wasn't about to stop him because I wanted it too. I finally let him press his mouth against mine. The warmth of his lips, combined with the way his hands gripped me, made me melt. I was vaguely aware that we looked like a couple of horny teenagers finally allowed to touch for the first time, but I wasn't about to stop it. It felt too good.

When his tongue slipped into my mouth, I knew I was done for. Every flick and move against mine made me shudder. Our bodies moved together, and as I sat on top of him, I thought about how it was borderline indecent the way we were teasing each other in public. Then, when his fingers grappled onto my hips and moved me suggestively against him, I felt the world drift away. I didn't want this moment to end, but I knew it had to if I wanted more.

"We should get out of here," I whispered against his mouth, flustered and hot. He nodded in response. "My place is only ten minutes away."

"Let's go," he said as he grabbed my hand and led me to the doors.

THREE
Reign

Banging against the wall, we fumbled into my measly apartment. If I weren't so drunk, I'd care more about my roommates and the smell of weed drifting around since they'd been smoking all afternoon, but that was the least of my concerns. The only thing on my mind was getting Cole into my bedroom and naked as soon as possible.

Granted, he seemed to be taking his time. My usual ten-minute walk home turned into a forty-five-minute tease fest where he'd stop me at every possible corner to make out. Not that I was complaining. Suffice it to say, I was completely drunk on Cole. And possibly the gin.

When he dipped to kiss my collarbone, I dropped my head back and hit the wall. "Sorry," he mumbled against me as his tongue grazed my skin.

I giggled when he nibbled my skin and grabbed his hand because I was tired of waiting.

Dragging him to the hallway, I hauled him through the living room, past my roommates—who were sitting on the couch with their mouths wide open—and straight to my room, slamming the door on my way.

"So, those were your roommates?"

Cole was behind me, his body only touching mine when he breathed in. I was staring at the door and smiled. "They don't matter."

I flipped the lock, and as I turned around, Cole encased me against the door. With his bulky arms on either side of my head, he was leaning in, staring down at me with hungry eyes. Biting his bottom lip playfully, he whispered, "Are you sure you want to do this with them just outside?" His eyes flicked over my head as though he could see them and then back to me.

I brought my hand to the nape of his neck, pulling him in for another kiss as I sealed our lips together. His lips caressed mine possessively, and all my inhibitions drifted as he devoured me. I moaned, completely forgetting about Gary and Rachel sitting just outside.

Crumpling his shirt in my hands, I melted into his touch, whimpering against his lips. He took the opportunity to slip his tongue into my mouth, igniting a burning need for him that spread all the way down to my panties. Releasing the tension in my hands, I teased my fingers down his chest, tickling his abs as I searched for the hem of his shirt. I was going to get this thing off him if it was the last thing I did.

When my hand relaxed against his warm skin, his body jerked, and I was burning inside because I wanted him so badly. I scratched at his abs as his hands dipped to my ass, squeezing as he brought me closer.

"They're assholes," I breathed against his lips, smiling because, in a way, this felt a little like revenge. "They let some guys steal my stuff last week." His lips curved into a smile when I unbuckled his belt, whipping it out of his jeans.

With my hands on either side of his svelte hips, I started to push the fabric of his shirt up, and he lifted his arms to make it easy for me to pull it off. It also gave me ample time to admire his chest without him knowing. The guy had muscle on muscle, and I couldn't wait to lick every last crevice. As my fingers traced across his muscles, Cole drew my attention back to him with a possessive kiss.

Without warning, his hands grabbed the back of my thighs, hoisting me up with a loud, deliberate bang against the door. The only thing I could do was wrap my legs around his waist to hold myself up. "Well then, I guess it's time for a little payback," he said in between kisses.

I disguised my moan with a giggle because in this new position, Cole's dick was rubbing right against my core, and it felt so good. So damn good.

When Cole broke our kiss, my lipstick was smeared across his face, and I loved it. He looked like he belonged to me, and for one night, he did. Still holding me against the door, he squeezed my thighs. "Take your shirt off," he commanded, and I complied, tossing the lacy fabric to the floor. His hands immediately clutched at my ass as he greedily took in my black, lace-covered breasts. His thumbs torturously rubbed the underside of the fabric before he curved down and put his warm mouth over the black lace covering one of my nipples.

"Oh god," I cried because every time his tongue swirled around the peak, the fabric would scratch against my skin in a way that made my whole-body tingle. We weren't even naked, yet I was slowly crumbling in front of him, so close to an orgasm I needed to get a grip.

He continued his torture by slowly rocking his hips into me and moved to my other nipple. My head lolled sideways, and I caught a glimpse of his smile as he watched my wanton reaction.

He crashed his lips against mine again, his fingers digging deeper into my ass and forcing our pelvises to mash together. He was so hard; I could feel him even through the thick fabric of both of our jeans. I was losing all self-control because I wanted him so badly. I could feel the whisper of a grin cross his lips as they caressed every part of me, waiting for my reaction to each touch. He kissed his way up my collarbone and slid his tongue back into my mouth. That was when my mind started short-circuiting, thinking about all the ways he could use that mouth all over my body. His tongue thrust to the same rhythm as his hips, hinting at what was to come once we finally got our jeans off.

Pulling me flush against his frame, he held me tight and walked us over to the bed. I squealed, excited at how strong he was and the way he commanded our clinch. This was exactly what I needed. Hot, animalistic want. He dropped me onto the bed before standing at his full height. With his jeans hung low and his button undone, I was dying to get my hands on that zipper and pull it down.

His breathing was labored as his hooded eyes took me in. "You're the hottest woman I've ever seen."

His heated glare made it feel like he meant it, and I felt more confident than I ever had before. So, I decided to take things into my own hands. Moving onto my hands and knees, I crawled across the bed back to him. The closer I got, the wetter I felt, because his hot gaze never left mine.

When I rested my hands on his jean-clad thighs, he groaned and threw his head back. Bolts of electricity flickered through me, knowing it was me eliciting that kind of reaction from him. My hands traveled farther up until they hit the top of his jeans. Then, ever so carefully, I curled my fingers around the loops and pulled them down in one quick motion.

I drooled when I saw his thick, muscular thighs and his tight black boxers, which was the only thing keeping his dick from me. The outline through the fabric was clear. He was a big boy, and I wanted to find out if I could handle it. My hand moved before I could think, and just as I palmed his huge cock, he growled, taking my hand and forcing me back down onto the bed.

Ignoring my whimpers, he brought my arms to the headboard, wrapping my hands around the slats. "Keep those there," he ordered as he kissed me hard, making me feel dizzy. As his lips dragged down my body, each touch felt like molten lava trickling down my skin.

When he got to the bottom of the bed, his face was directly against my crotch, hovering above the waistband of my jeans. Slowly and torturously, he played with the button and dragged them off my legs. I was left lying on my purple sheets in my bra and matching black thong. He licked his lips as his eyes roamed my body. "You're so sexy." His voice was husky with desperation, and my breath quickened when his heady hazel eyes looked into mine.

His deft fingers clutched at the sides of my thong before his lips curved into a wicked smile, and he pulled the fabric off. He gave me no time to feel self-conscious, and before I could register what was happening, Cole's mouth was on my center. "Cole," I yelped out as he rolled my clit against his tongue.

I could barely breathe, let alone think straight. Cole's tongue skated down to my center as he teased me for a few beats. By the time he slid a finger into me, he'd already worked me into such a frenzy; I knew it wouldn't take long to come. I was on the precipice, ready to ignite. His mouth sucked down on me, and I was so close it hurt.

My muscles clenched, my eyes scrunched, and I was chewing on my lip with anticipation because it was about to happen. Just as I could feel the first small pulsing wave, he stopped.

Nothing.

Just his breath tingling over me.

I wanted to throw something at him because I was so close.

When my breathing calmed and I was able to open my eyes, I was met with his curious look. "You were right there, weren't you?" He smiled. I couldn't answer because I was definitely going to throw something at him. He'd done it on purpose, and I wanted to grab his hair and force him back down to get the job done.

I didn't have to, though, because he started up again. Teasing. Licking. Adding another finger to his torture. Every time I felt my climax about to wash over me, he pulled back, kissing me just above my slit while his fingers came to a near stop. He was edging me, and I wasn't sure how long I'd last.

After the fourth time, I couldn't take it. I unfurled my fingers from the headboard, not caring that I'd broken his stupid rule, and ran my hand through his thick, dark hair, forcing his mouth back against me.

"Don't stop," I whimpered, and he let me take control as I rode his mouth while waves of ecstasy passed through my body.

Cole gently lapped up every ounce of my pleasure as he let me ride his tongue until my climax calmed and my breath evened. He kissed my inner thighs tenderly as I lay there, feeling like a pile of goo, relishing in the best orgasm a man had ever given me.

He crawled over me, draping his bulky body on top of mine as he removed my bra. Taking one of my nipples in his mouth, he swirled his tongue around the tip like he had just done on my center. He lavished my other nipple with the same attention, giving me enough time to recover that I was begging for more.

His velvety, full lips dragged up to my collarbone, where he nibbled my neck as his boxer-clad crotch ground against me. Even with the thin layer of fabric, I could feel every inch of his hard length.

"Can I return the favor?" I whispered, keeping my eyes closed so I could relish in the afterglow of hopefully my first orgasm for the night.

He did promise me multiples, after all.

He was fully on top of me now, his sweaty body crushing me in the most delicious way. My hands roamed his muscular back, feeling every move he made. He kissed and nipped up to my ear. "Tonight's about you," he husked, and just the mere tickle of his voice had me curling my back, trying to get closer.

The cold air hit me as he quickly got up, kneeling above me on the bed. He glowered down at my body, taking in my naked form with lusty eyes. He'd barely let me touch him, yet he'd given me a mind-blowing orgasm, and I was hungry for more. I glanced down at his crotch and licked my lips. He must be so hard right now. I wanted to feel it.

"Condom?" he asked. "I've got one in my jeans, but I don't want to find it."

Deliriously shaking my head, I leaned over to the bedside table and opened the top drawer. My hand tapped every object until I felt the smooth roll of the foil packets and tossed them his way. He caught the whole packet because I didn't have time or the brain capacity to rip one off.

Mesmerized, I gulped as he peeled his boxers off, revealing his long, thick cock. Cole's girthiness was definitely something I should have been worried about. My lips parted as he wrapped his hand around himself, lightly stroking as he watched my reaction.

I shivered, enjoying him squeeze and tease himself while he watched me. It was hot and feral at the same time, and something I'd never seen a guy do in the room with me. I pulled myself up because I didn't care what he said anymore. I wanted him in my mouth. Just as I got up, Cole moved off the bed and strolled to the end of it.

He grabbed my ankles and dragged me toward him, making me squeal. I was naked and compliant. Cole could breathe in my direction, and I'd probably have another orgasm. At this point, I felt like his little plaything. If he could make me feel as good as he did before, he could use me as he pleased. His moves were a far cry from the missionary sex I was used to. His dick was something to be worshipped. It. Was. Huge.

In one swift movement, he took both of my legs, crossed my ankles, and then rested them on his shoulder. Cole entered me in one smooth stroke, holding me in place as I withered beneath him. He filled me to the brim, and my back curled against my sheets, trying to feel everything. He was taking it slowly, trying to help me adjust. Like that would help. He was so big that I thought I might burst into a thousand tiny starbursts with every movement.

Once he felt my body adjust to his size, his hands held on to my thighs, clutching me as he jerked his body into mine. Faster. Harder.

"Cole," I cried, biting down hard on my lip because his short, fast pace had me breathless and dizzy.

Clutching the pillows, I tried my hardest to stay in place, but with every pound, I could feel myself moving up the bed. Deeper, faster. I so badly wanted to touch him, but he was too far away. He stared down at my breasts as they bounced with his movement, but I couldn't see him at all because my legs were in the way.

I could tell he was close; I could feel him pulsing inside me, and his thrusts were getting more frantic. I was close too, my body becoming a quivering mess, but I didn't want to come again without touching him.

Undoing my legs, I bared myself completely as I lifted myself up and scratched my nails down his chest. "Come down here," I purred.

Cole grumbled in displeasure but followed me down, nonetheless. As I wrapped my legs around his waist and my arms around his neck, he entered me again. Now, with his skin against mine, I felt more electric. White-hot heat was blaring inside me, and I was so ready to climax. Right on the precipice.

"Come for me, Reign," he whispered in my ear.

It was all he needed to say to break me. It was like a crescendo of euphoria crashing through my center. My body took over, jerking my hips wildly and clamping down on him as he continued to move inside me. He threw his head back, moaning my name as he thrust one last time before joining me in his release.

Cole collapsed on top of me, both our bodies sweaty and tired. With the only noise in the room our heavy breathing, I did what felt natural and kissed the salty sweat on his shoulders away. He, in turn, wiped a few strands of hair out of my face before kissing my sweaty brow. I was reluctant to move away from him, so we stayed there for a few minutes, reveling in what had just happened.

It was probably the best night of my life, but I wasn't about to scare him away and tell him that.

When I eventually realized that Cole's weight would probably crush me if I let him stay on top of me any longer, I unclasped my hands and legs, freeing him from my hold. He rolled to the side, lying next to me as we stared at the ceiling.

If he were anyone else, I might be embarrassed at the state of my room. What with the boxes everywhere and the giant water stain building up on my ceiling, but I was leaving here tomorrow, so none of it mattered. Not even the fact that we were so loud, I was certain Gary and Rachel would be able to describe the whole lewd act in intricate detail. I'd never see them again. I'd never see Cole again. Just how I wanted it.

Worried that Cole might have fucked out my ability to speak, I finally said, "That was intense." It was true. I never knew it could feel that good or I could climax that hard. Especially with someone I'd just met. I'd always thought it got better once you knew your partner's preferences. With Cole, it felt like he could read my body like a book and cheated by flicking to the back page.

He turned to look back at me, a smile wide on his face. "Did you think we were done?"

Before I could sputter out any response, he was back on me like a lion after his prey.

FOUR

Reign

Waking up, I felt absolutely wrecked. My body was still limp, and my muscles ached from overuse. Last night was indescribable. *Four times?* I didn't even think that was possible in one night. I'd only ever seen that happen on *The Bachelor,* and that involved a magical windmill. The only thing magical about last night was Cole's dick. Even after sleeping next to him, I still couldn't think straight because my body had become accustomed to his touch.

As sunlight streamed into the room, I squinted, trying to adjust to the light, and when I tried to rub the sleep out of my eyes, I realized I couldn't move my hand because Cole's hard, warm body was holding me down. His arm was draped across my body, his fingers laced with mine as though he wanted to keep me close. Had we been holding hands all night? Funny, after everything we did last night, I'd expect him to be groping me, but nope. He was just innocently holding my hand instead, and I liked it.

He pulled me closer to him, and I snuggled into the warmth of his body. It was strange to me how comfortable I felt with him. I was doing things with him I'd never do with Clay, and I was with him for five years. But now that it was morning and the sex-fest haze was fading, I didn't know what I was supposed to do. What was the etiquette after a one-night stand? Should I offer him a drink? Maybe a towel to freshen up? It all seemed so weird, considering I'd seen his ball sack and liked it.

But then I chastised myself for ruining the moment again. So instead of fretting, I focused on Cole's warm, snuggly body, burying my butt further into his crotch, and feeling him harden against me. His arms pulled me in tighter, and his breath tickled against my shoulder as he gently kissed my skin. Just a few touches, and he'd already prepped me. Ready for more. His hands skated down to my hips, digging in as he pressed himself against my butt.

"Good morning." His voice was husky with tiredness, and I responded with a muffled giggle, nuzzling my face into the pillow because I was enjoying his touch a little too much.

Unsatisfied with the greeting, he turned me around in his arms, and I looked up, careful to keep my mouth shut. Morning breath could be a real mood killer if I let it. "How many orgasms does a girl need to get a good morning?" He chuckled, kissing my forehead. A move that felt a lot more intimate than I thought a one-night stand should.

Swatting his chest, I tried to get away from him. "Stop!" I giggled as his fingers gripped my hips tighter, drawing me in.

Without the alcohol coursing through my veins, this whole interaction felt different. I buried my face in his neck, letting him hold me for just a minute longer because I knew this was going to be the last time, and I hadn't felt anything close to this connection in years.

Kissing my forehead again, he asked, "Did you have a good time?"

I wanted to laugh. Was he seriously asking me that? Surely it would have been obvious.

I felt his lips curve into a smile as they grazed my cheek, sending a shiver up my spine. Considering he gave me five orgasms in the span of a few hours, I was sure he knew the answer to that.

I opened one eye to peek at him, and he looked just as gorgeous as when I first saw him last night at the bar, save for one subtle change. His hair was tousled in every direction from sleeping. It was cute and made him look just a little less perfect. I could safely say that I liked a sleepy Cole.

His hooded eyes watched me, waiting for my answer.

"Yeah," I said wistfully, drawing circles on his abs.

I didn't have the guts to admit that was the best experience I'd ever had with a guy. That he was a unicorn among horses. That I had not only found a pot of gold at the end of his rainbow, but a whole damn cruise liner was there to take me on a round-the-world vacation. Yeah, that might be coming on a little strong.

His laugh reverberated through his chest straight into me. "That good, huh?" One of his fingers trailed up and down my back, sending hot sensations to my core. You'd think I'd be wiped out after everything that happened last night, but the minute he touched me, it was like my body immediately wanted more.

I giggled, resting my forehead on his chest so he couldn't see me blushing. "It wasn't what I was expecting. Let's just leave it at that."

"What were you expecting?" he probed, still lightly touching my back, going down a little further with every caress. I seriously considered shutting him up with a kiss, but I didn't think my body could handle another round.

"I wasn't expecting it to be so good," I squeaked out, slightly embarrassed at the omission.

"It was, wasn't it?" He rolled onto his back, firmly placing me against his side as he brought a hand up to support his head.

"Well, I guess you do this a lot, right? So, thanks for sharing your expertise." I grimaced the minute the words fell out of my mouth.

Really Reign? What the hell? Who says that?! And I could see from the look on his face that I'd just pissed him off. Not surprised. I did just imply that he whored himself around. I was shockingly bad at one-nighters, apparently.

"No, I don't," he said sternly, watching my reaction. "I told you before; this is the first time I've hooked up like this." He sounded quieter. More contemplative and less jovial than he'd been throughout the night. I didn't mean to offend him, but I couldn't believe a guy with his ability didn't get around. Where else could he learn to do that thing with his tongue?

"Oh, come on. You don't expect me to believe that?" I smiled, trying to lighten the mood after I bashed it with a hammer. He looked thoughtful as he lightly flicked a strand of my hair over my shoulder, keeping his hand touching my skin.

"Well yeah, I mean, I've slept with girls. Don't get me wrong, but I usually take them on a date first. I've never gone into it knowing it would be a one-time thing."

"Same," I drawled out. I wouldn't admit it out loud, but I kind of wanted to see that side of him. He was certainly a gentleman in the bedroom, so I wouldn't expect anything less out of it. But my stomach knotted because that wasn't the deal. We agreed on one night, and I was in no way ready to jump into anything.

But there was just something about Cole. He made me feel safe. Protected, even. But after everything that happened with Clay and my parents, I promised myself I would take some time out. To focus on myself instead of chasing the next high. I know now that I chased Clay because I wanted to keep my mind from wandering too far into my own thoughts. It was time now, though. Time to face reality and move forward.

After a couple of minutes of comfortable silence, curiosity got the better of me. "Can I ask you something?"

"Yeah?"

"Why were you on Covey Connections in the first place?" His face drew a contagious smile, and I stupidly started grinning back like a toothless child waiting for money from the tooth fairy.

"What do you mean?"

"You clearly don't need help to find girls willing to bang you." I took in his hard, naked body, remembering how I rode it for over twenty minutes last night. "And I don't buy that whole 'you're looking for a different type of girl' trash you spouted last night."

"Want the honest answer?" He bit his lip, and I wished it were my lip his teeth were sinking into.

"If we can't be honest with each other now…" I trailed off, pointing between our still very sweaty and very naked bodies.

"I was in a competition with the guys I live with. Who could get the most matches in twenty-four hours." I wished I hadn't asked. "But then you popped up on my screen. I thought you were cute, and I found the statement on your profile…intriguing, to say the least."

I couldn't even remember what I wrote. I knew it was something punny about a one "knight" stand, but I'd done it while drinking wine and watching *The Bachelor*.

Classy Reign. Real classy.

"Oh, okay." Because what was I supposed to say to that? *Great! I'm glad we matched because you only wanted me for your body count.* It wasn't like I was expecting some profound reason, but I guessed—no—I'd hoped that he felt the same way I did when I saw him. Like butterflies had escaped their cages and made a home in his stomach. "Did you at least win?" I asked, uninterested in the answer.

"No, of course not. I just downloaded the app, so they thought I was playing along. The minute I saw you, I stopped." I turned to look at him, and this time, he was staring at the ceiling. His face was stoic as he drawled out, "Kind of wanted to see if I could be your knight in shining armor." The sides of his lips curled, and I groaned, covering my face with my hands. "Do you get it? Because your name is Reign, and you wanted a one-knight stand?"

"Stop!" I mumbled into his chest, whacking his chest lightly. "How many times do you think I've heard that?"

"Not enough." His hands held mine in place, stopping me from whacking him and forcing me to look into his eyes. "Though after my performance last night, I thought you would promote me to the king of your heart." His eyebrows wiggled suggestively, and he made it hard not to smile t with that giant grin plastered across his face.

I held back, though, giving him a groan and an eye roll instead. "These are terrible. Please quit while you're ahead." I pulled the covers over my naked breasts and turned away, forming a tight ball, pretending to be annoyed. His corded arms wrapped around me as his breath caressed my ear. The warmth tickled my neck and made me giggle.

"Maybe you're more of a Khaleesi kind of girl?" he whispered. I turned around in his arms, letting them pull me in tighter because I kind of liked his embrace. "I guess my question is, are kings the only ones you slay?"

I brought my hand to his lips, and he gently kissed my finger while I held it there. "Okay, I'm officially stopping this." Amusement played in his eyes as his tongue darted out, licking my hand. I pulled away, wiping my palm down his chest and leaving it there to rest on his stomach so I could feel his slow, calming breaths.

"Why were you on the dating app?" he asked after several minutes of comfortable silence.

I shrugged. "I just heard it was the easiest way to get a no-strings-attached thing. You know?" I said coolly. I could feel his body tense slightly, and his hold on me relaxed.

"Why don't you want a relationship?" he asked, almost hesitantly. It felt like we were skating out of the realm of one-night stands with these questions. The cuddling had already brought us to the edge. "Most girls I've met at Covey U are looking for a serious relationship. You told me this was the first time you've done something like this, so I'm just curious," he elaborated, noting my pause.

"Honestly?" I was mimicking him. "I was in a relationship for three years, and it kind of ended badly. Like, really badly. So, I swore off men a year ago, and I still wasn't ready to dip my toes into the dating pool just yet. Sometimes, though…you know. You just need some…uhhh…" How do I put this without sounding like a total jerk?

"Assistance?" he offered, clearly seeing I was struggling with what to say, and I nodded in agreement.

Both our bodies tensed with that omission. The reality of what we did sank in. The way he was looking between my eyes and lips was too much for my heart to handle, and with daylight streaming in, I was way more self-conscious than I was with four glasses of gin in my stomach. I backed away, doing my best to avoid any more intimacy, scanning the room to find my clothes. They were nowhere to be seen, which meant I had no option but to take a pillow and try to cover as much of my modesty as possible.

I managed to get out of bed with a fluffy white pillow covering all the vital parts, and I could hear Cole snickering from behind. When I turned, I was met with his bemused expression. "You know I've seen it all already, right?" he asked with an eyebrow cocked and one arm resting under his head. With the other hand, he pointed to the small amount of fabric covering my modesty. "In fact, I'm pretty sure I've licked it all too."

Grabbing another pillow to hide my backside, I grumbled out a response, waddling toward the adjoining bathroom. "I'm well aware, Einstein. It's just different in daylight, okay?"

He shook his head, relaxing into my bed and closing his eyes. Why did he have to look so good mixed up in my sheets?

"You're right. You're even more beautiful," he drawled out, eyes still closed and a smile on his face as if he were remembering everything that happened last night. With my hand on the doorknob, I took one final look at his bulky frame and breathed in.

"I'm going to take a shower."

"Need company?" he cooed, moving to get out of the bed. My eyes grew, and my heart skipped when he lifted the covers off his legs. There was no way my body could handle seeing that anaconda in the daylight.

"No," I yelled louder than necessary, holding my hand up and letting the pillow in the back fall. "You stay right there." My voice was frantic as I tried to calm down. "Or go. Whatever you want."

I waved my hand, trying to act cool this time, and I watched him as I entered the bathroom backward, shutting the door behind me. I needed him to go soon because it was feeling less like a hookup and more like…I didn't know what. I just needed some space to free my mind. After turning the shower up as hot as I could get it, I hopped in and let it scald my skin. Just as I was conditioning my hair, there was a faint knock on the door. "What is it?"

"I was just going to…" Cole's voice was muffled by the spraying water and the door, which still seemed shut.

Pulling the shower curtain back, I stuck my head out and yelled, "I can't hear you." He slowly cracked the door open, and I could just about make him out among all the steam.

"Sorry," he said, louder this time. "I just wanted to let you know I was going to leave." He pointed his thumb behind him and casually leaned against the door with a lopsided smile on his face.

"Really?" I wiped my face down, trying to remove the water dripping over it. I probably looked like a drowned rat, and even though I was just trying to convince myself I wanted him to leave, there was an ache in my stomach. Why was I so disappointed he wanted to go?

"Yeah." Scratching the back of his head, he sounded confused. "I thought you wanted me out?"

Urgh, damn it. I was such an idiot. There I was, trying to act like I was cool with everything, and instead, I came across as a class-A bitch. "No, I'm sorry, I'm just a grouch in the morning. I need coffee to wake up properly." I couldn't see his facial expression through the mist, but his shoulders visibly relaxed. "Do you want to take a shower? I'm nearly done."

"Okay, I'll wait in your bedroom." He turned around and shut the door.

I quickly finished up, jumping out and wrapping the towel tight around my chest. I relaxed when I went into my bedroom and saw him sitting on the edge of my bed, playing with his phone. With just his boxers on, I could see every muscle flex in the light, and it made me a little hot. He really was gorgeous. His eyes darkened when I walked further into the room with my towel, fully capturing his attention. Much like last night, I enjoyed the way he looked at me a little too much.

Instead of acknowledging it, I tossed him a fresh towel, which he caught with ease. He thanked me with a kiss on my forehead when he walked past me into the bathroom. Yup, this was definitely moving away from hookup territory.

While he showered, I threw on a pair of jeans and a white T-shirt and tried to brush my wild hair. No amount of conditioner was a match for Cole's prowling hands, though. As the shower turned off, my mind started to vividly imagine Cole maneuvering himself around the tiny bathroom, water dripping down his chest, and patting himself dry with my towel. Just as my imagination was about to drop his towel, Cole sauntered out of the bathroom without a care in the world. My jaw dropped. There he was, standing there, droplets trickling down his torso, and I was thirsty, so very thirsty. Turning away, I shut my mouth and pretended to look at something on my desk, desperately trying to forget what was under that towel.

Then the most unbearable noise happened behind me. His towel dropped. Closing my eyes, it took all my restraint to stay looking at the desk and not in the mirror. As much as I wanted to gawk, I didn't know where this would end if I turned around.

"You know. I really did have fun last night," Cole mumbled while I heard the rustling of jeans.

"Same." It was all I could get out. I was too busy imagining his thick thighs and chiseled abs. He buckled his belt, and I sighed with relief, knowing I could focus. I turned around, fully expecting a clothed Cole in front of me. Nope. *Abort. Abort.* He was still topless, and I still wanted to trace his abs with my tongue. My eyes met his, and he tilted his head, giving me a crooked smile. For just a second, it was all I saw.

"I know the plan was for this to be a one-night thing, but if you ever need your itch scratched again, let me know." He spoke so casually while he shoved a shirt over his head like last night wasn't an amazing, godlike experience. While his face was covered, I watched every muscle of his torso flex as he moved.

"Yeah," I said wistfully. I was non-committal because I'd seen the movies.

They always start off as friends with benefits, but then one develops feelings, and then all hell breaks loose. I was not about to be another statistic, especially since I needed to be relationship-free for a while. To find myself and all that jazz.

He lifted his shoulder as he walked toward me. "I was just offering my services, but I get it. One night." He looked like he was about to head out, and I panicked. Was I supposed to offer him breakfast? I didn't think that was a requirement for a hookup, so I gave him a hug instead. A hug? Because that was even more normal for a hookup. *Why was I so awkward?* His body tensed. Yup, I'd screwed up again. He half-heartedly returned the hug and pulled away, leaving another lingering kiss on my forehead.

"I guess I'll see you around campus," I said, because what else was there to say now? *Nice dick. I enjoyed riding it.* Yeah, maybe not.

"Yeah," he replied thoughtfully, breaking the hug, and I reluctantly stepped back. "I'll show myself out. It was nice meeting you, Reign." He flashed his lopsided smile and walked out of my room. I heard him greet my roommates in a chipper tone before his feet stomped against the hard wooden floor, walking out.

"You, too," I called out, probably too late for him to hear. Just like that, we'd gone from lovers to strangers, and it all felt very finite. When I turned back to my room, I noticed his towel was neatly folded up on the side of my bed, the only evidence that he was here. There was a pang of something in my chest, but I didn't know exactly what. Disappointment? Confusion? Longing? I couldn't place it, but it wasn't an emotion I was used to.

Sighing, I looked around my room at the boxes stacked in the corner and all the work I had to do today. I was getting rid of most of the stuff, dwindling it down to two suitcases, and after last night, it all felt a little too much. I groaned at the idea of hauling my ass out of this apartment, but at least it meant I wouldn't have to face Gary and Rachel again. There was always an upside.

FIVE
Devin

"Hey, man," Adam greeted me as I yawned, stumbling into the house like I'd been drinking.

My energy was drained, and I had no desire to make idle small talk with my friend, and judging by the smirk on his face, he knew why.

"Good night?" he teased, watching me trudge up the stairs. Each step felt heavier than the last.

At this point, I was so wrecked from last night that I could only grumble out a response and give him a small wave. Plus, talking would use the vital brain capacity I needed to replay everything that happened last night. There was no way I wanted to dilute that memory with new ones just yet. Reign was a shock to the system. An unexpected storm on my sunny day, and boy, did I get drenched.

Opening my door, my bed was an inviting mess of black cotton sheets just waiting for me to jump on in. So I did. My head was still fuzzy from the ridiculous amount of hot sex we had last night, and I couldn't quite get it straight. The positions she let me put her in and the way she trusted me was so damn hot. I didn't think I'd ever be able to forget the way she moaned my name when she was right on the edge because it was the thing of dreams. I *hated* leaving without so much as her phone number, but that was what she wanted, and I didn't want to push my luck.

Granted, I tried. When I initiated a potential repeat this morning by dropping my towel behind her, I saw her shoulders tense, and I thought that was it. I thought she'd turn around, and we'd spend the rest of the day naked in her purple bed sheets, exactly where I wanted to be. But that didn't happen. She seemed happy to let me go, and I had to take the hint, even if I didn't want to.

Closing my eyes, I pulled the covers over my head, hiding away from my roommates so I could think about last night.

Reign.

Reign.

Reign.

That girl was all the things I'd ever dreamed of and everything I wasn't expecting. Sure, I knew what she looked like, but when I walked into the bar, my chest tightened seeing her sitting in that booth, biting her bottom lip, and fidgeting with her hands. She looked lost, and I wanted to be the place she felt found.

I felt like a giddy teenager as I walked up to her, knowing I was the lucky idiot she was waiting for. If I thought she was beautiful from afar, she was a goddess up close. Her makeup highlighted her catlike eyes, and even though she looked sexy as sin, I could feel the timidness radiating off her. I knew I needed to loosen her up, which was why I suggested Truth or Dare. I didn't want her running out on me before I'd had the opportunity to hold her.

But then, when I got the opportunity, I was like a kid in the candy store, devouring every piece of pleasure she'd let me have. Reign was beyond sexy, withering naked underneath me, and it would be a long time before I forgot the look on her face when she was coming all over my cock. In fact, I didn't think I'd ever forget how her nose scrunched when she realized how wide I was. I couldn't lie; her reaction made me feel like a god.

When she opened her apartment door, even though she was half-drunk, I was still surprised to find her living in a crack-den dump. She didn't seem like the type. She seemed way too studious for that, and I wondered why she was living with a couple she clearly hated. I didn't expect them to gawk at us while we ambled into her room, but I didn't mind showing her off as my prize. I especially didn't expect Reign to try to revenge fuck me against the door straight after; that was for sure. Not that I was complaining. She could take me any which way she liked, and I'd be there for it.

In the morning, while she was showering, I snooped around her room. Not much, just enough to learn a little more about her, given she'd hardly opened up in our game of Truth or Dare. Nursing books littered her shelves, along with air fresheners I assumed she'd hung to get rid of that slight weed smell covering her apartment. Sadly, it didn't work, and for a moment, I was thankful it wasn't football season because I most certainly wouldn't have passed a drug test after five minutes in there. It was sweet that Reign tried, though.

She had a few boxes scattered around; she mentioned she just moved, so maybe she didn't have time to unpack, but then again, she could have been a hoarder. But there was only one thing that gave me any hint of who she was, and that was the picture that sat next to her laptop on her desk. It was a picture of her, and I assumed her parents from a few years ago. I laughed because she still had braces on, and with black lipstick, it looked like she was going through a grunge phase. There were no other pictures anywhere in her room, though. No keepsakes. No mementos. Nothing. Something about it was off. The room seemed so empty when the girl occupying it was so full of life.

I couldn't help but think of Chloe and how I'd feel if I found out she was living in a place like that. I'd be so angry that I'd pay for a new apartment in a nice neighborhood myself. It made me wonder why Reign's family hadn't stepped in. She was from California, after all. Didn't she have a home she could have gone to? Wasn't there someone who cared about her?

My mind whirred with frustration as I thought about her past. Something happened at SLU to make her leave, and I would have asked more, but I stopped myself because, ultimately, it was none of my business. I shut my eyes, grunting as I rolled over and covered my face in my pillow, wishing they smelled like her. I couldn't save her either. I had enough females who needed my help. I couldn't bring home another one. Besides, she very clearly stated she didn't need saving either. It was just…I wanted to.

I forced myself to think of something other than her living arrangements, like her face, when I licked that perfect little pussy of hers. She tasted so sweet, and I loved the fact that even though I was barely touching her, she was so close that I could get all these breathy moans and stuttering pants out of her. She gripped my hair so tightly at one point I thought she'd pull it out. And now I was hard just thinking about her.

I kind of hoped screwing her four times would work her out of my system, and I'd be able to walk away satisfied. It seemed to have had the opposite effect, though. I couldn't think about anything *but* her. She was like sugar; the mere taste of her had me wanting more.

Taking my phone out of my pocket, I examined Reign's dating profile, focused on her face, and thought about how much I wanted to see her again. Not just for another screw. I wanted to know more about her. What kind of nurse did she want to be? Why was she living in a roach-infested apartment? What was she planning on doing for the rest of her life, and could I come along? Okay, maybe I was getting a little ahead of myself with that last thought.

Fuck it.

I was just going to put it out there. Coach always said, "*You* lose all chances you never take."

As I typed out a message, I sighed, remembering I'd need to explain that my name was not, in fact, Cole the next time I saw her. *If* there was a next time.

Cole: Had a great time last night. Was hoping I could get your number. You know, just in case you're interested in another round.

Smooth, Devin. I sounded like an ass. No, wait. I sounded like Aiden when he was trying to get into any girl but Alyssa's pants. The dude would sleep with a mailbox if it were shaped like a vagina. I assumed it was what Reign would expect from me, though. I accepted a booty call, after all.

Shaking my head, I groaned, remembering that I had football training this afternoon. I'd already missed a week's worth of practices, and I knew Coach was going to kill me if I skipped out on another. I had to go today, even if it was just to get bitched at by him. I was going to have to be honest with him about my family sooner or later. Right now, though, I needed to sleep; otherwise, the pounding from my teammates would feel twice as painful.

SIX
Reign

"Is it the house on the right?" my Uber driver asked, as though I should know.

I didn't. What I did know was that my new neighborhood was a hell of a lot better than my last one. It was a quiet residential street, only a five-minute walk from campus, and looked like one of those streets you see on Instagram or a postcard. The stereotypical Northern California neighborhood with white rockers on the front porches and beachy colors is a far cry from the sketchy apartment block I used to live in.

Transferring late has had its hurdles, like having no friends, not knowing my way around campus, and figuring out my new class schedule. But the absolute worst had been finding accommodations that worked for me. When I first met Gary and Rachel, they seemed super chill, and I could overlook the fact that they had mouse traps in the kitchen. The rent was cheap, and I had nowhere else to go, but it took me three days to realize they were super chill because they were always smoking pot and letting sketchy people sleep on the couch.

I stayed far away from any of them, preferring the solace of my room, and it kind of worked for a while. I did have to get a safe one day because my stuff went missing, but that wasn't a big deal; I could live with putting my valuables away whenever I left. The moment I knew I had to get out, though, was the day I woke up, and a dude was standing above my head, just staring at me. He was as high as a kite and had no idea where he was. The worst part was that he freaked the hell out when I tried to politely ask him to leave because he thought he was an orange and I was going to peel him. I was no expert, but I was pretty sure that something stronger than pot was in his system that night.

After that, I went straight to the hardware store and bought the most heavy-duty lock I could find because I had three months left on my lease. Thankfully, I found this place two months ago, and I had no idea how I lucked out. I met the other two girls, Alyssa and Laura, fully expecting something to be wrong with them, but they seemed like perfectly normal English majors. Granted, Alyssa, or Lyss, for short, was a little OCD, but nothing seemed as bad as living with Gary and Rachel.

"Umm," I stalled, looking for the house number on the front door. "It's number 56. Is that 56?" I should have probably come to look at the place, but after meeting the two other girls I was going to live with, I wanted to snap it up before someone else could.

The Uber driver rolled his eyes, taking his time to look at the screen next to him. "Looks like it."

"Okay, great." Hopping out of the car, the driver pulled my two suitcases out of his trunk with a thud and drove off before I could even mumble out a thank you.

Staring at the two suitcases, which were nearly my height, I was saddened to think that this was all my life had amounted to. Twenty-one years and all my possessions were in these two suitcases. No home. No family to be held back by. I guess that was what happened when you ran away from your problems. I left almost everything behind in the home my aunt held onto for a year, but when I was adamant I never wanted to go back, she sold it for me.

At the time, keeping memories of my parents was too painful. It was a constant reminder of what I'd lost and how I was all alone in the world now. With no brothers or sisters, I had no one to share the grief with or reminisce about the good times. All I had left were the memories in my mind and the hope that I'd never forget what their laughs sounded like. I wished I hadn't been so headstrong and saved more than my dad's watch and my mom's pearl earrings, but I had to accept that.

A wolf whistle echoed through the neighborhood, and a booming obnoxious voice yelled, "Fresh meat!"

If I moved next door to a frat house, I would kill Laura and Lyss for not telling me. I loathed jock parties. Although I couldn't deny noticing the topless guys as we drove past, I was too busy checking house numbers to give them my full attention. Ignoring the jeering and coughing coming from behind me, I contemplated how on earth I would get these two suitcases up the drive by myself. Being nearly my height at five foot three and also having a heavy backpack, I was going to make my walk up the drive look less than graceful.

Grabbing both of the handles, I sucked it up, rolling them up the rickety drive and doing my best to keep them straight, praying I didn't roll over a stone or something else that would throw me off balance.

Someone took control of one of my suitcases, and just as I was about to scream for help, a soothing smile broke through. It was one of the guys from next door. I knew because he was ripped and topless—apparently a requirement. "Let me help you with that." His soft voice was smooth like honey as he flashed me a dashing smile. He was charming in an unassuming kind of way.

One of his dark blue eyes winked, probably noticing my ogling, and he smiled, rolling one of my bags up the driveway. I cursed myself because I couldn't stop my gaze from flicking down to his bare chest and comparing it to Cole's. Both were just as chiseled, but this guy was leaner. Cole was built more like a surfboard, which was a good thing.

"Thanks" was all I mustered when I felt the other suitcase taken from my hand.

It was another one of them. They were popping up like flies to crap. This guy had deeply tanned skin glistening with sweat. I forced my eyes up because I spent too much time staring at his arms. I could have sworn they were the size of my thighs. It was fascinating. I didn't realize I had a thing for arms, but I learned something new about myself every day.

Looking up was a mistake; the guy had deep chocolate eyes and a smirk that looked a lot like trouble.

"No problem," the blonde one said, drawing my attention back to him. "I'm Adam, by the way." He pointed his thumb at the guy next to him. "And this is Jackson."

I stood there for a second, assessing my situation and wondering just how many hot guys there were at Covey U. It seemed they were all climbing out of the woodwork this week. "Nice to meet you guys. I'm Reign."

They looked at each other. I knew what they were thinking. "Like the weather?" Jackson asked, slightly bemused.

If I had a penny for every time I was asked that, I'd be a millionaire.

"No, my mom had a fascination with the British monarchy. I'm not the biggest fan of it." Mainly because I have conversations like this all the time.

"I think it's cute," Adam said, a dimple popping out when he smiled. Something about his stare made me feel flustered, and I couldn't help but gravitate toward him. I liked his genuineness and the way his eyes glistened in the light.

"Thanks." I could feel myself blushing, and as we walked to the front door, I glanced at their house, surprised at how close it was. Although the homes were detached, they looked connected. I could only hope they didn't have any loud parties. I needed to study if I wanted to make up some of those lost classes from Louisiana.

As I raised my hand to knock on the door, Jackson asked, "So, are you our new neighbor?"

"I guess so." My knuckles knocked against the wood, waiting for an answer.

"You know," Adam said after I'd knocked for the third time. "Lyss's car isn't in the drive. I don't think they're home." Laura did mention they would be coming back from a study group this morning. Maybe they were stuck in traffic. "You could always hang out at our house until they get home?" he offered.

I looked between them, both giving me a genuine smile and even though these guys seemed nice, there was no way I was just going to hang out in a house full of shirtless dudes I didn't know. I'd read one too many reverse harem novels to think that was a good idea. I was always left with one question every time I finished. How do the girls in those books handle it? I also refused to believe that five hot guys just happened to be best friends and open to the idea of sharing. Surely, they couldn't *all* be hot. There had to be at least one dud in there. Then it begged the question: did you take one dud so you could have four hotties, or did you take one hottie and miss out on the other three? Anyway, I digress.

"It's okay; I'll just wait here."

Plopping down on the concrete step, I balanced my elbows on my knees and rested my chin on my palm. It was a lovely day, and Lyss had a nice porch, so I didn't mind waiting. When I looked up, another two shirtless guys were making their way to us. Maybe I was too hasty in my reverse harem decision. These two were just as hot as the last two.

I cocked my eyebrow when Adam dropped next to me. I guessed they were staying too.

"Guys! Are we gonna play or what?" the one with jet-black hair and steely-blue eyes that cut me with his narrowed gaze asked his friends while he trudged over reluctantly.

"We were just trying to get to know our new neighbor here," Adam said. His words came out casually, but I could tell from the other guys' faces that there was some kind of implication behind them.

Leaning over, Adam pointed in their general direction. "The guy with the black hair is Aiden, and the one with the blue cap is Matty. They also live with us," he explained.

"How many of you are there?" I asked with a raised eyebrow, bemused.

"Five. Devin is sleeping upstairs. He had a late night and is still recovering."

Jackson sniggered. "Don't you mean an early morning? He didn't come home until this afternoon. He hasn't left his room since."

I knew how Devin felt because my thighs still ached from Cole's touch. Just thinking about all the positions he took me in made my belly burn with need. I squeezed my eyes shut, trying to rid my mind of his memory. I couldn't date, so it wasn't like I'd ever see him again. "Either way, sounds like he had a good night," I deadpanned.

"I'm sure he did," Jackson jeered. "Come to think of it, when *was* the last time Devin was with a chick?" he asked Adam, whose mouth hung open in surprise.

I interrupted before I found out the answer. "Don't you think it's weird that you're talking to a girl that you've just met about your roommate's sex life? I haven't even met the guy."

Nodding, Jackson stifled back a snort, revealing his super-straight teeth. "Oh, don't worry, you'll get to know him very soon."

I wrinkled my nose, looking up at the mischief twinkling in his eyes. "What does that even mean?"

"You'll see." Adam's lips curled up on the edges, bringing my attention to the light freckles dotted across his nose. I couldn't deny how gorgeous he was. The perfect symmetry of his face was almost unnerving, and it reminded me of those old Abercrombie and Fitch ads.

I pursed my lips, squinted my eyes, and studied his face. "I don't think I like that smirk."

"So, Reign." Adam leaned back, scooting closer to me. He had a hint of a smile on his face while he stared at his feet, shuffling them against the concrete. "Can I take you out sometime?"

My body stiffened while my brain processed his words. That was forward, but the fact that he asked me in front of all his friends didn't sit well. It screamed a pissing contest, and I was no fire hydrant.

"I…uhh…" I stumbled, trying to think of a witty answer, when Matty interrupted.

"You're going to have a fight on your hands, you know?" He was staring at Adam. So yeah, I was right. He was marking me like a dog. Romantic. "She's got Devin written all over her."

I grimaced at the way they were talking and stood up, coming face-to-face with Matty. Unfortunately, Matty was at least a foot taller than me, so any chance of appearing intimidating quickly dwindled. I poked him in the chest. "Excuse me?! What's that supposed to mean?"

Matty's mouth hung open; his floppy brown hair draped over his face as he looked between Adam and me, not sure what to say. He raised his hands, backing away. "I'm sorry. I didn't mean anything by it. It's just. Well, Devin has a type." He paused, looking down at me.

"Hot, tiny, and tanned brunettes." Aiden stared with sharp eyes. "You obviously fit that," he said with no hint of humor in his voice. He just stated it like a fact, and I wasn't sure if I should be complimented or confused.

Before I could retort, a shiny BMW rolled onto the drive. Lyss was glaring at us from inside; her face was the same shade of cherry red as the car. Her narrowed eyes and scowl were directed squarely at me.

What the hell did I do?

She jumped out of the car before it had even stopped moving; Laura barely batted an eyelash in the driver's seat.

"Uh oh. The she-devil is back," Aiden muttered, elbowing Matty.

"Is that your new pet name?" Matty asked, holding back his laughter.

Lyss looked between us, and then her gaze landed on me. "Reign! What are you doing?!" Brows crossed, she stomped over at a pace I'd only seen at the Olympics. I could have sworn her whole body was vibrating with anger. The guys didn't flinch.

I backed away from the guys, raising my hands in innocence. "What do you mean?"

She stood in front of Aiden, standing toe-to-toe. He watched her every move with an amused smirk on his face. "You can't fraternize with the enemy, Reign," she said simply, still staring at Aiden.

When Adam snickered next to me, Lyss whipped her head to him, narrowing her eyes. "Back away from my new roommate, Adam," she said calmly, but her tense jaw told a completely different story. Adam didn't move, staying defiantly by my side.

After a couple of minutes of staring, Lyss rolled her eyes, grabbed my arm, and pulled me away from the guys. "I hope you didn't tell them anything."

"Ummm," I stuttered out because I couldn't think straight.

When I didn't answer, she stopped and stared at me with wide eyes. "Oh god, you did, didn't you?"

"Don't worry, Lyss, she didn't say a thing," Jackson teased as he backed away.

The other guys had already gone back to playing football in their yard, except for Adam. He still lingered on the edge of the porch. "Is there something you need?" Lyss asked him with a questioning glare.

He bit his bottom lip, holding back a smile. "No. No. I'll see you around, Reign," he said, giving me a subtle wink before jogging back to join the rest of his roommates. I watched, doing my best to ignore the little ball of anger standing next to me. There was a tiny moment when I wished

I could go over and join them. Maybe I could embrace the reverse-harem life.

Lyss turned to me. Her face was as red as a baboon's ass, and her fists were clenched like she was trying to squeeze an orange. Clearly, I'd done something wrong, so I lifted my hands in defense. "Hey, all I did was wait outside for you." When she looked at me, she closed her eyes and finally relaxed her body.

"Ugh, I'm sorry." She sighed, glancing over at them throwing a football. Her gaze lingered on Aiden for a little longer than I thought necessary. "It's not your fault," she said, still looking at him. "We just don't get along."

I had a feeling there might be a little more to the story. "Why? They don't seem like bad guys. A little moronic, but find me a guy that isn't in college."

She laughed, and when I glanced over my shoulder, the guys were still playing football. Adam smiled when he saw me looking, and I gave him a small, inconspicuous smile back because I didn't want to tick off my roommate before I'd even gotten my bags through the door.

Laura had quietly joined us from the car, clutching her purse and inspecting her nails. Like the guys, she seemed unfazed by Lyss's reaction. "It's a long story." She sighed, wrinkling her nose and taking one of my bags. She was lugging it up the stairs before I could stop her. Just as I went to pick up the other one, Lyss swatted my hand away, taking the bag and bringing it into the house, up the stairs.

"Thanks," I mumbled, feeling a little sheepish.

"Are you sure you don't need any help, ladies?" Aiden hollered over, jeering with the other guys.

Lyss's back went ramrod straight, and she rolled her eyes. Ignoring the comment, she pulled my bag in, urging me to follow her.

My jaw nearly dropped onto the wooden floors. This place wasn't only huge; it was beautiful. The kitchen and living room were connected, creating a perfectly laid-back great room, and the house was decorated in white and blue, evoking a coastal vibe. I wanted to jump in excitement because I was more than happy to be living here.

After hauling my stuff up the stairs, Laura stood outside a door that I could only assume was the entrance to my bedroom. Her hand lingered on the doorknob, and she seemed hesitant to open it. She looked over my shoulder to Lyss before starting, "So, there's something we didn't mention about your room." She widened her eyes, guilt staining her irises. My shoulders slumped, and my stomach rolled. I knew that this place was too good to be true.

I closed my eyes, taking a deep breath. "What's wrong with it?" I was bracing myself for the worst. Maybe Lyss had an unhealthy obsession with cats, and they lived in the room, or she'd painted all the bedrooms red because she really liked *Fifty Shades of Gray*. Whatever it was, I'd already planned on embracing it. I needed to live somewhere, and it couldn't be worse than my old room.

She was looking down at her hand, fiddling with the gold knob, pushing it down. "There's nothing wrong with your room. It's a double as advertised. It's just that your window has an interesting view."

I raised my eyebrows. "What kind of view?"

"One of your windows looks into the guys' house."

Blowing out a breath, I thought about it. I could handle that. All I needed to do was shut the curtain. Easy peasy.

"Into one of the guys' bedrooms, to be precise."

My eyes widened.

"Don't worry. You've got thick curtains that you can draw at night, and Devin's always at football practice anyway, so it shouldn't be too much of an issue."

I laughed to myself. That explains Adam and Jackson's comment earlier. "Is that why you were so keen on me signing the lease before I saw the room?" Not that I pushed to see it myself.

"Yup," Lyss quipped with no ounce of remorse.

I thought about it for a second. "Okay, open the door. Let's see the damage." I couldn't back out now, and I didn't want to. Closing a curtain was much better than living with my crackhead roommates.

When Laura opened the door, I gasped at the big, beautiful room. It was light and airy, with double-aspect windows. There was a bay window facing the front of the house with a window seat, and sheer curtains billowed in the wind. The room was clean, fresh, and everything I'd wanted. To the left, there was a large window that converted into a Juliet balcony.

I walked past the large double bed toward the window. "Is it this one?" Laura nodded, and when I got to it, I gasped. There was another Juliet balcony less than two feet away, and I could see Devin's entire room. Well, I could if his curtains were open. Thankfully, his thick black curtains currently covered my view. "Oh wow. I didn't realize I'd be able to have a conversation with the guy."

Laura stood next to me, shrugging. "Yeah, it's not so bad once you get used to it, and at least you have the nice front windows." She pointed to the other side of the room, and I cocked my eyebrow. She pursed her lips, trying to hold back a laugh. She knew she was grasping at straws and that I was desperate.

It can't be that bad. I'd make it work by keeping the curtains shut. It would be fine. This little mishap wasn't enough for me to decline the room.

"We, uh, also recommend that you lock your window every time you leave the room," Laura added, showing me how to lock it.

"Why?" I didn't know why I bothered asking since I knew the answer would be something ridiculous.

"We're in a prank war with next door," Lyss answered flatly. "If you don't lock it, they'll come over and set up pranks around the house."

"What do you mean, a prank war?" Could this be worse than crackheads?

Laura waved her hand nonchalantly. "We prank each other every so often. It started last Halloween when the guys gave us what we thought were caramelized apples as a gift. When we bit into them, it turned out they were onions." I winced, my mouth tasting bitter at the thought. "Took us a week and a hell of a lot of mints to get rid of the bad breath. We got them back, though. We relabeled bait spray to air freshener and sprayed it all over their house. Their parties didn't last long that week, since the house stank of fish. They started out as harmless pranks, but slowly they're getting more extreme. So yeah, just make sure that you lock your window."

Okay, that doesn't sound *that bad*. My old roommates were definitely worse. I could deal with a few pranks. Maybe I could even get them back. They wouldn't see it coming.

"We'll leave you to settle in, but if you want any help, just call us up." Laura smiled while she and Lyss strolled out of the room.

Standing in my bedroom, I looked around. Yeah, it wouldn't be that bad at all. This house was amazing, and my roommates were friendly. Yes, Lyss seemed a little high-strung, but that was nothing I couldn't handle.

Since Devin's curtains were closed, I opened the window to let in the cool breeze. Laying my backpack on the bed, I pulled out my laptop, tablet, and phone, placing them on the desk. When I checked my phone, I noticed there was a notification from Covey Connections.

Cole.

I smiled because, in all the hassle of moving, I'd hardly had time to miss him. What was I thinking? How could I miss him? I'd only just met him.

Cole: Had a great time last night. Was hoping I could get your number. You know, just in case you're interested in another round.

I grinned at the message before forcing my face into a frown. I had a good time with him. A *great* time with him. But I couldn't give him my number because I liked him too much. If we met again, I could get attached. He'd already been occupying a little space in my mind since our encounter, and I was certain I'd fall for him if we spent any more time together.

Turning the phone off, I placed it on my desk and headed back to my suitcases on the bed. I opened one with a sigh, looking at all my neatly packed clothes. Hopefully, this would be the last time I'd have to unpack until I graduated.

Pulling out some of my clothes, I started putting them in the dresser sitting next to the open window.

"Reign?" a confused, husky male voice said, and I lifted my head up in shock because I couldn't forget that voice.

What the hell was he doing here?

SEVEN

Devin

"Reign?"

My voice was hoarse with sleep, and I still wasn't fully awake. I narrowed my eyes at the familiar form in front of me. It couldn't be her. Why the hell would she be there? It made no sense. But when my eyes drifted to her jeans, I knew it was her. I'd be able to recognize that ass of hers in a lineup if I needed to. I was clearly hallucinating; it was the only explanation for her standing in my neighbor's room. The same room that had been empty for the last three months.

Yes, that had to be it. It was because I had the best sex of my life with her, and my brain was short-circuiting, still trying to process it. I'd been seeing her everywhere since I got back from her place, and this was no different. She was clearly a figment of my imagination. I refused to close my eyes because I was concerned that if I did, she might disappear, and I wasn't quite ready for that.

She slowly stepped on her heels until she was facing me. Her perfect pink lips parted as they came into view, and her intense chocolate eyes stared at me in shock.

It was official. I was losing my mind. I was imagining her.

Scrunching my eyes shut, I scrubbed a hand across my tired face. Stubble prickled my palm, confirming that I was, in fact, awake. When I opened my eyes, I fully expected to see an empty room and to have to call Coach and let him know I needed to see a doctor tomorrow because I was having delusions.

Welp, she was still standing there, wearing a tattered high school sweatshirt and staring at me like I'd killed her pet dog. Was she a dog person? Maybe she preferred cats. *Get it together, Devin. Stop thinking about her favorite animal.* By some miracle, she was standing across from me, and I needed to focus on that.

"Cole?" she whispered it like a prayer. Her mouth was parted, and there was a slight blush on her cheeks as she stood there, stunned and confused.

The air was warm, but a fresh chill made its way down my back. Why did seeing her flustered turn me on so much?

I didn't say anything. I just watched as her eyes drifted down, taking in my bare chest and gray sweatpants. I didn't feel the urge to put a T-shirt on because she'd seen me in less, and I guess I liked watching her gawk at me.

When her eyes stopped at my thighs, they stayed there. Was she hoping my sweats would magically disappear? All she had to do was ask, and I'd gladly remove them. After a few minutes, she lifted her gaze to meet mine. When she did, she was biting her lip in restraint. I scratched my chin, hiding my smile because I enjoyed her greedy glare.

"Cole?" she whispered out again. "What are you doing here?"

Her voice. It was still as smooth and buttery as I remembered. California with just the subtlest hint of a drawl. One you'd only notice if you knew she lived in Louisiana for a few years. I took a step forward, taking my time to lean against the railing of the balcony because I liked the way she took in my chest. Resting my elbows on the railing, I was surprised at how close I was to her. My hands were basically inside that room.

Reign glanced behind her before she shuffled her way toward me. That South Point High sweatshirt she was wearing was too big to be hers, and I forced my hands to relax. They nearly clenched at the thought of her wearing another guy's sweatshirt. I needed to chill. It was a high school sweatshirt. It must have been from years ago.

"I live here." I tilted my head back at the identical room to the one she was standing in behind me. Albeit, mine was a little more modern. Aiden's dad renovated it before we moved in. "What are you doing over there?" I cocked my eyebrow, still trying to hide my smirk. I wanted to see her again, but I didn't expect it to happen so soon and for her to be delivered straight to my window. It had to be a sign.

"Well, I live here." She pointed back. Yeah, that was definitely a sign. I watched as she slowly took in the situation. Her brows pinched, her pink tongue poked out a little to swipe her bottom lip, and then her mouth dropped. "Wait a minute. Have I moved next door to you?"

I nodded, hiding my grin and excitement. We practically lived together. There was no way she could ignore me now.

She jumped, moving around the room, rambling incoherently to herself. I was going to interrupt, but I kind of liked watching her pace. It was cute. She suddenly stopped in her tracks, eyes wide and lips curved. "Wait a minute." Running back to the balcony, she poked at my chest with a broad smile. "You don't live there. That's Devin's room." That loud chuckle she did at the bar last night came out in full force and eventually turned into a fit of giggles. "You're good. You got me. This is all a joke, right?" She looked around the room and behind me, expecting Devin to pop out, I assumed. I only felt slightly guilty that I was about to dash all that hope in her eyes.

Taking in a long breath, I scratched the back of my neck before I mustered up the courage to respond. "Yeah…uh…about that…can I come over? I think it would be better if we spoke about it without the whole neighborhood hearing." I couldn't be certain that they could hear us, but I had a theory that the small gap was making some kind of echo chamber, and everyone would know our business soon.

When she tucked her bottom lip behind her teeth, I held back a groan, remembering the last time I saw her do that. It was when her legs were on my shoulders, and I was pumping inside her. "Okay, let me go downstairs and let you in." She swiveled on her heels and walked toward the door. I was too impatient to walk all the way down. Plus, I didn't want to reveal the fact that I already knew her to Laura and Lyss.

She turned away, and I watched her ass sway for a few seconds before jumping over the railing. Something I'd done countless times before.

Reign jumped when my boots thumped against the wooden floor. She quickly turned around; her face paled when she saw me standing next to her. "What the hell are you doing?! I was going to go downstairs and let you in through the front door like a normal person." She adjusted her hair, looking flustered at my presence.

Yes, I was still only in my sweats, and the closer I got, the pinker her cheeks became. "This was quicker."

She laid her hands on my arms, checking me for bruises, or at least, that was her excuse. "You could have hurt yourself."

I shrugged. "But I didn't. Look, there's something I need to tell you." I felt like an ass. Being in her presence again, with her hands innocently wrapped around my arms, reminded me how much I liked her. This omission was going to be hard to admit.

"What is it, Cole?" I winced when she stressed the name. It was like she was inadvertently taunting me. The way she looked up at me with those dark eyes and long lashes, fluttering, it was like she already knew the truth and was judging me for it. Waiting to see how long it would take for me to tell her.

But how was I supposed to break it to her? I liked her. A lot. More than I should, and I didn't want her to hate me. She was still staring at me. I needed to rip that baby off like a Band-Aid. "About that. I'm actually Devin. My middle name is Cole." Short, quick, and to the point. How could she be mad?

There was a moment of silence as she processed my truth. "WHAT?!" Her shrill voice shocked me, and I jumped back, looking for cover. There was nothing around, so I kept a comfortable distance between us. I thought she'd be upset. A little touchy, maybe. I didn't realize she'd be that pissed. She looked angrier than Lyss when she found out Aiden put hair removal cream in her face wash. Although that could be because Lyss didn't have any eyebrows, which made it hard to tell her facial expression.

I massaged my neck, easing the tension. "I had to change my name on the app," I said to the beat of her tapping foot. "It was part of the game."

"The game?" she spat out disgustedly. I had a feeling Reign could be a ball-buster when she wanted to be.

"Yeah, with my team. Remember? I told you about it this morning." Her eyes flicked to the floor, and her shoulders relaxed. "We couldn't put our real names on the app because the girls on campus know us. We wanted to see who would get the most matches without the extra help."

Reign toyed with the sleeves of her sweatshirt before dragging her eyes slowly up to me. "So, what you're telling me is that I had sex with you, and I didn't even know your name?" she said calmly, but I felt a storm brewing behind those dark chocolate eyes of hers.

"No. I'm Devin *Cole* Walker. You knew my name. Just not the first part," I surmised, hoping that helped the situation. Judging by the hurt look on her face, it didn't.

"Why didn't you tell me? You know, after we…you know?" she whispered, sadly pointing between us. I wanted to make a joke and ask after which time, but it wasn't appropriate.

With her knitted brows and shoulders slumped, what I did felt a lot like betrayal.

Pulling my ear, I shrugged. "You told me we were a one-time thing. I didn't think there was much point if that was it." It was only now, after seeing how upset she was, that I realized that was a mistake. I should have told her, probably before the first orgasm. Definitely after the second, but I didn't. It wasn't like there was a good time to just come out and mention it. Imagine if I'd brought it up while my cheeks were rubbing against her thighs. Yeah, that wouldn't have gone down well either.

"Then why did you bother sending me a message today?"

My lips twitched. "So, you got my message, then? I'm still waiting for you to respond, but yeah, I sent it because I thought I'd try my luck. It worked the first time." I leaned closer to her. Our faces were inches apart, and she looked at me, flustered.

"How was this house design ever signed off?!" she yelled, releasing some of that tension and backing away. She trailed the room back and forth. "How did this happen?" Reign started pulling at her hair, pacing faster now with the shake of her head. "I'm not that girl. I don't go around having sex with guys I don't know the name of." She stopped in her tracks, giving me the once-over. "Well, I guess you changed that for me."

I felt a slight flush on my cheeks. I didn't mean to tick her off. When I didn't answer and gave her an apologetic smirk instead, she started babbling incoherently again. I couldn't watch her freak out anymore. "Calm down. It's okay, Reign."

"No, it's not! We basically share a room!" she cried, looking back at the door as if she was worried that Lyss and Laura would hear. It wasn't like they'd care. I was almost positive Aiden had slipped through that window more than a couple of times to visit Lyss. Besides, this room has been like a revolving door over the past year. They couldn't keep anyone in it longer than a couple of months. Not because I was a lousy roomie or anything, but I guess all those pranks hadn't helped.

"You say it like it's a bad thing." Best. News. Ever. I could just imagine sneaking into her room at night and…

"It is!" she shrieked. "This." Pointing between us. "Was supposed to be a one-time thing. I was never supposed to see you again."

"Clearly, fate is bringing us together." The only response I got to that was a low, aggressive growl. I tried to ease the tension. "Or maybe you're a creeper and found out where I lived. If you wanted me, though, you didn't need to go through all that effort. Maybe it's just fate, but then again, I could imagine you doing something like that."

"Shut up, Col-Devin!"

"Look. If you're that stressed about it, you know you can lock the window and shut the curtains. I won't bother you if that's what you want. You won't see me. Well, except when I'm outside, or you're outside…but you know what I mean."

She looked back at me, calmer now, and as she approached, I couldn't help but look at her lips. They were so plump and soft. Kissable. She relaxed a little, and for a split second, I considered leaning down and kissing her, easing away all her concerns, but the creak of my door stopped that thought. I knew the rooms were close, but I had no idea it was possible to hear that from over here. It was more like sharing a room than I'd expected.

"Someone's coming," I whisper-shouted.

Her eyes widened. "Hide," she whispered back, pushing me to the side of the window, out of view. I didn't care if the guys found out about us because I didn't want any of them making a move, but that was something I'd worry about another time.

Scratching the back of her head, she pretended to look in the mirror beside the window and completely ignored my presence. She played with wisps of her hair as her eyes flicked to my room. A faint smile brushed her lips at whoever was in there.

"Oh, hey, Reign." It was Adam. How the hell did he know her name? Why did he sound like they were old buddies? And most importantly, what the hell was he doing waltzing into my room when I wasn't there?

Reign tucked a strand of hair behind her ear and walked closer to the window. "Hey." She fucking smiled at him. That cute, coy smile that girls did when they were interested in guys.

What the hell did I miss? Clenching my jaw tightly, I did my best to calm my annoyance, reminding myself that I was in her bed last night. Not him.

"I'm guessing you haven't met Devin yet?" He chuckled.

She crossed her arms over her chest, pursing her lips. "Nope. Not yet." She enunciated the words and then pointed at the railings. "Thanks for the warning," she deadpanned.

I heard him shuffling; Adam didn't take confrontation well. "Sorry, I thought you saw the room before moving in. They've had trouble filling it. No one lasts more than a few months." Why was he still talking to her? I figured he'd leave once he realized I wasn't here. Wait a second. Is he here *for her*? I'm getting a lock.

There was a moment of silence between them. Reign flicked her gaze at me and shifted her weight from side to side.

"Maybe I should ask Devin to switch rooms," he muttered. Was he flirting? I was seriously considering giving him a black eye when I got back over there.

What happened next disturbed me more than that time I accidentally walked in on Jackson changing. That dude had a Mickey Mouse tattoo on his ass, and I still couldn't get the image out of my head. Reign giggled at Adam. *Giggled.* It was all cute and flirty. Did she *like* him? Did they *like* each other?

"The good news is you know what you're getting with Devin. He's the quietest one. Always studying or sleeping." Well, I guess that was a compliment unless he was trying to paint me as boring.

Her lip quirked, and I knew she said the next line for my benefit. "Oh, I'm not worried about Devin. It's him who should be worried about me. I like to watch *The Bachelor* with twenty of my middle-aged single friends on Mondays. It sounds like he'd be some good eye candy." Dear Lord, I hoped she was joking.

Adam chuckled. "I'll make sure to stop by sometime for that." Somebody hollered inside our house. It was too far away for me to make out. "Hey, I've got to go, but I'd love for you to think about that date."

Date? He asked her on a date. Okay, I would definitely chop his balls off and feed them to him when I got back over there.

What.

The.

Fuck?

When did he even have time to ask her on a date? I thought he was obsessed with some chick back home? What was her name? Harley? Harper? Hannah? I didn't know. Either way, there was no reason for him to be sniffing around my turf. Only he didn't know it was mine.

Reign looked at me and laughed with uncertainty. "Uh-huh." That was it. That was her only response. She ignored his question. Was it because she didn't want to let him down in front of me?

My stomach dropped when something more sinister played in my mind. What if it was *me* she wanted to let down gently? Surely not? She rode me like an expert cowgirl last night. That just wouldn't happen if you weren't interested in someone.

After saying goodbye, she pulled her curtains closed and gave me a crooked smile. "Sorry about that."

"Date?" I wasn't even subtle. I needed to know.

She waved off my concern. "It's nothing. Adam was joking with the guys earlier and made a comment."

"Sounded pretty serious to me." I was pissed and couldn't hide it. She either didn't notice, or she ignored it.

"Well, it's not. Like I said to you before. I'm not in a place to be in a relationship." I so badly wanted to ask who hurt her so I could find them and rip them to shreds. "Anyway, you aren't here to talk about my relationship with Adam. You're here to talk about what happened between us."

Lifting a finger to my chin, I pretended to think for a second. "You know what? I can't remember what happened. Maybe we need to recreate it. That might help jog my memory."

She whacked me on the arm. "Stop it. This is serious." I was serious too. "Look. I've had a rough time the last year, and I really need this room to work out. I don't know what Lyss has against you guys or what's going on between all of you, but I think it would be best if we maybe keep our encounter private."

"Private?"

"Yeah. I just don't want anything to come between me and this room."

"Trust me. No one else wants this room. You're safe."

She closed her eyes, taking a deep breath. "Maybe, but like I said, a lot of things changed for me in the last few years, and I could really use some stability. I'd rather not have to explain to everyone our extremely bad luck."

"Bad luck, good luck, potato, po-tah-to."

She tilted her head, and it was the first time I noticed just how tired she was. Not physically, but mentally. Her deep eyes looked a little dull. It was a little like there was pain swimming through her irises.

What happened to this girl?

"Sorry," I breathed out. "Sure." I agreed because I'd do anything to see that carefree smile she gave me when she woke up in my arms again. "It's not a big deal. We'll just keep what we did a secret. It was supposed to be a one-night thing, anyway." That last part stung to say, but it wasn't about me. It was about her.

Her shoulders relaxed; I could almost see the tension leave her body. "Thank you so much," she whispered, giving me a hug. "So, we're going to pretend we've only just met today and that we're friends." *Friends.* It was like poison to any of my future hard-ons.

"Sure, friends."

Well, I could already tell this wasn't going to end well.

EIGHT
Devin

Trying to sleep that night was agonizing. Every time I rolled over, my eyes wandered to the window, and I stared at it, thinking about Reign. Knowing she was only a few feet away, probably snoring lightly while she slept, had my mind racing with thoughts. Naughty thoughts. What I wouldn't give to jump the railing and convince her to throw caution to the wind and try something with me. Especially now that I knew Adam was sniffing his big old honker around.

When I woke up this morning, I'd had all of two hours of sleep. Not the best way to start my weight training session, but I survived. It was the offseason, so Coach was a little more lenient. He'd still get pissy if I missed practice altogether, though. So I went, and I lifted a few light weights. I was useless. He knew a few of us were entering the draft in April, but he asked that we respectfully continue to work just as hard until that happened. The reality of it was that even if some of us entered the draft, not all of us would get picked, and then we'd have to play another year to prove ourselves all over again. Therefore, slacking before the draft wasn't an option.

Hauling up my heavy gym bag, I walked into the house, making a beeline for the kitchen. Adam was there, hunched over the counter, reading a textbook, and taking notes. My keys clinked on the granite as I tossed them across the counter and rubbed the back of my neck, trying to rid it of tension. Tension that developed from being so close to Reign but not being allowed to touch her.

"Hey Adam," I drawled out, much more Southern than usual. It happened when I was tired.

He mumbled out a soft greeting, his hands stuffed in his hair while he concentrated on the page in front of him as I stepped past him to the fridge, looking for a snack. "So, were you going to tell me about what, or should I say, *who* kept you out so late the other night?"

Thankfully, I was staring at some leftover lunch meat instead of my friend's face when he asked that question. I took my time looking for anything that could be considered a snack while I gained my composure. It was my chance to stake my claim on Reign. He'd back off. He owed me. The only problem with my plan was that Reign wasn't mine to claim. Even if I thought she was interested in me, she hadn't actually expressed any interest beyond a quick lay. If I told Adam, then he'd ask her because he was a blabbermouth, and I wouldn't want her thinking I'd been talking about our situationship with other people.

When I finally emerged from the fridge with a drink in hand, Adam was staring at me, his eyebrow quirked with a smug smirk on his face. He thought I was going to tell him all the sordid details. If it were anyone but Reign, I probably would. Hell, I'd done it before. This time, though, he was getting nothing. I kept my lips flat and emotionless. "Just someone." I shrugged it off, pretending it wasn't a big deal.

"Is it the same *someone* you were drooling over on that Covey Connections app the other day?"

I should have known this was coming. He was there. He saw my reaction, but I didn't think he'd bother asking me about it. Frankly, I thought he might have better things to do.

I changed the subject. "What's your weird obsession with wanting to know about my sex life, creep?"

His smile grew wider. "Oh, you're admitting you've finally got a sex life?"

I said nothing, annoyed at myself for that slip-up. Admittedly, it'd been a while since I'd been with a girl, but it wasn't like I'd been rolling in free time. What, with my family issues, training, and schoolwork. Hell, I would have been as happy as a priest on Christmas without any more action for the rest of the year if it sorted out all my problems. I didn't ask for Reign; Reign came to me.

"Hey man, I'm happy for you." He offered me a genuine smile. "I don't think I've ever seen you with that dazed look on your face. It's nice to see the man of steel has a chink in his armor." If he wasn't my best friend, I'd punch him in the nose for being so sappy.

"Don't you have something better to do? Like, think about your own love life? Isn't there a girl back home?" I purposely asked.

When I first met Adam in freshman year, he had a girl back home he was obsessed with. Like absolutely in love with. He hadn't mentioned her in a while, and I was curious to know why. I wondered if it had anything to do with why he asked Reign out.

He looked at me with disdain. Probably because Aiden walked in just as I asked the question. There was no way Adam would admit anything in front of Aiden, who seemed to hate women who didn't fall to their knees in front of him. Adam went back to reading his textbook. "There isn't one," he ground out. That was a lie. "I've moved on. Who knows, Reign's hot and seems nice. Maybe I'll ask her out."

My whole body tensed, and I tried to control my breathing. Well, that answered my question. I was conflicted. I wanted to tell him to back off. That he was wasting his time because I'd already slept with her. Only if I did that, I might not be able to sleep with her again.

Aiden taunted us with a snort. "Looks like there might be some competition." He glanced between the two of us, putting the pieces together before Adam could. For all of Aiden's faults, his perceptiveness was one of his better qualities. It was why he was a good quarterback. Right now, though, I did not need him pointing anything out.

"Dev's not interested. His head is in the clouds over some girl he met the other night." He was right on the one hand. On the other hand…

"Yeah, about that girl." I should just tell him.

"Guys, as much as I want to sit here and talk about our feelings, we've got more important things to do. Come with me," Aiden said, striding out of the room.

I looked back at Adam, and I was about to tell him the whole truth.

"Hurry up!" Aiden yelled one more time, and we reluctantly followed him out.

Walking into the bathroom, I stopped in my tracks. There, in the middle of the room, was a giant catapult aimed out the window. "What the hell is that?"

"A catapult," he said, as though it were simple. "I ordered it from China two months ago, and it finally arrived. The girls are sitting outside with pizza; it's the perfect opportunity to use it."

"Uh, what are you planning on throwing at them? Rocks?" Adam asked. I was sure he was feeling as uneasy about this as I was. This prank war that Aiden and Alyssa had going on was getting old.

"No! I may be an asshole, but I'm not a killer." At least he admitted it. "Matty made water balloons." He pointed to the bathtub full of bright-blue balloons. How did I miss that when I walked in? I guess the giant catapult drew my attention.

I looked between the catapult, the balloons, and Aiden. "Maybe we should wait for a couple of days. You know, because it's this girl's first week in that house. We've already helped to run off three other roommates. Maybe we should give them a break," I said, pretending I didn't know Reign's name.

"Don't pretend to care, Devin. You just want to get in her pants," Aiden spat out, looking out the window while Adam shook his head. "Perfect." He grinned and waved his hands at us. "Come on, have a look."

When we got to the window, we could see the girls below. They were sitting at their picnic table with a welcome banner for Reign. It was such a sweet gesture and a welcome I was certain Reign would love. I didn't know much about her, but I sensed she needed a few people on her side. Hopefully, she'd get that with Laura and Lyss.

A pang of guilt passed through my veins as I looked at the girls and then at Aiden with his maniacal grin. "Aiden, I don't know. I feel bad about ruining their dinner…"

Adam scratched the back of his neck, his face contorted. There was no doubt he was feeling the same guilt as me.

"Don't be ridiculous. We'll buy them more pizza after. It gives us an excuse to go over there, and we can watch Adam and Devin fight it out over the new one." And there we had it. Aiden was coming up with any excuse to see Alyssa. Even if it meant tormenting her. Adam had this drunk smile on his face, and I was starting to worry he might have already developed feelings for Reign. I really should speak to him. I just needed to figure out how.

"More like an excuse to hang out with Lyss," Adam retorted.

"Whatever. I just like seeing how angry she gets with our pranks."

"Do us all a favor and sleep with her already so we can stop these stupid games," Adam added.

"Nope. Not gonna happen."

Adam and I groaned in unison. He was like a damn dog with a bone sometimes.

"You're a stubborn ass, you know?" I said.

Aiden shrugged past me. "Aren't I always? Be back here in ten. I'll get Matty and Jackson, and we'll start this up." He walked past us, rubbing his hands together like he was an evil genius. *Idiot.*

Adam and I were standing in the room together. As he inspected the catapult, I tried to think of a way to tell him about Reign without explicitly telling him. Then, when he moved to the window, I noticed a goofy grin fall across his face.

Well, shit.

I bet he was watching Reign. Studying how her cheeks dimpled when she laughed or how her forehead creased when she asked a question that she was genuinely interested in. Yeah, I knew I had it bad for her already, but I couldn't let Adam fall in too deep. "So, the new girl…" I started, not sure how I was going to end the sentence. All I needed to do was admit I'd slept with her. Four times if we were being technical.

"She seems really sweet." I wanted to whack that stupid smile off his face.

"Oh yeah? You've talked to her?"

"Jackson and I sat with her while she was waiting for the girls to come home." That explained when he had time to ask her on a date. A little desperate if you asked me, but who was I to judge? I stalked her on an app first. "Have you spoken to her yet?"

"Yeah, we practically live in the same room."

"I figured." He looked like he was concentrating on something. What, I don't know. But, as his eyes glanced back at me, I could tell there was a question on the tip of his tongue. Maybe he was taking all those hints and coming to the conclusion that I was interested without me having to explicitly say so. That might help.

Our conversation was cut short when Aiden, Jackson, and Matty entered the tiny bathroom. Five large football players should not be in here at one time. "Are you ready?" Aiden asked, eyes gleaming with mischief. We were actually going to go through with this. Jackson took one of the giant water balloons and set it in the catapult's well. The sheer size of the balloon made me feel uneasy.

"Aiden, are you sure about this? It could seriously hurt someone," I interjected.

"It's just water, and I'll shout so they have time to get away from the impact."

"Wait, you're agreeing that this could hurt someone?"

"It won't, dude, don't worry." He patted me on the shoulder, like that was supposed to make me feel better. "Right, the girls are all down there now and eating. It's the perfect time."

Adam and Jackson held the balloon in place while Matty ordered pizzas for the aftermath. Aiden was leaning out the window, watching the girls, and I stood there looking like an idiot, waiting for the whole thing to play out. "Devin, you need to hold the handles to position it," he ordered, and I foolishly followed his lead. I wish following the captain hadn't been drilled into my brain since birth. "Lean it slightly to the left…too far. A little more to the right. Perfect. Okay, Devin, slowly and carefully pull back the balloon. Adam and Jackson hold the catapult steady."

I pulled the balloon back and held it in place. "I think it's ready to go, Aiden."

"Okay, on three. One…two…three!"

With that, I closed my eyes and let the balloon go. Before I could even register what had happened, the giant blue balloon was flying out of the window and heading straight for the girls.

What had I done?

NINE
Reign

A loud voice boomed in the distance. "Incoming!" That was when everything moved in slow motion.

Lyss and Laura's eyes grew wide as they looked at something behind me. Their screeching chairs moved me into action, and when I turned around, there was a big blue ball floating in the air. As much as I wanted to move out of the way like Lyss and Laura, my brain couldn't focus enough to move my feet. I was frozen on the spot, and all I could do was watch a giant ball hurtling toward me.

Closer.

Closer.

The ball was getting bigger, and finally, my mind snapped back to reality. There was no way I had time to get away from the table, so I did the only thing I could think of. I covered my face with my hands, held my breath, and braced for the impact.

I didn't see what happened next, but I heard a loud burst as the balloon hit the table and the plates clattered around it. The cold water stole my breath. My entire body was drenched, and I couldn't move at all. I was stunned and found myself asking what the hell I'd gotten myself into. Even the warm California heat couldn't stop my shivers, and I kept my eyes closed, just in case another water balloon was coming my way. The silence around me was deafening; everyone was just staring, lost for words.

As I slowly gained the courage to wipe my eyes and open them to assess the damage, the first thing I noticed was the hot pink of my bra blaring from under my white sundress. Folding my arms over my chest, I covered as much as I could. It wasn't much, but it was all I could do.

Torn blue latex covered the table, right above our now-soggy pizza. Plates were thrown everywhere; quite a few had cracks or were broken completely. In a way, I was lucky it was only the water that got me.

"Oh my god!" Lyss screeched. "I am so sorry, Reign." Bone dry, she and Laura headed back to the table, cleaning up the mess in front of me. "We should have warned you that the guys like to make sneak attacks."

Laura rolled her eyes, shaking her head as she carefully picked up the broken shards of plates. "I'm sorry, Lyss. I think these are unsalvageable."

Lyss stopped, looked down at the remnants of the china, and frowned. She flicked her gaze up to a laughing Aiden and Jackson. "This was your idea, wasn't it, you arrogant poop sniffer?" she screamed at Aiden, shaking her fist like it would do anything. The only thing it did was make the guys laugh harder. "I'm going to kill you."

When Aiden finally stopped laughing, he said, "Try to come back from that, Alyssa!" He drawled out her name like a taunt.

"You could have waited. It's Reign's first day!" Laura yelled.

Squelching out my now-wet hair, I sighed. "It's fine, guys. You have to admit it was pretty funny," I said to Lyss and Laura. Then I glanced up at the guys, mainly focused on Devin, who had popped his head out and was watching me. "How the hell did you throw that with such precision?!" I asked loud enough for them to hear.

"We have a giant catapult," Jackson responded. Aiden nudged him, throwing a threatening look his way.

"Maybe next time, try throwing it toward Aiden," Laura muttered, and Aiden barked out a laugh as he backed away from the window without a care in the world.

A flash of blonde appeared, and Adam's friendly face beamed down. "Chill out, guys. We've ordered more pizza; it should be here soon. We'll come down and join you." He winced when we made eye contact. Yeah, I looked like a wreck. Drowned rat didn't look good on me, but did it look good on anyone?

"Maybe we don't want you here!" Lyss retorted, marching into the house and slamming the door behind her like a toddler having a tantrum.

"Aw, come on, Alyssa, you gotta admit that was a good one!" Aiden softened, poking his head back out and talking to her, even though I was almost certain she couldn't hear him. She'd been inside for a couple of minutes now.

When Lyss came back out, she had a trash bag in her hands, ready to clean up. She tried to look unimpressed, but I noticed her nose was red and her cheeks were rosy. Had she been crying? "I'm sorry, Reign. I can't believe they couldn't just give us a night off so we could enjoy some time with you." She looked over at me with an apologetic smile. It was hard to pretend I didn't notice how blotchy her skin was.

"Honestly, it's fine. Come on; it's pretty funny when you think about it. That catapult they have must be huge to have thrown a balloon that size." I tried to lighten the mood a little.

"Aiden probably bought it to make up for his other shortcomings," Lyss muttered.

"Don't knock what you can't have." Aiden opened our fence door, grinning proudly from ear to ear. He and Adam walked in like they owned the place, and Lyss didn't stop them. I did notice one of her eyes twitching, though. She kind of looked like a malfunctioning robot.

Aiden tapped her on the shoulder as he walked by, and she narrowed her eyes with a scowl.

"Here. I brought you this," Adam said behind me. He fanned out a fluffy white towel, and I noticed his cheeks redden as he looked down at my dress, only to immediately flick his eyes away. The white skirt of the dress was clinging to my legs, no doubt showing an unflattering image of my bright pink underwear underneath. Like a little kid, I walked into the towel and his embrace as he wrapped his arms around me, covering my whole body. The warm citrus tones of his aftershave tickled my nose.

His hands rubbed up against my arms, trying to dry me off. His warm breath hit my cold, wet shoulder when he whispered into my ear, "You're shivering."

He was right, my teeth were chattering, and I needed to take a shower before I caught a cold. But I also needed to get out of this backyard with some dignity intact. "Thanks," I mumbled out breathlessly.

When I turned to look at him, his blue eyes peered down at me. The light dusting of freckles played on his cheeks as he smiled; his hand was now rubbing my back. I must admit, I was surprised at how affectionate he was. It seemed to come easily to him.

"Get a room, why don't you?" Aiden hollered from across the yard, making me instantly snap away from Adam and look for Devin. Why? I didn't know. I just seemed to look for him.

I held the towel across my chest as I pointed toward the back door. "I'm just going to head inside and shower." I offered Adam one final smile before opening the door.

He nodded, holding his lips tight. "Make sure you come back down, though. The pizza should be here soon."

"Okay. Sure."

Just as I turned around to head back to the door, Adam said, "And umm, sorry…"

I glanced over my shoulder, meeting Adam's eyes. "For what?"

"Getting you wet," Aiden interrupted with a chortle.

Laura slapped him upside the head, which was impressive in its own right, considering he was at least a foot taller than her.

I hurried to my room because I could hear the water dripping off my dress. A lot of the stuff in Lyss's house looked like antiques, and I didn't want to ruin anything. When I got to my room, I shut the door and dropped my towel.

Knock. Knock.

Devin was at the window, leaning over the balcony and waving with a lopsided grin. His eyes drifted down my dress, taking me in. I didn't bother covering up because, frankly, I liked the heat behind his eyes, and I thought he needed a little payback after yesterday when he strolled in here with nothing but a pair of sweatpants on.

I walked up to the window, unlocking it and then opening it up. "Nice prank." I smirked, leaning against the railing.

"Nice bra," he retorted, looking down at the pink poking through. "You should probably shut your curtains before you take your dress off. The house next door is full of a bunch of horny college guys." He motioned his thumb behind him.

"Mhmm, it's okay. You'd protect me, right?" Was I flirting with Devin? Of course, I was. He started it with the bra comment, and he was looking at me with those gorgeous, smoldering eyes. I couldn't help it.

"Why would you think I wouldn't be watching too?"

I leaned over, closer to him, fully aware of how much I looked like a melting panda, but I didn't care. He was still looking at me like I was delicious, and that gave me enough confidence. I could hear the dripping pools of water puddling around my feet. "You've already seen it," I whispered, trying to speak with as straight a face as possible.

"Doesn't mean I don't want to see it again." He licked his lips, and my heart skipped a beat.

He was only saying it to get a rise out of me. He wanted to see me melt at his feet. Instead of swooning and letting my legs give out like they wanted to, I bit my bottom lip, taking him in. Damn his dark wash jeans and white shirt. They hugged him in all the right places. I got so hot just looking at him.

"Not gonna happen," I teased. I turned around, doing my best to saunter into my room with sass and leave Devin wanting more. Sadly, it didn't work. I slipped as I walked over the puddle I'd created earlier. I felt the wind blow through my hair as I landed on the floor with a loud, hard smack.

I stayed on the floor, lying there. What would be more embarrassing? Looking like I'd passed out from falling in my own pool of water or trying to get up only to fall over again because I couldn't get a grip? Before I could make a choice, Devin, ever the white knight, was crouched next to me. He either climbed through that window really fast, or I actually passed out and had a concussion.

"Are you okay?" he asked as he tried to push away some of the wet hair from my face.

Did I forget to mention that my wet ponytail smacked me dead in the nose like a whip? I hadn't had time to remove it, so I was just lying there with all my hair in my face. Yeah, I must have looked super hot.

"I'm fine," I lied, even though I was pretty sure it wasn't just my ego that was bruised from that fall. My back was aching, and I wasn't sure I'd be able to get up.

As if he read my mind, Devin grabbed my hand, pulling me slowly up to my feet. His arms wrapped tightly around me, making sure I didn't fall again.

Once I was standing, I fell into him from the full force of his pull and braced myself by placing my hands on his chest. At that moment, I lost my breath. Memories of when we were in bed came flooding back. I wanted to rewind to that night and replay it over and over again.

"Thanks." I couldn't look at him. I didn't want him to know what sort of dirty thoughts were going through my mind.

He leaned to the side, grabbing the towel that Adam had given me, and placed it on the floor below as he wiped the wood. "Wipe your feet on the towel, so they're dry."

I obliged, letting him capture my feet in his towel-clad hand as he massaged them. Something about him being on his knees, serving me, was mildly erotic.

"Why don't you go take a shower? I'll dry the floors for you and then meet you outside," he suggested, taking the towel and my thoughts away with him.

"Okay."

I really wanted to ask him to stay with me and wait, maybe even join me. But I didn't. It would sound a little desperate, and I wasn't desperate…well, maybe a little…for him. Which I shouldn't be because I already told him we should just be friends. Nothing more could happen between us. So, I walked ahead into the bathroom, feeling weird that I was leaving a hot guy in my bedroom to clean my floors. That didn't happen every day.

My room was dry when I'd made it out of the shower, and Devin was gone. His curtains were shut, and for a split second, I thought my mind was playing tricks on me. All the moments I had with Devin felt like a vague memory in the back of my head. I only wish I could bring them forward and relish in them.

After brushing my hair, putting on a pair of shorts, and one of Clay's old sweatshirts, I made my way downstairs. The laughter and chatter from outside floated into the house, and it sounded like the pizzas had already arrived.

Our backyard was now empty and clean. The only evidence that we were attacked with balloons was the still-wet patio stones. I followed the voices drifting over the fence to the guy's backyard.

When I unlatched and opened the door, I was met with the smiling faces of my new roommates and our next-door neighbors with enough pizza to feed the college for the day. Even though I was just a victim to a pretty cruel prank, they were all smiling and happy to see me. It was the first time in a long time I'd felt somewhat normal. No one viewed me as anything other than the college girl I was. A feeling I hadn't had since high school before my parents passed away.

I headed over to the bench and took the last seat available between Devin and Adam.

"Sorry about earlier, Reign." Matty smiled apologetically. "We didn't want to do that on your first week, but Aiden insisted." He took his black cap off, running a hand through his chestnut hair, and scowled at Aiden.

I just shrugged, grabbing a piece of pizza. "Ah, it's not a problem. I thought it was a good prank." I took a bite of the cheesy pie as Matty relaxed back into his seat. "Just wait until we get you back," I said quietly.

"Is that a challenge?" Aiden piped up, his eyebrow cocked with a smile growing on his chiseled face. A guy that wicked shouldn't look so much like Superman.

"More of a promise." I winked.

His brows knitted together in surprise. Maybe he thought he could intimidate me. He didn't scare me in the slightest.

"You're a feisty one, aren't you?" Adam elbowed me, pushing me directly into Devin's arm. That small connection sent shivers straight down my spine, directly to my panties.

"I've been called worse in my day." I took another large bite and lifted the leg next to Adam up to create a little more room between the two guys. The seats were wide, but the guys were bigger than the average person. In fact, I was surprised they could fit through door frames. Lifting my leg was the only way to claim more space.

As I chewed on my pizza, Devin choked loudly. Adam took no time to reach around me to pat him on the back. "Dude, are you okay?" Adam asked, and Devin nodded, holding a hand to his mouth and still partially coughing. Then, with tears streaming down the corners of his eyes, he looked at me with urgency. His gaze flicked down, moving between my face and thigh a few times. It took me a few seconds to register that he wanted me to look down.

I gasped. Purple, red, and blue marks covered the top of my inner thigh.

I shoved my leg back under the table, pulling my shorts down as far as I could. Devin had given me not just one hickey but a plethora of them leading directly to my center. How had I not noticed?

My cheeks heated at the memory of him nibbling toward my center and the way his tongue teased me right before he gave me everything I ever wanted. But I was quickly knocked back to reality when Adam's arm rested on my shoulder. Instead of bringing it back after patting Devin's back, he draped it around me. Not sure what to do with that. If I moved it off, I'd embarrass him in front of his friends, so I just left it there for now.

The conversation continued as I munched down on the pizza, noticing Adam's hand trailing down my back and rubbing my shoulder. It was awkward. What, with Devin sitting right on the other side, but I couldn't deny his warm hand felt nice. Clay never touched me so freely, and it wasn't like my parents were around to offer me hugs anymore. His arm gave me a sense of comfort in a way. That was when the guilt started to settle in, but I shouldn't feel guilty. It was just a hand on my shoulder. Devin was just a guy I'd slept with. We'd made no promises to each other. Nothing was going to happen between us.

"So, how did you guys meet?" I asked, pointing between Aiden, Jackson, Matty, Adam, and last, Devin. I held my gaze with his for a second longer than I probably should have because his hazel eyes always dragged me in.

"Football," they grunted in unison. Most of them were more concerned with eating than answering my question.

"Should have guessed that, right? Have you always lived together?"

"We moved here last year when Aiden joined the team," Matty replied. "We wanted to live off-campus away from the frats and their parties."

"It means we control the guest lists," Aiden griped out, looking at me pointedly. As if I wanted to go to his stupid jock parties anyway. They sounded worse than those two-on-one dates that happened on *The Bachelor.*

"Ah, so I guess you just focus on the jocks and cheerleaders, right?"

"They come, but they aren't the only ones we invite," Jackson added. They probably only invite other girls because they'd been through all the ones on the cheer team.

"Rest assured, princess; you'll always be invited. You can be my plus one," Adam whispered in my ear.

Princess? No one called me princess, but I nodded along, focusing on how good the pizza was instead of my new nickname.

"Speaking of, are you girls going to come to our party on Friday?" Laura and Lyss responded with a few grumbles that I guessed were a yes.

Devin leaned in. "I'd love to see you there," he muttered, only loud enough for me to hear. I bit my bottom lip to hide my smile.

"What are you studying, Reign?" Matty asked before I had to respond.

"Nursing," I answered quickly.

"That's admirable. What made you choose it?"

I shoveled a little more pizza into my mouth, taking my time to think of an answer. My parents dying in a car accident wasn't exactly something I wanted to share with the group. Talk about killing the mood.

"I just want to help people," I replied. "What do you study, Adam?" I asked him quickly because he was the one who was looking at me most intently, and I wanted to get the focus off me.

His eyebrow lifted in surprise, and he cleared his throat. "I study business economics. Are most of your courses in the Farrar Research Building?"

I nodded.

"I'm surprised I've never seen you there. All of mine are in the Coates Building next door."

"It's probably because I'm a recent transfer."

"Where'd you transfer from?"

"South Louisiana University."

"A Southern girl without an accent." He laughed. "What made you leave?"

"I'm originally from California. I'm just coming back home." I could feel Devin's eyes on me. He knew more of the story than any of them, but he wasn't going to admit that.

The conversation moved away from me, and I quietly ate my pizza, lost in my own thoughts. So many things happened in the last few years at SLU that it made it hard for me to trust and connect with people. Clay and Ally were the biggest blow to my confidence, and I wasn't sure if I was ready to let anyone get that close to me again or if I wanted to.

Devin's thigh nudged mine, and when I peered over at him, the corners of his lips were upturned slightly, making tingles burst in my belly.

Maybe eventually I'd be able to let someone in.

Later that night, as I was lying in my bed watching the moonlight pool on the wooden floor, I heard Devin's door open. I looked at my red flashing clock. One a.m. I hadn't seen him for hours, not since we finished dinner, and I'd wondered where he'd been. Watching him, I felt bad that I'd left my curtains open and was now technically invading his privacy. I couldn't bring myself to shut them earlier because I kind of liked the feeling of his presence.

He was standing in the middle of his room, looking down at his phone wearily. Running a shaky hand through his hair, he sighed heavily before stuffing his phone in his pocket. Pacing back and forth, I could feel the frustration from here. He still hadn't noticed me. Probably because there were no lights on in my room, and I was peeking from under my covers.

I should stop looking. This would definitely be considered an invasion of privacy, but when he pulled his shirt off, I couldn't keep my eyes off him. Muscles in his stomach rippled as he revealed his tanned, toned torso. My inner thighs tingled and my face flushed. I had it bad for the boy next door—that much I knew.

I shimmied farther under the covers, watching him unbutton his jeans and pull his pants down, excited that I knew what was hiding under there. It was official; I was a pervert, or at least a sexual deviant.

A burning desire churned in my belly as I continued to watch every contraction of his muscles. If only he were just over the balcony in my room, then I could show him some appreciation.

When he turned, I gasped and quickly clasped my hand against my mouth, crushing my eyes shut. He didn't hear me, did he? When I gained enough confidence to open my eyes, he was making his way toward the curtain, and all of those excited tingles turned to dread.

Embarrassment flamed across my cheeks.

Did he see me watching him?

I slumped further into the bed, so only one eye was visible, and watched. My nerves had calmed with the protection, but there was still something brewing in my belly as Devin walked to the window. I was hoping it was trepidation and not lust. He lifted his hand to the curtain, holding it for a minute while he looked out—directly at me.

Oh god. He saw me.

His fingers twitched against the fabric, as though he was contemplating his next move. I took a deep breath in preparation because I knew for sure he was going to shut the curtain and out me for the voyeur that I apparently was. Instead, his lip quirked before he dropped his hand, turning back to his room and sitting on his bed. After dropping his phone onto the bedside table, he laid back on his bed, sighing.

Did he want me to keep watching? Maybe that was his way of asking me to join him.

I shook my head, ridding myself of all the wayward thoughts, and rolled over. Closing my eyes, I did my best to think about anything except how hot and flustered my new neighbor made me feel.

TEN
Reign

I shut the front door, relaxing against it as I breathed in the fresh jasmine scent of my home. Sucking in a breath, my eyes opened in surprise. *Did I just say that?* Did I just call this place my home? It'd only been a week. That label should have felt premature, but strangely, it didn't. I've felt more at home here than I had anywhere else over the last few years. Once my parents passed, my house was empty. All those once-happy memories crumbled into dust. It wasn't my *home* after that. I hadn't had one since. Don't get me wrong. I was so thankful that my aunt took me in after everything, but her house was never my home. I was in a different state, living my cousin Ally's life. Little did I know how literal that sentiment would become.

When I got back to California a few months ago, I wasn't sure I'd made the right decision. I was still lonely, but it was a fact that I had to live with now. I was alone. That was my reality now. It was me against the world. Only me, and I needed to get comfortable with it.

I could hear Laura and Lyss chattering in the kitchen, and although they weren't family, they somehow made me feel a little less alone. They'd been nothing but kind to me since I moved in. We'd already had a couple of movie nights, and Laura loved to cook, so as long as I pitched in for the groceries, I'd had a meal most nights.

Things were falling into place. The messed-up life that I was leading over the last few years was coming together. No longer was I living like a ruined canvas, with colors that had been muddled together to create a brown, lifeless painting, because nothing made sense. Now, it felt like the chaos was slowly bleeding away, leaving me with a lightheartedness in my chest that I hadn't felt in a long time. No, this didn't feel the same. This house was different. These people were different. Maybe even *I* was different. It was too soon to tell, but I was hopeful.

As I walked farther into the house, the laughter in the kitchen grew louder. The girls were unloading some groceries, and I quietly greeted them as I walked over to help.

"Reign! Just the girl we were waiting for," Lyss cooed through curved lips.

Something about the way she spoke made my stomach fill with trepidation. I was sure she wanted something; I just wasn't sure what.

"What's up?" I opened the plastic bag, pulling out some fruit.

Laura shrugged, fiddling with a carton of orange juice. "Nothing major. We're just figuring out our next prank on the guys."

"Nothing major?!" Lyss grunted. "I would say that is pretty major since Aiden broke Nana Lou's plates." Then, pursing her lips, she didn't look at either of us, too busy stewing in her own anger against Aiden. That explained why she was so upset when she saw the state of the table after the balloon bomb.

"What's your revenge plan?" I asked, putting the fruit in a bowl.

They gave each other a smirk, then Laura answered, "We've got a few ideas, but we thought we'd pass them by you before we started prepping."

"What's your best one?"

"Glitter," Laura quipped with a broad grin. I cocked an eyebrow, waiting for more.

"Just glitter?" They both nodded proudly. "So what? You want us to throw glitter in their faces when they open the door?" It didn't sound great.

"No, of course not." Lyss rolled her eyes, flipping a strand of her wavy blonde hair over her shoulder. "Everyone knows glitter is the herpes of the crafting world. It gets everywhere, and just when you've spent days cleaning, and you think you've managed to get rid of it all, sparkles start shining from between your butt cheeks."

I wrinkled my brow. "Do I want to know where you've been using glitter?"

Lyss closed her eyes, sighing in annoyance. "Not the point. The point is, we're going to use it to tick the guys off. We're going to stick it in places they'd least expect it, so when they start to notice glitter, they'll have no idea where it's coming from, making it that much harder to get rid of." She cackled at the idea.

Okay, now it sounded better. "Where were you thinking of putting it?"

"In their drawers with all their clothes, especially their boxers. We should also stick some in their washing machine. That way, when they go to wash their clothes to wash it off, they'll make it worse."

"And don't forget how much glitter sheds. It will be all over their carpet," Laura added.

Lyss pointed with a nod. "Exactly. And I doubt they even own a vacuum, so every step they take will be a constant reminder of us." She cackled, throwing her head back to the ceiling. "They'll have hairy, glittery dicks for months." Where Laura and I cringed at that thought, Lyss was unfazed. She almost looked happy about their decorated penises.

"Hold on a minute. If you just stick it in their drawers, wouldn't it be obvious that someone came in and tampered with their stuff? If we want this prank to work, we need to hide it in places where they'd never expect to find it." I thought about it while putting the yogurt away. "I got it. We should stick it in the condom pockets of their jeans."

"Condom pockets?" Laura's brows furrowed.

"You know, those little pockets within the big pocket at the front?" Lyss and Laura shared a bemused glance. "Aren't they called condom pockets?"

Laura shook her head. "You two. Glittered cocks and condom pockets. That is a good idea, though. It won't move too quickly around their stuff, and it will be hard to pinpoint where the glitter is coming from, with the added benefit that it will be a bitch to get out."

I clapped, picking up my bag. "Cool, so there we have it. We will fill their denim with glitter. We just need to figure out a time when they're all out."

"Tomorrow morning, they're all at practice," Lyss pointed out. I couldn't help but question how she knew that. I had a feeling there was a lot more going on between her and Aiden than this weird prank war. "Let's aim for that."

"Alright, guys, I'm glad we have a plan, but now I need to head upstairs and write a paper." I grabbed my bag from the counter and made my way toward the stairs.

"Be ready at seven a.m."

I swiveled on my heel to make sure they weren't joking. "Seven a.m.?"

"They go to practice early. Surely you knew that. What do you and Adam talk about, if not football? You're connected at the hips."

"We aren't *that* close?"

"Uh-huh, sure." She sounded unconvinced. "Because it's totally normal for a guy to go to campus in the morning for training and then come all the way back just to walk you there."

I clutched at my bag straps. "I didn't know he did that," I admitted, feeling rather stupid.

On my first day walking to campus, Adam was waiting at the end of the drive. He wanted to show me the quickest route. We'd been walking to class together ever since. We even had the occasional lunch when our schedules matched. I had no idea he was coming all the way back just to walk me in, though. I'd need to talk to him about that. "I gotta go. I'll be ready at seven," I said, taking the steps two at a time to get up the stairs quicker.

When I got to my room, I scrunched my nose and groaned. My brain was fried from all the assignments I needed to finish. It didn't help that I now felt terrible about Adam. On that first day, I was thankful he was there, and I'd really enjoyed hanging out and getting to know him over the last few days, but that didn't mean I wanted him to go out of his way for me. I didn't have time to worry about that now, though. Now, I had a date with my laptop and a paper to write.

Sitting at my desk, I rolled my neck, ridding myself of the tension that had accumulated from hunching. I'd been working for hours; my eyes were burning, and my head was throbbing from the lack of light. I'd been so engrossed in my assignment that I only had my small desk lamp to work with. Just as I was about to turn the computer off, I heard the distinct creak of Devin's door opening. Scrunching my face, I was already feeling embarrassed because I knew I'd have to explain myself.

The last time I saw him was when I ogled him in the dark. I hoped and prayed he hadn't seen me, but that question was answered when I got up the following day. I eagerly woke up, fully expecting to see him in all his chiseled glory, stretching and getting out of bed.

Disappointment and embarrassment burned through my belly, creating an intoxicating feeling of regret when I was met with his black velvet curtains instead.

His curtains.

He *shut* his curtains.

I had to take it for the hint that it was. He knew I was a voyeur; I acted worse than a bachelorette watching a *Magic Mike* stage show. At least they were open with their staring. I needed to accept that he wanted nothing to do with me. I just wished I wanted nothing to do with him either. I could hear him rustling around the room. I had no restraint. Not when it came to him.

I tilted my head, trying to peer at Devin through the corner of my eye while keeping my head facing the laptop. I nearly fell off my chair when I caught sight of him. He was scrubbing a towel into his dark, wet hair, and a pair of gray sweatpants hung low on his hips. Did he run out of shirts or something? His abs were on full display *again*. I bet if I turned all the way to look at him thoroughly, I'd see a droplet of water trickling down his muscles, calling out for me to lick it off.

Apparently, I'd learned nothing from the other night. With my eyes already aching, I knew I should look away. Give Devin the privacy that he so clearly hinted at wanting, but I couldn't drag my eyes back to the laptop. Maybe this was how all voyeurs started off? Just a few innocent glances until the thrill was part of the thing that got them off.

The way those sweatpants hung on his hips left little to the imagination. Not that I had to imagine much. I knew exactly what he was packing under there, and I wanted to feel it all over again.

I bit my lip because I was getting hot and uncomfortable watching him. I very slowly and discreetly started rubbing my thighs together to ease the throbbing that was building between them. Why the hell did I agree to a one-time thing? The way he set me on fire was unhealthy, and I needed a good dose of vitamin D to ease the burn.

All my thoughts stopped when his eyes met mine and his lip curled. He caught me watching him, and he knew it. All that tension left his body as he slowly walked toward the window, making sure his chest was puffed out. He was giving me a show and a whole bucket load of mixed signals.

As he leaned over the railing, he placed a hand on the glass and gently pushed my window open. "Hey, darlin'," he slurred, and I had to ignore the butterflies in my stomach when I heard his thick, throaty accent. I hadn't realized how much I missed it.

"D." I gave him a tight smile, hoping he couldn't tell he was making me hotter than Las Vegas in my panties. He watched my every move as I stood up to meet him at the window. As I approached, I noticed his tired eyes and pale skin. "Are you okay? You look a little down." I asked, placing my hands on either side of his. We were barely touching, but I felt the electricity all the way down to my toes.

His smile softened as he relaxed, looking down at the floor, then back at me. "It's not been the best day," he admitted quietly. His hazel eyes were swirling with tiredness mixed with a little sadness. "But just seeing you has made it all a little better." I could tell he was giving me a forced smile.

Ignoring the tingles, I let my thumb gently rub the side of his pinkie finger. "Do you want to talk about it? I'm a great listener."

His pinky moved, wrapping itself around my thumb as he thought about it for a minute. "Not really." He sighed, and as he edged closer, his musky cologne filled my nostrils, instantly relaxing me.

Devin's the quiet one. Quieter than any of his friends who are almost open books. When they were joking and laughing the other day, I noticed he was pensive as he sat there watching the group. It was like he was lost in his own world. One I wanted to learn more about because, even though we'd shared the most intimate parts of our bodies, it felt like I didn't really know him. And gosh, did I want to.

I leaned back from the railing, giving him the space I thought he needed. I smiled, noticing he watched my body with interest. It was nice to think that I might have the same effect on him as he had on me.

"Do you want to hang here?" He scratched the back of his head, giving me a lopsided smile. A quick thrill ran down my spine because this was the first time I'd been invited to spend time with him, in his space. "We could watch a movie," he suggested.

A dark room, alone with Devin.

I was in.

"Are you sure? I don't want to disturb you," I asked, more out of politeness because the last thing I'd want to do was force him to hang out with me when he just wanted to be alone. I couldn't deny the idea of being in his bedroom was sending all kinds of excitement through my body, though.

He grinned, and I was sure he could hear the eagerness in my voice. I had a feeling if I went over there, things might end in a more than friendly kind of way, but I didn't mind. "I'd love the company."

I held back a squeal of excitement. "Okay, great. Well, let me just put my pj's on, and I'll come right over."

He nodded with a wide grin on his face. Was this really going to happen again? Had I somehow manifested it through all those dreams last night?

After I turned around, I glanced over my shoulder. Devin was still leaning against the railing. He was slow to move because he was watching me intently. I may have added a little swag to my walk for good measure. I grabbed a pair of shorts and a T-shirt from my bed and headed to the bathroom to get ready for my night with Devin.

ELEVEN
Devin

Well, that was easier than I expected. I'd always believed blackmail would be the only way to get Reign into my room after we agreed to just be friends. *Friends.* I scoffed at the sour taste that word left in my mouth.

I saw the way she watched me when she thought I couldn't see her. When she was tucked under her covers, anxiously waiting for me to drop my boxers. Oh, she was tempting as hell that night. Unfortunately for her, she had no idea that my light reflected into her room, giving me the perfect view of her lusty gaze. When I walked up to the window, I was ready to jump over and show her exactly how *friendly* I could be. But I didn't. I respected her wishes and turned away, leaving my curtain open for good measure, of course. She wanted me as much as I wanted her; I just needed to get her to admit it, especially after such a crappy week.

The minute she shut the door to the bathroom, I spun on my heel, scanning the room for wayward socks and boxers. I picked up a couple of pairs of dirty white tube socks and threw them into my almost overflowing laundry basket. I wasn't a neat freak like Adam, but I certainly didn't like living in a pile of dirty clothes, especially when a hot girl had the perfect view of my room.

Learning from last time, I locked my door. No one was going to interrupt my time with Reign; more specifically, *Adam* wasn't going to. It'd been so hectic; I still hadn't had time to tell him about Reign. I'd only seen him at practice and dinner with the guys, and it was a subject I'd rather not broach with anyone else around. I knew he was interested in her. Hell, I heard he started going back home to walk her to campus after morning practice. Of course he would. He was the chivalrous type. Always trying to be the white knight. But he seemed to be misinformed. He was in the wrong fairy tale. Reign wasn't his high school sweetheart. He couldn't swoop in and impress her with his kindness. Reign was *my* girl, whether she knew it yet or not.

Rubbing my chest, it was only then I remembered I was standing in the middle of my room without a shirt on. As much as I enjoyed watching Reign drool all over my chest—yes, I noticed—I didn't want to scare her away. I also didn't want her to think I was just a horndog. Truth was, there was so much more that I wanted from her than to see her naked again. I wanted to be with her, learn everything possible, and win a quiz on her. I just wanted her. All the time, every time.

And that was the problem. I didn't have time for this newfound obsession. Reign was a distraction to my goals, and I wasn't sure she felt the same way. I found one of my old high school shirts and threw it on.

"Devin?" Her faint voice reached my ears. She was standing by her railing, timidly smiling because she'd been watching me again. Her beauty took my breath away. She wasn't in anything special, but she looked so…so snuggly. She wore a gray hoodie which swallowed her petite frame and delectable curves, with a pair of red flannel shorts that were so baggy, I was sure I could fit in them with her. Something I wouldn't mind trying later. That sweatshirt would have to go, though.

She shifted on her heels, making my eyes drop to a set of black fuzzy socks that were pulled up to her calves. Snuggly was definitely the right word to describe her, and I wanted to get involved.

Shuffling over, I offered my hand out before I got to the window. "Let me help you." She took my hand and pulled herself up, letting her feet gain traction on the metal railing. She was still a little short, so I leaned over, ready to haul her over myself.

I grasped onto her hips over her sweatshirt, but my fingers slipped when I tried to pick her up. "I can't get a good grip," I told her honestly. She nodded silently, giving me permission to lift her hoodie up, revealing a small sliver of her tanned, toned stomach.

She took a sharp inhale of breath when my hands touched her warm skin, and she dropped her head down, watching as goose bumps prickled across her skin. Instinctively, my thumb rubbed circles across her hip, the same motion I'd done when she was riding me. Catching her eyes, I noticed the slightest tinge of pink on her cheeks. She must have been thinking the same thing. When she looked at me like that, all coy and pouty, all I wanted to do was pick her up and throw her on my bed.

I didn't, though.

No. I restrained myself. Instead, as she bent her knees, I lifted her over the railing. She was lighter than the weights I lift to warm up at training, so it was easy to drag her over to my side.

As she fell into the room, I pulled her toward me, wrapping my arms around her back, still under the hoodie. I pretended it was to help balance her, but really, I just wanted an excuse to get her this close again. She still had that fruity scent I remembered from the first night we met, and her hands were twisting against the fabric of my T-shirt.

Breathing heavily, we stood there watching each other for a minute. She was biting her bottom lip, and her gaze flicked between my lips and eyes. I forced myself to think about anything except Reign. Fred the ferret, Aiden's weird obsession with watching that pimple-popping show…anything to make sure my dick didn't make an unwelcome appearance between us. She was close enough that she'd definitely feel my hard-on, and I didn't think she'd appreciate it.

"You okay?" I asked, because she seemed breathless.

"Yeah." She sighed, pulling out of my hold and straightening up. "You, uh, put a shirt on?" she blurted, covering her mouth with wide eyes.

I chuckled at her awkwardness since I guessed she didn't mean to say that. "I thought you might be more comfortable if I put one on. I can take it off if you'd prefer?" I played with the hem of the shirt, pulling it up slowly and revealing just the slightest hint of my abs.

She sucked in a breath, her eyebrows popping up, and her mouth gaped open. "No. No! It's okay." She jumped from side to side, sounding disappointed with herself.

"Are you sure? If you want me to get naked, all you'd have to do is ask." I smirked, dropping the shirt, and toyed with the waistband of my sweatpants instead.

She rolled her eyes, groaning. "Am I going to have to go back to my room?" She swiveled on those fuzzy socks that reminded me way too much of a hobbit. I wrapped my hand around her arm, dragging her farther into the room. She wasn't leaving now that I'd gotten her here.

"Nah, you're good. Do you want a drink or anything?"

"I'm okay." She smiled awkwardly as her eyes darted across my face, studying me. "But I'd like to give you this." Without warning, she torpedoed herself into my chest, wrapping her arms around my waist and squeezing. She was hugging me. My torso was too wide for her to reach all the way around, and I wondered how she was breathing since her face was squashed so tightly into my chest, but I didn't care much. I had her in my arms, and that was all that was important. I caged her in, placing my hands on the small of her back.

She breathed me in, and even though she was doing this for my benefit, I thought she might need this hug more than me. "I'm sorry you've had a shitty day. I won't force you to talk about it, but I want you to know that I'm here for you." At least, I thought that was what she said. Her voice was muffled since she was talking into my pecs.

I took a long exhale, closing my eyes. She made me feel calm without trying. Just being around her, thinking about her, was like a soothing caress to my soul. "I'd rather watch a movie if you're interested?"

She tipped her head up, resting her chin on my chest as she looked up at me with lazy eyes. "I'm interested."

I got the urge to drop a kiss on those perfect lips of hers. Just a short, quick one, one that she'd hardly notice. But she wasn't mine to do that to. I answered the urge instead by kissing her forehead.

"Sorry, the only seat I've got is the bed. Is that okay?" I nodded over to my clean navy sheets and paused before adding, "That wasn't a line. I promise."

"I know. You're too much of a sweetheart to use lines." She unwrapped herself from me, plopping down on my bed tentatively. *Sweetheart.* Just what every guy wanted to be described as. Instant boner killer.

"Thanks, darlin'," I grumbled, taking a seat next to her. We pushed back, so we were both leaning against the headboard. Our shoulders rubbed and our thighs brushed. I did my best to ignore how good it felt to have her here, in my bed.

"Let me know if you see anything good." I leaned into her while she played with the laces on that stupid, raggedy hoodie. She barely noticed any of the movie choices. "Can I ask you something?"

"Anything." She dragged her eyes away from her fiddling hands to smile, revealing the smallest of dimples on her right cheek. God, I wanted to lick it.

"That South Point High sweatshirt." How do I put this? "Is it your boyfriend's?" Subtlety wasn't my strong point, and I was ninety-nine percent sure she didn't have one since she slept with me that first night, and she's in my bed now, but I wanted to make sure. For my own sanity. I'd seen her in that hoodie one too many times now for me not to think it meant something to her.

She dropped her head, pouting her lips and pulling on the laces. She was thinking about the answer, which made me feel a little uneasy. "It's my ex-boyfriend's," she confirmed, but looked almost disappointed at the admission. She'd alluded to a bad ex the first night, but if he was that bad, why would she still wear his sweatshirt? "He. Uh, well, I caught him cheating on me a few months ago."

"I'll kill him," I said calmly. So calmly that Reign hopefully thought I was joking. I wasn't. I was seething on the inside and already planning the murder. Who in their right mind would cheat on this girl?

She smiled softly, swatting me on the chest. "It's fine. You can put your He-Man tendencies away. I'm over it." From the pink on her cheeks and the somber look on her face, it was fair to say she was not over it. "I just wished it wasn't my cousin I caught him with." She twiddled her fingers now, refusing to make eye contact after that bombshell.

If I was furious before, I was seething now. How could you do that to your own family? "Are you serious?"

She nodded with pinched lips. "Yeah, I moved to Louisiana in my junior year of high school to live with my aunt. That's when I met Clay." She crossed her legs, making her look even more tiny and vulnerable than she did before. "We dated the rest of high school and decided to go to SLU together. My cousin Ally and I shared a dorm, and well, one day, I found out we shared more than that."

I dragged her into a hug without thinking, and she seemed surprised at first but then melted into my touch. "I'm so sorry." What was I supposed to say? *I'd never do that to you. Let me show you how a real man acts.* But those were promises I wasn't sure I could keep considering everything plaguing my life right now.

Her next words were muted. "It's okay." When she pulled herself away from my chest, she looked into my eyes with grit and determination. "Honestly, it was probably the best thing that ever happened to me. I'd been running away from my problems ever since." She paused, biting her lip. "Ever since junior year, but I'm back home in California now. Where I should have been all along."

I noticed her eyes welling up. I had a feeling there was more to this story, but I wasn't about to push it. "Is that why you don't date? Because of those two assholes?"

She shook her head, making her whole body vibrate with movement. Straightening her shoulders, she looked me directly in the eyes. "Partly. A lot of stuff has happened in the last few years."

"What kind of stuff?" I know I said I wasn't going to pry, but she was alluding to something else. I couldn't exactly help her if I didn't know what that was. Taking her small hand in mine, I rubbed my calloused thumb across her palm, trying to comfort her. "You don't have to tell me if you don't want to."

"I mean, I guess you'll find out sooner or later." She was trying to show nonchalance with that statement, but it held more weight than I thought she realized. She was always planning on telling me this, which meant she trusted me with it. "My parents died in a car accident when I was a sophomore in high school. Since I wasn't eighteen yet, it meant I had to move to live with my aunt."

"Reign." It was hardly a whisper, because what the hell else do you say to that?

She held her hand up. "Please. Don't feel sorry for me. I've had more than enough of that to last a lifetime." She bit down on her bottom lip so hard it looked like it hurt. Maybe that was her way of controlling her emotions.

I didn't know what to do. I wanted to hug her, but that wasn't what she wanted.

"It's been five years, and I know they'd want me to be happy and move on, so that's what I've been trying to do. I just wish I hadn't put all my eggs in Clay's basket. I hear he and my cousin are dating now. If anything, maybe I helped bring them together." She shrugged it off like it wasn't a big deal. Like it didn't take a lot of strength to be the bigger person when you were already dealing with some pretty crappy cards. She smiled through that heartbreak; this time, both her dimples popped, and something about her innocent grin squeezed at my heart. She was everything, and she didn't even know it.

"You're the strongest person I've ever met." I didn't dwell on what she told me. She didn't want me to. I hoped one day she might feel strong enough to tell me about her parents, but I was happy to wait until she was comfortable.

"Thanks," she mumbled.

"I don't mean to sound rude, but why do you still wear that idiot's sweatshirt?"

Picking at the nail on her index finger, she said, "Being my first love and all that jazz, he's the only guy who's ever given me one to wear, and I like wearing it. It makes me feel safe and protected." Did she just inadvertently admit that I was the second guy she'd had sex with? I shook that thought out of my head because it wasn't important. What was important was making the girl sitting next to me feel special.

"Not sure how that jackhole can make you feel protected anymore. How about you take one of mine instead?" I uttered before I could stop myself, groaning inwardly at my incessant need to insert myself into every part of her life, even though I shouldn't. I didn't have time for a girlfriend, and she wasn't in the right mindset either. But I kept pushing.

Her head turned sharply. Squinting, she examined me, most likely trying to understand my motives for the offer. I gave her a smile instead of an explanation, because that usually got me out of trouble.

"Uh." I hopped off the bed and went to the bottom drawer of my dresser, rooting through the five sweatshirts I owned. I didn't have many, but I knew I wanted her to have one.

"I've got a couple of gray ones, a couple of black ones and a red one. Any of those work for you?" I asked, turning to look at her deer-caught-in-the-headlights expression.

"Oh no, I really couldn't."

"Don't worry. I'm not going to get any ideas. I just think it's better for you if you're not constantly reminded of your ex every day." I paused for a beat. "You're just borrowing a friend's sweatshirt. That's all it is," I reassured her, which seemed to make her relax a little. "Once you're done with it, you can just throw it over the balcony."

"If you're really okay with it?"

"I wouldn't have offered if I wasn't."

"Um, alright, well, how about one of the gray ones?"

"Perfect choice."

She caught my old high school sweatshirt with ease, studying the emblem. "West Lake Tigers, huh?" She smiled.

"Yup. I'll forever be proud to wear the stripes, and now you will too."

She smiled wider and took her ex's sweatshirt off, revealing a white tank. I turned on my heel before I could see too much. I knew she wasn't wearing a bra; I felt it when I helped her over the balcony, but if I wanted to keep this interaction PG, I couldn't see her nipples.

"Thank you." Her voice was muffled by the fabric. "What do you think?" I turned back around, and my jaw dropped. If she looked small in her ex's hoodie, she looked minuscule in mine. She flicked out her hair from underneath with a smile. I couldn't stop myself. All kinds of fantasies swirled in my head. The main one was me touching her breasts underneath while she straddled me on the bed. So much for PG. I scraped my hand over my face, hoping it would scratch the thoughts away before I did something stupid.

"You look great." She snuggled further into my sweatshirt, and my chest constricted watching her. I put it down to a hard chest day at the gym and not to my potentially growing feelings for this girl. She took her place back down on the bed, bringing her legs under the sweatshirt and holding them tight across her chest.

"Are you cold?"

She half-nodded and half-shrugged.

"You can get under the covers if you want. I washed my sheets yesterday."

She seemed hesitant at first, but when I raised an encouraging brow, she slipped her legs under.

When I joined her on the bed, I lay on top of the sheets. As much as I wanted to be under there with her, I didn't want to make her feel uncomfortable. She edged a little closer to my side, leaning her head on my shoulder, and let out an audible, relaxed sigh. I considered wrapping my arm around her; with that confession earlier, I felt like we bonded, but I decided better of it. I tossed her the remote.

"I can't decide on what to watch. You pick something."

She silently picked an old movie I'd never heard of. It looked like some romantic teen comedy. I didn't care at this point; I knew I wouldn't be watching or concentrating on it. "In case you want to change it," she offered, resting the remote on my thigh.

As we sat in silence, the only noise came from the TV, and I tried my best to concentrate, but I couldn't. I had so much on my mind before Reign opened up that now my brain was exploding with all my other problems. Covering my face, I sighed in frustration, wishing I could take a break from my thoughts. But, as always, I couldn't.

My sister, Chloe, called me this morning. She was yelling frantically, and I couldn't make out what was wrong because she was ranting hysterically on the phone. I skipped my classes, hoping I'd be able to sort out her problem. When I finally got through to my mom, she told me Chloe had gone out drinking again and called me in a hammered-induced haze. At the ripe old age of seventeen, my sister was an alcoholic. She wasn't even legally allowed to drink, but somehow, she'd always find enough to lose herself. How do you try to explain that to anyone without them thinking you come from an abusive household?

We didn't, by the way.

In fact, before all of this happened, we were just your usual run-of-the-mill family. Loving wife with a doting husband and two kids. Now, it was temper tantrum after temper tantrum with Chloe, and it was exhausting, to say the least. It killed me that the town blamed my mom. None of them were there to see how hard she worked to try to help Chloe. It wasn't like she didn't have her own shit to deal with either. Her husband, my dad, left us. When the going got tough, my dad left, and now it was up to me to try to mend the broken pieces of our family. It was the least I could do after everything my mom did for me.

Chloe hadn't been the same since her best friend died of an overdose. You'd think that would make her stop drinking altogether, but it seemed to fuel her on. When I'd confronted her about it in the past, she'd say that alcohol was the only thing that got her mind off it. When she wasn't out trying to find someone who would buy her a beer, she'd be home, raiding the bathroom cupboards, looking for mouthwash to use as a shot. She had a problem, and we knew it was one we couldn't fix on our own. We'd tried everything to help her over the last couple of years, but it was almost like she didn't want to change. It was like she didn't care about anything. Not even my mom and me.

She needed professional help. It was to the point now where we couldn't control her, especially when I wasn't around to chase away those idiots she hangs out with. My entire body shriveled when I thought about how we'd pay for the help if I didn't enter the draft early. I didn't think my family could wait another year for a solution. A couple of months already seemed like a big ask.

When I got Chloe back on the phone, I convinced her to stay home and take a nap instead of going out and partying. That was only today, though. It was a temporary solution. She would go out and get drunk again. It was only a matter of time. She was broken, and it broke me that I couldn't be there to help her more. We were so close growing up, but now it felt like I was talking to a hollowed version of her. She was a shadow of herself, and I wanted to get my sister back.

A soft snore interrupted my thoughts. Without noticing, Reign had snuggled into my torso; her little hand rested on my chest as her cheek used my bicep as a pillow. A smile grew on my face as I watched how relaxed and comfortable she must have been to fall asleep on me.

And just like that, I'd forgotten about everything. The only thing that mattered right now was the two of us.

Me and Reign.

I carefully placed her head on my pillow so I could get up and get ready for bed. I figured I'd leave my shirt on because I didn't want her waking up tomorrow thinking I'd taken advantage of the situation.

Removing my jeans and turning off the TV and lights, I pulled the covers from the other side of the bed and got in. Lying on my back, I stared at the ceiling and looked over at Reign. She was nestled into one of my pillows, looking like she belonged there. Twiddling my thumbs, I felt her roll over toward me. She was like a kitten looking for warmth as she curled herself into my side again. Her leg draped over mine, and I raised my arm so she could rest her head on my chest.

Even though her hair was tickling my face and all I could do was breathe in the sweet smell of her shampoo, I didn't move her. This was the happiest and most relaxed I'd been all day, and I wasn't about to ruin that.

TWELVE
Reign

Pain shot down my neck; the hard pillow below me did little to soothe it. Groaning, I whacked the pillow, hoping to fluff it up a little.

"Ouch."

My eyes bugged open in shock as my pillow moaned in agony.

"Good morning to you too, darlin'," Devin husked out, rubbing his eyes. I immediately jumped up and looked down at the silky black sheets that were definitely not mine. Devin was casually lying next to me like this was no big deal. I raised my brows in question, but he was too busy rubbing the sore spot on his chest to answer. His rock-hard, warm chest I was just sleeping on. Damn, even groggy, he was the sexiest thing I'd ever laid eyes on.

"I'm sorry, D, I didn't realize you were under me," I said, my eyes watching his shirt the entire time as it gently rode up, showing the light dusting of hair close to his navel. My fingers tingled, wanting to skate them across that sliver of skin. "Or that I stayed the night." As I dragged my eyes up to his face, I stopped at the little wet patch where my mouth was on his shirt and felt my cheeks heat. Thankfully, he was too busy waking up to notice the drool patch I'd left behind.

Finally, his eyes squinted opened as he looked at me with that gorgeous, crooked smile of his, making my heart skip. "You fell asleep during the movie. You looked so peaceful; I didn't have the heart to wake you." He shrugged while scratching the back of his head.

He was right. Apart from the crick in my neck, it was a fantastic sleep, one I didn't think I'd have if I hadn't opened up and told him everything. It was the first time I'd told anyone since Clay, and I honestly thought it would be more monumental than it was. It just felt normal. It was like I was telling Devin something he was always supposed to know.

"Thanks for letting me share your bed." *And my secrets,* I mumbled, trying to keep my eyes off the gorgeous man lying next to me. The sheets rode low on his hips, framing that perfect V leading down to his…

Stop. I shouldn't be thinking about him like this. We were *friends.* That was all. If there were something more going on between us, he would have told me what was bothering him. But he didn't.

"I should probably go," I lied, because I needed to leave for my own sanity. Being around him was making me itchy. Itchy to fling those sheets off and see what was going on under them. "I've got class soon."

He looked at me skeptically, and that was when I realized it was Saturday morning. He didn't call me out on it, though. "No problem, I've got practice in thirty minutes, anyway." He smirked, throwing the sheets off his bed and revealing those wide thighs tightly held by his boxers.

Memories of the first night we slept together came crashing back, and it took all my self-control not to straddle Devin and kiss the crap out of him. I couldn't do it, and it was my own fault. I was the one who friend-zoned him.

My center tingled at the mere thought of him between my thighs, and I bit my bottom lip hard, hoping the pain would refocus my attention.

"Are you okay?" he asked, leaning closer to me; his musky, manly smell invaded my senses and made my brain go a little fuzzy.

"I'm fine," I whimpered. "I, uh, just need help to get over the railings."

I let out a squeak when he unexpectedly scooped me into his arms and carried me over to the window as though I weighed nothing. My stomach turned. In a good way. Not like I was about to vomit on the guy or anything, but the feel of his hands skating across my bare skin was making my body throb. I was so glad I'd be in my room and away from him soon. I needed space.

He gently placed my butt on the railing, letting me slide across and land safely on the other side. With the two windows between us, I felt the sanity seeping back into my brain. "Thanks for last night. I had a great time," he said, his hand lingering on my arm.

Following his touch, I noticed he was fingering the sweatshirt. *His sweatshirt.* The one I was still wearing and slept in. He probably wanted it back, and I would have a hard time giving it to him. "Do you want this back?" I reluctantly asked as I played with the bottom. His eyes immediately dropped to my thighs where the sweatshirt ended and focused on my hands, as though he was waiting for me to take it off and reveal what was underneath. Hopefully, it wasn't just me who had those thoughts.

"No, darlin', I told you to keep it for now." He smiled as his hazel eyes flicked back up, melting my chocolate ones. The shiver it caused to run down my spine was undeniable. "Thanks for taking my mind off my problems for a little while." He sighed, making my heart ache.

I wished he would talk to me. I wished he would let me in and let me know what was going on. I wanted to help him. To make him feel better. It was a privilege I didn't have, though. Because he wasn't my boyfriend, he wasn't my anything. And that was why I needed to maintain a healthy distance.

"Anytime. If you ever want to talk, you know I'm here," I offered.

His lips curved slightly, still looking sadder than usual. "Sure. See you later, darlin'." He winked, and just like that, he disappeared into his bathroom, leaving me there thinking about his naked, wet body. Ugh. I needed to get out of this little microcosm of a world we'd built between our two bedrooms and see sense.

Shoving a pair of jeans on, I grabbed my phone and earbuds, fully planning on going for a long, sobering walk. Only I was stopped in my tracks. "Reign!" Lyss cried as she heard my feet coming down the stairs.

I grunted out a response, hoping she'd take the hint that I was in no mood to talk; I just wanted to get out of this house and not think about Devin for a few hours. She didn't, though. Wrapping her arm around my shoulders, she walked me toward the kitchen. Laura was sitting on the island, looking at me apologetically, and I was shocked to see it was covered in bags and bags of glitter. All different colors and sizes. They must have raided the craft store last night. "The guys are leaving in five minutes for practice, which means they should be out for a couple of hours. That gives us plenty of time to fill their house with glitter," she explained, with a somewhat crazy glint in her eyes.

My forehead creased. I remembered talking about this yesterday, but I didn't think she'd be ready with supplies. "You weren't joking? We're actually going through with this?" I asked them both, particularly looking at Laura. I thought she would have talked some sense into Lyss while I was gone.

"Why wouldn't we be?" Lyss stated matter-of-factly. She checked her watch and then shoved a giant bag of gold glitter in my hand. "Come on. We don't have much time if we want to thoroughly ruin their sex lives." She grabbed her own bag and motioned for us to join.

Laura and I diligently followed her to my room, where she proceeded to put my desk chair next to the railing, making it easier to jump over. "Hurry," she whisper-shouted while she jumped the ledge with ease. My heart pounded. I didn't leave Devin that long ago, and there was a chance he was still in that bathroom. Lyss landed with a thud, and I closed my eyes, waiting for her to get busted. Only she didn't. She was still just standing there, waiting for us.

Laura was next to jump over, and I followed. Standing in Devin's room, I looked around, making sure there was no evidence that I had slept there last night. Even if there was anything, the girls didn't notice because they were too busy shoving pink glitter in Devin's pants, his drawers, and his sink. Poor guy.

"Reign!" Lyss shrieked. "What are you waiting for? Come on! We need to split up to hit all the rooms in time." She scurried out, Laura rolling her eyes in tow.

Walking down the hall, I picked the room next to Devin's and pushed open the door. This place was neat-freak central. The idea of getting glitter all over his perfectly pressed sheets had my eye twitching. He didn't deserve this kind of torture. Unless it was Aiden. Then he did. I surveyed the room, searching for the owner, and a smile crossed my lips when I saw a photo frame on the desk.

It was Adam in his graduation gown with a girl by his side, smiling. He looked happy, content even. He'd never mentioned a girlfriend, and it definitely wasn't his sister because the way she looked at him was anything but familial. Who was she?

"Reign!" Lyss yelled, making me jump. "Hurry up." I gently put the picture down and made my way to his drawers. Guilt seeped through me as I stuck the glitter in his jean pockets.

"Crap!" I accidentally dropped the bag, leaving a giant pile of gold glitter on his perfect gray carpet. I didn't have time to fix it because Lyss was fretting outside, muttering to herself, and waiting for me.

Padding out of Adam's room, I walked farther down the hall. My hand was on the knob of the next room when Laura spoke. "Umm guys." She ran out of the front room, Lyss doing the same on the opposite side.

"Adam's car has just pulled up," she said, pointing her thumb at the window.

"WHAT?!" Lyss screeched so loudly that I was sure they could hear her outside. She pushed Laura out of the way so she could look out the window. "Reign, go downstairs and create a distraction. Now!" My feet were already treading down the stairs as she spoke. "We'll finish with the glitter up here. Just keep them distracted for at least twenty minutes." I could only hear her feet shuffling at this point. "Go! Go! Go!"

As I got to the front of the house, I saw two shadowy figures walking to the door, and my heart was beating faster. How the hell was I going to explain why I was here? The door opened before I could hide or think of an excuse, and right there, in my face, was Aiden, staring down at me. Confused and angry. "Reign?"

"Uh, hi." I fumbled, shifting from side to side.

"What are you doing here?" Adam asked with a smile, coming up behind Aiden. I immediately felt terrible. If only he knew what I just did to his most sacred pockets.

I did the only thing I could think of. I threw my arms around Adam, forcing him to hug me. "I've been looking for you, obviously," I said, watching Aiden stalk further into the room, sharply surveying it. He didn't trust me; I wasn't surprised or offended.

"How did you get in?" he asked with a hint of annoyance.

"Uh, Jackson let me in before he left." My arms were still around Adam, who'd now let his fall to my hips.

His mouth moved to my ear, his breath tickling my neck. "So, you've been waiting for me for over an hour?" he teased as his fingers pressed into my side.

"Yeah…" I trailed off, trying to think fast. Aiden was still looking around, more suspicious than before. I needed to keep him down here as long as possible. As I stepped back, I noticed there were some steps behind me, and finally, an idea came to mind. Keeping my eyes focused on Adam, I slowly stepped back, away from him. "I just wanted to talk to you about that date you mentioned." Smiling, I kept walking backward, knowing the steps were coming soon.

Adam followed me, his smile widening. "Oh, yeah?"

"Yeah." My heel was on the edge of the step. It was now or never. Forcing myself down, I pretended to fall to the floor, screaming the entire way dramatically. Even if they thought I was faking it, this should give Lyss and Laura more than enough time to get out.

"Reign!" Adam was kneeling by my side in a second, brushing the hair away from my face. "Are you okay?"

Nodding. "Yeah, I'm fine. I'm just a klutz." I wondered how long it'd been. Five, seven minutes? I needed to keep them down here for longer. "Ouch!" I squealed, moving my foot. "It hurts so much," I whined.

"Jesus! You can't sue me. You were in this house without my permission." Aiden held his hands up, watching Adam tend to my foot.

Adam scoffed at his friend as he manipulated my foot, testing different pressures. I watched him intently, so I knew when I needed to wince. "Shut up, dude. We need to help her. Get some ice." He draped my arm over his shoulder and then lifted me up in a bridal carry. He dropped me off on the kitchen counter, and without warning, he took my shoes off, inspecting my foot. I grimaced. *What if he fainted from the smell of my feet?*

Aiden threw him a dish towel filled with ice, and Adam gently applied it to my fake injury. "It looks like you've rolled your ankle," he said, and, at that moment, I realized I must have naturally fat ankles if he thought it looked swollen. I added a pained whimper for effect when he pressed the ice down.

"I don't think I'll be able to walk to my house. Will you both be able to carry me?" I'd never been the type to act like a damsel in distress, and giving them puppy-dog eyes was forced, but it seemed to work.

Aiden groaned. "I'm sure Adam can do it himself."

"It will be quicker if we do it together," Adam answered for me.

I kept pouting at Aiden, wondering if I could melt that icy-cold heart of his. Grumbling, Aiden didn't say anything else, just ambled over and lifted me up easily. I thought Devin was tall, but Aiden was enormous. He wasn't bulky like Devin, but lean and muscular, like a championship racehorse.

"Or you can do it yourself." Adam chuckled, following behind us.

When we got to my house, Aiden kicked the door open. Lyss and Laura were both sitting in the living room watching TV and acting like nothing happened at all. Mock shock crossed both of their faces.

"Reign. Are you okay?" Laura asked, running up and inspecting me.

"What did you do?!" Lyss, as per usual, accused Aiden, using her index finger to push his shoulder.

He grumbled, walking past her. "*I* did nothing. She did this all by herself." He plopped me down on the sofa and, without another word, left the house. Adam was still standing by the door, watching me.

"If you need anything, just let me know," he said, rolling on his heels.

"Thank you for your help, Adam. I owe you one."

He stuffed his hands in his jeans, and his cheeks reddened at my compliment. He ran a hand through his blond hair as he said, "Maybe next time we can talk about that date?"

There was a chorus of coos from Laura and Lyss, heightening the embarrassment I felt. I was kind of hoping he'd forgotten about that.

"Oh yeah, sure." I gave him an awkward smile. I needed to talk to Devin about how we handled this. Adam was cute, but I doubted he'd be interested in me if he knew I banged his best friend, which wasn't something I was willing to admit in front of everyone. I needed to talk to him soon. He was a great guy, and he deserved someone who wasn't lusting after his friend.

"Alright, I'm going to head out. See you guys later." He waved, shutting the door behind him. I spent the next few minutes convincing Laura and Lyss that nothing was going on between Adam and me. Luckily, we were disrupted by a threatening message from Aiden, who had discovered the glitter almost immediately. Apparently, we should sleep with one eye open because things were going to get a lot worse.

I still had no idea how I ended up in this stupid prank war.

Later that night, when I was lying in my bed, I looked over at Devin's room. The light still hadn't come on. It was midnight, and he had yet to set foot in his bedroom. All the other guys came back within an hour of Aiden and Adam, except Devin. My mind immediately thought the worst. *What if he was in an accident? Or he was lying in a ditch somewhere needing help?* Surely the guys would be more panicked if that were the case. From what I could tell, they were all still inside the house, playing games. They could be completely unaware of their friend's demise.

I gasped involuntarily, my whole body shivering. What if they weren't worried because he was with another girl? It wasn't like he'd touched me sexually since that first night, and maybe all of those stolen glances and sexual tension between us was in my head. He had calmed his flirting since I'd turned him down. Maybe he was out there sowing his wild oats without giving me a second thought, and I was the one sitting in my room, wearing his sweatshirt and waiting for him like a puppy. It was my own fault. I was the one who told him we were nothing, when in actual fact, I was hoping we might be something someday.

Rolling over to the other side of my bed, I stared at my bathroom door, running through all our interactions. Apart from the occasional flirty comment, he'd given me no sign he was still interested in me, and I shouldn't be this invested in a one-night stand. That was what I had to remind myself. At most, we were friends because he was doing exactly as

I asked, keeping what happened between us private. I could handle friends, but I couldn't handle seeing him with another girl.

I closed my eyes, forcing myself to sleep.

It was three days before I saw his light come on again.

THIRTEEN
Devin

Walking up to the rickety porch steps I planned on fixing the next time I was home, I saw a figure rocking on the swing, sobbing into her palms. My heart was instantly destroyed hearing my mom's cries, knowing that she had to deal with this alone. Without me. Or my asshole of a dad. All of this fell onto her shoulders, and she couldn't handle it.

"Ma," I whispered as I took the first step onto the porch. Her eyes darted up, startled that I was standing in front of her. When she called me after practice, I doubted she was expecting me to come all the way back just to help her. Hell, I wasn't planning on it myself, but when Adam saw my face after getting off the call with her, he all but forced me to explain what was happening and told me I had to go home. I didn't even feel guilty putting that small fortune of a flight on my credit card. I needed to be here. With my mom.

"Devin. What are you doing here?" she asked, getting up from her seat and clasping me in a tight hug. I just stood there, holding her as she clutched one of Chloe's toy rabbits close as she sobbed in my arms.

It was the right decision to come home.

I could feel my mom's tears seeping through my shirt, and I forced the lump in my throat down. "I came because I wanted to help you find Chloe."

This wasn't the first time Chloe had gone missing after a Friday night of illegal drinking. However, this was the first time that she'd left her phone at the bar she was illegally drinking at, and we had no idea where she was. Maybe she left it by accident, or maybe she finally realized we installed a tracker on it, so we knew where she was at all times. Either way, this was the first time we had no idea where she ended up, and we had to resort to calling the police to report her as missing just to get an Amber Alert issued.

My mom looked up at me. There was a moment in all kids' lives when they saw their parents for who they really were and realized that they weren't as unbreakable as they believed. This was that moment for me. My mom had held back so much. Had tried to be strong for Chloe and me. Even when my father left her with nothing last year, she barely showed any pain. She just got another job and dealt with it. Now, looking into her glazed hazel eyes, I saw all the torment and pain these last couple of years had brought her. It was a painful reminder that I'd been away for most of it. "You didn't need to come all the way home." She tried to put up a stony mask, but it was too late; I already saw the cracks.

"Yeah, I did, Ma." I led her back to the porch swing, sitting down next to her, never letting go of her hand. "I went down to the police station before I came here. They said they've got no more leads, which is frustrating." She nodded, and I had no doubts that she'd been on the phone with them every thirty minutes, asking for updates. "So, I took things into my own hands and went down to Chloe's ex-boyfriend's house. Got a few addresses for her friends."

"Chloe's going to kill you when she finds out," my mom said with just a hint of amusement. I couldn't laugh, though, because something was making my chest feel tight. All I could think was *if* she found out. What if I was already too late to save what was left of my family?

Shaking the thought out of my head, I looked back at my mom. "That will be the least of her concerns once she's back home. I went to a few of her friends' houses, and it seems like she dropped all the good ones right around the time Grace overdosed," I explained. She'd been shutting us out for a while, but I didn't realize just how much until I came face-to-face with it today. "I managed to find out some of her new friends." Friends was a term I used lightly. Those guys had so much grease in their hair; it looked like they hadn't showered in weeks. "They told me they saw her a couple of hours ago, and she was with some new guy." My hands tightened at those words. I hated thinking that someone was taking advantage of my sister, and I was helpless to do anything about it. "I searched all of Willow City looking for her but came up short." I slumped at the admission.

"I'm sure she'll be home soon. She always comes back," my mom reassured me, even though I didn't think she believed it. She placed her palm on one of mine and looked down at my hand with a gasp. "Devin Cole Walker," she chastised me; I knew I was in trouble when she used my full name. "Have you been fighting?" Holding my hands up, she showed me my bloodied knuckles as though I hadn't noticed them.

"Nah, ma, it's from football," I lied. I may have had to hand out a few bloody noses to get as much information as I did from the greasy duo.

She squinted, knowing I was lying, but didn't press me on it. Probably because we had other things to worry about. "Come inside. We need to put some ice on your knuckles." She scrunched my hair like I was still a ten-year-old and not double the size of her in both height and width. I followed her into the house like that diligent ten-year-old. "Have you been getting enough sleep? You look like you've been chewed up, spit out, and stepped on."

I sat down on our threadbare couch, picking at a string hanging off it. "A redeye flight across the country will do that to you."

She fiddled around in the kitchen, and when she came back with an ice pack, she said, "No, sweetheart. There's more behind those tired eyes than just a flight. You've been worrying too much and holding it in. I know you like to pretend you've got two backbones, but occasionally, you need to remember you're only human, like the rest of us."

Sighing, I let her ice my hand. "I know, Ma. I just want to make sure you and Chloe are okay."

As I looked around the room, memories of my father came back. We hadn't heard from him since he left us high and dry one night while my mom and sister watched me play.

"What we need is for you to be okay," she said.

She was right. The only way we were getting out of this mess was if I got drafted, and in order to do that, I *needed* to be okay.

"I know, Ma. Have you looked at any of the facilities I sent through?" I quickly changed the subject because I didn't want to talk about myself. It was a wasted effort since I already had a plan. Chloe was the one that needed work, and we'd been looking at different places to send her for treatment for a few months now, trying to decide what was best for her.

She gave me a small smile, the first hint of hope I'd seen since I got home. "Yes. I think you're right; out of state would be best, and I liked St. West's because you're close by." It was two hours away from Covey U, which meant I could at least see her on the weekends. "But we can't afford it," she replied resolutely.

"Let me worry about that."

"No, Devin. You're my son. I need to deal with this."

"She's *my* sister, and I've already agreed to a generous payment plan with them." They agreed to six months of treatment payable at the end. Sure, a large interest charge was tacked on for the pleasure, but it would be worth it if Chloe got better. "Now, it's nearly four a.m., and I'm sure you haven't slept at all." I know I hadn't. "Go and at least try to get some sleep. I'll wait out here for Chloe."

After planting a small kiss on my forehead, she made her way to her bedroom. Sadness pitted in my stomach because I'd never seen her like this. She was exhausted and on the brink of giving up. The stress was aging her faster than her years, and I hated watching her decline. It was exactly why I needed to focus. I couldn't let these two women down. They were all I had.

When I checked my phone, the battery was nearly drained, and the screen was dimming. I cursed myself because in my rush to get here, I didn't have time to bring my charger or pack any clothes. I'd have to wear some of my old high school stuff if I wanted to change tomorrow.

Anger coursed through my veins as I sat back on the couch, waiting for Chloe. I was certain she'd be home soon because she'd need more stuff. If only she had some help. I couldn't suppress the guilt I felt over leaving her here unsupported. Even coming home tonight made me feel useless. She still wasn't home, and I'd never forgive myself if something happened to her.

Before I could think about it anymore, the front door flung open, and my head shot up.

"Chloe," I breathed, staring at my little sister like she was a ghost.

She was standing there with her back to me, waving at some guy driving off on a motorcycle. I was certain the idiot could see me, and I glared at him until he drove away. "Where were you?" I ground out, and she turned in surprise, nearly tripping on the loose floorboard as she did.

"Dev-Devin?" she drawled out, confused.

Heading to her, I clasped my arms on her bare shoulders, annoyed that she was wearing next to nothing in a crop top and hot pants. She looked like a stripper, not an underage minor.

It took her a few minutes to focus on me because her pupils were dilated, and she was obviously on something other than alcohol. Her head swayed, and she giggled, ending it with a snort. "What are you doing here?"

All my fight was gone because my little sister was broken. I led her to the sofa, making sure she was sitting before I headed to the kitchen to get her a glass of water.

She didn't notice that I didn't answer her. Instead, I just headed back to where she was and sat on the coffee table in front of her. "Drink this," I demanded. "You aren't leaving this room or going to bed or whatever the hell you plan to do until you've had this."

She took the drink from me. "Uh, okay," she mouthed off. If she were in her right mind, I'd yell at her, but right now, all I wanted to do was convince her that she needed to listen to me. Chloe slowly swigged the drink, and it took her all of five minutes to finish it. "Happy?" she asked, showing me the empty glass like it was a trophy.

"Mildly." I moved the glass away from her and took her in my arms.

"What the hell are you doing?" Chloe squirmed, but she was a little thing, and I was used to holding back much bigger men on the field, so her tiny punches and little kicks were no match for me.

"Taking you to your room," I said, taking one step at a time.

"I can walk. Thank you very much." Ever the smart-ass, even when she was high on something.

"I know you can, genius. Ma's sleeping, and you're about as clumsy as a newborn calf right now. Considering the countless nights you've kept her up, I'm not letting you wake her tonight." That seemed to shut her up. After I placed her on her bed, I walked to the bathroom to fill up another glass of water and forced her to drink it, too. I then went into my old room, grabbed a pillow and sheet, and made a bed on her floor.

"You're not really going to stay there, are you?"

"Chloe," I said in the calmest voice I could. "I know you'll deny it, but it's obvious you took something tonight." She tried to speak, but I raised my hand before she could. "I'm not leaving you alone until I'm certain whatever is in your system is out of it."

She grumbled, but knew it was a losing battle to fight with me, and dramatically threw her blanket over her head. I rolled my eyes, and in less than two minutes, she was snoring away. I didn't leave her side until about ten a.m., when I could smell my mom cooking breakfast downstairs.

Chloe stayed asleep, only gracing our presence a few hours later. "Hey." She sheepishly smiled as she padded into the kitchen, looking for food and something to drink. I handed her a glass of orange juice, and she mumbled out a short "thank you" before sitting on the island and pulling her long, dark hair into a bun.

"Chloe, we need to talk," my mom said. There was no hint of the sadness from last night, and she had that tone I remembered from when we were younger. She was pissed, and she wanted Chloe to know it.

"Yeah," Chloe squeaked out. Her eyes widened; thankfully, her pupils were back to normal, her high having worn off in the early hours of the morning. "I think we do," she admitted, pursing her lips. "I'm sorry. I shouldn't have left my phone."

"Leaving your phone is the least of your issues," I snorted. "You do realize we called the police? There was an Amber Alert on you?" Her mouth popped open in confusion. "Yeah, that idiot that dropped you off on his motorcycle could have been charged with the abduction of a minor."

"But he didn't abduct me. I *chose* to go with him."

"Doesn't matter. You disappeared, and when you came back, you were high as a kite. What were you on last night? Cocaine? LSD?" Her head lowered in shame as she watched her fingers twiddle. "What happened to you?" I asked, a little more gently this time.

"I'm sorry, Devin. We aren't all perfect like you," she sniped back, but I shrugged it off. She was trying to start a fight to deflect, which wasn't going to happen. There was a stark silence as my mom sat down beside Chloe, holding her hand. Chloe shoved her other hand in her hair, staring down at our linoleum countertop, thinking. I leaned against the counter on the other side, hanging my head down, waiting. "I'm sorry," she finally whispered. "It's just I feel too much, and I don't know how to stop it without help." It wasn't a new revelation. We'd known Kate's death had been tough on her, and she wasn't coping, but that didn't make her antics okay.

My mom and I shared a glance. "Chloe, Devin, and I have been talking," my mom started. "And we've found a place that can help you…"

Chloe looked up, puzzled. "Help? But…" she stammered, looking between my mom and me. "We can't afford it." I wanted to ask how she was affording all the alcohol and drugs, but I had a feeling that the guy on the motorcycle was the answer.

"Don't worry about that, Chlo," I butted in. "I've dealt with it." I held my hand up, stopping her from finishing her sentence. "All I need is for you to pack a bag and be ready to leave for California in three hours."

Her brows furrowed. "California?"

"Yup. You're leaving these new friends behind and coming home with me, where you'll be away from boys with motorcycles and guys with greasy hair and bad intentions." I left no room for an argument. We'd been through this so many times with her. She wanted to get better; she just couldn't do it on her own.

Chloe pursed her lips, closing her eyes and nodding. Well, she took that a lot better than I expected. Maybe it was the fact that her brother came all the way back to host this intervention or that the bags under our ma's eyes were noticeably bigger, but something had changed her mind, and I wasn't going to question it. My mom held Chloe in an embrace. A single tear rolled down her cheek, and as she stroked Chloe's hair, she mouthed "thank you" to me.

I gave her a small smile back because this was the least I could do.

That night, Chloe flew with me to California. Her hands were jittery, and she scratched her skin the entire flight, but she didn't complain. I skipped my classes for the day, arriving at the facility first thing Monday morning to help her settle in. After spending a few hours with her, I felt more confident about the change in environment. She looked happier and more relieved than I'd seen her in a long time, and that made this whole thing feel worth it. Even if it burned a thirty-thousand-dollar hole in my pocket.

I ended up standing outside of the facility for an hour longer than I needed to. The process of leaving her there was harder than I thought, but I knew it was for the best. I rested my head against the car seat, closing my eyes for just a second. I'd barely slept in the last three days, and it was taking its toll.

Opening my eyes, I connected my phone to the car and let it charge. When it came to life, I was shocked to see twenty missed calls. All from Reign. Adam probably told the guys not to worry about me but wouldn't think to tell her because he thought I barely knew her.

Devin: Hey, Reign. Sorry I've been out. I'm alive and heading back. See you soon.

I pressed send and threw my phone in a cupholder as I started the engine, ready to finally make my way back to campus.

By the time I pulled up to my driveway, it was close to midnight, and I needed sleep. My head was pounding with everything that happened these last few days, not to mention that Coach would blast me in the morning for missing so much training. I didn't want to think about that right now. All I wanted to do was fall into my pillows and sleep.

Sighing, I opened the door, walking into the house as inconspicuous as possible. The guys were playing on the Xbox when I came in.

"Hey, D," Aiden yelled, hardly taking his eyes off the TV.

"Hey," I mumbled, and the other guys gave me a nod in acknowledgment, not one of them questioning where I'd been. Walking past, I trudged up the stairs, holding the railing tight because I was so tired; there was a very real possibility that I would fall down them if I wasn't careful.

As I opened the door to my room, my desk lamp illuminated the shadows, and I was startled to see Reign sitting on the edge of my bed. Her shoulders were shaking as she quietly sobbed into her hands.

What the fuck? Who the hell hurt her?

I was tired, but if she needed my help, I would be there for her. When I dropped my bag at the door, her head popped up in surprise. Her watery eyes met my bloodshot ones, and I felt something deep in my chest again.

Frowning, she jumped up, stomping toward me. "Where have you been?" she yelled in my face, or I should say in my chest, since she was so tiny. I held back a chuckle because the fierce look on her face made my balls shrivel.

Still wearing my sweatshirt, I had to wonder if she'd taken it off since I last saw her, but that furrowed look she was giving me told me it wasn't the time. Her foot tapped because she was waiting for me to answer, and if this were any other time, I would find the fact she was so worried about me charming and tease her mercilessly. Right now, though, all I wanted to do was lie in my bed and sleep for the first time, not worrying about Chloe.

Fourteen
Reign

"Reign." Devin sighed, rubbing a hand down his face, and I immediately felt guilty. "I've had a tough few days, and I don't want to argue with you. All I want to do is lie in my bed and try to get some sleep." His bloodshot eyes pleaded with me.

What am I doing here? Why am I acting like this? I must look crazy. We weren't even dating, and here I was yelling at him for not telling me what he was doing. If that weren't bad enough, sitting in his room and silently crying to myself was surely grounds to get me sectioned. But I couldn't help myself. Throughout everything, I'd grown to care about him, and when he disappeared without a word and didn't respond to my messages, all these emotions and feelings that I'd boxed up started hurtling back. Back to the day I said goodbye to my parents, thinking it was like any other day, and then I never saw them again.

I stepped away, giving him space to roam his room. "I'm sorry, I was just…" I couldn't find the words to complete that sentence. *I was just worried about you. I was just missing you. I was just thinking about all the ways I didn't tell you I liked you more than I said at the beginning.* And that was what all this came down to really. Me finally admitting to myself that I did like Devin. I liked him so much that when he was gone, I felt like he'd taken a little piece of me with him.

As he sat down on the bed, he spread his legs out and rested his elbows on his thighs, gazing back at me, and the words got caught in my throat. He must have taken pity on me standing there because he opened his arms, inviting me in. Any frustration or fear melted away when I wrapped myself in his warm body and perched on his thigh. He squeezed me tight; it was like he needed the hug just as much as I did.

"You don't have to explain anything to me." I burrowed into his shoulder. "I'm sorry for getting in your face. I'm an idiot. I just…" I paused, still not sure I could say it. After all, it probably wasn't the right time to express my innermost feelings. "I was just worried about you, that's all. I was so nervous when I hadn't seen you around for a few days, and when I finally asked Adam, he said he didn't know where you were. I guess I just freaked out." I spoke into his jacket, too embarrassed about admitting how worried I was when, clearly, he was fine.

He threaded his hand through my hair and whispered, "It's okay, Reign. It's sweet that you were scared, and I'm sorry I didn't text or call." His breath sent shivers down my spine. "I really need some sleep, though. I've been up for almost three days."

His voice was hoarse, and he backed away slightly so he could look me in the eyes. His hand was still in my hair, our noses almost touched as he looked down at my lips, then back up to my eyes. My breath hitched, hoping he'd edge closer and kiss me, but he didn't. He just eased the tension by smoothing down a few of my errant hairs.

I wanted him to get some sleep, but something about his expression made me want to stay with him while he did it. "Would you like some company?" I asked quietly and laughed when his eyes widened. Was he really all that surprised? Wasn't this where we'd been heading the whole time? "Just so you know, you aren't alone," I clarified, and the deep grin on his face as he squeezed my hip was enough of a sign that he knew this was where we were going too.

"Sure, darlin'." I couldn't help but notice his accent was a little thicker than last time I saw him. "I would love some company." He smiled, gently kissing my cheek. He was letting me comfort him, and I *wanted* to be that person for him. As his lips drifted away from my face, I thought this just might be the turning point in our relationship. The night where we threw caution to the wind and finally admitted how we really felt about each other.

I reluctantly moved off his lap and gestured to my worn-out denim jeans and Devin's sweatshirt. "I'm just going to hop over to grab my PJs." He clutched my hand tighter, pulling me back to the space between his thighs, and placed my hand on the crook of his neck.

He rested his head on my shoulder, then his palms fell to my hips, gently stroking me. "Or you could just wear one of my shirts," he offered. His lips grazed across my neck, and he refused to look at me. When I didn't back away but tilted my head to the side, he pressed his lips a little more firmly. I was sure it was his way of testing the waters, and by not backing away, I gave him permission.

Nodding my head, I said hesitantly, "Yeah, that sounds like a good idea." Had we just silently agreed to more? Letting go of me for just a second, he walked to his dresser, grabbing a white shirt and throwing it my way.

"Do you want me to turn around?" he offered as I stared down at his shirt, nervous because I couldn't remember what underwear I'd put on this morning.

Awkwardly, I smiled. "Nah, I guess you've seen it all before." It didn't stop me from shifting when I dragged his sweatshirt off my body. The cold air of the room reminded me I only had a thin lace bralette on. I threw the shirt on and then quickly took my jeans off, noting that, thankfully, I was in a pair of respectable boy shorts.

Turning back to him, I smiled because Devin had his back to me. He pulled his own shirt over his head in one swift movement. *How do guys even do that?* Every single muscle in his back worked as his arms fell back down. I wanted to run my hands across them and feel them flex. Then I heard his zipper lower, and my heart stopped. He bent over, and I gasped. His butt was just perfect.

He straightened up, looking over his shoulder. "Everything alright?" he asked with a cocked eyebrow.

"Yes. Yes. Sorry. Everything is fine," I squeaked out as I watched his eyes flit to the bottom of the shirt, which grazed my upper thighs.

Instinctively, I pulled the shirt down, and that was when I noticed how very see-through it was. He could easily see my bralette outline.

He sauntered over, taking my hand as he pulled the covers of his bed back. He slid under, bringing me with him, and as I relaxed down, he rolled the cover back over us. Resting my head on his chest, he wrapped his arm around me, and his hand absentmindedly played with my hair, and his brows furrowed in concentration.

"I'm always here for you, D. I hope you know that," I whispered, holding back what I really wanted to say. *Tell me everything. Let me make it better.*

"Thanks," he whispered back.

I took the hand resting on his chest and waffled mine with his, hoping this would show him exactly how I felt. His thumb drew circles around my palm as we lay in each other's arms. Devin took a heavy breath. "Something happened this week," he started, still looking at the ceiling, and I kept my gaze focused on our connected hands, letting him talk. He told me everything. About his sister, his dad leaving, and how he'd been trying to scramble enough money together for rehab. How he brought his sister back with him and could barely handle the idea of leaving her at the facility. How he hoped this would be the thing to work for her, but he couldn't be too sure. About how he didn't care how much it cost, he just wanted his family back.

I didn't say a thing. I just listened the entire time because it felt like Devin had a lot of things to say but no one to hear it. When he'd finished explaining everything, I could feel his heart rate slowing and his breath becoming shallow. I raised our waffled hands to the place on his chest, just over his heart. "You're one of the most resilient men I've ever met." I looked up at his slightly glassy eyes. "Your mom and sister are lucky to have you." Because what else could I say? No words would fix what was on his plate, and I hated how many people said "I'm sorry" when they heard about my parents, as though it was something they did. As though it was something they could fix. It wasn't. It was my burden to bear, and I didn't want people to feel sorry for me. Sometimes situations sucked, and it was just the act of sharing what happened with another person that made it easier to manage.

Unclasping our hands, I squeezed him tight, forcing my whole body against his side. He squeezed back as he gently kissed the top of my forehead and rested his hand on the small of my back where his shirt had ridden up. A small zing of electricity ran straight to my core. "Thanks for listening, Reign." He sighed, closing his eyes and letting his pinkie finger lazily stroke the top of my lace boy shorts. There was something between us; I knew he could feel it, too.

Devin's breath quickened as I raised my lips to his ear. "No problem, D," I whispered, lowering myself down to his neck. I gently placed a small kiss on his jaw. When he didn't object, I kissed his jaw in a few more places. He was stiff underneath me, but his fingers were still dancing across my back. As if he couldn't take it anymore, he clasped my chin, bringing my mouth to his. The kisses were slow, tortured, and lazy as his tongue slipped into my mouth, and I whimpered in pleasure.

This was finally it. I wanted him. He wanted me. It was clear.

His hand on the small of my back sank a little lower, covering the swell of my butt as he gave it a small squeeze, bringing me closer and making my core grind into his thigh. That was all the indication I needed to slink my hand under the covers, dragging it down to the bottom of his stomach, right next to the waistband of his boxers. Groaning, he asked between kisses, "Do you know what you're doing to me?" Giggling, I nuzzled further into his side, feeling the heat radiate off his chest.

A small gasp escaped my lips when he grasped my hips and dragged me over his body to straddle his waist. His soft, velvety tongue still played with mine as his hips moved deliciously over my core, grinding his hardness against me. I flicked my tongue across his lower lip, and his fingers clutched me harder, biting into the flesh of my hips. Then, reaching down between us, I played with the elastic just above his waist. His eyes were glazed over, and I wanted to make sure he got a good night's sleep after this.

I shimmied down his body until I was sitting just above his knees. My hands grazed the top of his thighs as I bent forward and licked across his abdomen, all the way to the light dusting of hair just above his boxers. "I think I have a favor to return." I smiled mischievously before leaving a trail of kisses across his navel.

Teasing him, I watched his muscles tense with anticipation, and as I drew my hand further up his thigh, he let out a low, guttural moan. When I gently brushed my hand across the fabric over his crotch, he groaned, "Reign, please." His voice was gravelly now, and his hips were bucking, urging me on.

Thumbing the side of his boxers, I yanked them down, seeing his hard cock with a pearl of pre-cum already waiting for me. He hissed when I gripped the base of his length, slowly smoothing my hand over him, moving it up and down, letting my thumb tease the tip whenever I passed it.

I lowered my mouth onto him slowly, maintaining eye contact the entire time. When his thick cock reached the back of my throat, he threaded his fingers through my hair, holding me in place as his hips shifted deeper into me. My cheeks hollowed as I sucked and moved him in and out.

When I got to the tip, I swirled my tongue around it and gripped the base of him hard. I knew he liked it because his fingers held onto my hair tighter, and he couldn't speak. As he watched me with heady eyes, I felt myself getting more aroused. Something about having his cock in my mouth made me feel powerful, and I was wet just watching him. I wanted to touch myself to relieve some of the ache, but I didn't want to detract the attention from him.

"Reign," Devin moaned. "It's too much." Without warning, he sat up, gripped me by the hips and flipped me around. Then he quickly pulled my boy shorts off. I was, *oh my god,* completely bare and sitting on him. On his *face.*

Popping his cock out of my mouth, I squealed. "What are you doing?" I asked nervously, trying to squirm away from his roaming eyes. His grip on my thighs tightened, holding me firmly in place.

"I need a distraction, or I'm going to come too soon," he said, his hands wrapped around both thighs, and I looked between us; I could see he was looking up at my pussy eagerly. I felt so self-conscious right now. He could literally see everything. Only my waxer had seen this side of me, and it all felt a little too exposing.

"I've, um, never done this," I admitted with flushed cheeks. I'd never felt comfortable with the thought of sitting on a guy's face before. The idea that my butt was right in their eye line was enough to put me off it.

The only thing I could see was the curve of Devin's smile. "Well, then relax and enjoy the ride, darlin'," he said before forcing my core down to his lips, flicking and twirling my clit like his life depended on it. The euphoric feeling went a long way toward helping me relax, but I still couldn't stop the anxiety, so I drew my mouth back to his cock, hoping that would distract me enough.

Gripping his cock, I slid my mouth up and down, moaning as his warm tongue entered me and his thumb flicked my clit. He thrust up and muffled something inaudible while his lips were on me. I was riding his face so hard, and I was surprised he was able to breathe, let alone talk. His hips jerked, and his balls tightened. I knew he was close. That was when I forced him further into my mouth. He groaned as hot, salty liquid rushed down my throat. I did my best to swallow every last drop, surprising myself at how comfortable I found it.

The entire time, Devin didn't let up on me, feasting on my pussy like it was his last meal. Then, when I finished lapping up his cum, he grabbed both of my hands and hauled me up, so I was literally sitting on his face. *Dear Lord.*

"What are—"

"Ride me, darlin'," he interrupted, his tongue driving me wild as I carefully moved against him. I gripped his chest, and I moaned out his name breathlessly. When his tongue went inside me, I couldn't hold back. I was coming. On. His. Face. *Hard.* The feeling was so intense that I tried to move away from his touch, but he wouldn't let me. He held my thighs down as I quivered around him, lapping up all my juices. No one had ever attended to me quite like that before.

When my climax subsided, I fell to the bed like a boneless rag doll. I was so lost in my own world I barely noticed Devin lying on top of me, kissing my neck and nipping at my ear. "You'll have to keep it down for round two," he whispered. "I'm sure the whole house heard that."

I didn't listen. All I was focused on was, "Round two?"

"You thought we were done?" He laughed.

He groaned into my ear when my nails dragged up his back. "I thought you needed to sleep?"

"Oh, I'm wide awake now," he growled as he led my hand to his already growing cock. Without another word, he slid into me and rocked my world again.

++++++++

By the time morning came, I was absolutely wrecked and in need of another few hours of sleep. As much as waking up in Devin's sheets was quickly becoming one of my favorite past times, we didn't exactly have a talk about what this was between us. We just got naked again. It felt good to let go, but was I ready for the potential letdown if he thought we were just friends with benefits?

Ever since my parents passed, I'd found it hard to open up, in fear that I'd get hurt all over again. It took Clay a year to convince me to go on a date with him, but once I did, I could feel myself opening up and thinking that maybe having friends and other people in my life wasn't so bad. And it wasn't bad for a couple of years. I started to feel a little more like my old self every day, and it was getting easier to think that maybe I could move forward without my family.

That was until I came home to our apartment from a particularly tough day at SLU. I couldn't believe my ears when I opened the door and heard the moans coming from our bedroom. My hands trembled against the knob as I twisted it open. Then, right in front of me, the world I thought I had created came crashing down. Clay was naked, plowing into Ally, who was on all fours. I wanted to throw up, but there was nothing in my stomach. Instead, my heart sank straight to my toes and slithered through the floorboards. I vowed never to feel like that again.

I left the apartment and Louisiana in less than a week. I hardly had a plan; I just knew I needed to get back home and face my demons. When I picked up my stuff, Clay was there, wanting to apologize, but I didn't bother listening. It should have always been Ally for him. I was there by mistake, a glitch in the matrix that was there when I should have been here—my home. There was a nagging feeling in my stomach as I questioned if I'd set myself up for failure again by not defining things with Devin before riding his face like a bull last night.

By the time I'd poked my head out of Devin's sheets, he was nowhere to be seen. Besides his woody scent clinging to the blanket, all that was left of him was a small yellow note with his scribbles letting me know he had football practice and would be back by lunch. I took advantage of the fact that the whole house would be at practice and sunk into his silky sheets, savoring his scent and getting lost in memories of his touch.

One thing was for sure: it never felt like this with Clay. Devin made me feel like I was on fire, and I found it hard to concentrate on anything except how to get him naked when he was in the room. He made me dizzy, and I ended up forgetting about everything except us. It felt different, and I kind of liked it.

When I finally decided to reluctantly pull myself out of Devin's bed, I noticed patches of pink glitter spewed out on the floor. I giggled, thinking about him putting his sweats on, confused about where the stuff was coming from. Padding across the room, I picked up the clothes that had been strewn across the floor last night and put them on before doing my best to jump over the balcony.

The minute my feet hit the floor in my room, Lyss's piercing screams penetrated my ears, and I was thankful I let myself sleep a little longer before coming back to this nuthouse. I showered and changed before heading downstairs with my books for the day in hand. She was still screaming at that point, and I was fully expecting to see her having a meltdown in the kitchen, but she wasn't in the house. Instead, the noise was coming from the front yard.

When I finally found her standing outside, she was flailing her arms, dramatically screaming and shaking her fists at the guys' house. Laura was doing everything she could to calm her friend, but Lyss was too riled up, stomping her feet and yelling like one of those desperate housewives who just caught their husband cheating. It took all of two seconds to register what had her so angry, and then it took all the strength I had inside me not to burst out laughing.

"Oh, no. What's happened?" I managed to say, mildly hiding any hint of humor.

It seemed that the guys, or I should say Aiden more specifically, had covered Lyss's car in bright pink and yellow Post-it notes, which in itself was annoying because imagine trying to remove them all. But what made it worse was that the paper colors had been contoured in such a way that there was a bright pink penis across the side of her car and some boobs on the hood. Walking around the vehicle, I got a better look at the outline in the back too. There was an impressive amount of detail, considering they probably had to do this in the middle of the night. Aiden must have drawn out a plan beforehand to be able to do it so accurately.

"What do you think happened, Reign?" Lyss asked sarcastically. Her face was cherry red; she was pissed. I guess if I had a car and someone did this, I'd be angry too, but stomping around like a toddler wasn't going to help the situation. "I hate you, Aiden!" she screamed at the house again. It probably wasn't the right time to mention that I thought he was at football practice with Devin, so he couldn't hear her. Laura stood next to her friend dutifully, eyes closed, rubbing her back. I honestly didn't know how she put up with this on the regular.

After a few minutes of ranting and raging at the empty windows of the house next door, Lyss turned back to Laura and me, shoulders slumped.

Her face was flustered, and her hair was a mess. "I'm sorry, guys. It's just I can't let him win," she said, shaking her head. Well, at least she was regretful about her outburst.

"What's with you and Aiden?" I asked because, to be frank, two households had been brought into their weird rivalry, and no one even knew how or why all of this started.

"Here we go…" Laura grumbled, for the first time turning away.

"Nothing is going on with *us,*" Lyss stressed.

Hauling my bag further up my arm, I pressed on because I wanted to know what I was fighting for. "I'm just curious how you both got to a point where you want to kill each other and you don't care about the collateral damage?"

"They dated," Laura said flatly.

My mouth dropped, and my eyes widened. I wasn't expecting that. "What?! When?"

Lyss clarified, "We did not *date.*" She started to remove the Post-it notes, letting them flutter to the ground as she pulled them off. I'd offer to help, but after I heard her story, I needed to head to class, or I'd be late. "We went out once when we were freshmen. Last year, Aiden kindly told me during that one outing that he would rather fornicate with a dead fish than me." She pulled off that last Post-it Note extra hard.

"Ouch!" I winced. "I don't get it, though. That's clearly not true. He's always trying to get your attention."

"The guy is a man whore. I don't care about what he said or what he does anymore."

I snorted. She obviously did; otherwise, they wouldn't be doing this to each other.

"Are you sure about that?" I questioned with a cocked eyebrow.

She ignored me, her eyes darting like crazy, as though she was already plotting and planning her next move. I couldn't help but think that she would have already graduated if she had put this much dedication into her college work.

Still working her way through the Post-it notes, she declared, "I'm going to come up with the perfect plan to get him this time."

With that, I decided it was probably best to head to my classes instead of encouraging her crazy ass.

Just as I waved goodbye, Adam met me on the sidewalk. Lyss was grumbling about something, which I was sure was directed at me for fraternizing with the enemy again, but whatever.

"Hey, Reign. Are you walking to campus?" he asked, noting the books in my hand. "Shall we walk together?"

"Aren't you supposed to be training?" I narrowed my eyes, taking in his preppy outfit. A polo shirt with jeans combined with that pop of blonde hair, he reminded me of a Ken doll.

"I had to skip this one because of a class clash. I will make up for it later in the week," he explained. I wasn't sure if that was strictly true after

Laura told me he would come back to walk with me, but I thought I'd let it slide.

"I'm going to get you, Adam," Lyss shrieked, and Adam ignored her threat. Instead, he offered her a small wave, chuckling.

"I'm guessing she didn't like the Post-it notes?" he asked with a little mischievous glint in his eyes.

I couldn't help but smile broadly as we walked to class. "Nope. She is apparently planning something even more spectacular."

He shrugged. "It will be hard to top the glitter. That crap is still everywhere. I think she put it in Aiden's shampoo. His hair has been glistening for days." He laughed. "And she got it all over my boxers, too. Did you know glitter itches?" He adjusted his crotch to make a point.

Blushing, I think back to that day. It was me who filled Adam's drawers with glitter and roamed around his room, uninvited. I wanted to tell him and ask him who the girl was in that picture, but I bit my tongue instead. I already felt guilty for being the glitter culprit; I'd feel worse admitting that I snooped around his room.

"Devin looked like he'd been hanging around in a strip bar last night. His biceps were glistening," he joked. How I wish he'd woken me up for that. "I wish Aiden and Lyss would get it over with and screw already. I'm tired of all these pranks," he said, and I scrunched my nose. Something about the way he said screw felt weird. Like he was too nice to use that word.

I cocked my eyebrow. "Did you know they went on a date when they were both freshmen?"

"What? No." His eyes widened. "Have they been screwing this whole time? Is this some weird form of foreplay for them?!"

Raising my hands, I giggled at his facial expression. "I didn't say that. I have no idea; I just think there's more to the story than we know."

He winced. "More than I ever want to know." Then, draping his arm over my shoulder, we walked the rest of the way to class, laughing and joking.

FIFTEEN

Devin

Slamming the car door, my bones were aching, and my head was throbbing. After getting bitched at by Coach for the better part of an hour because I missed three days of practice, he proceeded to put me through an extra round of grueling drills. A part of me wanted to tell him where I was just to spite him, but I kept it to myself. He would've been fine with it if I had told him *before* I missed practice, especially since it was the offseason, but I didn't bother, and that was on me. Plus, I'd never bothered him with personal stuff, believing it should be kept off the field, so I sucked it up instead. Since I was hoping to get drafted in two months, a tough day of training wouldn't matter in the long run, anyway. Not even the classes I'd been working my ass off to pass would matter. But I wanted to do well just in case my NFL career only lasted a few years; then, I could at least come back and do something useful with myself.

I grabbed my books and gym bag out of the car and walked to the door, feeling absolutely exhausted. I'd never looked forward to getting back to my bed more than right now, especially since I had a tiny hope that a little brunette might still be under the sheets, waiting for my arrival. Preferably naked, in my sweatshirt if not.

All hope of that was lost when I heard Aiden, Jackson, and Matty yelling at the TV, playing some stupid game on the Xbox. I doubted Reign would have the courage to stay in my bed with these idiots milling around.

"You wanna play?" Matty asked in greeting as he leaned over the sofa.

"Sure, let me just drop this stuff off upstairs." I gestured to my bag.

"If you're planning on seeing if that girl is still in your room, she's not. I checked," Aiden said, eyes not moving from the screen, face completely flat. Sometimes I wondered if he was a psychopath. Matty smirked, turning around. I ignored the comment because, frankly, we'd all heard him do much worse over the years. I knew Reign was loud last night, but I thought they were too busy Post-it noting Lyss's car to notice. Maybe it was round two that gave us away.

Aiden laughed as I walked past them to the stairs. When I got to my room, I threw my bag on the bed and instinctively checked her window. All the lights were off, probably because she was still busy on campus. I couldn't imagine a nursing degree was easy.

Even though I was disappointed, I headed back downstairs to my roommates and sat next to Jackson on the giant sofa while I watched them play a simulated football game. The comfortable silence was broken when Matty asked, "Where's Adam?"

Jackson shrugged. "Last I saw him, he was walking onto campus with Reign again."

My whole body froze. I remembered he offered to walk her once, but I didn't think they were that close. She hadn't mentioned him to me at all. My fists clenched, and I forced myself to relax. *It was just a walk.* That was all it was. I was inside her last night; that had to count for something more than walking next to her.

"Has he hit that yet?" Aiden asked, still refusing to remove his eyes from the TV, too focused on beating Matty for the fifth time today.

"Was he going to?" I stupidly hoped no one noticed the hesitation in my voice.

Matty piped up this time. "He mentioned he liked her, and she's hot. I guess he's laying the groundwork."

I knew it. He mentioned it when she first moved in, but it'd been over a month, and he hadn't said anything to me since. I figured he wasn't interested anymore. I should have said something then instead of waiting. Now, my best friend was trying to woo the girl I slept with last night. If she were that interested in him, surely she would have said as much before putting my dick in her mouth and sucking harder than a vacuum.

But we hadn't talked about being exclusive or dating at all, for that matter. What if she wanted to keep her options open for Adam too? It wasn't like I had a claim on her, and I had enough on my plate with Chloe and my mom as it was. I didn't need or want a girlfriend. I didn't think so. Unless it was Reign...

"You upset about that, D?" Aiden finally paused the game, making Matty and Jackson groan. I wished I could wipe that smirk off his face.

"I was winning that," Matty grumbled, but Aiden kept his eyes focused on me.

"Why would I have an issue with it?" I called Aiden's bluff. The only thing he knew was that I brought a girl home last night. That was it.

Aiden's grin grew wider. "Don't you think it's funny how none of us saw Devin bring the girl to his room?" He elbowed Jackson and glanced at Matty, both of whom had lost interest in the conversation and were playing on their phones. "And how no one saw her leave. It's almost like she had a different entry point into the house." He cocked an eyebrow. *Shit.* He was smarter than I'd ever given him credit for.

The front door opened, saving me from coming up with some lame-ass excuse, and Adam walked through the door with his laptop in hand. "Hey guys," he chirped. The stone in my stomach dissolved, knowing he was home and not with Reign. "I'm going to order a pizza tonight. Do any of you want in?"

There were chants and cheers as Adam sat down on the sofa. He seemed happier, lighter maybe, and that ticked me off. Reign certainly made me feel happier, but I hated the idea she did that for him, too. "You're in a good mood," Jackson muttered my thoughts.

"Yeah, I've had a good day." He had this annoying smirk on his face, and he looked drunk.

"Anything to do with Reign?"

"A gentleman never tells." He smirked, still looking delirious.

What the fuck was that supposed to mean? Whatever. It didn't matter. Reign was mine.

After an extraordinary amount of pizza, I headed upstairs to my room, fully intending to write a business essay that I'd been putting off over the last week. When I got there and saw Reign's light on, though, I had different ideas. My lips curled just thinking about her, and as much as I tried to repress it, I couldn't.

Her curtains were open, and I could clearly see her throwing a bag full of stuff on her bed before walking to her bathroom. As she shut the door, I checked my teeth and hair, then made my way to the railing, silently waiting for her to return. If she wasn't naked underneath me last night, this might be considered a creeper move. But luckily, we were past that.

As I heard the crack of the door open, I watched her walk out of the bathroom. Her hair was in a loose bun, and she had this tight white top on with tiny pink shorts. To top it off, she was wearing long tube socks to her knees. If she didn't already have my attention, she had it now. I adjusted my junk, checking it was all in place, before I gently tapped on her window. She jumped a little, but when she saw it was me, her face softened, and she glided over, opening the window.

"Hey D, what's up?" she said sweetly, leaning on the railing.

I forced my eyes to stay on her face and not down at her squashed boobs against the metal.

"Nothing, just wanted to see what you were up to." Looking over her shoulder, I could see she was planning a night alone in her room. "Wine and popcorn? Are you having a movie night?"

"Umm, not exactly." She backed away, and then her gaze flitted down at the floor as though I'd caught her in some sort of sordid act.

"What are you doing then if you've got wine and popcorn?" I asked with a hint of a smile. She was squirming underneath my gaze, and I loved watching it. It made me feel powerful because all she had to do was look at me, and I'd fall to my knees.

"Just a TV show," she said casually, but her cheeks were flustered like it was some kind of dirty pleasure. I needed to know what she was watching now.

"Can I join?" I asked, giving her a slow smile and her lips pursed. A little tuft of hair fell from her bun, and I reached over the railing, putting it behind her ear. That move caught her off guard, and she took a sharp breath. She turned to the room, then back to me, contemplating whether to let me in. When her eyes met mine, I gave her a wink for good measure.

"It's probably not your type of show." She looked anywhere but me and scratched the top of her bun.

"What kind of show is it?" My eyes widened at the thought. *Reign wouldn't watch that, would she?* "Are you watching porn? Is that why you need the wine? A little Dutch courage?" I teased, and I didn't think her face could get any more flushed, but it could. I barked out a laugh because she was as red as the wine she was planning on drinking.

"Clearly not, because that *would* be your kind of show."

I shrugged. She wasn't wrong.

"Ah, it can't be that bad. Come on." I cocked my eyebrows and held onto the railing, hinting that I was coming over. When she moved out of the way, I took that as my invitation and jumped, stepping into her room with ease. She stared at my arms, still in the white shirt and gray sweatpants I put on this morning.

"It's rude to stare," I joked, flexing just slightly and watching her lazy stares.

She shook her head and looked back up at me. "I wasn't staring at your muscles. I was staring at the glitter."

"Ah yes, I hear I've got you to blame for this." I pointed at the pink sheen on my biceps, which got me a lot of looks in the locker room this morning. "I should thank you. It's had the ladies staring at my arms all day." She rolled her eyes at that comment. "Cute pj's, by the way." I sat down on her desk chair and took my shoes off. I didn't know if that was the correct etiquette after inviting yourself over, but I figured it would be harder for her to kick me out once they were off.

"Thanks," she mumbled, turning on her heel and walking further into the bedroom. I followed behind as she shuffled over to the bed and took a seat. She moved high onto the purple comforter, a different one from the first night we spent together, and patted the spot next to her. Following her lead, I moved up the bed, resting my back against the headboard and holding one of her fluffy pink pillows to my chest.

She grabbed the fuzzy white blanket from the foot of the bed and brought it over her body, covering her perfectly toned legs, which was disappointing. "Do you want under?"

I knew she meant the blanket, so I nodded, pretending my filthy mind didn't just take me to another place entirely because, yes, I would very much like to be under her again. It was a small blanket, so while it covered her, it only barely skimmed my thighs.

"What are we watching?"

She tucked a bowl of popcorn in between us, and I grasped a handful, shoving it in my mouth, fully expecting the buttery taste to melt on my tongue. Only there was a tangier taste to it because she'd melted cheese on top, making it that much more delicious. I made a beeline for another handful, but she smacked my palm away, shoving her hand in.

After she swallowed the popcorn, she looked over, giving me those wide doe eyes. "If you're staying, then we have to share."

"I'm always up for sharing, darlin'."

She bit into her bottom lip before she gained the courage to speak again. "Okay. So if I tell you what I'm watching, you have to promise not to judge me before I tell you." Her gaze flicked down, and she started picking at some of the fuzz on her blanket, staring at it as though it had the answers to all her problems. She was so cute when she was embarrassed.

"You're actually watching porn, aren't you?" I cocked my eyebrow, stopping the corners of my mouth from lifting too much. If she wanted to watch porn with me, who was I to deny her that pleasure?

"Shh, no." She smacked me playfully on the arm, and I rubbed my bicep, pretending it hurt. "Just promise you won't judge," she repeated, still more focused on the blanket than my face.

"Okay, I promise." Raising my hand, I gave her my scout's honor. Of course, I was never a scout, but she didn't need to know that.

"The Bachelor."

"The Bachelor?" It took me a moment to process what she said. "It's not the worst thing, I guess." I was expecting something much more sinister, but a bunch of hot chicks vying over one guy didn't seem that bad.

"You don't have to stay." She looked at me as though she was expecting me to throw this blanket off and run for my life, but I was with her, in her bed, eating cheesy popcorn. As if there were anywhere else to be. "*But* if you do stay, you can't judge me, and you have to play my drinking game." Her eyes skittered over to the bottle of red.

Normally, I would say no to drinking like this after the whole Chloe debacle, but tonight, I might just let loose. It was only one bottle of wine. It wasn't like we could get drunk on that, and we were in the comfort of Reign's bedroom. What was the worst that could happen?

"Deal?" she asked, pulling out her hand, and I dutifully accepted.

"Hanging out with a pretty girl on a school night…doesn't sound too bad to me." I winked, and she giggled softly. "Now, what's this game?"

"The rules are simple. Rule one: anytime the host says 'dramatic,' you take a drink." She held up the cheap bottle of wine she bought for herself. "Rule two: anytime a contestant cries, you drink twice. Rule three: anytime you hear someone say, 'right reasons,' you drink. Finally, rule four: when someone says 'love' or the bachelor kisses a contestant, drink twice."

Chuckling, I tried to remember everything she had just said. "There are a lot of rules for a simple game," I pointed out, and she pursed her lips, unfazed by my response. "Were you planning on playing this on your own?" I knew she was in her room, and she wasn't planning on seeing anyone, but the idea of her getting drunk by herself had me feeling uneasy because it was something Chloe would have done if my mom and I weren't monitoring her.

"Yes," she responded sheepishly. "I wasn't expecting to be judged," she defended.

"I'm not judging." Okay, I was judging. I couldn't help it.

"Studying nursing is hard, and before moving here, the only time I got to relax was Monday night with a glass of wine." My heart immediately sank; she did it because she was alone and didn't have anyone else to do it with.

"You're right. I'm sorry." I couldn't bring my own prejudices against her. She wasn't Chloe. "How about we switch the rules up?" I suggested.

"What do you propose?"

"You drink whenever the host says 'dramatic' and a contestant cries. *I* drink when someone says 'right reasons,' 'love,' or there's a make-out session. That way, the wine might last longer." At least this way, we could still play her game, but I wouldn't feel quite so bad about how much we were drinking.

"Well, I originally thought it was just me watching, so I assumed I would only need one bottle, but if we run out, I'll go down and get some more." She grabbed the remote and leaned against my arm. I motioned to put it around her, but she leaned forward, grabbed the wine, and put it in between us. Unsubtle hint taken. "Have you watched *The Bachelor* before?"

"No, but the concept is easy. Guy picks from a bunch of hot women, right?"

"Yes, but not just any guy; this guy is Shawn. He's a fireman from North Carolina, and he had his heart broken by Carly on *The Bachelorette*. His wife died four years ago, and this was the first time he tried to date. He was ready to introduce her to his little boy, but then Carly broke it off because she had stronger feelings for Ben." It sounded like *she* wanted to date Shawn.

"Why would you go on *The Bachelorette* after something like that happened to you?"

"Because you might find your true love." I cocked my eyebrow in disbelief. "Or you might end up the bachelor, and then you can pick from all the women. That's why there's always such talk about 'right reasons' on this show." She laughed, stuffing some popcorn in her mouth. "Shawn is definitely here for the right reasons, though," she clarified before I got any ideas about his intentions.

"Sounds riveting."

"Says the guy who I bet only watches sports."

I shrugged. "Sports is an easy watch. You always have a team to root for, and you don't need to watch every game to know what's going on."

"You don't need to watch every episode of this either. They go over the important stuff at the beginning."

"Mhmm."

She pointed her finger at me, her mouth curving up on one side. "You're judging."

"I'm not judging." I raised my hands, laughing. I was definitely judging. "Just don't know why you'd want to watch this show. It feels a little backward."

"I like it because it's funny. There's a lot of drama, and I like being drawn into their ridiculous world for a couple of hours a week. It gets me out of my head."

She looked down at the popcorn, picking at a few of the pieces. There was definitely more to that statement, but I wasn't going to push her. I hoped one day she'd feel close enough to me that she could tell me everything, but until then, I would just make sure I was there for her.

"Well, thanks for letting me join you." I elbowed her lightly. Her gorgeous dark chocolate eyes looked up at me, and she licked her lips, which moved my gaze down. Man, I wanted to kiss her again. I still hadn't had "the talk" with her because I still wasn't sure if it was appropriate to do it. Yes, we slept together last night, but we'd had casual sex before. Maybe she was only looking for that, and I'd rather be friends with benefits than raise the topic and get shot down completely.

"Let's wait and see; you might want to jump back to your room after the first ten minutes." That's definitely not happening. I was staying here as long as she'd have me.

Unfortunately for Reign, this episode was particularly *dramatic*. Shawn left one of his girlfriends—his term, not mine—in the desert because she was too busy bitching about one of his other girlfriends. It all felt a lot more like an episode of *Sister Wives* than a dating show. The girlfriend he left in the desert cried, and they repeated that scene at least twenty times, which meant Reign had downed over two-thirds of the bottle of wine by the time we'd watched the first half-hour of the show. Her little hiccups and giggles were a telltale sign she was hammered. I wasn't surprised; she was like four foot nothing, and just drank her daily quota of liquid in alcoholic form. I knew this was a bad idea.

I watched her reach for the remote, pausing the TV and then looking at me. Slowly, I turned to look at her and was met with a devilish smirk, and this glint in her eyes I knew could only mean trouble.

"Devin," she whispered, leaning closer.

"Yeah?"

She brought her mouth next to my ear and did a very loud, very drunken giggle. On any other girl, it would be annoying. On Reign, it was cute.

"I think we need more wine." She fingered my chin, leading my face to hers. Our mouths were only inches apart, and I knew what she wanted me to do. She wanted me to catch her lips in mine and kiss her senseless. But, unfortunately, the wine on her breath reminded me she wasn't in her right mind, and I wasn't about to take advantage because that wouldn't make me any better than those guys Chloe hangs out with.

Covering the hand she rested on my cheek, I gently moved it down to her side and placed it there. "I don't think that's a good idea, darlin'."

She jumped off the bed at the speed of a mountain lion. "What do you mean, D? I think it's the best idea I've had all night." Then she did that super-sexy giggle-hiccup thing again. I swore she was the only girl in the world who could still look hot when she was drunk as a skunk. She skidded out of the door, and I held my breath, waiting for the thud as she fell down the stairs. Thankfully, I heard nothing, so she either made it down the stairs safely or she passed out before getting there.

A few minutes later, she was back, clutching the neck of a white wine bottle in her hand as she slowly walked toward me with half-lidded eyes. I couldn't be sure if she was trying to be seductive or if she was genuinely having trouble walking at this point. It was probably the latter, but the way her eyes darted across my body and the way she bit her lip made me think she had ideas for something else.

Her eyes stayed trained on me as she approached the end of the bed. Then, hauling her knees up, she crawled over, eyes focused on me the entire time. Well, that confirmed it. She was trying to seduce me, which wouldn't take much on a normal day around her, but tonight was a little different. There was no way I was taking advantage of this situation.

My legs were parted, and she crawled between them. The view of her cleavage wasn't helping matters, and for some reason, I felt frozen on the spot in her bed. Probably because she planted her hands on either side of my hips, blocking me in as her chocolate eyes pierced through mine. I wasn't going to deny that part of the reason I came over tonight was because I wanted to get into her pants again, but doing it like this just felt wrong.

Thankfully, she didn't stay in that position long, choosing to lie next to me instead. She picked up my arm, wrapping it firmly around her shoulders, and then rested her head on my chest. If sex wasn't on the cards tonight, I was glad snuggling was.

Still clutching that bottle of wine like it was her firstborn child, she turned the show back on. This I could deal with. She'd fall asleep soon, and I'd sneak out before she could remember I was even there.

The show was getting more ridiculous as it went on. I stopped pushing the fact that the host said "dramatic" again because, frankly, I didn't want her to drink anymore. Luckily, she seemed to have missed it, too busy twirling her finger across my chest. I said loudly, "Oh! Shawn just said, 'right reasons.' I guess it's my turn to swig." Taking the wine bottle out of her hands, I pretended to take a drink. She poked me hard, laughing, and failed to notice me putting the bottle on the nightstand, out of her reach.

As Shawn made another contestant cry, Reign's hand traveled up my chest, over the thin cotton of my shirt. I watched her hand carefully because I thought she was reaching for the wine, but when she didn't and instead used her long nails to lightly scratch at my pecs, I lost all focus.

Shit.

Now all I could think about was the last time she did that. When her tongue was down my throat and her other hand was in my pants. She glanced up to look at me, fluttering her eyelashes with a small grin on her face.

Shit.

She knew what she was doing.

"Devin, do you remember when I said that we should just be friends?" She draped her leg over my thigh, using her foot to rub my calves. Her whole body was flush against mine, and the thin cotton material of her tank and shorts did nothing to hide the feel of her curves brushing against me. Was she really going to have the talk right now?

I nodded, feeling uneasy and unable to say anything because she was still drawing those damn circles on my chest.

"I think I might want more," she whispered.

Yes. We were going to have this conversation now. When Reign was drunk and wouldn't remember it in the morning.

"More in what way?" I shifted uncomfortably underneath her, trying to get some breathing space. I tried to gently swat her hand away from my chest, but she was persistent. She kept it there and then gently grazed my nipple, causing my dick to stir.

"Whatever way you'll have me," she admitted, exasperated. Normally, those words would have me hard as a stone. I'd part those legs of hers and show her exactly how I'd have her. But right now, Reign was so hammered,

I couldn't tell if she was horny and just saying it. Either way, I knew it was off the table tonight. She was biting her bottom lip, and it was taking all of my self-control not to bite it for her.

"Maybe this is something we can discuss in the morning, darlin'. When you haven't drunk so much." If I wanted to actually date her, which I thought I did, I couldn't be an asshole and take her tonight.

"Fine," she pouted, and I breathed a sigh of relief. At least drunk, Reign was reasonable. "I'm tired of talking, anyway."

Before I could process anything, she crashed her lips against mine, and without thinking, I reacted. I kissed her back; the feeling of her warm, soft lips was what I'd been craving all day. She wound her arms around my neck and moved across to straddle me. Her hot center rocked against mine as her tongue darted across my bottom lip, making me growl. I placed my hands on her hips as she started grinding faster. Those tiny cotton shorts meant I could feel every inch of her against my sweatpants. My body started reacting, and I could feel myself hardening underneath her. She felt it too because she ground down harder, making me moan into our kiss. I grabbed her hips tight and forced her to stop.

"What's wrong?" she asked, leaning her forehead against mine. "Don't you want this?" She tried to move her hips again, but my grip was too tight, and I kept her in place.

"We can't do this right now." I took several long, slow breaths to center myself. If that ocean breathing didn't work now, then it was useless. Her lips were red and pouty, and it was taking everything in me not to kiss her again.

She pouted out her bottom lip in annoyance. Her legs were spread on me, and those socks did little to tame my thoughts, especially when she shifted over my crotch. "But we did it last night." I groaned at the memory. We did do it last night when she was fully in control and not drunk over watching a guy hand out a bunch of roses to a thousand women.

"Let's talk about this in the morning, Reign," I whispered, gently kissing her cheek, hoping that would soften the blow.

"What if I want to talk about it now?" Her lips scorched my skin as she kissed my neck, traveling down to my shoulder. I loosened my grip on her hips for just a second, letting her grind against me again.

"I don't think it's talking you want to do, darlin'," I drawled out and closed my eyes as she nipped at my collarbone. She knew exactly where to lick and bite me to get a reaction, and I wanted her so badly.

She let out a little giggle as her hands ventured to my shirt, crinkling it up to just below my armpits. "Did I tell you the first night I saw your chest, all I wanted to do was lick the lines?" She bobbed her head down, and I knew exactly what was going to happen if I didn't stop her. She was going to give me head, or I was going to fuck her senseless, and when she'd wake up in the morning, she'd regret it.

The minute her hot, wet tongue hit my belly button, I clasped her shoulders, hauling her up. "As much as I love hearing that, I still think we should discuss this in the morning." She finally glared at me, her eyes half-lidded, and moaned like a child, but that final blow seemed to have worked. "It's been over an hour, and I still don't know who Shawn gives his roses to," I explained, and her eyes widened as if she'd just remembered she was missing out.

"Fine." She reluctantly resumed her position next to me. I opened my arm so she could tuck herself under, and her hand went straight to my chest where she proceeded to draw lazy circles. That I could handle. Her wet tongue skating across my chest? Nope.

We finally got to the part of the show where Shawn narrowed it down to his final ten. "I can't believe he's still got so many," I muttered. "I could get rid of at least another five right now." I glanced down at Reign, expecting a response, only to realize that she'd fallen asleep on my chest. She'd left the tiniest puddle of drool on my shirt, but I'd still bang her. However, it left me wondering how long I'd been watching this show by myself when I didn't have to.

Taking my time, I gently lifted her off my chest and onto the pillow beside me. She hardly stirred, which was unsurprising since she was out like a log. I pulled her fuzzy blanket over her petite frame and kissed her forehead lightly. "Good night, darlin'," I whispered, and as I was getting off the bed, a stack of bright pink Post-it Notes caught my eye. After going into her bathroom and getting her a glass of water, I wrote her a note, leaving both on her bedside table.

Reluctantly, I headed to the window, ready to sleep in my own bed. Just as I gripped the railing, her voice broke the silence. "Are you leaving?" I didn't turn to look at her because I knew if I did, I'd go straight back and join her. I wasn't prepared to keep hooking up, like last night. Next time I have my way with her, I want us to be officially dating. I shook my head because I couldn't believe how willing I was to throw my no-dating rule out the window for her. It wasn't her fault she was perfect.

"Because you need to rest, darlin'," I said over my shoulder, still staring at my room. It was dark and uninviting, but there was no turning back.

"I'd rest better if you were here." There was a hint of sadness in her voice which killed me. I'd sleep better with her too.

"Just knock on the window if you need me." There was a momentary pause, and I took the opportunity to glance over my shoulder, and she was already asleep. "Good night, darlin'," I whispered one more time before climbing out of her room and into my own. Taking one final look at her, I smiled.

I couldn't wait to talk to her in the morning because it felt like we were on the same page. I wanted her. She wanted me.

How difficult could this whole dating thing be?

Sixteen
Reign

Thud. Thud. Thud.

The pounding bass throbbed against my ears as I opened my eyes. Bright light flickered in. *What time is it?* More bass thudded in between my ears. *Was this another one of Lyss's pranks?*

I threw the covers off; the cold morning chilled my legs as I shifted to get out of bed. That was when the thudding turned into throbbing, piercing my brain with every move my body made. That pounding wasn't a prank. That pounding was inside my head.

Slowly and ever so gently opening one of my eyes, I reached for the glass of water next to my bedside table and opened my drawer for some painkillers. After swallowing them and gulping down the water, I fell face-first back onto the bed. Shoving a pillow over my head in hopes it would block out some of the light until I felt human again, I closed my eyes, urging myself back to sleep. I may have had a few essays to finish today, but I wasn't in a state to do them just yet.

After getting up an hour later, the pounding felt much more like a tepid tapping. Even though the throbbing was lighter and a little less intrusive, I knew today was going to be a fragile one for me. When I threw the pillow to the other side of the bed, a pink piece of paper caught my attention. I plucked the soggy Post-it Note from under the glass of water and could only just make out what was written on it because of the smudges.

Reign,

Sorry I had to go.

Hope you feel better this morning,

Devin

My brows creased, studying his scribbles. Devin? When did he come over, and why didn't I remember? I tried to think back to what happened last night, but it was blank because of my red wine haze. I definitely watched *The Bachelor.* That was something I always did on Mondays, but anything beyond that escaped me.

Trudging to the bathroom, I let the warm water of the shower wake my bones. It was only while I was brushing my teeth that memories from last night came flooding back. I remembered drinking a lot. Devin was there, watching TV with me. We were snuggling like last time. My lips curved into a smile, thinking about being in his arms. But then I frowned when I remembered more. Me straddling Devin; me throwing myself at him; the look of disgust on Devin's face; Devin pushing me off him.

I slowed the movement of the toothbrush, staring at myself in the mirror in shock. Devin rejected me. White foam dripped from my mouth as it hung open in disbelief. I threw myself at him, and he gave me a hard pass.

Spitting out the minty toothpaste, I wiped my mouth and shook my head because I was trying to make sense of it. I wanted to talk to him about us, and he said no. But the night before, he wanted me. We wanted each other. We *had* each other. My feet moved on their own accord, straight to the railing, because I was ready to talk to him about everything.

It was nearly midday, and his curtains were still shut. It wasn't like he was asleep; that entire house all had football training in the morning, so he'd been up for hours, which left me with one conclusion. He'd shut them on purpose again. To shut me out.

Embarrassment flared from the apples of my cheeks down to the tips of my toes. Did I read the signs all wrong? My heart was beating wildly, and my breath quickened when I remembered last night. I ground against him while telling him I wanted more than just a friend-with-benefits kind of situation. We needed to talk, but dry humping him against his will wasn't exactly how I wanted that conversation to go. God, I must have looked so desperate.

Snippets of our conversation came back to me. When I told him I wanted more, he just kept stalling, telling me we would talk about it today. The same day, he shut his curtains. *What was I thinking, opening up like that?* Clay was the only other person I'd opened up to, and look how that turned out.

It was so obvious now. Devin only ever wanted a fuck buddy. Where I thought we were headed for a relationship, he thought we were just having a good time, just like I said I wanted. And I gave him that. Until I wanted more.

My body vibrated with annoyance. God, I am so embarrassed. Was this why guys didn't want me? Was it because I pushed them too far, and then I gave them no option but to push me away? Shaking my hands, I walked to my closet, shoving on the first outfit I could find. I needed to get out of this room.

I threw my hair into a ponytail, grabbed my purse, and stalked out of the room. I didn't care what I looked like. I just needed to do something to get my mind off this situation. Skipping down the stairs, I tried to ignore Laura and Lyss in the living room, but they noticed my presence immediately.

"Reign, there you are." Lyss smiled, holding a large bag of I don't know what in her hands. "I figured out the perfect way to get back at the guys." She lifted the arm holding the bag, waiting for me to ask about it. I wasn't in the mood, and I genuinely wondered when she had time to take her classes with all the crap she and Aiden pulled against each other.

Clutching my purse to my hips, I said, "Sorry, Lyss. I've already planned something today." I left it at that, hurrying out the door before she could get to me. There was no way I wanted to spend the day sneaking into Aiden's house. No. I needed to get out of the neighborhood. I needed to breathe.

Lyss muttered something under her breath. I knew she was disappointed, but I didn't care. I couldn't stay here. With my head tipped down, I watched my feet shuffle out of the door, and then I stopped. *Where was I going to go?*

"Reign," Adam's familiar deep voice called. He was leaning against his car, holding a bag, as his bright blue eyes twinkled at me. I didn't want to talk to Adam or anyone. I started walking again, not acknowledging him. "Where are you off to in such a hurry?"

It was like he could read my thoughts. I had nowhere to go, and there were no sidewalks to walk on. I swiveled on my heels. "Hey," I said casually. "I'm just going for a walk." I turned back, head held high, and ready to walk on the street if I had to.

"There isn't that much in the way of a walk in that direction," he said, his voice laced with curiosity. "Unless you like walking beside the highway." Fiddling with the strings of my purse, I slumped, looking back at him. "It's not that pretty, and to be honest, I'd rather not end up in a police investigation because I have no doubts if you head that way, I'll be the last person to see you alive."

I huffed out an annoyed breath. "I'm not going to die."

He raised a brow. "You are in that direction."

"Fine. Is there anywhere I can go that isn't on campus and is walking distance from here?" I asked with my head hung low. I didn't want his help, but it seemed like I didn't have a choice.

"Not much." He shrugged. "Are you okay?"

Looking back up, I was met with his perfectly straight smile and a cute little dimple on his left cheek. Adam was such a nice and open guy. Just being around him instantly made me relax and forget about my problems. "I'm fine. I just need to get out of here for a while."

"Wanna go for a drive?" He gestured to his car, and when I hesitated, he raised his hand. "Hey, I'm just offering you a way out of here for a while that doesn't involve walking around some haunted woods."

Pursing my lips, my shoulders dropped because I asked the universe to help get me away from my thoughts, and this was clearly them answering. "I'm sorry, Adam. I didn't mean to be rude. If you're not up to much, I would love to come out with you." He smiled at that, immediately opening the door for me. Without another word, I slid in, and before I knew it, he was backing out and driving down a nondescript road.

After what felt like hours of driving in silence—which was probably only thirty minutes—Adam pulled up to a rickety old diner. "I'm starving," he said, turning his car off and opening the door. He paused, looking back. "You coming?"

"Uh, I guess." What else was I going to do? Sit in the car on my own?

It turned out that Adam could eat like a horse. I'd watched him chow down on sweet potato fries, cheese fries, a cheeseburger, a chocolate milkshake, onion rings, and a hot dog. All in the span of twenty minutes. As he took the last sip of his milkshake, he cocked a questioning eyebrow.

"What?" He smirked. "Haven't you ever seen a guy eat before?"

"Oh, I've seen guys eat, but this is another level kind of crap. Where do you put all of it?" I asked, unintentionally checking out his body. It was all hard edges and sharp lines. He grinned when my gaze met his.

He laughed. "It's the offseason, so our training isn't as vigorous. Means I can have a cheat meal a couple of times a week."

"That wasn't a meal. That was a full week's worth of calories."

His eyes dropped as he smiled. "For you. What are you? One hundred and twenty pounds when wet? I bench more than that on an off day." I rolled my eyes, balling up a napkin and throwing it at him. He dodged it easily, watching it fly to the booth behind him and hit an older gentleman.

The man made a disgruntled noise as he got up. Adam straightened in his chair, watching as the man walked away, and eyed him angrily. "I'm sorry, sir," Adam coughed out, sounding sobered and embarrassed.

He winced at me when the man left. "That's your own fault," I whispered, stifling a giggle and shoving one of his fries into my mouth.

Shaking his head. "You're the one who threw it!" He snatched the next fry that I was about to put in my mouth and ate it. "Now that you seem to be in a better mood, are you going to tell me what had you running out of your house like it was on fire?"

Sinking my teeth into my bottom lip, I wondered how honest I could be with Adam. Even though he and Devin were close, I was almost certain Devin hadn't mentioned anything about us.

Us?

What was I thinking? There wasn't an us. I was just a good time for Devin.

"Nothing much, really."

"Didn't look like nothing much. If Aiden wasn't at the gym, I would have thought you'd seen him naked. Now, *that* is something to run away from. Believe me. I've seen it one too many times." He shivered.

"It can't be that bad. I heard a lot of stories about the great Aiden Matthews before I knew who he was. He's a legend around the Covey campus." It was true. When I first enrolled, I heard some girls talking about him and his wild parties. It didn't take me long to realize it was the one and only Aiden who lived next door that they were talking about. Maybe that was why Lyss hated him so much, because everyone else seemed to love him.

Adam's face straightened, and he looked at me dead in the eye. "Is that your way of telling me you're interested in him?"

"God, no. Besides the fact that Lyss would kill me if I ever had that thought, I'm kind of getting over someone."

His whole body relaxed. "Well, that explains why you dodged my date request."

I was left speechless for a few seconds. I almost completely forgot about that because I was too busy thinking about Devin. "I didn't dodge it. I reminded you about it. Don't you remember?"

He tilted his head, scratching the slightly blonde stubble on his chin. "You mean when you were trying to create a distraction so you could put glitter in my pants?" I pursed my lips. "Yeah, I thought as much. Being rejected by you was bad enough, but did you have to destroy any chances of getting a girl to date me at all?" He adjusted himself in his seat as though he was thinking about all the places the glitter was still clinging to.

"Hey, some girls like the whole Edward Cullen vampire vibe." I smiled.

He shrugged, shoving another fry into his mouth. "You probably did us both a favor. Neighbors dating would never have worked, anyway."

My body tensed, thinking that was exactly what I said to Devin those few weeks ago. If only I had trusted those instincts, then I wouldn't be here. Alone and pining. "I wouldn't say that," I said defensively. Maybe if Devin and I had met in different circumstances, it could have been different.

"Oh, yeah?" Adam's lip quirked while he played with the straw in his milkshake. He looked happy, more relaxed.

"Yeah," I confirmed, checking my watch and slumping down into the seat. "I think I should probably head back home. I've got a paper that I've been avoiding for the last week," I whined reluctantly. "Thanks for saving me from myself and bringing me here."

Adam still had a wide grin on his face. It was the kind that was contagious and made me smile back. I guess if anything good came out of the fiasco with Devin, it was that I had Adam as a friend. Conversations with him were easy, and it felt like we'd known each other for years, something I didn't have with many people.

"No problem. I had a great time," he said, distracted.

As we headed back to the house, there was a warm silence between us. We didn't need to talk to feel comfortable in each other's presence, which was another thing I liked about Adam. We didn't have to talk aimlessly to fill the air, and we could just be. When we pulled up to Adam's driveway, both houses looked empty, but when we opened the car doors, we could hear an argument.

Lyss and Aiden were screaming down each other's throats, and it was so loud it was echoing through the neighborhood. Adam rolled his eyes and gave me a lazy smile. "Here we go again."

"Are they ever going to stop?"

"Not until one of them is naked," he deadpanned, rushing to the backyard. I followed closely behind so I could drag Lyss away. When he opened the back gate, Lyss and Aiden were toe-to-toe, face-to-face, yelling over each other with a ferocity I'd only ever seen on nature programs when chimpanzees were having a conversation.

That wasn't the main thing drawing my attention, though. No. I couldn't concentrate on them because there was a boatload of foam frothing from the pool behind them, multiplying by the second, and sliding its way across the concrete to them.

"What the hell?" I whispered in awe. The more they argued, the frothier the foam became, overtaking the backyard. I'd never seen anything like it.

"Guys, calm down." Adam tried to get in between them. He was met with sharp head turns and narrowed eyes because they'd only just noticed his presence.

"Oh, look who it is, your little puppet." Lyss laughed bitterly, focusing her attention back on Aiden. Aiden didn't look at us long; instead, he turned back to Lyss and shouted over her again.

"Aiden is going to kill her." Adam leaned over, only speaking loud enough for me to hear. "Look out," he yelled, grabbing me and pulling me into his chest as something flew past us. The empty box fell to the floor, bouncing against the modern gray tile and rolling to a stop. The bright white words "Dish Soap" etched across the red box caught my eye. That must have been what she used to bubble the pool. I thought back to this morning and the bag in her hand. *Was this her plan all along?*

"You are paying for my fucked-up pool filters," Aiden shouted. Lyss was tall like a supermodel, but with her shoulders hunched and her detached gaze, it was the first time I thought she ever looked small. Fragile even.

"Your filters will be fine, frat boy," Lyss yelled with an uncaring laugh at the end. "How about you pay for my Nana Lou's plates that you wrecked with that stupid water balloon? Oh, that's right, you can't. *They* were priceless."

With each word, the air thinned, and her voice cracked. Adam and I gave each other knowing looks. There was a sheen to Lyss's eyes that no amount of fake grinning could hide. I remembered she seemed a little upset about the plates at the time, but I didn't know just how much.

Aiden looked down at her, and for the first time, he looked anything other than menacing. He was quiet, with pursed lips, a far cry from his usual cocky attitude. It seemed, as much as he hated Lyss, he hated seeing her upset more.

Lyss didn't bother with a second glance when she shouldered past him. She didn't acknowledge us as she walked out of the gate with her chin held high, either. Aiden, Adam, and I just watched.

The foam had doubled in the time it took for her to stroll out of the yard. Yeah, she'd definitely wrecked the filters, but Aiden didn't seem bothered anymore. His gaze locked onto Adam and me, and it was as though he'd just registered our presence. His back straightened, and he looked between us with a smirk. "Have you two finally boned?" he asked, that human side of him completely gone, replaced with his usual roguish attitude.

"Shut up," I snarled. The way he could turn off his emotions and not care in the slightest how much he hurt Lyss made me angry.

"What the hell happened to the pool?" We heard Devin's voice before we saw him. He opened the back door, rushing out, shocked and confused. My heart skipped a beat, seeing his beautiful, chiseled face, then dropped, remembering how he left me high and dry. He didn't want me.

He scanned the backyard, waiting for an answer, and stopped when he saw me. For the slightest of seconds, I saw something in his eyes. Anger? Annoyance? Frustration? I didn't know. All I knew was that it quickly turned to disgust and confusion. Probably because he was wondering why I was following him around like a lovesick puppy, humping his leg like one, too. His eyebrows crossed, and he swiveled on his heel, walking back into the house, shaking his head. "Whatever," he mumbled, loud enough for everyone to hear.

"What was that all about?" Adam posed the question to no one in particular. I broke away from his embrace, bowing my head to hide my crimson cheeks. Devin was so embarrassed by me and what happened last night that he couldn't even acknowledge me.

"I gotta go." It was all I said before scurrying out of their backyard to find Lyss. I couldn't bear to look at Adam because I knew he'd somehow get me to admit everything to him. I didn't need another person getting involved in my and Devin's complicated relationship.

I rolled my eyes, annoyed at myself for using that word. There was no relationship. There was nothing between us, and I needed to get that through my thick skull. Getting into the house, I looked for Lyss because if I couldn't feel good about this situation, the least I could do was check on her.

SEVENTEEN
Devin

I looked down at the red bucket I was holding. Full of balls and string, I wondered what the hell I was thinking when I agreed to sneak into our next-door neighbor's house with Aiden and Jackson. The house was old but in immaculate condition, and this prank was stupid. This prank war had gone too far. The pool filter cost over two thousand dollars to fix, something Aiden just tossed money at like it meant nothing, and he spent the rest of the night planning his next diabolical deed to get Lyss back. She'd made him lose all his sense, albeit he didn't have much there to lose to begin with, but still. In times like these, I really wish we had more vigorous football training to keep Aiden busy. Idle hands and all that crap.

We didn't even question why Aiden had a spare key to their house when he confidently waltzed in. He'd tell us it was because he was a good neighbor, probably say that Lyss wanted him to look after her plants while she was away, or something. It was all a lie, because I can guarantee that

Aiden would be the last person Lyss would want in her house. I'd bet money I don't have that he got the key copied so he could sneak in here and pull some stupid crap like this.

As he stomped up the stairs, the walls shook around us. The dude was like a bull in a china shop. As I felt the weight of his feet in the room above me, I realized he must have been in Reign's room.

Fuck.

I dropped the balls. "I'll be back in just a minute," I called to Jackson, who could hardly hear me because he was filling a bucket with water, and I ran up the stairs. Passing the fake body on the landing, I headed straight to Reign's room, knowing my sweatshirt was still in there. If he saw it, we'd be found out, and he'd tell everyone. I didn't care if everyone knew, but Reign did, and I couldn't do that to her.

When I opened the door, her familiar fruity scent engulfed me, sneaking into my lungs and taking hold of my bloodstream. Damn, I needed to get a grip. Aiden was by her bed, tossing fake spiders under her sheets and then throwing the comforter back into place.

"Need something?" he asked, moving to the bedside table and sticking bug outlines onto the inside of the lampshade. Even though he hadn't shown any passing interest in Reign, I was surprised he wasn't snooping. For blackmail purposes, more than anything. "Or are you just here to make sure I don't ruin any of your lover's stuff?" He laughed to himself.

I discarded his comment, scanning the room for my sweatshirt, which was nowhere in sight. A pang of pain hit my spine. Why did I bother checking? It'd been over a week, and she hadn't spoken to me since we watched *The Bachelor* together. I came back from the gym fully ready to talk to her about being exclusive, only to find our pool overflowing with foam and her wrapped in Adam's arms. Entangled in his embrace like he was her protector.

The worst part about that day was finding out they'd gone out on a dinner date just before. A date…the thing she told me she didn't want to do the first time we met. God, did I want to punch Adam in his perfectly angled face when he smiled deliriously at me. I left for all of three hours, and she'd already apparently moved on to my best friend.

The only saving grace was that I didn't sleep with her last night, even if the taste of regret was souring everything I ate. I thought about talking to her about it, but she'd barely been in her room since everything went down, and when she was in there, she made sure her curtains were shut.

"Nah, you're good. I came to check on what you wanted us to do with the buckets." I waved him off with a lie. I'd been so lost in thoughts about Reign and Adam that I only just noticed he was staring at me with one eyebrow raised.

"Were you not listening to our briefing before we came here?" Yes, we had a briefing about setting up the pranks. Aiden gave us our parts and initiated the play. Once a quarterback, always a quarterback. "You put the buckets on top of the doors," he said simply and slowly to make sure it sank in this time. "So, when they come home, they get drenched with water."

"Maybe we should fill the buckets with whipped cream instead."

He narrowed his gaze at me. "You're a kinky dude, aren't you, Walker?"

Clutching a hand to my chest, "I just don't want to get arrested if all of this goes wrong. We don't live in *Home Alone*. We could seriously hurt someone."

He waved me off dismissively, still planting fake spiders across Reign's room. "Do whatever you want. Just get it done in the next ten minutes."

Padding down the stairs, I told Jackson the plan and did my best to find some whipped cream in their house. They didn't have much, and the stuff they had was slightly yellowed in the back of the refrigerator. We decided to improvise and added some marshmallows as well. At least that way, we were potentially avoiding a lawsuit.

Four buckets full of cream, marshmallows, and chips later, we'd positioned the buckets over doors and were ready to get out of there. Aiden's feet stomped down the hall, scanning the room, and checking out our setup. There were plastic balls all over the floor, rolling under every piece of furniture. We'd wrapped their TV in newspaper and switched out the sugar with salt. "Upstairs is set up. Did you guys finish down here?" He inspected the work with a smug, satisfied smile.

"Yep, we're just stringing up that web," I said while wrapping the remaining white string around the column in the living room. It would be impossible for them to walk in without walking straight through it.

Aiden rubbed his hands together with a smile. "Good work. This should defeat them and be the end of this."

Jackson laughed. "What would be the end of it would be not retaliating when Lyss tries to get you back."

"Or Aiden sleeping with Lyss," I mumbled back, narrowing my eyes at Aiden.

Aiden tipped his baseball cap, glaring at me from under the bill. "Yeah, I guess finally fucking her would be the best prank of all." I winced. Not exactly what I meant. "But she'd enjoy it too much. I can't have her taking pleasure in any of this." I rolled my eyes. Sometimes, I just wish I could pull his head out of his ass. He glanced down at his watch. "Come on. They'll be home soon. We need to get out of here."

He stalked toward the entryway, careful to avoid the balls strategically placed there, snaked around one of the doors with the bucket on top, and smiled as he opened the front door.

When we were outside and walking on the grass to our house, I cleared my throat. "Aiden, can I ask you how you got the keys to their house?"

His smile broadened as he breezed up the porch steps. "She may have given them to me in a moment of passion."

"Passion or rage? Given or stolen?" Jackson clarified, not believing a word he said.

"Aren't those one and the same?" Aiden emphasized as his hand curled around the knob of our door. He peered inside before opening it. "Mhmm. Looks like Adam's got a new lady friend over." He grinned over his shoulder, wiggling his eyebrows suggestively.

"Reign?" Jackson echoed the same thought that was going through my head. Only his fists and jaw weren't clenching. That was just me.

Aiden shrugged. "Doesn't look like it." I didn't know what was worse. That Adam took Reign on a date the night after I slept with her, or he was now treating her like garbage while he hung out with another girl in our house. "Maybe she was a pump and dump." He cackled, watching me with beady eyes.

I held it together with a surprising amount of restraint because I didn't want to prove Aiden right. I followed behind Jackson and Aiden as we walked into the house. "Yeah, I'm looking forward to studying math." Her sing-song cadence hit my ears, and I shoved past the guys further into the room. *What the hell was she doing here?*

Adam's eyes darted to me from above her head. "Here he is." He smiled, pointing as the little brunette spun around.

I could feel the blood draining from my face. If I was going to faint, it couldn't be now because, yet again, I needed to sort this mess out before it escalated. Chloe was standing next to my best friend, bleary-eyed and pale, giving me a small, apologetic smile.

"And so, the plot thickens," Aiden muttered.

Adam was the only one who knew about her, and as much as I'd like to keep it that way, Chloe had just screwed all of that up.

"Guys, this is my *sister,* Chloe," I emphasized, my eyes never leaving her.

Her backpack was resting on the chair next to her, and I wondered how on earth she got here. She had only been in rehab for a week and had another six months to go. Shouldn't they have called me if she'd gone missing?

Fishing the phone out of my jeans, I did indeed have several missed calls and messages from the facility. It'd been on silent for my lectures, and I'd forgotten to turn it back on because I was too distracted by Aiden's prank. Stalking over to her, I clutched her arm and dragged her up the stairs. "If you will excuse us, we've got a few things to discuss."

When we got to my room, I shut and locked my door before turning back to her. "What the hell are you doing here, Chlo?" I was trying my best not to sound angry. I needed to be the responsible one. Be the helpful, bigger brother. If I sounded like I was trying to be Dad, this wouldn't work. She'd just scream back, and we'd get nowhere. My arms crossed as I waited for her to answer.

She sniffled slightly. "Dev, I missed you." Was she high? I saw her last week, and I was planning on seeing her in a couple of days. She was stalling; her fidgety hands and darting eyes told me as much. Had they even had time to start working on a withdrawal program for her? I suppose I should be thankful that she came here and didn't just decide to run away completely.

"Why aren't you in rehab, Chlo?" I whispered, hoping the guys weren't eavesdropping on the other side of the door. All I got in return was the shrug of her shoulder. I sighed, trying to think of how to get the answer I wanted from her. "You know, I've gone into debt to pay for it?" Guilt-tripping used to work wonders when we were kids.

Her eyes drew down, looking at the tips of her black boots as she shuffled them against the gray carpets. "I know, and I'm going back." The relief that washed over me was like a tidal wave. "I just." She paused, pursing her lips as she dragged her eyes up to look at me. "I guess. I kind of felt like we left everything on a bad note."

Tilting my head, I studied my sister for a moment. She hadn't looked this vulnerable since she was eleven. For the first time in a long time, I could see the hurt and pain brewing behind her eyes.

"We didn't leave on a bad note, Chuck."

She snorted at the mention of her old nickname.

"You could have called me if you wanted to talk about something. You didn't need to leave the facility."

Without warning, she strode past me, collapsing on the bed, and covered her face with her hands. Small, desolate sobs came out. "I'm sorry, Dev."

It was all I could make out through the muffled cries.

I sat down on the bed next to her, rubbing her back as she sobbed. "I don't need an apology, Chlo. I just need you to get better." She nodded her head and looked up. All I saw was pain behind her bleary eyes, and I hoped that would change soon. She wrapped her arms around my shoulders, and I held her as she cried. It was more emotion than I'd ever seen from her, but that was a good thing. She needed to let it all out.

"Being alone in that room, all these thoughts and feelings came over me," she managed to say after another few minutes of quiet crying. I ran my hands through her hair, silently listening to her. "There was no one there to take those thoughts and feelings away. I had nothing to numb myself. All that was in the room with me was the black hole that Grace left when she died." It took her a long time to get all the words out, but I listened, and my heart broke for her. "And then I ruined our family. I'm the reason Dad left. I'm the reason you're leaving college early and losing out on your degree. I've not only fucked up my life. I've fucked up everyone else's around me."

For a moment, I couldn't let her go. I just held her tighter, hoping my love for her radiated through my arms. When she didn't stop crying, I clasped her shoulders, pushing her away so she'd have to look at me. "Don't you dare feel guilty about Dad leaving us. He wasn't a real man. He left us right when we needed him the most, and that's on him. Not you. Could you have dealt with your grief better? Yeah, probably. But that doesn't mean you're the villain of this story. You're just trying to make it in the world as best you can. Like we all are."

She smiled solemnly, hardly registering what I was saying. Instead, she chose to focus on her chipped black nails, a subtle reminder of who she tried to be.

Aiden's booming voice interrupted our moment as he cheered downstairs. He was probably congratulating himself on winning a game on the Xbox or something stupid like that. "Things have been tough for us. We know that. But all Ma and I want to do now is help you through this. It's going to be tough, and you're going to have to face things you don't want to. But you will get better. That's all Ma and I want for you. It's what Grace would have wanted for you, too."

She remained quiet, preferring to give me a slightly upturned lip and a reassuring head nod. She leaned her head on my shoulder, and I rested my arm across her back, placing a gentle kiss on her forehead. "I'm sorry for all this, D. I just needed you."

A throaty chuckle escaped me. "Yeah, well, next time you need me, just call. I'll always pick it up for you. You don't need to break out and travel for two hours to get here. How did you even get out of the place?" I asked with a curious lilt in my voice, trying to break the tension.

She curled into herself as she groaned softly. "I may have stolen a nurse's uniform and walked right out of the building." That was all I needed to hear, because I knew there was a nefarious story about how she got it. One I didn't want to know in case it actually was a felony.

"Right. Well, don't do it again. I need to call the facility and let them know I've found you. You're still a minor, and we can only hope there hasn't been another Amber Alert for you." I left her sitting on the bed while I called the facility and arranged to drop her off in the morning. At least it wasn't too far to drive, and I was thankful that she was here because I was the only person she could run to.

"I'm sorry, Dev," she mumbled as she toyed with the cuffs of the black sweatshirt I let her borrow after explaining the plans. "I won't leave again. I promise. I want to make this work too." Her voice was laced with conviction. For the first time in a long time, I believed her.

"Good. Now let's get some food. I'm starving." I grinned, hoping to see her relax a little. She squealed, jumping up and hooking her arm around me.

As we left the room, she said meekly, "I love you, D."

"Love you too, Chuck."

EIGHTEEN
Reign

I wiped the whipped cream off my face, confused and surprised at just how stupid I must have been to miss that when I opened the door. I already knew something was up. What with the plastic balls rolling out onto the patio and the cobweb I had to crawl under, but somehow, I missed the red bucket gently placed on top of the pantry before it doused me.

Still standing in the pantry, the gooey white substance clung to me as I padded over to the kitchen sink, washing my hands. The white froth came off, only to be replaced with some weird blue dye. By the time I'd found a paper towel and wiped as much of the dye off that I could, it looked like I'd spent the afternoon torturing, then killing a Smurf. The only thought running through my mind was how angry Lyss was going to be when she saw this.

I didn't have to wait long to see her reaction as the front door creaked open and she yelled like a wailing hyena. The loud thud made me hurry to the door, only to find her sprawled out on the floor, scowling and cursing Aiden's name. Laura stood behind her with pursed lips, stifling a laugh. "Are you okay?" I asked tentatively. Her eyes whipped to mine; she held her hand out, asking for help up because she'd slipped on a few of the errant balls.

"I'm going to kill him," she muttered to herself as she stomped into the kitchen, making the room shake with each step. Unfortunately for her, she was so lost in her plans for revenge, she walked straight into the cobweb, getting tangled in its mossy texture. Now it was me holding back the laughter. Her long arms flailed in the air as she pushed through it, grunting her way up the stairs.

Her shrill scream forced Laura and me into action. Lyss was at the top of the stairs, throwing a plastic-covered figure down them. "I hate him," she grumbled, looking more deranged than I'd ever seen her. I caught the bag, which felt like it had old clothes stuffed into it to give it the shape of a man. I must admit, the dedication Aiden and the guys had put into this one really impressed me. Something I'd never say aloud because I'd rather live to see tomorrow.

Laura and I cleaned up the downstairs rooms, careful to avoid any more traps as we did it. I was certain we'd find a rogue plastic ball rolling around the house in a couple of weeks, but for now, it was safe and habitable. Lyss hadn't left her room since she stormed off earlier. "I guess I should go check on her." Laura sighed, resigned to the fact that she had to talk Lyss off the edge. "I hear toothpaste is good at removing food coloring." She gestured to my hands. I'd nearly forgotten about the streaky blue stains that had dripped down to my elbows.

"Yeah, I'll give it a go." I smiled, but already resigned to the fact that I would probably have to wear evening gloves to school tomorrow. Making my way up to my room, I stealthily checked the door before opening it, not wanting another bucket of whipped cream tumbling down on me because last time, it really hurt my head. Luckily, it was all clear. I hurried into the bathroom, showering for over thirty minutes, scrubbing my skin raw, trying to get rid of the bluish tinge to my arms. I came out looking worse than I did going in. The blue dye had somehow streaked down my body, and it looked like a terrible fake tan job in blue. *Great.*

I dried off and wrapped a terry cloth robe tight around my waist as I sauntered back into my bedroom. As I brushed my hair in the mirror, movement in Devin's room caught my eye. My ears pinkened at the mere thought of facing him after he rejected me. Sure, I expected it to be awkward, but I didn't expect him to look so disgusted by my presence like he did when I was in his backyard with Adam the other day.

I hadn't been able to look at him since, keeping my window closed and hiding out downstairs until the last moment before bed. Today, though, my eyes couldn't help but look and linger at the sight in front of me. It was as if someone pulled my heartstrings, tied them in a knot, and then yanked them until they tore, falling to the ground like little tendrils.

Devin had a girl in his room.

I crouched closer to my mirror, hoping that it would obscure their view of me as I watched them.

My heart was beating like a drum. She was absolutely gorgeous. Like supermodel-level gorgeous. The kind of girl you'd never actually see in person, but only in pictures that you assumed were photoshopped. Her long chocolate hair cascaded down her back where it met her even longer legs. Disappointment coursed through my veins when I noticed she was wearing his hoodie. One of the hoodies that Devin offered me before. All kinds of rational thought went out the window as I watched the scene play out in front of me.

She was sitting on his bed as though she'd done it a thousand times before. He joined her. Like *he'd* done that a thousand times before, and then he rubbed her back, comforting her as she moved to hug him. I couldn't hear them because both our windows were shut, but his facial expression said it all. He loved her. *Who was she? Was she the real reason he brushed me off? Was she actually his secret girlfriend, and he was using me as a side piece? One he got bored with very quickly.* My heart beat faster now, the tingling making my fingers shake. Could I self-combust? Because right now, it felt like a real possibility.

God. I was such an idiot when it came to guys. Why did I always believe all their lies? Of course, someone like Devin wouldn't want a relationship with me. He just wanted to use me as a fuck buddy. The words made me feel sick, like someone punched me in the gut from the inside. I banged my head against the wall and closed my eyes, trying to regulate my breathing. This wasn't how it was supposed to go. Moving here was supposed to be my shot at redemption. Now, I'd just dug a hole bigger than the Grand Canyon into that plan because my heart was breaking all over again. This was why it *should* have been a one-night thing. No strings attached. Why did I try to tie those damn strings back together? I'd only hurt myself with miscommunication.

Did he set up this whole thing on purpose? Did he want me to see this so I would leave him alone? There was no way I could sit in my room while Devin hung out with another girl in his. Kissing. Cuddling. Gutting me from the inside. A lump of vomit was already working its way up my throat. Sitting here, I was just torturing myself unnecessarily. I stood up, grabbed some clothes, and made my way to the bathroom. Once dressed, I didn't bother looking out my window again; instead, I opted to text the one person I knew who could get me out of here.

"So, are you going to explain why you look like the genie from Aladdin?" Adam's gaze swooped over my arms and across my neck as he stifled a laugh. I grumbled, crossing my arms in the seat next to him. I wasn't in the jovial mood to talk about Aiden and his antics.

"I thought you were involved with this."

"Oh no, I can't claim any of that. I believe it was the handy work of Aiden, Devin, and Jackson." Hearing his name sent a shiver down my spine. "I had class. I didn't manage to get a briefing on what they actually did because something came up."

"What came up?" I asked, curious.

He waved his hand dismissively. "Some stuff with Devin." That sinking feeling returned to the pit of my stomach. It has to do with the girl in his room. I was sure of it. I waited for Adam to elaborate, but he didn't. The loyalty to his friend was stronger than to me, obviously.

Tired of the silence, I leaned forward, pressing the buttons on his radio. "Don't tell me you're going to program in Taylor Swift." He chortled as his eyes focused on the road. When I texted him, asking him to take me to the grocery store, he said yes immediately.

"Please. I'm sure I can find something else." I pressed his pre-programmed stations, surprised when one piqued my interest. Old-school Blink 182 blared out from the speakers as Adam bared his brilliant white smile, mouthing along to the words.

"I'm a little old-school with my music tastes. You know, the stuff from the early two thousands?" he explained when he noticed my knitted brows.

"Oh, I know." I laughed. "This is some of my favorite music too. My mom used to play it to me when I was a baby," I said before really realizing how much I admitted to him.

As he turned the corner, he said, "Although this is an odd choice of music to play your baby daughter. I can safely say that she's a badass for doing it." My stomach pitted out. My mom *was* a badass. "Explains why you're such a badass."

I cackled at his words. "Please, I am so far from a badass."

He shrugged, pulling into a parking space. "You're badass enough to ask me to take you to the grocery store on short notice with blue arms," he joked. "What's your favorite album? *Take Off Your Pants and Jacket* or *Enema of the State?*"

"They both have their merits." I sunk my teeth into my bottom lip. "But I prefer their self-titled album."

"Controversial," he quipped as he opened the door, sliding his way down to my side of the car, opening the door for me.

"'I'm Lost Without You,' is one of my favorites," I explained, but didn't go into detail about how much it reminded me of my parents.

"It's a good song; I won't deny it. Obviously, I'm biased, though. 'Adam's Song' is mine." His lip upturned, and we walked into the supermarket together. "Now, what is it you need?"

My heart rate quickened, trying to think up something on the spot. "I need some macaroni and cheese," I blurted out; he paused, waiting for more. "And, uh, ice cream."

"The essentials, then?" We walked swiftly through the doors, heading to the frozen aisle. "Did Lyss or Laura say something to you? Because this is the second time in almost as many days that you've wanted to get out of the house."

I shook my head, trying to think of a way to answer without giving away too much. "No, they're fine. I mean, Lyss is crazy, but you already know that." He nodded. "It's just being stuck in that room sometimes makes me a little claustrophobic. My mind goes places it shouldn't, and going somewhere new just gets me out of my head."

"Who's got you so wound up?" I stuttered for a second; he watched me with narrowed eyes. "Don't lie to me. I can tell it's a *who* and not a what just by looking at you."

"An ex," I said, because it was kind of true. "I just thought something might happen between us, but it didn't. I'm moving on, though."

His eyebrows arched, and I swear I saw some confusion there. He opened the freezer door, allowing me to pick my ice cream. I perused the options, settling on rum raisin. "I get it. I have an ex like that at home too," he said, shutting the door behind me as we strolled down the aisles. That easy feeling I always got with Adam breezed over me—the same feeling I used to get when I hung out with my cousin Ally. Before she slept with my boyfriend, of course. I hadn't spoken to her since.

"I chased her throughout high school, and we dated in my senior year. Then she dumped my ass right before graduation." His sneakers skidded across the polished tile floors. "Tried to contact her for a while, but gave up at the beginning of this year. Made a promise to myself to finally move on."

My mind flashed back to the day I filled his drawers with glitter. I wondered if the girl in the picture was the one he was referring to. I couldn't ask, though, because that would be admitting I was, in fact, the one traipsing around his underwear, not Lyss.

"Moving on is important. Don't you think?" He tilted his head as he asked.

"Yes." My throat felt dry as I tried to swallow the lump stuck there. He ignored the hesitancy in my voice as he draped his arm around me, walking me to the checkout, making jokes the whole way. He really had a knack for cheering me up. We spent the journey back analyzing Blink 182 songs, and when I got home, my cheeks hurt from smiling so much. I really did feel better.

I walked past Lyss and Laura, who were already planning their next prank and went straight up to my room. When I shut the door, I leaned against it, smiling with my eyes closed. For just a few hours, I was carefree and away from my thoughts. My eyes swept over to the window. It was second nature at this point. The sting in my heart came tumbling back when I saw the gorgeous girl leaning out of the window, smoking a cigarette. She looked comfortable and happy in a pair of Devin's shorts and his T-shirt.

Striding over to the window, I ignored her glances and shut the curtain, vowing to never open them again. I was officially done with Devin and how he made me feel.

NINETEEN
Devin

Ever get that feeling that someone was ignoring you? The feeling that the last time you saw them, you did something unforgivable, like a fart in an elevator? Yeah, well, that was me. Every time I thought about Reign, I got this constant nagging feeling gnawing in my stomach. In fact, if I didn't know better, I'd think she'd moved out. In the morning, the first thing I did was check if she'd opened that damn curtain, blocking my view of her. She'd kept the window closed too, so it wasn't like I could hear when she was in there either. When I'd get home from training or classes, I couldn't help but look over at her house, wondering if I should just go over there, burst the door down, and kiss the shit out of her.

Am I a stalker? Maybe?

Am I a creeper? Definitely.

I couldn't help it. This girl had me tied around her little finger, and she didn't even know it. The more days that went by, the more I wondered if rejecting her when she was drunk was the right thing to do. Maybe I should have laid all my feelings out there for her. Maybe I should have told her that even though I was probably leaving in a couple of months, I wanted to spend every free moment I had with her. That even when I was off, hopefully playing for some NFL team, I wanted her to visit me.

But I didn't say any of those things because what if the only reason she said those things was because she was drunk and horny? What if she was just doing her best to get me to sleep with her again because she was finally taking me up on my joke offer? Of being my fuck buddy. The way she'd been acting over the last week and how much she'd been hanging out with Adam would have me believe that narrative.

I scrubbed my hand across my face, tired of thinking about this. She was just a girl. A girl who only wanted me for my dick. I didn't have time to worry about her. Spinning my phone in my hand, I considered calling Chloe again. I'd been calling her at least once a day, trying to make sure she wasn't going to seduce any more employees to get access to the supply closet. On the drive to drop her off, she gave me intricate details about how she escaped the first time and she could give James Bond a run for his money. I couldn't help but point out that if she had put as much effort into getting better as she did to escaping, maybe none of us would be in this position right now.

Did she like hearing that? Nope. It sobered the mood as badly as COVID on Christmas, but I needed to give her a reality check. This was serious stuff that would affect the rest of her life if she wasn't careful.

When I dropped her off, she cried into my shoulder for the better part of an hour. Every time I called her, I'd get the same silent sobbing. Her psychiatrists told me it was all normal, just her way of working through the grief. So, I let her. Today, she actually talked, giving me more hope than I'd had in a while. Things would be okay with her. I just knew it.

I tossed my phone to the side. Chloe would call me if she needed me. I, on the other hand, needed to get this essay done. It was probably the last one I'd write as a college student, which was a weird feeling. If everything went well, I'd be drafted before my next assignment.

I was the only one in the house who was entering the draft this year. Aiden, Matty, and Jackson weren't eligible, and Adam decided to stay for his final year. If I didn't have the financial worries, I'd probably do the same, just to make sure I had a college education to fall back on, but I needed to do what was right for my family right now.

I scratched my head as I read the same line in my textbook over and over again. Every time I tried to think about writing, my mind wandered back to Reign and those perfectly pouty lips of hers. That infectious laugh and the way I felt like a calm river whenever she was around. I'd tried texting her with a few jokes to see if that would break the ice, but I'd barely gotten a response out of her. I knew she was in her room at night because I could see the light pouring out from under the curtain. Was that her subtle way of telling me she wasn't interested in me anymore? Maybe, but I wasn't giving up without a fight or at least a discussion.

I padded down the stairs, abandoning my essay for the time being, hoping some donuts would help me think. Matty and Jackson were sitting at the kitchen table, going through some of their class notes together. I quietly waved as I raided the pantry, hoping to find the cakey goodness in there. After finding what I was looking for, I sat on the kitchen counter, munching my way through the chocolate.

The front door creaked open, and Adam strode in with his backpack slung over his shoulder and a stupid grin on his face. I wanted to smack that smile off his face, and the feeling only intensified when he greeted us brightly.

"You're in a good mood," Jackson pointed out. Matty had barely taken his eyes off his laptop to notice.

"Yeah," Adam replied wistfully, throwing his bag over the countertop. I'd never seen him so happy. Maybe that chick from back home had finally taken him back.

"Hanging out with Reign again?" Matty surmised, still focused on the screen in front of him. My jaw twitched as I continued to slowly chew the donut. I didn't want anyone to think I cared, but I also really wanted to hear his answer.

He didn't respond, though. Not with words, at least. Just some weird "mhmm" noise like that was supposed to be enough of an answer. Interesting, nonetheless. He'd been hanging out with Reign while she ignored me. Maybe *he* was the reason for the sudden snub.

Jackson made his way to the fridge and pulled out a soda. "You've been spending a lot of time with her recently," he said, and even though it sounded like a statement, I was eager to hear Adam's response.

"Yeah." There it was again. That stupid, wistful tone and response. What was Adam? A fifteen-year-old girl? He looked like that damn heart-eyed emoji right now as he leaned his elbow on the kitchen counter, blowing out a breath and looking between Jackson and me.

"What's going on with you two, anyway?" I asked with a cocked brow, hoping they couldn't hear the eagerness in my voice.

"Nothing really." My clenched hands unfurled. I didn't even know they were clasped until then. "We just hang out a lot now. She's a cool girl." He was trying to act calm, but I knew my best friend. I could see in his eyes just how much he liked her. It made me want to smack that pretty face of his into oblivion. A feeling I'd never had before. Nice to know that while I was dealing with my sister, he was keeping Reign busy.

"You okay, Dev?" Jackson asked as he slapped my shoulder, forcing me to walk forward.

"Yeah." Adam pointed directly at me. "How are things going with that girl from the app?" he asked with a wolfish grin. "Aiden mentioned you had her over the other night?"

I sighed because I really wished Aiden hadn't heard that. I mumbled out a non-committal response and told them I was going back upstairs to work just so that I could avoid any more questions about Reign and our relationship. Or lack thereof.

As I opened the door, my pulse quickened because her curtains were open for the first time in a week, and she was in the room. Her hand was threaded through her hair as she sat at her desk, typing on her computer. Looking at her made me feel like my insides were burning. This was surely a sign she wanted to talk to me.

Screw it.

I was tired of not talking to her. I missed her, and I needed to figure out if she was drunk babbling or if she wanted more with me before this thing with her and Adam went too far.

Striding over to the window, I opened mine quietly and then gently knocked on hers. Her shoulders visibly tensed, and her eyes dragged over to me, taking their time. She gave me a weak smile as she walked over. When she unlocked her window, the smell of her fruity shampoo escaped, reminding me of the time I was lucky enough to see her after her shower.

She was in a tight black tank and track pants, no makeup, and she still looked as beautiful as the first time I saw her. She leaned against the railing, making it impossible for me to jump over even if I wanted to. Which I did. Badly.

"How you doing, darlin'?" I asked, drawing it out, hoping that my accent would make her melt like it did the first time.

She stared down at her hands, refusing to show me those beautiful chocolate eyes of hers. "I'm okay. How about you?" Her body moved as though she were shuffling her feet, like she was nervous to talk to me. As though we haven't seen each other buck naked before.

I ran my hands through my hair, trying to dispel all the nervous energy coursing through my veins. "I'm good." I sighed. "It's been a long week." There was a beat of silence, as though every second that we didn't talk, another brick was added to a wall that was being built between us. I didn't like it. It made me edgy. "Do you have another episode of *The Bachelor?*" I asked. "I'm dying to know who Shawn ends up with," I joked, hoping it would lighten the mood.

Her head finally lifted to look at me. "I've watched this week's episode already," she said, biting her perfect bottom lip. She glanced over at her desk and then back. "I'm actually kind of busy with work tonight. I should probably get back to it." She pointed her thumb back at the desk, and I inadvertently nodded.

Just as she was about to turn away, I reached over and clutched her arm, ignoring the hair on my arms rising. "Reign," I said. My voice sounded strained and desperate, but at this point, I didn't care. "I think we should talk about what happened between us last week." I came out and said it.

Her eyes widened, and she choked out a laugh, waving me off. "What's there to talk about? I was just drunk, that's all." Something about her answer didn't feel genuine. Maybe it was the way her cheeks flared at the memory of that night.

"Are you sure? Because I thought you wanted to talk about you and me," I pushed.

Her body stiffened, and she snaked her arm out of my grasp. "There is no you and me," she quipped. "We were just fuck buddies." I winced at her cursing. It wasn't something I was used to hearing from her. "It's not like I actually thought anything was going on between us," she huffed out, her lips straight. "You can keep getting with girls, and I can get with guys too."

I backed away from the railing, surprised and confused. She was talking as though I'd been seeing other people. Like I'd had the time to think about anyone else but her. Or I wanted to. I wanted to tell her just that, but she shut the window and the curtain before I could get another word out. I stood there for a few minutes, hoping she'd realize her mistake and come back to the window, but she didn't. Spinning on my heel, I fell down onto my bed, trying to figure out what on earth Reign was talking about.

TWENTY
Reign

I was speechless. As I stood in our living room, I wondered when I lost my mind and my self-respect to agree to do this. How did I get hauled into this mess? A little over a month ago, I had no idea who any of these people were. I was happily going to class, avoiding my apartment as much as possible. It wasn't great, but at least Gary and Rachel didn't pull me into their shenanigans. Now, I was front and center of some weird drama, or foreplay, between two people I barely knew.

"Lyss, you're kidding, right? This is all just a joke. Have you moved on to pranking me now?" I asked, my voice flat and resigned. My hands rubbed across the velvet fabric clinging to my stomach, trying to soothe the uneasy feeling ricocheting through it. The outfit was so tight, and I could hardly breathe.

"Why would I joke?" Oh, that's right, I forgot she had tunnel vision. All she was focused on was taking down Aiden. Or going down on him. I still hadn't decided which urge was controlling her actions more. I was just another casualty in their fight. "Come on. It's not *that* bad." Her hand clasped the top of my shoulder as she squeezed reassuringly. *Not that bad?* I hadn't looked down in the last twenty minutes in fear that my boobs might suffocate me. They were hoisted so high it felt like I didn't have a neck.

"Says the woman not wearing it," muttered Laura beside us.

I raised my hand, nodding in her direction. "Thank you. Why don't you put it on?" I aimed at Lyss, shrugging out of her hold, trying to adjust the bottoms which were riding high up my ass.

She cocked an eyebrow, her lip curling on one side. "There are two very good reasons I can't." She raised her hand, pointing one perfectly manicured nail up to the sky. "Number one." The same finger was then directed down to me. "That costume barely fits you. Ergo, there is no way I'm going to fit in it." She was about a foot taller, to be fair. "Number two." That talon spikes back up, this time with another one joining it. "The cake is too small for any of us *but* you. You're like the size of a stamp. No one else will be able to jump out of it."

My gaze swept over to the giant fake cake Lyss had made. She didn't order it. She *made* it. Out of what, I didn't know. But she had essentially hired me out as a stripper for the night without asking first. "Why do I have to do this in the first place? Isn't there another way?" I pleaded, wobbling on my six-inch patent leather heels and scratching at the fishnet tights covering my legs. Normally I could get away with heels, but Lyss had picked ones with a particularly vicious spike at the end, making it hard to balance.

She shook her head. "Unfortunately, I've exhausted all my options. This is the only one with an element of surprise. There is no way they'd ever expect this from us." Of course, because who would be caught dead in this outfit when it wasn't Halloween? Reality started to settle in; my breath heaved because there was little room for my lungs under this corset, and I was getting hot. Is this what a panic attack felt like?

Laura was right by my side. "Relax, Reign. No one will know it's you. I promise." I think her words were supposed to soothe me. They didn't.

"How are they *not* going to recognize me?" I snorted out, still trying to hide my freak out.

Lyss smugly smiled as she walked over to a bag and pulled out a piece of fabric. "Because you'll be wearing this." She shoved a black latex mask in my face. I held it up, inspecting it with interest and wondering where in the hell she bought it, but that was one search engine history session I didn't want to go down.

"This only covers half my face, though. The guys have seen me enough that they could tell it's me."

"Not after I put this blonde wig on you." She held it up proudly. "And some bright red lipstick." Lyss really had thought of everything. Any kind of hope I had to get out of this was dashed as she stained my lips with a color as red as Satan's tail. I couldn't think of any other excuse not to do this.

"Is there a reason you didn't just hire an actual stripper?" It was my final out. The only thing that might make her see sense. I couldn't dance. I most certainly couldn't be seductive. Yet she expected me to go out there and shake my tail feathers like I was in a Jamie Foxx music video.

She squinted. "I didn't have time to hire one, and I can't risk the stripper targeting the wrong guys. You know exactly who you need to keep the attention of." Words escaped me for the second time that night. "It's not that big of a deal. All you need to do is pop out of the cake and dance close enough to them so you can grab their phones out of their pockets. Laura will do the rest. Simple." She shrugged, making it sound so easy. So effortless. I guessed she had thought of everything, and I supposed most jersey chasers wear less on a Thursday, so maybe this wasn't so bad. Maybe I was just being a prude.

"Adam's seen you in less, anyway." Laura waved off the hesitation I was about to voice. My head shot in her direction. "Oh, don't act so surprised. We know you've been bumping uglies since you moved in." She smiled, elbowing me when I gave her a furrowed brow. "Don't be embarrassed. It's obvious."

My mouth hung open. Confused. I thought about all the times she could be talking about. "No, we haven't."

She eyed me suspiciously. "Who did you have lunch with today?" I didn't answer. She already knew. "And who did you walk home with?" Silence.

"Is there a reason you're stalking me?" I asked rhetorically. "As you both know, it's his birthday today. I'd always planned to take him to lunch, and we live next door to each other. It would have been weird not to walk home with him." My rationale made perfect sense in my head, at least.

A slow smile grew on her face. "Sure. Whatever makes you feel better." She was quiet for a minute, and when I thought I was out of her line of questioning, she asked, "Didn't he ask you out on a date the first day you moved in?"

"Yeah," I replied, but we'd moved past that now. "That was because he didn't know me then. He knows me now. We're just friends," I explained, and it was true. Adam made things easy. He made me feel safe, like I'd known him my whole life. It was like I could tell him anything. But not in the way that I *needed* to tell him everything. It wasn't the way I felt when I was with Devin. He could sizzle my soul with just one hooded look. And there goes my stomach again. I'd been doing that every time I'd seen or thought about him recently. Mainly because I hated how things ended with us. *Ended.* It was such a final word. We didn't even start. He'd already moved on to his next fuck buddy. I just wished I'd said something when I had the chance.

How could it already be over between us?

My stomach had been rolling so much that I ended up shutting my curtains, refusing to see him for a week, in hopes it would act like an antacid and I could move on. In reality, I thought I might die if I accidentally saw him with that girl again. Thinking about his hands all over her, his lips kissing her skin, his body on top of hers. No, thank you. He should be kissing and touching me like that. Only he didn't want to. Not anymore, at least. He got his fill.

Yesterday, I stupidly thought I was over everything. We just had two nights together. That was it. I was a big girl. I moved on from Clay, and I was with him for years. I could move on from this too. When his knuckles rasped on my windows and I saw his ruffled dark hair and cheeky grin, I could have kicked myself for thinking that. I reluctantly walked over to what felt like the death march. I'd never known I was walking into a "break up" conversation before going into it. I chickened out and avoided it. I didn't need him giving me all the reasons he didn't want me. I'd been thinking about our situation a lot since it happened, and the whole thing became glaringly obvious.

I wasn't the girl you settled down with. I was the practice one. I was the girl guys had fun with. The one they hung out with until they found the one. I didn't think that was me until Devin and Clay proved it.

Sadness was heavy in his glare, and I knew—I just knew—he was trying to let me down gently. The idea of him sitting in my room while he told me he didn't want to be serious with me because he was, in fact, with someone else made me want to vomit. So, I did what any sane person would do; I told him we were nothing, and I was too busy shutting the curtain in his face to hear his reply.

Even hearing his name in passing today at lunch had my bones tingling. I wish I didn't crave him like a starved dog, but Devin just felt like the right guy. And now I was going to his best friend's birthday party and pranking them.

I wanted to fall into a puddle on the floor, but I was a big girl. I'd been through worse, and I needed to move on.

This whole thing might be good for me. Devin was probably going to bring his new plaything to the party tonight, and seeing them together might make me feel better. Like ripping a Band-Aid off. I inwardly rolled my eyes. What an idiot I was to fall for him. He just made it so damn easy.

"I'm sure he wouldn't say no to more." Laura elbowed me with a grin on her face, forcing me back into the room with them. Adam. Right. We were talking about him. *Not Devin.*

"Adam's great." He is. He was gorgeous and funny and smart and everything a girl could want. "It's just—"

Lyss raised her hand. "We don't have time for this, guys," she interrupted me, draping the wig over my head and stuffing my hair underneath it. "Reign needs to get this cake in the next two minutes before the two frat guys I've paid to wheel her in get here." She snatched the mask from my hands and wrapped it around my face. Then she stepped back, adjusting my blonde wig as it tickled against my thighs. I had no idea how I was going to dance in this with such long hair, but I'd figure it out.

With lightning speed and little less than a warning, Laura and Lyss lifted me over the top and into the cake. Now that I was closer, I could smell the cardboard, and as they shut the lid on me, I was thankful I wasn't claustrophobic. It was dark and tiny, and I was counting down the minutes until I could get out of it. I clutched my legs tight, nervous that I might break the cardboard too early if I moved.

Here goes nothing, I guess.

I tried to adjust my pants. The wedgie was getting bigger with every bump on the road the frat boys rolled over. I could hear them complaining about the weight of the cake until they found something to roll it on. Holding my body tight and spitting out strands of the synthetic wig, I thought about how I ended up here. That this was, in fact, where my life had taken me. Who knew that every event in my whole life was going to lead me to this moment? Wearing a black crushed velvet costume that was at least a size too small and a mask with an ear stuck on the tape holding the cake together. No boyfriend, hardly any purpose, and a wedgie. Yup. I was really winning at life today.

How am I going to do this?

I'd have to capture the attention of five guys, all the while making sure no one saw me steal their phones. It would be a miracle if this worked. "Hey guys." I heard a muffled voice. "What's this?" The person choked out a laugh. That was exactly what I was. A joke. One of the frat boys holding the cake gave him some generic answer, and that was when I felt the cake being lifted. I could only hope I was being carried into the party.

The crowded room filled the silence as the bass bounced through the cardboard. The party was already in full swing. Adam invited me to his party at lunch, and I wondered if he'd noticed when I didn't arrive when Laura and Lyss did. There was raucous cheering when I felt the cake dropping on the table. If only they knew a terrible Dita Von Teese impersonation awaited them. I still hadn't figured out how I would pop out of this cake in any way that could be interpreted as sexy.

The song "Birthday Sex" blared, and that was my cue. I had two options: I could just not jump out of the cake and hope no one opened it up trying to find me. That idea was out the window, though, because I knew Lyss would open the cake and force me out herself. The other option was to push through the cardboard and do my best to seduce our neighbors with the best interpretive dance I could. It was interpretive because I was not a natural dancer in flats. Add the heels, and there was a potential hospital visit in my future. We were halfway through the party. Maybe everyone would be too drunk to notice the stripper's inability to dance anyway.

"Here goes nothing," I whispered to myself, as if I'd ever be ready for this. I took a deep breath in and pulled myself up, pushing through the top of the cardboard cake, hands first.

TWENTY-ONE

Devin

I pretended to chug a beer, swallowing my own spit in annoyance. This party stunk. My lips were curved in a fake smile since it was Adam's birthday after all, and I wasn't a dick. I wanted the guy to have a good time. The house was full of jersey chasers, all looking for their next boyfriend or meal ticket. Purple and white uniforms crowded the space, and I was surprised at how hyped everyone was. The girls were giggling, sending coy waves our way if we caught their eyes.

Short skirts and butts shaking should have been enticing, but as per usual, it wasn't. I somehow ended up pussy-whipped by my next-door neighbor, and yet she had no interest in me. I shouldn't berate myself too harshly, considering she seemed to have the same power over Adam.

I strolled over to Jackson because I figured there was safety in numbers and the girls would be less likely to hit on me if I wasn't on my own. He tapped my beer with his as I made myself comfortable next to him and leaned against the kitchen countertop. The great room was full, and I surveyed it, looking for the one girl that mattered the most, but I couldn't find her.

Strange. I had no doubts that she'd be coming tonight. It was Adam's birthday, after all, but she was late, and that didn't seem like her style.

"Not a bad party." Jackson tilted his head up at a few of the smiling girls. He was known as the ladies' man of the house, always smiling and never saying no to a hot lay. "Waiting for someone?" He raised his brow.

I grunted in response because it seemed everyone in the house knew about my obsession with our neighbor, except for Adam, of course.

Jackson took a slow drag of his drink. "They haven't kissed if that's what you're worried about." He winked at a girl, not looking back at me.

I chewed on my tongue, biting back the questions I wanted to ask. *What has Adam told you? How far have they gone? What happened on their date?* I'd save it because if it were my business, Reign or Adam would have told me. On the bright side, since they hadn't mentioned anything *and* they hadn't kissed, I guessed that meant it was all still to play for.

Maybe when she walked in, I would take matters into my own hands and force her to talk to me. Or I'd just grab her wrist, drag her upstairs to my room, and show her just how much I'd missed her these past few weeks. But she wasn't here, so it wasn't like I could do it.

An idea popped into my head, and a smirk grew on my lips. If she wasn't here, then she was at her house. Alone. I scanned the room one last time, just in case I missed her. Laura was near Matty, who was talking to some hot blonde. Thank God Olana and Fred, the ferret, weren't here, otherwise, she'd be making a scene. No surprise, Lyss was chewing on ice, scowling at Aiden, who was flirting with a set of twins. So, if Lyss and Laura were both here, then Reign was definitely alone. I didn't have long. I was taking my chance.

"I'm going to head out for a few minutes."

"You can't bail, dude. It's Adam's birthday." Jackson looked over at the birthday boy himself.

Adam was relaxed on the couch with several hot girls vying for his attention. He didn't seem interested, though. Probably because he thought he had a chance with Reign. But why couldn't he just be interested in one of them? He had enough admirers to leave Reign alone. She was mine for all intents and purposes.

"Looks like Adam is doing just fine without me," I ground out.

Cheers and hollers interrupted our conversation as a giant cake came into view and was placed directly in front of Adam.

"Who ordered the stripper?" Jackson elbowed me in question.

I shrugged. "I didn't. Probably Aiden. He's such a horn dog."

The music got louder as the cheering took over, and we all waited in anticipation to see what was going to happen next. Maybe I could sneak out once the stripper was in full flow. Everyone would be distracted then.

The sound of ripping cardboard overtook the room, and the first thing to pop out were two delicate hands dancing. Nothing else happened for a good thirty seconds. Just hands daintily moving to the beat of the music. Finally, the hands grasped at the sides of the cake and up popped a pair of black bunny ears. Slowly, so slowly, the bunny rose to reveal a sexy blonde.

Every part of her face was covered except for her bright red, heart-shaped lips. They looked familiar, but I couldn't quite put my finger on why.

As she emerged from the cake, she fumbled around, finding it hard to get her grip because the cardboard cake started ripping around her. It was about as sexy as a baby traveling through the birth canal. Awkward and messy. She must be new to this.

"Help her out, Adam," Aiden jeered from the side. "She's your gift, after all."

The girl struggled to stand as Adam reluctantly made his way to the cake, looking around the party. Probably hoping Reign couldn't see him. He stepped onto the table where the cake was resting and reached over, picking the girl up like it was nothing and helping her out of the cake with at least some of her dignity still intact.

It was the first time I could get a real look at her. She was a tiny little thing in an incredibly hot, vintage Playboy bunny costume. I didn't think they even sold those anymore. I couldn't keep my eyes off her curves. Her lips. Something was drawing me to her, but I couldn't quite put my finger on what it was.

Adam looked uneasy as he stood next to her. The tips of his ears pinkened when the bunny wrapped her arms around his neck, expecting him to move her off the table. This wasn't our type of thing, especially as there were a lot of uncomfortable-looking girls here. I wondered why Aiden arranged this, but then I noticed he wasn't paying attention because he was too busy arguing with Lyss across the room. Nothing new there. I wouldn't be surprised if he arranged this just to specifically tick her off.

There wasn't much dancing from the bunny because she was clasping on to Adam for dear life as she slowly rocked her hips against him, moving her hands down his chest. Her nails scratched as they trailed down. I played with the neck of my beer, watching the interaction with amusement. He looked shell-shocked, and she looked awkward. After a few minutes of uncomfortable dancing, the bunny turned around, whipping her long blonde hair to one side.

The bunny scanned the room for someone until she whipped her head back to Adam, who'd backed away. She didn't let him get far and tiptoed toward him. The crowd roared when she planted both of her hands on his chest, forcing him down on the sofa behind him. He nearly dropped his beer in surprise, and it splashed across the leather. He obliged her, more out of fear than anything else.

Flitting around, she ground her ass into his crotch, and, ever the gentleman, he looked in the other direction. It wasn't just Adam who found this display uncomfortable. Everyone in the room felt it. I was certainly ready to upchuck my lunch at the visual. A sick part of me hoped Reign would walk in right now and dump his ass before they could become a potential couple. Yes, I was a dick. Tell me something I didn't know.

Something about the girl's face irked a memory in the back of my mind. That mouth looked familiar as she awkwardly smiled away, forcing Adam to hold her hips while she curved her body into his. In an instant, she turned around and leaned her hands on the tops of his thighs, dangerously close to his crotch. The crowd jeered as she gave the audience a full view of her ass. Adam squirmed underneath her and was going redder with every passing second.

I leaned into Jackson, who was chuckling at the performance. "Do you think the bunny looks familiar?" I asked, trying to get a better look at her face.

He dragged his eyes toward me and quirked a brow. "Nope. Have you been visiting the strip bar, Behind Closed Doors, without me?" he teased.

I shook my head, watching the bunny closely again. "No. I've seen her before, though. I just can't pinpoint where."

Jackson watched as Adam leaned farther away from the bunny. It was funny for a while. Now, it was just awkward. "Maybe she goes to Covey, and she's just trying to pay her tuition," Jackson suggested with a shrug.

The bunny leaned forward, her face inches away from Adam's as she poked her ass out further. Her panties, not quite a thong but not quite briefs, rode up high. I grimaced, thinking about how uncomfortable that must be. It didn't stop me from scanning the curve of her ass until my eyes stopped, and I swore my breathing did too. Right on that delectable ass was a very familiar birthmark. It was the same birthmark I spanked and bit that first night we slept together. I remember it well because it was the best night of my life.

Reign?

My mind couldn't keep up with all the thoughts running through it. What the hell was she doing here dressed like that? Why the hell was she giving Adam the most awkward lap dance of his life? She wobbled just standing up in those heels. Was this a surprise for Adam? Why the hell would she put on a show like that for him in front of everyone? It couldn't be her. She wasn't like that. There had to be another explanation.

My gaze searched the room, noticing Laura was close to Adam, watching Reign with interest. Lyss was still with Aiden, but they weren't talking now. Instead, they, too, were mesmerized by the terrible lap dance. This has got to be part of some elaborate prank.

Reign turned back around, and I couldn't believe it took me so long to figure out it was her. Those tits. Those lips. Those thighs. I was an idiot. My dick got hard watching her because I wanted her so badly. I was too busy looking at her body to notice she was eyeing me up, watching me as she bit her bottom lip. I knew those lips were familiar. I'd thought about them wrapped around my cock at least ten thousand times. I felt Aiden's presence as he walked across the room, about to leave. She immediately perked up, watching him, and hastily hurried away to follow Aiden. Adam looked relieved, shaking his head and scrubbing his face.

Jealousy coursed through my veins as I watched her saunter—as best as she could in those heels—toward Aiden. She tapped him on the shoulder, waiting for him to turn around before lifting her chest in his direction. My friend licked his lips, taking her in.

I saw red.

The idea of her grinding against him was too much. I needed to stop this, but it wasn't like I could call her out in front of everyone. No one knew it was her, and I'd bet my college tuition that she wanted to keep it that way.

Aiden skated his hands down to Reign's hips, pressing his fingers there as his head dropped to her shoulder.

"Where are you going?" Jackson asked. I hadn't even noticed I'd already started walking in their direction.

"It's my turn with the bunny," I mumbled, more to myself, but I heard him laugh from behind. Striding over to them, my eyes burned holes in Aiden's hand. His pinkie was going a lot further south, but he straightened up when he saw me coming.

"Hey, D," he scoffed. I ignored him completely and focused solely on Reign.

My mouth met her ear. "Can I get one of those dances, darlin'?" I whispered, hoping she would know I recognized her.

Her body shivered at my voice, and I could see her breath quickening. She was affected by me. There was something between us. She just needed to stop all this bullshit with Adam so we could get on and live our happily ever after.

Her hands dropped from Aiden, and she turned, looking at me. How can no one recognize her? Those deep chocolate eyes gave her away immediately. She nodded slowly, still focused on me.

"Devin, you dirty dog. Begging like that." Aiden laughed.

I hardly noticed. The heated look in Reign's eyes was enough to burn an entire rainforest down.

I held my hand out to her, and she gracefully accepted. All I could think about was how badly I wanted to kiss her again. It didn't help that she kept biting her bottom lip. My plan was to walk her out of the room, get her alone, and ask her what the hell she was doing. She didn't give me that option, though. She pulled me back and led me toward the couch, still in full view of everyone. Her eyes swept over my roommates. For some reason, she wanted us all in here.

She pushed me down onto the leather sofa; Adam still sat off to the side and watched every move of this display. She swung a leg over me and sat her plump ass down on my lap. A sight I loved seeing without the audience.

Her perfectly peachy ass sat right on top of my groin, and her boobs begged for attention. I could only hope my jeans were thick enough to cover how hard I was getting. Laying one hand on my shoulder, she ground into me, getting into the music and the crowd. This was the least awkward she'd been tonight, and I'd like to think it's because she was with me.

She leaned closer, grabbing both of my hands and placing them on her butt cheeks. It was done with expert precision, and it was only when she reached back behind me that I realized what she was doing. She was trying to get the phone out of my pocket. I could stop her now and expose their prank, but in doing that, I'd expose her as the bunny. There were too many cameras recording this for her to be comfortable with that.

Instead, I stayed calm, splaying my hands over her ass so no one else could see it. I wasn't going to deny how nice it felt cupping it, though. I gave it a squeeze for good measure. Yup, just as soft as I remembered. She squealed at me as she tried to suppress a smile. Her lips grazed my collarbone, and my hand instinctively went through her hair, only to pull on her wig. That made her back away, looking around the room. I pushed it back, pretending not to notice.

Once my phone was on the sofa, she popped off my lap, leaving me with a hard-on and a surly attitude. She walked over to Matty, who had a look of fear in his eyes. Not because he was afraid of her. No. It looked like his girlfriend Olana had arrived—sans Fred—and if she saw him interacting with Reign, she'd make him pay in unspoken ways. Reign didn't get the memo, though; she danced around him while he was stiff as a board, looking between Olana and that blonde he was talking to earlier. Anywhere *but* Reign's semi-gyrating body in front of him. I had a sneaky suspicion this was her trying to booty pop, but sadly, it looked more like she'd broken her ankle.

It seemed most people had gotten bored with the bunny's antics, but I couldn't stop watching Reign, wondering how far she was going to take this. When she was done with Matty, she spotted Jackson, sauntered over to him, and opened his legs up so she could place herself between them. A surprising move. Jackson looked shocked for all of two seconds, then embraced it, dipping his face into her neck. That was it. I was done. All I saw was red. I would kill him if that hand went any lower.

Striding over to them, I gave Jackson a pointed glare. "Hey, man. You, okay?" Jackson asked as Reign's hand ran through his dark hair.

I didn't respond, choosing to focus on the need to unclench my jaw, or I wouldn't have any teeth left. She turned in Jackson's arms, grinding her ass into his crotch, barely noticing me. What a crappy turn of events.

That was it. I'd had enough. A low growl emanated from my throat as I grabbed her, forcing her into my chest. She stumbled on her heels, and her little hands found balance on my pecs. When she gawked up at me with her big almond eyes and bit her lip, man, did my cock stir again. That bunny mask was so hot, and it wasn't like I had time to recover from her earlier dance with me. She balled up my shirt with her fists and moved her hips to the dirty R&B track playing from the speakers. She didn't even notice how crazy she was driving me.

Guys around me cheered, calling me a dog as I kept hold of her ass. At this point, I didn't want anyone else touching her. Anytime she tried to move away, I dragged her straight back to my chest, keeping her firmly attached to my front. If this were any other girl, I wouldn't care. But Reign was mine, whether she wanted to admit it or not. She yelped when my fingers grabbed her ass a little harder.

"You look hot as a bunny, darlin'," I whispered in her ear, and she let out a breathy gasp. I was fairly certain she knew I was in on it now. Digging my fingers into her ass cheeks, I smiled. She had to know I knew. I did that exact move both times we slept together.

She looked around and then back at me. "I've got to go," she said, in a random British accent.

Was she trying to throw me off? She squirmed her way out of my grasp, wobbling toward the cake, and when she got there, the same two frat guys helped her back into the broken cardboard. Just like that, she was gone, and all the guys at the party were booing. I looked over at the sofa, remembering that I needed to get my phone, but it was gone when I went back.

After the cake was rolled out, unsurprisingly, Laura and Lyss disappeared. So now I was phoneless and confused, with a hard-on.

About ten minutes after I watched Reign retreat into a cake—words I never thought I'd utter—she walked back into the house as though she wasn't just dressed up as my wildest fantasy. One I only knew I had after seeing her. Her jeans hung low on her hips, and the fluffy sweater she wore hid any kind of bad girl bunny vibes she had been rocking before. She waved to people as she walked through the crowd. Nonchalant as fuck.

I walked to the kitchen, grabbing a Coke to waste some time, contemplating when it would be appropriate to go over and talk to her. When I turned around from the fridge, she leaned against the counter opposite me, throwing me a shy smile.

"Hey," she said in her usual voice. A voice I didn't know I missed so much. "You dropped this over there." Placing the phone on the counter, she pushed it toward me. Did she really think I was that drunk that I didn't know she took it?

"Thanks." I grabbed the phone, eyes focused on her the whole time, wondering what on earth she did to it. "Do you think we could talk, darlin'?" I asked her.

Her body bent back. "Maybe some other time. I've got to wish Adam a happy birthday."

Her eyes didn't meet mine, and I didn't bother mentioning that I knew she'd already spoken to Adam today. What was the point? She was giving me clear signals she wasn't interested in me anymore. It was Adam she wanted now. It didn't matter how much I asked her to talk; she didn't want to.

I sighed, opening my phone. The first thing I checked were my messages, ready to do damage control. Luckily, they didn't mess with that. The next thing I checked were my social media accounts. Nope, nothing there. My brows furrowed; maybe they couldn't get into my phone because it required facial recognition. I shoved it into my pocket, looking back up at Reign one last time. She was hugging Adam, giving him one of her perfect smiles. The ones I thought were reserved for me. I spun on my heel, going up the stairs to my room. I didn't plan on staying down here to watch him get with the one girl I wanted since arriving here at Covey.

TWENTY-TWO

I balled up the piece of paper in my hand as I opened the door to the house, trying desperately to keep my emotions in check. This would not break me. It was just a stupid prank. Lyss and Laura were just my roommates. They weren't friends. I just wished I had said that to myself before ever agreeing to be a part of their stupid games. I hardly knew them, yet my need to be liked by them overruled my need for self-preservation. Their laughter echoed down the hall, and I found myself stomping into the kitchen.

"No. No. This is the best part," Lyss snorted as she paused the video. They were huddled over her phone, and I knew exactly what they were watching. "Watch Adam's face when she bends forward."

Laura leaned in closer; the noise of the video took over the room as they laughed like hyenas. At me. Holding my lips together, I closed my eyes, trying to suppress my rage.

Too engrossed in the video, they didn't notice me entering the room or standing there for several minutes waiting for them to turn off the replay of my biggest humiliation. After another fit of giggles, I threw my fist down onto the table with the balled-up piece of paper.

"That's enough," I roared, clearly not keeping my anger in check. "Did you know there are wanted posters around campus?" I pushed forward the piece of paper so they could see the screwed-up picture with my bunny-clad face on it. It was a new game around campus; people were trying to find out who the bunny was. My mother would be mortified if she knew this was what my college experience amounted to.

Laura and Lyss looked up at me with gaping mouths. No doubt they were surprised by my outburst, but they weren't the ones who had to wear that stupid costume. They weren't the ones humiliated for nothing. That's right. FOR NOTHING. Turns out, when Lyss got the phones, she didn't consider that they'd have passcodes or face recognition to access them, which meant we had to give them back. No prank whatsoever. Therefore, everything I did was for nothing except for *my* embarrassment.

"Reign, I—" Laura started, her breath slightly caught.

I raised my hand. "Birthday Sex" continued to play in the background, taunting me with its undulating tones. I couldn't count the number of times the video of me dancing from every angle had been reposted online. "Save it. I don't want to hear your apologies." I turned to Lyss, fury burning in my eyes so bright, I could feel the heat. "This is me tapping out of your stupid pranks. Do your own dirty work next time. I'm done with this." *And I'm done with you.* It was what I wanted to say, but something held me back. Maybe it was her sad, wide eyes as she stared back at me, or it was the fact that I would rather not say anything than leave saying something I might regret later. I'd learned you never know when your last encounter might be with someone, and ending it on a bad note can gut you like a fish.

After a moment of silence, one I'd stunned them into, I turned on my heel and marched to the steps toward my room.

"I will stop the pranks. I'm sorry," she croaked quickly, as though her Band-Aid of an apology would be enough to fix this mess. "I never intended to hurt you."

But you did. And you didn't care. I stayed silent, just walking up the stairs, counting each step as I went. Something I was taught to help reduce my anxiety.

When I reached my room, I checked that the curtains were still closed, a reflex at this point in fear that Devin would be there, waiting to tell me he had a girlfriend or something. When the coast was clear, I fell onto my bed, letting the pillows suffocate me for just a moment. I was angry. Angry at myself for ever agreeing to Lyss's demands. Angry that I let Devin get under my skin. Angry that Clay and Ally forced me to start all over again. And angry at the trucker that took my parents away. The burning heat that built up in my chest was new. I'd learned to suppress my anger by shoving it deep down inside me and focusing on the future. On things I could control. Not on people. People inherently let you down, whether they meant to or not.

Maybe I was overreacting. The bunny mask kept my identity hidden the entire time, and so far, no one has guessed it was me. It was just seeing the wanted signs and hearing students I didn't even know laughing about my inability to dance was too much. I felt cold and angry inside, like I'd been duped into it. The only two people I could talk to about it were the same two people who put me in the costume in the first place. It'd been over a week, and I thought things would die down by now, but everyone was still talking about it.

It made me feel like Laura and Lyss didn't care about me or what happened. I thought I was helping them out. Being a good friend and roommate, but somehow, I ended up being the joke again. They just used me for their own gain and laughed about it afterward. It felt like it was the same old story for me since I moved to Louisiana. Clay and Ally used me. I guess Devin used me to get his rocks off, and now Laura and Lyss used me too.

I threw the pillow off my face, letting it fall to the floor. Sitting around this room and feeling sorry for myself was not something that helped my mood. All I was doing was replaying the entire situation over and over in my brain and making myself angrier. The worst thing for me to do was sit here and think about it. I needed to get out.

I stared at the ceiling, contemplating where I should go. An idea popped into my head. My heartbeat slowed. It was something I needed to do since the day I got off the airplane from Louisiana. I'd been avoiding it, but I knew I had to do it soon. The festering feeling decayed in my chest, eating its way through my heart with every day that passed, and I didn't do it.

Did I want to go there in this state? I wasn't sure, but there was nothing more important than visiting them. Maybe it would help give me some clarity. Maybe I'd feel more connected, and gosh, did I yearn to feel connected. I grabbed my phone, ordered an Uber, and stalked out of the house, ignoring Lyss and Laura's pleas as I did.

Standing at the end of the drive, five minutes felt like five hours. The Uber driver was running late, and I was running out of patience. My body stiffened when I heard him.

"Reign?" Devin wasn't trying to soothe me, but the minute his husky voice reached my ears, I melted. "Are you okay?" he asked, his hand clasped on my shoulder, urging me to turn around.

I didn't. I knew if I looked into his eyes, every part of my being would want to wrap myself around him and never let go. *He's just my friend.* Why would he want anything more with me when he could have his pick of women?

"Reign," he persisted, moving around me instead and chucking my chin up with his thumb, so I was looking at him.

"I'm fine," I said, my gaze still focused on the ground. His hazel eyes had a way of disarming me without trying, and I needed to be of sound mind for what I was about to do.

"You don't look fine," he whispered.

The screeching of tires echoed down the street. "That's my ride," I said with no emotion. All I was focused on was how I would get out of there and into the car without revealing anything to Devin. He stayed silent as he watched the car pull up and opened the door for me like the true gentleman he was. I mumbled out a thank you before dropping into the seat.

His bulky body pushed me into the car as he sat next to me. My mouth hung open as he shut the door and smiled, ignoring my shock. Before I could protest, he said to the driver, "We're ready to go." Tapping the headrest in front, he glanced over to me and winked. I nearly lost my breath. It was a normal occurrence around him these days, but he was unfazed by it. He leaned his back against the seat, getting comfortable, and then turned to look at me with a smug smile.

"What are you doing?" I asked, too dumbfounded to protest.

He picked at his nails. "You look like you could use some company, and I've got some time," he said, still pulling at a cuticle.

What on earth did he think he was doing? I didn't ask him to come. He couldn't know where I was going. No one could. It was too raw. Too real.

"I'm fine. Can you stop the car?" I directed the driver. Devin's hand enclosed mine; his warm heat traveled through my body and snapped my resolve like a pencil. I needed someone for this, and although I didn't want to admit it, I needed him. I was connected to him. We were connected to each other in unspoken ways.

"Darlin', either you let me ride in this car with you, or I'll follow behind. You choose. I'm not leaving you alone, though." His thumb rubbed at my palm reassuringly; his voice soothed the aches in my bones. *Did I want him to know where I was going?* I guess he would find out sooner or later.

I huffed as I leaned back against the seat, telling the driver to keep going. We sat in silence for the entire forty-five-minute journey, and he held my hand the whole time, squeezing it gently every time he heard my breath hitch. I didn't know what he was doing or how he popped out of thin air, but I was happy it was him who found me.

The wheels crunched at the gravel pit below, and I wished I had the nerve to look at Devin's face right now. He had no idea what he got himself into, that was for sure. His hand didn't waver from mine as the driver informed us we'd arrived, and the realization set in on what we were actually doing. What *I* was going to do. Devin's hand was still the pillar of strength, holding on to me tighter, making sure I didn't slip into my own sadness.

He opened the door for himself, never letting go of my hand as he pulled me out of his side of the car. Without a word, he wrapped me in his arms. I froze for a moment because the sheer act of this hug was more intimate than any other moment we'd shared together. I hadn't been hugged like this—like I mattered—since their deaths.

I wrapped my arms around his wide torso, hugging him back and feeling his strength oozing into me.

"Who are you here to see?" he asked softly, not moving from our hold. His breath tickled my neck, warming me up from the inside.

Could I do it? Could I say the words out loud for the first time since it happened? I thought I was over it. I thought I'd moved on, but everything came crashing down like a tsunami and hit me all at once when the car parked and we stood outside the gates. "My parents," I squeaked out. I didn't have to say it again. Devin already knew; he just wanted me to say it. "You didn't have to come." *But I'm glad you did.*

He tucked me under his arm, holding me against his hard body. "Yeah, I did," he said, walking me toward the wrought-iron gates and pausing when we were through the entrance. "I'll wait out here for you," he said decisively, letting go of me.

My body felt like a limp noodle without his iron rod backbone to hold me steady.

I stumbled like a newborn deer, trying to walk farther into the cemetery but making little headway. I looked over my shoulder, and he smiled at me encouragingly. "Would you come with me?" I asked, because the idea of walking on my own terrified me.

His hands were in his pockets, and he tilted back on his heels until he smiled confidently at me. "Sure. I can't wait to meet them," he said as he took a few steps to get to me, tucking me into his embrace again. This time, I wrapped my arm around his waist, letting him take most of my weight as I led him farther into the gardens.

As we walked toward the tombstones, the memory of the last time I was here ran through my mind. My aunt held my hand on one side while Ally was on the other. They were all I had left as I cried into my aunt's shoulder, wishing it was me that had gone instead of them. I was an orphan. I had no one to love me. No one to talk to. I was leaving everything behind, not because I wanted to, but because I had nowhere else to go. I was sixteen and had to start all over again as the girl whose parents died.

I was expecting a ball of vomit to roll in my stomach at the thought, something I was used to getting from time to time these days, but somehow, the wave of emotion was easier to handle with Devin comforting me. He may never be mine, but I'd take this moment with him and treasure it forever. We stopped right next to the cherry blossom tree that shaded my parents. It was blooming, with the flowers floating down to the ground in the wind. *Drew and Hayley Pennyworth* was etched on the stone, and it felt so permanent. It'd been four years since I'd been here. Four years too long, but I was too afraid to come, worried about how I'd cope. Devin squeezed my hip, reminding me he was here for me. Unbeknownst to him, he was the only thing holding me up right now.

I dropped to my knees in front of the gray stones; the wet mud squished into my jeans as I reread their names like it would change something. Like it would make me feel different. There was so much I wanted to say to them, but words escaped me. Instead, I just sat with my parents for the first time in years, letting the tears flow down my cheeks as I quietly thought about them.

I wish they were here to talk to. I missed talking to my mom about the latest gossip from the Royal Family, and I missed my dad's mundane chats about the Giants and the 49ers. I missed being normal. I missed having a family unit around me that cared for and protected me. But mostly, I just missed being in their presence and their hugs. Being hugged like you were the most precious thing to someone was rare, and I missed that. I missed them. God, I'd never missed something more.

A tear dropped onto my hand. Feeling foolish in Devin's presence, I wiped my cheek, and I felt him sit next to me. He gently draped an arm over my shoulder, letting me lean my head against his chest while we sat there watching the tree sway in the wind.

"Will you promise to tell me about them one day?" he asked with hope and sincerity lacing his voice.

"Mhmm," I quietly agreed as we sat staring straight ahead.

Devin's slow breaths kept me grounded, reminding me how lucky we were to be alive. How lucky I was to have a friend who would follow me out here even though he had no idea where I was going. Devin was special. I already knew that. I'd always cherish our friendship because I feared that was what we were destined to be to each other. A fact I'd have to accept.

We watched the sunset; Devin didn't pressure me to move. It was the groundskeeper who informed us they were closing that made us leave. Our jeans were soggy from sitting for so long. He held my hand again, leading me to the entrance.

"What do you want to do now?" he asked as he bent over, wiping any remaining tears from my cheeks.

"We should probably get back."

Coming here gave me clarity and time to think. As much as I didn't want to admit it, the way I left things with Laura and Lyss didn't feel right. I needed to get back and talk it out. I couldn't keep walking away from my problems, hoping they'd fix themselves.

He nodded, giving me a small smile as he took his phone out to order a ride. The entire time, his thumb circled over the palm of my hand. As we waited, I looked back at the park, watching the birds fly overhead. It was in that moment that I realized something. My parents never left me. Their bodies may be buried in this park, but that wasn't where their souls were. Their souls were with me. In my heart. A place they would never leave.

The drive back to our homes was a blur. We didn't talk. We didn't need to. I'd shared some of my most intimate moments with this man, and I'd never felt calmer about it. Not once in our little journey did he ask me what was wrong or where we were going. I suppose to him it didn't matter. He just wanted to be there to make me feel better. He knew what I needed before I did. A smile drew across my lips because I couldn't ask for anything more than that, could I?

He opened the door for me, holding his hand out, waiting for me to accept. "Do you want me to come in with you? Beat up Laura and Lyss? I assume that's why you were upset," he joked. I guessed he saw me slam the door as I left. "I'm in the mood for hunting some wabbits." He chuckled.

I smiled, feeling a lot less hysterical now than before I went on this little adventure. "No. It's okay. I need to speak to the girls on my own. We have some unfinished business." I sighed.

There was no way I was telling Devin the full truth about what happened between us. He was all over me when he thought I was some blonde in that costume, which was yet again further evidence he didn't want me as anything more than a bed buddy. It would just be awkward to mention it was, in fact, my ass he was grabbing. No matter how much I enjoyed it.

"Thanks for coming with me today," I said. My voice was low, and I couldn't look him in the eyes. There was so much more I wanted to say, like, *Thank you for being there for me when no one else was. Thank you for seeing me when no one else did.* The words sat on the tip of my tongue, never to be said, too afraid if I did, he would run for the hills or tell me the truth. That I was just his friend, and that's all we'd ever be.

My head was still bowed when I felt his arms draw me closer.

"Get over here, Doc," he mumbled, pulling me into another hug with a chuckle.

His manly scent took over my senses, and I melted into his arms. This was what I'd been missing all those years. This hug. This man. This was where I felt I belonged; I just wished he felt that way, too.

"Devin, are you drunk?" I asked, tipping my head up to look at his goofy smile. He glanced down at me, his lips curling up on the sides.

"No. It's nothing," he quipped, shaking his head. "I guess I've just got a thing for bugs."

I tilted my head, confused, and he ignored my questioning brow, choosing to kiss my forehead instead of elaborating.

"I'll let you go." His lips moved down, kissing me on my cheek and leaving my skin tingling when he left. He walked backward, watching me the entire time, and just when he was about to turn, he winked and laughed. Our moment together was fleeting; it left me wanting more because no matter how much time I spent with him, it never felt like enough.

I watched him walk up his driveway and then took a deep breath, bracing myself for the shitstorm that was about to go down. I didn't want to fight. I had little left in me. I just wanted to forget about today and hope that the bunny dance would soon be forgotten.

"Reign." Lyss and Laura rushed to the door.

I fell back from the unexpected move, only to be caught by them in a hug.

"We're so happy you're back." Laura's words were muffled into my shirt. I was only gone a few hours, but they were acting like I'd been missing for days.

Lyss pulled away, raising her hand, when she noticed I was about to speak. "Please. Let me talk." She took in a deep breath. "I'm sorry, Reign."

My shoulders dropped. Lyss wasn't the type to apologize.

"I went a little crazy in my quest for revenge against Aiden. I shouldn't have asked you to do it in the first place. It was selfish, bitchy, and pathetic. You're my friend, and I will not let a vendetta against Aiden ruin it for me."

Friend. It wasn't like I had many of those, and hearing it come from her made it feel a little more real.

"We've done it," Jackson hollered from the kitchen. He was hunching over Matty, who was concentrating on the computer screen. "It's all wiped."

"What's all wiped?"

Laura squeezed my hand, leading me into the kitchen. "After you left, Lyss and I knew we had to make this right. We shouldn't have laughed and let it go viral." Regret filled her face as she looked down at the screen in front of Matty.

Jackson clasped Matty's shoulder. "Matty here is a technical genius with computers."

"I wouldn't say genius." He rubbed the back of his neck, still looking at the screen. "I have a friend from back home who taught me a few tricks. That's all. The video is wiped from social media. I've set up bots to report it if it's uploaded again. I may have also deleted it from all the clouds I could get into."

Jackson chuckled, looking up at me and smiling. "See. I told you. He's a genius."

"What did he do?" I was still a little confused, even though the rest of them were smiling at me.

"Matty got rid of the video before it truly went viral," Lyss said. "Laura and I spent the last couple of hours walking around campus, taking flyers down, and threatening anyone who was putting them up." My eyebrows rose in surprise.

"Seriously?"

She nodded. "Yes, Reign. God, I'm so sorry about it all. I promise I will never ask you to get involved in my crap again. Once we got back from destroying the flyers, I went to Aiden's house and called a truce." She smiled proudly. Well, crap. If I had known that was all I needed to do to get them to stop, then I would have walked out weeks ago.

"What's a truce with Aiden look like?"

Jackson and Matty chuckled beside me. "Doesn't matter," she quipped. "What matters is that I'm sorry, and I will never pull you into anything like that again."

"Just please, please, please don't leave us," Laura begged. "We really want you here." There was a momentary pause. "Not just because we hated the last four roommates. Which we did. But because we actually like you." Lyss nodded along.

"I took it all a little too far. I'm sorry." I rolled my eyes because they were one please away from getting on their knees and looking ridiculous. I bit my lips, holding back a smile.

"As long as I'm not involved in any more of that crap with you and Aiden, I'll stay." I left out the fact that I didn't exactly have anywhere to go, but that was beside the point. They were both remorseful, and they both took steps to make it right.

Lyss beamed. "No way. I'll keep it all to myself, and every time I see the video, I'll report it."

"You don't need to do that," Matty interrupted. "I've got it covered. Anyone who shares it will get reported and their account shut down for a couple of days. It's the perfect deterrent."

I looked between them. "Guys, thank you." I gave each one of them a hug, relishing in this new sense of tranquility after seeing Devin. In his own way, he reminded me that there were more important things in the world—like hugs that could make you feel alive—than your reputation online.

"We ordered some Chinese if you would like to join us?" Laura gestured to the unopened boxes on the table. "We were kind of waiting for you."

Of course I agreed, and we ended up spending most of the night together, watching TV and talking about random crap. I may not completely trust them yet, but they stopped the video from spreading and walked around campus for hours just to remove the posters. They at least deserved a second chance.

It was late when we finished; I was yawning into my hand, ready to crash onto my bed. "I'm calling it a night." I stretched my arms above my head, sinking softly into the sofa.

"Alright, just do me a favor and make sure that window of yours is closed."

Lyss smirked, and I quirked an eyebrow. Did she know about my late-night catch-ups with Devin?

"I may have sworn Matty and Jackson to secrecy over your identity as the bunny, but if Devin somehow finds out it was you, all hell is going to break loose."

"Why?" I stood up, padding my way to the stairs.

"I'd never seen him so invested in a girl before. He was following your bunny butt around like you were Jessica Rabbit or something." She barked out a laugh. "I don't know what he'd do if he knew it was you under there."

I took one step at a time, slowly digesting what she said, and then I halted, staring at the cream carpet. *Wabbit. Doc. Bugs.* Devin had used all those words before dropping me off. Aren't all of those Elmer Fudd references? Was that his way of hinting that he knew it was me underneath? *Oh my goodness. I was an idiot.*

My heart beat out of my chest. Was that why he was so pushy, getting me to sit on his lap and taking me away from others when I was dressed as a bunny? Was he trying to help me? I rushed to my door and stood in front of it, caught up in so many questions and needing an answer.

It was already midnight, and Devin's light was off. He was probably exhausted from catering to me all day. I quietly walked over to the window, unable to see into his room because it was too dark. I should let him sleep. My questions could wait until tomorrow. That was when I'd give Devin the real grilling.

Twenty-Three

Reign

I threw my bookbag onto the sofa in front of me. The house was empty, and after hours of classes, all I wanted to do was talk to Devin. I could barely concentrate the whole day because I was busy running through every conversation we'd had since we met. Last time he wanted to talk to me, I brushed him off because I was worried he would tell me about his girlfriend, but what if I was too hasty? What if he wanted to clear the air between us?

After everything that happened yesterday, I knew it was time for us to talk. I was ready to lay my feelings on the line. I had so many questions for him, and I couldn't wait for a straight answer. My head whipped to the side when I opened my bedroom door, hoping I'd see him sitting at his desk or lying on his bed in that sexy way he did. He wasn't there, though. Just his dark, empty room, and my heart dropped, knowing I'd have to wait longer.

I plopped down on my bed with a sigh as I planned to snuggle into my pink fluffy blanket and forget the world until I heard Devin enter his room. As my head hit the soft pillow, I closed my eyes and felt something cool roll across my lids. I jumped with curiosity when I realized it was a rose skimming across my face. Studying the perfect red petals, it reminded me of the ones on *The Bachelor.* An ivory note was resting on my pillow with my name scrawled across it in messy man writing.

Plucking the envelope, I ran my hands across the back to reveal a handwritten note inside.

Reign,

I feel like somewhere along the road, we somehow got off track.

Let me take you to dinner tonight.

I'll be at your house at eight.

There was no signature. It didn't need one because I knew exactly who it was from. No one else had access to my room. I felt like my face was going to crack with happiness. Devin wanted to take me out. I jumped out of my bed right then on the spot with excitement. My very own bachelor wanted to take me out, and I could hardly breathe. I ran the rose across my face, holding back a squeal. What a good choice, and maybe that was his way of acknowledging that was the night that things went off track.

Was this why he wasn't in his room? Did he jump over to leave this note? Maybe he didn't want to see me until I opened the front door to him. I couldn't hold it back; I squealed loudly. I'd never been this excited to go on a date with anyone before. It was the first time I felt butterflies in my stomach, and I didn't know what to do with myself.

Flicking my eyes at my phone, I panicked. It was already six forty-five, and I didn't have much time to get ready. I wanted to look good for him. After all, if things went the way I wanted them to, I'd probably invite him back to the fantasy suite, a.k.a., my bedroom, later.

When I finished my shower, I styled my hair with perfect wavy tendrils at the bottom and added some smoky eyes to my makeup. I knew exactly what I wanted to wear before I even looked in my closet. My short, gold sequined long-sleeved dress hung on the back of my chair, sparkling at me. I'd bought it for a formal at Clay's frat house, but that never happened. Well, it happened, but he took Ally, obviously. Thank God. Now I could wear it for someone who mattered instead.

Picking up the dress, I smiled at the low back. Devin would love it. This is what I'd wear if I were on *The Bachelor*, going to one of those evening cocktail parties. I grabbed my pair of gold, strappy Jimmy Choos, ones I bought on eBay because they matched this dress perfectly, and put them on. As I checked myself in the mirror, I swore I could see my legs trembling and my knees knocking. I was actually going to go on a date with Devin. *A real date.*

I checked his window one last time, out of habit more than anything, and he still wasn't there. That had to mean…

Ding-dong.

I jumped as the doorbell chimed, and my breath hitched with excitement. He was treating this like an actual date, coming to the door and everything. He wasn't going to jump over the railing like I'd grown so accustomed to. I grabbed my purse, doing my best not to giggle with excitement as I walked down the landing.

Laura had already opened the door. My grin was so wide that I could give the joker a run for his money. Devin was standing there, holding a giant bouquet of roses. There were so many, they covered his top half. All I could see were his suit bottoms and shiny black shoes. He'd dressed up for me, too.

Laura laughed at something he said, and I hurried down the stairs because I couldn't wait to get to him. When my toes hit the wooden floor at the bottom, I stopped in my tracks.

Keep smiling. Don't falter.

My mouth was aching with how wide I was pulling it. I knew it didn't look natural, but I tried my hardest since my heart was currently withering into nothing. Devin wasn't holding the roses.

It was Adam.

He looked gorgeous in his black suit and baby-blue button-down shirt underneath. One that made his blue eyes sparkle.

"Reign," he said my name breathlessly as he took in my outfit.

My heart wasn't the only thing crumbling, my insides were turning to dust with every look. Adam was amazing; it's just…I was expecting Devin.

"You look gorgeous." He walked toward me, holding out the roses nervously. "I got these for you."

I clutched the roses like they were my lifeline, and they were the only thing holding me back from having a full-blown meltdown. Yet again, I'd somehow convinced myself that Devin was into me. How many times did he have to clarify that we were just friends before I took the hint and backed off?

I wanted to stomp upstairs and cry like a child in my room for the rest of the afternoon. But I couldn't. I had to hold myself together and blink away the tears threatening to fall from my eyes.

"Thank you, Adam. These are gorgeous." My smile was still forced as I bent down to smell the roses. It was exactly what I needed to do right now. I needed to focus on the gorgeous guy in front of me who wanted to take me out. Even if I thought nothing could come between us, I'd at least go out with him and break it to him gently. I didn't have to do it in front of Laura.

No more thinking about Devin.

I brought Adam into a tight embrace because if I couldn't clutch the roses all night, I was going to need something to help me stand. As I pulled away, his smooth lips kissed me on the cheek, and I was devastated.

Can I really go through with this? Wouldn't it be just as bad as Devin leading me on?

Since Laura was still loitering, I had to keep quiet for now. Adam followed me into the kitchen as I filled a vase with water. "How did you know roses were my favorite?" I gently put the flowers into the vase one by one, smelling the sweet scent.

He paused, leaning against the counter and watching my hands dip the roses into the vase. "Well, they are timeless, beautiful, strong, and elegant." I looked up when he took a deep inhale. "All attributes that reminded me of you." His eyes were hard, laced with sincerity, and his cheeks flushed just ever so slightly. Why did it feel like someone was pulling my toenails out with a rusty set of pliers?

I laughed deeply. "Oh, Adam. I didn't know you were such a cornball." I didn't acknowledge his extremely kind words because I was too embarrassed.

He laughed, barely noticing my awkward behavior, chucking his own chin as he looked me up and down. "You look gorgeous." He got up from the counter and sauntered over, putting his hand on my hip and gently placing another kiss on my cheek. Shivers ran down my spine, but it wasn't the good kind. It was the kind that made me nervous and guilty.

Where did I go wrong with this? Was I too busy thinking about Devin to realize I'd inadvertently led Adam on? God, I thought we friend-zoned each other after our first outing. I didn't realize this was a possibility.

His fingers loosely connected with mine as a slow smile grew across his face, and he backed away. "Now, are you ready to let me take you on this date?" My stomach pitted out when he said the word "date." I flicked my eyes over Adam's shoulder, and Laura smiled broadly, giving me the thumbs up.

Adam was standing in front of me, trying to make me feel special and doing a fantastic job of it, while I was fretting over his best friend. His best friend, who had made it clear countless times that he wasn't interested in me except for sex. Oh, and also was his roommate.

"Sure," I said with a small smile. I *should* go because he'd made all this effort, and we were friends. That wasn't something I was willing to lose, and I could talk about things with him at the restaurant when it was just the two of us.

He held out his arm, and I slipped my hand through, resting it close to his elbow. He reached over with his other hand, placing his palm over mine and walking me out.

I felt sick to my stomach the entire time.

Pulling the side of my dress up, I looked around at all the couples, smiling and kissing affectionately. Their loving gazes were a constant reminder that I was here with the wrong guy. Not that he knew it yet.

We were in one of the fanciest restaurants along Covey Beach, sitting on their outdoor patio on the edge of a cliff, with the waves crashing down below us. The twinkling lights echoed against the night sky, and all I could think about was how hopelessly romantic this whole thing was. I'd never been on a date like this. Clay and I dated in high school, so after the initial flurry of dates in the first year, it eventually became pizzas and sleepovers.

The only other person I'd technically dated was Devin. Okay, that was a stretch. No matter how much I tried to convince myself that what Devin and I had was special, it wasn't.

This should have been special.

I glanced over at my date; the candlelight flickered against his almost perfectly symmetrical face. He really was dashingly gorgeous. Adam had an air of dream boyfriend mixed in with a perfect prince, ready to save the day. He just wasn't *my* prince.

"This place is beautiful," I whispered into the night.

He mumbled out a soft thank you as he toyed with the napkin on the table.

"How did you find it?" I was trying my best to make small talk because Adam seemed more muted. He wasn't his usual carefree self tonight.

"I googled it," he said, running a hand through his tousled blonde hair.

He fiddled with the menu nervously until he met my gaze, deep blue eyes boring into mine. He was nervous; the jittery hand told me as much, which surprised me. We hung out almost daily before this. It'd never felt forced or awkward. Until tonight.

I placed my hand on top of the one he was resting on the table. His eyes drew up to mine. "Are you okay?"

He chuckled softly, narrowing his eyes just a little. Was my dress too shimmery and making me hard to look at? "Yeah, sorry. It's stupid." He leaned back in his chair, waving off my hand. There was something on his mind, and I wanted to get it out of him.

"Come on. I can tell something's up. Your jaw's twitching."

He gave me a half-smile as he watched his own fingers tap against the wood of the table. "I haven't actually been on a date in a long time," he admitted on an exhale.

"Neither have I. I was with my ex-boyfriend for so many years, I almost forgot what it was like to date again," I said, ignoring my most recent heartbreak.

"The guy from Louisiana?" he asked. Adam and I had talked a lot, and I'd mentioned Clay in passing a couple of times, so he knew about him. Just not the extent of what happened. I nodded. "How long were you with him for?"

"About four years." I snorted at my own stupidity. "What a waste of time." Shaking my head. Waste of time, a waste of breath, a waste of brain capacity. "What about you? How long were you with your ex?"

His head snapped up at the question. In all this time Adam and I have hung out, he'd only talked about his personal life once, and that was to tell me about the girl that broke his heart right before he went to college. "Um, we kind of saw each other on and off for the last couple of years of high school." His lips thinned as he recalled the memory. "She broke it off almost immediately after senior prom." His hand tapped faster against the table as he silently recalled the memory.

I did the math in my head. Adam was a junior, which meant it'd been three years since he broke up with her, and he hadn't been on a date since. He must have been fighting the girls off all this time. It also seemed strange that he'd still have a framed picture of her on his desk.

How did I not think about this before?

Relief washed over me, and my shoulders relaxed as I smiled at Adam. He looked at me with curiosity, only to be met with my laughter. Adam wasn't in love with me. He couldn't be because he was still hopelessly in love with *her*. "What's so funny?"

"Nothing." I waved my hands up, apologizing and straightening up. "How long have you been in love with her?"

It took him a minute to register my question. When he did, he scrunched his brow. "I'm not still in love with her." It sounded more like he was trying to convince himself than me. "She's been dating the quarterback from our high school for years now, anyway."

And there it was. The real reason he asked me out in the first place. He needed a rebound. He needed someone to make him forget about the girl he was really in love with.

"Did you ever tell her how you felt?" I placed my elbows on the table, resting my chin on the palms of my hand as I watched Adam unravel his thoughts.

He snorted and shook his head. "Oh, believe me, she knew exactly how I felt about her." His acidic tone was hard to ignore. "She didn't care. I was never her end game. The quarterback was." He slumped into his chair, regret in his eyes. He'd pretty much completely forgotten that this was supposed to be a date between us, but I was thankful for that because it meant I didn't have to turn him down.

"Who was the quarterback?"

"Some dudebro named Jarod. He slept with half the school, but Hayden didn't care. She still acted like he pissed liquid gold." He shook his head, annoyed, and whipped his head up with wide eyes.

I held back a grin, knowing that the same thought just ran through his mind as it did mine. We were just friends. He was telling me this because that was all we were. And that was okay.

He chuckled lightly. "I'm sorry. We're supposed to be on a date, and here I am getting wistful about some other girl."

I waved it off, laughing. "I think we can both agree; this probably isn't a date anymore." He scratched the light stubble on his chin, looking uneasy. "Don't worry, Adam. That girl has no idea how lucky she is to have a guy like you so invested in her. Even after all this time." He didn't look convinced by my answer, but he offered me a small smile.

"I feel like a jerk."

"Don't be. Honestly, Adam, I was surprised when I found out it was you who'd asked me on a date anyway. I kind of thought we'd moved past all that."

He shrugged. "Maybe we had. I don't know." He pointed between us. "I guess I kind of thought this might help. I couldn't stop thinking about how beautiful you were the first time I saw you and how much you didn't look like Hayden." He paused, meeting my eyes. "That was a first for me. I haven't been able to look at another girl since her. Not that I've tried particularly hard. I just didn't click with anyone the way I clicked with you."

"I felt that click, too," I offered, but left out that it was more of a friendly click than anything.

"Yeah. When we started hanging out, I thought you were cool. I may not have had the same feelings I had with her, but I thought maybe something could grow between us. If I was lucky."

I grimaced. "When you have to rationalize it like that, doesn't that sound like a lot of work?" He bit his bottom lip, and I grabbed his hand back in mine. "Adam, you are an incredibly awesome, gorgeous, and sweet guy. I like you a lot. But I think we're meant to be friends, don't you?"

His lip curved. "Friends sounds pretty good to me."

"Maybe I could help you find a girl to get you over Hayden?"

He laughed wickedly. "Let's not go too far."

"Have you guys decided what you'd like to order?" the waitress interrupted, spoiling the moment.

We took our time over dinner, and I let Adam monopolize the conversation, telling me all about Hayden. He was like a dam. The minute his walls broke, he couldn't stop talking. My heart nearly burst, seeing how wide his smile got when he talked about her. It made me hopeful that one day I might find someone who loved me just as much.

By the end of the night, I knew the most mundane things about Hayden because Adam wanted me to know everything. It wasn't how I thought our dinner would go, but I wouldn't change it for the world. It seemed Adam and I had an unspoken bond, one I didn't share with many people. We were firm friends, and I knew that wouldn't change. "Can I ask you something?" Adam asked, and I nodded as we put our jackets on. "Who did you think was coming to take you on a date if it wasn't me?"

"Who said I thought it wasn't you?" *How did he know? Did my facial expressions give it away?*

"You." He laughed. "Earlier, you said you were surprised it was me when you came down the stairs. You were definitely expecting someone. You wouldn't dress like that for anyone, and your smile was so genuine." He cocked an eyebrow, and I could feel my face reddening. I'd been caught, and I couldn't think of a way to get out of this. "Come on. You've just listened to me talk about my long-lost love for over an hour. Give me something."

I pursed my lips. "Just a guy," I said, brushing it off. "We met on Covey Connections, but I think he has a girlfriend." I didn't want to lie to Adam, not after everything he admitted to me tonight, but I wasn't ready to spill my guts over sleeping with his roommate.

Adam draped his arm over me as we walked out to the parking lot together. The awkward tension completely gone between us now. "Sounds like Devin." My eyes widened, and my back stiffened as I immediately tried to think of an excuse. "He met some chick on that app. He's been obsessed with her ever since." He laughed, shaking his head. "That app is cursed, I swear. I'm still getting angry messages on there from girls I didn't respond to after Aiden made us play a stupid game," he said flippantly.

"Oh, yeah?"

"Yeah, they're like hungry dogs. I think Devin found the only sane one on there. He hasn't told the other guys or me much, but I can tell he likes her. He keeps his cards close to his chest, but whenever I ask him about her, he gets all hot and flustered, like it's his first crush. My guess is he's taking it slow and doesn't want to jinx it." Or he was just keeping our promise. "I'm not sure if he's still dating her, though. Over the last couple of weeks, every time I've asked him about her, he just grunts like a caveman. But he does look at his phone like a desperate addict waiting for his supplier to call back, and every now and again, I wonder if it's her he's waiting to call."

Adam opened the car door, gesturing for me to get in. I dropped my head to make sure he didn't see my reaction. As he shut the door and walked around the car, I fretted. *Was Adam talking about me? What about that girl in Devin's room? Didn't he meet her?*

"I thought Devin had a girlfriend?" I asked when Adam relaxed into his chair. I tried not to act too eager, but I wasn't sure I was hiding it well. "I could have sworn I saw a girl in his room the other day."

He narrowed his eyes, tilting his head as he studied me. I may have blown my cover. "Devin hasn't had a girl in his room for months. They're repelled by the smell."

So, he didn't know about our late-night hookups. That was good.

"Oh, wait." He rested his head against the headboard, rolling back to look at me. "Do you mean Chloe?"

My stomach dropped down to my toes. I felt empty. She had a name. A nice normal one to go with her gorgeous face and incredible body.

Chloe.

Bet she didn't have dead parents like me. She probably took Devin to the movies instead of graveyards. God, I'm pathetic.

"Did you see her?"

I shot up straight, pursing my lips with a nod.

"Tall with dark hair? Kind of a Gothic vibe?"

I nodded again. Each movement of my head felt worse than the last.

"That's not Devin's girlfriend. That's his sister."

It took a few seconds for that to sink in.

His sister?

"The one in Texas? What's she doing here?"

Unease took over Adam's face, and he squirmed in his seat. "That's, uh, not something I should talk about. It's personal for Dev. You could ask Dev if you want the details." He was right, of course. If Devin's sister's here, then something's happened that he hasn't told me about. "Why does it matter?"

"Huh?"

A smile spread across his face as he took in mine. "Why does it matter if Devin has a girlfriend?" He spelled out the question for me with a hint of humor in his voice. This time, I was the one squirming.

"It doesn't." I shook my head aggressively.

"Oh, it totally does," he teased, pointing at my face. "You're going red. Is there something going on between you guys? Is that why Devin would clam up every time one of the guys would ask me about you?"

"He clammed up?"

Then it hit him; he gasped with realization. "Are you the girl from the app?"

With my body slumped, I dropped my gaze to my hands, toying with my fingers as I nodded. There was no point in hiding it now.

"No wonder Dev's been weird with me." He shook his head and looked at the roof. "If he had told me you were the app girl, I'd have backed off immediately." He turned the engine on, and, as he started to drive away, he said, "I'm an idiot for not seeing this sooner. Of *course,* it was you. The weird, dazed stares, the groping of the bunny, the disgruntled noises he'd make when he walked up the stairs. It's because it was you." He laughed. "I'm an idiot."

"I told Devin not to say anything," I replied sheepishly.

He just laughed it off. "Come on. We've got to get you home before Devin finds out I took you out. I need to be explicit and tell him it wasn't a date. Then apologize. Have you seen the size of that guy's arms? He could do some damage to the walls…or my face."

Twenty-Four
Devin

"Where's Adam?" I asked Matty while I munched on some chips and watched the game. I was surprised he wasn't here. The Carolina Jaguars were playing, and he rarely missed a game, especially when they were winning.

Matty barely heard me, too focused on the drive. "Didn't you hear?" Aiden snickered at my side. "He's out with Reign." He dragged her name out, letting that sink in. "On. A. Date." He very carefully enunciated every single word as though I needed clarification. Dick.

Crunch.
Crunch.
Crunch.

My teeth were grinding against the salty chips as I tried to keep my cool. I wanted to blow out a breath to save myself from blowing out a wall, knowing that would draw too much attention in this room.

"Something wrong, D?" Aiden asked with a smirk playing across his face. When I looked up, all the guys were watching me, concerned. In all my attempts to calm down, I had apparently destroyed the bag of chips, crunching them into nothing but a tiny ball.

Screwing it up further, I threw it on the table in front of me and leaned back against the sofa. "I'm fine," I said with a clenched jaw. I knew I didn't look or sound fine. I was pissed, and everyone knew it. Here I was thinking that Reign and I were making progress. You could forgive a guy for thinking that yesterday might have meant something to her.

I'd just come back from seeing Chloe, in one of the best moods I'd been in a long time, and I was ready to knock on Reign's door and force her to talk to me. That didn't happen, though, because when I pulled up, all I saw was Reign's petite figure standing on the edge of the driveway. Her face was red and eyes were puffy. My stomach lurched. I didn't know exactly why she was upset, but I could guess.

The bunny had come back to haunt her. Flyers with her face were hung around campus, and everyone was talking about who the bunny was. I tore down as many of them as I could, but I had to leave campus; otherwise, I'd miss Chloe's visiting hours. I'd planned to come back and take down the rest later, but I was too late.

Judging from the sniffles, I was sure she'd already been to campus and seen them everywhere. It wasn't like they were bad photos. Just the side of her face with a bunny mask and her cute ass, which was mostly covered by my hand. No one could tell it was her, but I had a feeling that wasn't a thought that would comfort her.

But as I watched her shoulders shake and hiccup through a sob, I didn't feel like I had much of a choice. I couldn't leave her alone. Reign always seemed to be on her own. Even when everyone was around her, she always looked alone, in her own world, doing her own thing. She needed someone by her side for once, and I knew that person would be me.

Did I get a shock when I realized she was going to see her dead parents? Sure, but I didn't let it show because standing by her side and supporting her felt right. When her sobbing settled, I clasped her hand, squeezing it tightly. I thought that moment with her meant as much to her as it did to me.

Hell, by the time we got back, she was smiling. Smiling enough that I could make a joke about rabbits with nice asses, and she'd laugh. I didn't go that far, even though I knew I could.

But yet again, I was wrong. I was always wrong with her. Maybe it was the universe telling me to let her go. I had less than a couple of months of classes left, and I avoided getting involved with any girls for the last three years. It's probably best for me to stop chasing Reign and focus on my future. For Chloe. For Mom.

I couldn't even say I was angry with Adam. I never told him how I felt about Reign. He'd mentioned countless times that he was interested in her, and I said nothing. He was just doing what I should have done in the first place. I should have been honest with Reign and asked her on an actual date instead of getting naked with her. Especially that second time. She was just so damn tempting.

I shook my head, trying to dispel some of the anger coursing through my veins. This was not how I envisioned my night ending.

"Are you upset that your bunny found a new mate? You do know where the phrase fucking like rabbits comes from, don't you? I guess she's just doing what comes naturally." Aiden cackled, and if we were alone, I would punch the living shit out of him for disrespecting Reign.

I couldn't do anything to him with Jackson and Matty watching—too many witnesses. Any drama could get back to potential scouts, and punching your team's quarterback was a surefire way to ruin your career before it had even started.

I needed to remain calm. I clicked my knuckles, glancing at Jackson and Matty, who both looked apologetic.

Did they know about my mild obsession with the girl next door?

"Lyss told Jackson and me that Reign was the bunny," Matty clarified, his ears turning pink.

That was one of his tells. He knew something was going on, but he wasn't going to outright confront me about it. He hated getting into drama, and that piece of knowledge put him firmly in the middle of it. Did Adam know she was the bunny? Was that why he finally decided to ask her out? If I wasn't already interested, I knew I would be after seeing her pert little ass in that thing.

"She was?" I played dumb, not in the mood to explain my relationship with Reign to these guys.

Jackson nodded. "Yeah, Lyss and Laura asked for some of Matty's technical skills to take off the videos that had been uploaded on social media." Well, at least Matty was good for something. "Apparently, Reign was really upset."

No shit, Sherlock. I knew. I was the one who comforted her. Not Adam.

"How long have they been gone?" I stared at my shoes because I didn't want to meet any of their gazes. It was the first time I think I'd ever felt embarrassed. I guess I wasn't as subtle as I thought when it came to Reign.

"A couple of hours," Jackson replied.

A couple of hours?

What the hell were they doing for a couple of hours? Kissing? Getting naked? I was most certainly going to throw up later.

"Reign looked hot," Aiden interjected. He knew what he was doing. He'd known something was going on between us since the first day, choosing to taunt me over it instead of confronting me. That was Aiden. He liked to play with his food before eating. Sick fuck.

"I'm sure she did," I quietly ground out.

Reign always looked hot. That was never a question. The only question I had was why Adam had to pick the same girl to be interested in as me. He'd barely shown interest in any of his one-night stands since we met. A relationship wasn't even on the cards for any of them. When he finally wanted to date someone, why did it have to be the same girl I wanted?

Aiden's door notification chimed on his phone, and he picked it up. "Oh, look who's just arrived home." He laughed, glaring at me. Who shit in his Cheerios this morning? He was more spiteful than usual today. "Looks like Adam's pulling Reign out of the car."

That's it. I'm out.

There was no way I was going to sit here, torturing myself while Adam gushed about his night with Reign. Or worse, he brings her in, and I have to watch him take her upstairs to his room, where they unintentionally proceed to fuck my sanity away.

"I've gotta call my mom," I muttered, more spite coming out than intended.

The air was thick with tension, but no one said anything. Probably because my fists were clenched, and I was ready to punch a window if it reflected the light in the wrong way.

I stalked out of the room, refusing to hide my feelings anymore. Everyone knew that my best friend somehow weaseled his way into my girl's heart.

When I got to my room, I couldn't help myself. My fingers were twitching, and the only way to satisfy the itch was to look out the window. My jaw clenched when I saw Adam help Reign out of the car, her face beaming, wearing this hot little gold dress. A definite date-night dress intended to impress. She wrapped her arms around his neck, hugging him. Her dress rode up her thighs, and she looked like she didn't have a care in the world. She looked happy. Did I ever make her look like that? Her little giggles echoed from here, and Reign shut the door, leaning her back against the car, giving him the same smile she gave me yesterday. He placed a hand on the door above her, grinning down. She laughed at something he said again.

And I was done.

I shut the curtain before I could watch them make out. I was a tortured soul, but I had to draw the line somewhere. I lied on my bed, staring at the ceiling for all of two seconds, before I got my phone out and turned on Covey Connections. I didn't know why, but I needed a distraction, and this felt like the perfect one. I didn't bother looking at the messages Reign and I had exchanged; instead, I went straight for the meet new people section, hoping that someone else could get my mind off her.

My thumb swiped left again and again.

No, Reign's hair is glossier.

Left swipe.

Nope, Reign's smile is more genuine.

Left swipe.

She's going to be a nurse. The only nurse I want treating me is Reign.
Left swipe.

Just not for me.

Left swipe.

I sighed in frustration. It didn't matter what I did. No girl was going to match up to her. I already knew that, but something needed to take the pain away.

A knock at my door startled me into sitting up. "What?" I grumbled, annoyed that someone would disturb me while I wallowed in my own misery. I thought they all got the hint when they choked on the tension I left behind.

"D, it's me. Can we talk?"

I cracked my knuckles again because it was better to do that than crack his pretty-boy face. The only thing that made me feel less like I wanted to throw him out the window and watch his body twitch on the ground was the fact that if he was behind my door, then he wasn't with Reign. That was a win.

He jiggled the handle and knocked again when I didn't respond. "D, please." I could hear the strain in his voice, but it made me no less willing to open up. He probably wanted to come in here and gush about his date with her and how much he liked her to his best friend. *Ex-best friend.* Thank God I was leaving this place soon. I couldn't handle hanging around here and watching them be blissfully in love for the rest of the year.

I inwardly groaned when he fiddled with the handle again. I wondered if Reign told him something happened between us. She was too sweet not to. He was probably desperate to get in here because he wanted to ask permission to date her. Well, screw that. I wasn't going to open the door and let my heart get decimated until it was pounded into dust. Let them feel guilty about this shit. Because that was exactly what it was. A big steaming hot pile of shit. Horse shit mixed with cow pat, to be precise.

"I'm busy," I husked out, balling the sheets in my hand.

"It will only take a second. Let me in." The door jiggled again, and I wondered if the rest of the guys were out there, watching Adam as he pleaded against my door. I bet Aiden was there, the sadistic fuck.

"I'm jacking off," I ground out, hoping that would get him to go away.

"No, you're not."

He chortled. *Chortled!* I was in no mood to laugh with him.

"Come on. It's about Reign."

That was all the confirmation I needed. That door was not opening for him. Not today. Not tomorrow. Not until I'd boxed up my room and was leaving for my new team, whoever it was. Hell, I'd be happy to play for the New Jersey Lions if it meant I was out of this room.

"Not in the mood. I just got back from seeing Chloe." It was my trump card. The only thing I knew would make him go away because he was a sensitive guy, and he knew handling her was difficult. I was beginning to regret opening up to him the first day I came back with Chloe. He had donuts, and it wasn't like Reign was talking to me at the time, so I told him more than I'd told anyone else. "I need to call my mom."

He audibly sighed on the other side of the door. "Fine," he grumbled, his steps getting further and further away. My shoulders relaxed; I didn't know I was so tense.

It was midnight before I calmed myself enough to walk to the bathroom and brush my teeth, shedding all my clothes. I had no right to be as angry as I was. If Reign and Adam made each other happy, I should be happy for them, right? In another sixty days, I'd be gone, and they could act like I never existed. Three years of friendship with Adam and a couple of hot sessions with Reign meant nothing to me. I could get over it.

As I lay in my bed, I spent another fifteen minutes on that stupid dating app, trying to force myself to get Adam and Reign out of my mind. I swore by the time I was done that I'd swiped left on every single girl on campus. I didn't know what I was hoping for or what I was expecting to see. The only girl sitting in my matches section was still the only one I wanted.

But she wanted my best friend.

I dropped my phone to the floor, closed my eyes, and let myself drift off. I did my best not to think about how hot she looked in that bunny costume, but that plan failed miserably.

TWENTY-FIVE
Devin

"You okay, D?" Jackson asked, lightly knocking on my door as he stuck his head in. He knew, like everyone in the house, that I'd been avoiding Adam like the plague for the last couple of days. It wasn't the mature thing to do, but I never said I was.

This morning, I'd snuck out of the house at six a.m. and had breakfast on campus so he wouldn't walk to training with me. When I got to the gym, I started early so I could finish before Adam arrived. I got a good workout, though, because I may or may not have imagined Adam's face the entire time I was punching the bag. Those perfect teeth were knocked out, and he had a couple of shiners under his eyes. It was cathartic.

"Yeah, I'm good. Just trying to get this essay done." I pointed at my desk and lied. I'd finished it last week, but I knew he came in to ask me about Reign, and I didn't want to answer. I liked to think that the knockout session had brought me some clarity. Not enough clarity to be happy for the both of them, but enough that I could walk into my house without breaking a window.

"Cool. Cool. Well, we're going to watch the game in an hour if you want to join?"

I closed my eyes and bit down on my tongue. Adam would be there, obviously. I still had no idea what would happen when I saw him. I picked up my phone. "Ah, I can't tonight. I've got a call with Coach and then my agent to discuss my next steps."

That *was* the truth. Things had progressed since my performance at the Combine, and I was getting more attention. Granted, not enough to be considered for the first round, which was partly because of my defensive position. Teams always went for quarterbacks and tight ends first, but there was interest in me nonetheless. Both Coach and my agent thought I had a good chance of getting picked in the second or third round.

I'd be more than happy with that result. Second or third round would give me enough cash to pay for Chloe's treatment and buy my mom a house in the state I end up playing in. These were the two most important things and what I needed to focus on.

Not Reign and Adam.

The future king and queen of the Covey campus. Ugh. It made me want to wretch just thinking about them. In less than two months, I'd most likely be happily drafted, far, far away from them.

They'd still be here. *Together.* And didn't they deserve to be happy? I'd be long gone. Most likely in another state, focused on winning for my team and getting paid. Reign needed someone to rely on. She needed someone here. And as much as I hated to admit it, Adam was the most loyal and caring asshole I'd ever met. They were perfect for each other, really. Something I should have noticed when all of this started.

Jackson's fingers curled around the wood. "Sure, man. Good luck with the calls. We'll be downstairs if you finish them early." He smiled before shutting the door and leaving me to my own thoughts.

My phone buzzed, and I grabbed it, ready to talk to Coach. Only it wasn't him. It was a message from Reign.

Reign: Hey D, I was wondering if you wanted to watch *The Bachelor* with me tonight? I've missed watching it with you.

She knew how to rub salt in the wound, didn't she? She missed it last night because she was too busy going on a date with Adam. Did she really think watching that stupid show while playing drinking games with me was appropriate now that she had a new boyfriend? She was probably trying to soften the blow. Get me drunk to tell me she was in love with my roommate, and they were having hot sex. Hotter than her riding my face, which I doubted was possible. I shook my head, dropping my phone back down to the table and focusing on my work.

That text was helpful. The more Adam and Reign pushed me, the more annoyed I got, and the less I cared they were bumping uglies. Okay, that was a lie. I would always care who Reign was bumping uglies with. Especially if it wasn't me. But at least the more they pissed me off, the more I was looking forward to leaving this place.

The phone buzzed again, toying with my emotions like I was Woody from *Toy Story*. I itched to check it, but I knew it was her wondering why I was ignoring her. I shouldn't check it. I shouldn't. I should just focus on the draft. Burly football men. That was who I was going to be hanging out with for the next few years. Burly men. Not soft, sweet curves that I wanted to touch and play with. Nope. Not those. Just smelly, strong men. With thick lumberjack beards. And bad breath.

My hands moved before my head could stop them. Apparently, the prospect of hairy, burly men motivated them into action. Like I suspected, it was another message from Reign.

Reign: Are you ignoring me? Because I spoke to Adam last night, and he told me you were ignoring him too.

I groaned. She just had to bring Adam up again, didn't she? It was like she was trying to shred every piece of my heart.

Reign: I think you've got the wrong end of the stick, D.

She continued messaging. Ignoring the fact that *I* was ignoring her.

Reign: Open your window.

I disregarded her last request. I needed to stay strong. I heard a light tap against my curtain-covered window and scrubbed a hand down my face. *Ignore.* My phone buzzed again. *Ignore.* Another tap. *Ignore.*

"Devin!" her voice yelled through the paned window. "Check your damn phone," she shrieked, and my lip quirked at hearing her curse. Not something I was used to. Lifting my phone, I did as she said, checking her last message.

The phone dropped from my hand in excitement, confusion, shock, and any other emotion that I couldn't think of right now because she just fried any working brain cells I had left with that last message. I bent back down, picking up the phone again to see if the picture was still there or if it was all in my imagination. It was still there. I think my heart stopped beating.

My mouth watered as I looked over the picture of her in that bunny costume, staring down at the camera. The phone was tilted up in a hot girl selfie angle, giving me a great view of her boobs, and my goodness, did they look good in that corset. The words "What's up, Doc?" were plastered above the bunny ears. She was trying to kill me. It was the only explanation for sending me a picture like that. Although, I couldn't deny that being suffocated in her boobs would be a pretty awesome way to go.

"I know you've seen it." She spoke loudly through the glass again. "I can see the blue ticks. Will you please open your curtain?" After saving that picture three times and screenshotting it for good measure, I reluctantly walked toward the curtain. I wasn't sure if I should be excited or pissed at this whole thing.

Of all the things I was expecting when I opened the curtain, I was not expecting Reign to be standing there, her bottom lip tucked under her teeth, in my gray sweatshirt and heels. "Where are your pants?" I blurted out, staring at her bare thighs, remembering when they were wrapped around my face.

She looked down and then back up at me with a smirk on her face. She shrugged while tilting her head. "Whoops. I guess I forgot."

My hands were trembling because they wanted to touch her so badly. I stuffed them in my pockets, leaning back on my heels, thankful for the railing between us. "Maybe you need to put some on," I muttered, eyes focused on the ground, too confused to look at her.

She laughed. "Maybe you should stop being a stubborn ass and get over here." She opened her window wider, leaving plenty of space for me to make my move. She turned around, walking further into the room. The heels made her butt stick out, and I couldn't help but follow. I jumped the railing with such ease; she was surprised to hear the thud of my boots connecting with the wooden floorboards so quickly.

She jumped and looked over her shoulder with a smile. "Shut the curtain," she instructed. My brows furrowed, but I did as she asked. The only light now illuminating the room came from her desk lamp. "Why have you been ignoring me?" I swore she purred it out like a hot little pussycat.

I couldn't answer straight away, assuming that "because I'm obsessed with you" might be an awkward response. "I've been busy," I mumbled, running a hand through my hair, looking anywhere but her face.

"Mhmm." She tipped her head up, sitting down on her bed, the sweatshirt riding fist-clenchingly high. *Was she wearing anything under that?* She was trying to make me sweat; I could tell by her cocked eyebrow and grin. I forced myself to look down at my feet and I shoved my hands in my pockets again, in fear that they might touch things they weren't supposed to.

"Too busy to talk to me?" She pouted, sticking that big, plump bottom lip out. I eased my hips back, hoping to hide the tent growing my sweats just thinking about her. "Last night, I wanted to talk to you."

I rubbed one hand over my face, preparing for disappointment, but my dick was still hopeful, it seemed. She wasn't wearing pants after all. She languidly rose from her bed, walking back over to me. "I'm here now. We can talk," I quipped. I might as well get this over with. Just in case it was going to be the most disappointing moment in my life.

"I'm not dating Adam. I was never dating him," she stated. My head tilted as I studied her beautiful face. "If you had let Adam talk to you last night, you would know that. You would also know that I'm only interested in you, you idiot."

I could feel my mouth hanging open. "But why did you—"

She shook her head, biting her bottom lip as she glanced at me. "Uh-uh. I think we're done talking for now." She cupped my cheeks, lifting her mouth to mine, and kissed me gently. It was tender and tentative, as though she wanted to check if I was okay with this. I was frozen. Thousands of questions were running through my head, but none mattered when she brought my bottom lip into her mouth, sucking it lightly. Her eyes stared into mine, still looking for permission.

Hell yes.

Her hesitant pecks and nipping weren't enough. I was greedy. I wanted all of her. I threaded a hand through her hair, forcing her lips to open against mine, making it easier to slip my tongue in. She lightly bit down on my lip when I rested my other hand on her bare ass, making her squeal. I was straining against my boxers, knowing that she wasn't wearing anything under my sweatshirt.

Her hands moved to my chest as she kissed my jaw, moving down my neck and nibbling when she got there. It seemed Reign was as greedy as me. Her hands grasped at the edges of my shirt, trying to magically force it off. I grabbed the back of it, pulling it over my head as her hot mouth kissed down my chest, licking the crevices as she bent to get lower down, giving me a great view of her ass and the tiny white lace thong she had on.

The trail of her tongue teased my skin. Her hands were resting just above the fabric of my sweats. I watched her eyes widen as her gaze lowered to my gray sweatpants, seeing how hard I was just from her kisses. Her lip upturned as her fingers lingered at the hem of the pants, her nails tickling my abs, torturing me slowly.

She was making me so hard it hurt. I let out a sigh when her fingers dipped past the elastic of my boxers and wrapped around my cock. I had to think of ice baths and Aiden's hairy ass just to stop myself from coming on the spot like an inexperienced teenager.

She watched my reaction as she did something completely unexpected. She dropped to her knees, her face directly in front of my cock, and licked her lips. I dug my fingers into the delicate flesh of her shoulders, salivating at the thought of what was to come.

She skimmed my pants down, only enough to free my cock. I barely felt the cool night air on my dick before Reign shoved it in her mouth, devouring my long, thick shaft like it was a lollipop. This was how I wanted to die, with her thick lips moving up and down my cock, watching my reaction.

I closed my eyes, tilting my head back and letting my hips jerk into her hot, wet mouth. She released my cock with a pop, wrapping her hand around the base and tickling the tip with her tongue as she eagerly lapped up my pre-cum. My whole body trembled when she lowered her mouth back down, inch by inch.

Holding the back of her head, she let me control the speed. She swallowed when I pushed myself down her throat, and I was close. Standing was making me much more sensitive.

"Darlin', I'm going to come," I warned, letting go of her head so she could get back up, but she didn't flinch. When she didn't get up, I glanced down, seeing a soft smile forming at the corner of her lips. She held me firm in her mouth, hollowing out her cheeks and sucking me hard. She wanted me to come in her mouth. That thought alone made it impossible not to come immediately.

Stars flooded my vision, and my hips jerked uncontrollably as her nails dug into my thighs. She was milking me dry. Swallowing every last inch of me, licking up my shaft just to make sure she didn't miss anything. "Fuck." My legs trembled, and I took no time lifting her up, crushing her lips against mine.

We made out frantically, as though we weren't just standing there nearly naked, and I didn't just blow my load in her mouth. I could get lost in her kisses all night if that was all she wanted to do. Thank God it wasn't. She pulled her lips away from me, licking her lips as she pushed away.

Reign confidently walked over to the bed, sitting down with her legs crossed.

"I want you," I whispered as I looked at the apex of her thighs and the shock of white lace fabric covering exactly what I wanted to do.

She just smirked, leaning back on her forearms and opening her legs, showing me everything I wanted to see. I growled, kneeling in front of her and pushing my sweatshirt up so I could slide my hand across the curve of her breast as I took the other one in my mouth, nipping and sucking at the tip. She moaned, arching her back to my touch.

"Devin. I need you," she whined out, her head falling back as her hips rocked against my groin, trying to find any friction she could. I smiled, loving the way I was making her feel. My hands traveled to her hips, grasping at the fabric on either side and pulling it down, past her knees, to the floor.

Her pussy was perfect—pretty, pink, wet, and just for me. I licked my lips, anticipating what I was going to do next. I moved back, kissing just behind her knees and working my way up to her thighs. When I'd get close to her center, I turned my attention to her other thigh, kissing my way up, ignoring her tortured moans.

She opened her legs wider, trying to force me to touch her, and that was when I dragged my thumb along her slit, teasing her until I slowly pushed two fingers inside her. Her hips rose as my fingers went deeper into her warm heat. I couldn't help myself; I dipped my head down and licked her swollen clit, watching her eyes close at the touch. I didn't let up, flicking her clit over and over, hearing her get louder and louder.

Her hands gripped my hair as she screamed loud enough to alert the whole house of my presence. Hopefully, Lyss and Laura were out for the afternoon. She rocked her hips against my mouth as I lapped up her juices, growing hard again just from watching and tasting her.

My name left her mouth every time I flicked her clit, working her faster and faster until I could feel her clenching around my fingers and her body withering at my touch. I watched her breathing increase as I tasted every inch of her. She was delectable.

Her cheeks flushed, and she tightened her legs around my head, rocking her body against my mouth as the orgasm took over. I was in heaven. I take back what I said before. This was what I wanted to die doing. Licking Reign's essence as she comes on my face.

I watched her come down from the high and kissed her thigh, wiping my mouth as I stood. I wanted to be inside her. Now. "Do you have condoms?" I asked. She opened her eyes, half-lidded, shaking her head.

I thought I might faint because all the blood was rushing to my head.

"I'm on the pill. I'm clean," she muttered. "Are you?"

I nodded. Even though I knew I was clean because I got tested regularly for football, I'd never been with someone long enough to forgo condoms. "Are you sure?"

"Yes. Please, I need you." Her hands clasped my shoulders as she tried to force my body on hers, but she was no match for me. I took my time, moving up her body, resting my elbows on both sides of her head, and kissing her mouth as I wrapped her legs around my waist. Grasping my cock, I rubbed it up and down her slit, indulging in the feeling of her wet pussy against it without a condom. "Please," she whined, and I centered myself as I eased into her smoothly. Her wetness made it easy, but as she gripped at my cock, my thrusting became haphazard. It'd never felt this warm, this wet, this good. When I got used to the feeling, I thrust into her over and over, loving being inside her bareback. She clutched the sheets as I growled, nipping at her neck, her skin sticky from the sweat.

I moved against her, grabbing her ass and pulling her closer. She held on to my shoulders, biting on her bottom lip, trying to hold back. Her nails bit into my shoulders, and I knew she was close because I could feel her body tensing. "Dev, I'm…" That's all she got out before her orgasm took over. She trembled beneath me as her pussy clenched my cock, and the feeling alone set off my own climax.

After a few final thrusts, I collapsed on top of her, breathing heavily and taking in what we just did. I lifted to press my lips against hers one last time before I rolled off to the side to lie next to her. After a couple of minutes of just breathing, I smiled at her. Her dazed chocolate eyes connected to mine as I watched her chest heave. My sweatshirt was still scrunched up above her armpits, and she looked well and truly fucked. *She was perfect.* "Does this mean you'll finally let me take you out on a date?"

Her plump lips parted with a laugh as she pulled my hoodie down. "We've done it all backward, haven't we?"

I took her hand in mine, waffling our fingers together as I lifted them to my mouth, kissing her knuckles softly, feeling more connected to her than I've ever felt with anyone before. "Doesn't make my feelings for you any different," I whispered.

She looked up at the ceiling, a smile still etched across her face. "Devin Walker, I would love to go on a date with you."

"Well, then be ready tomorrow." I grinned, already thinking about where I was going to take her. I wanted to treat my girl because that was who she was now. *My* girl, and I was going to treat her right.

TWENTY-SIX
Reign

"Why are you so nervous?" Lyss snorted as she looked down at my tapping toes. "It's not like you haven't already seen him naked."

I could feel my cheeks turn pink at her words. I didn't realize they were home last night, and I may have been a little too vocal. I couldn't help myself. Devin was making up for lost time and took me in all kinds of positions. When I emerged from my room in the morning, Lyss and Laura were waiting in the kitchen with smirks on their faces and all kinds of questions.

"Tell me, Reign, does he have a six or eight-pack?" Laura asked from the kitchen, making herself a coffee while Lyss and I sat in the living room. Lyss's eyes narrowed as she scrutinized my every move.

I ignored both of their questions, choosing to straighten out the crinkle in my paisley dress instead of making eye contact with either of them. Just because Devin had probably licked every inch of my body by now didn't mean I couldn't still be so nervous about going on a date with him. To me, he was perfect, and I felt like vomiting. He was taking me out on an actual date. Not a one-night thing or a quick screw in his bed. He was taking me out to get to know me. We'd talked before, and something shifted between us on the day he joined me to see my parents, but what if I screwed it up by blurting out something stupid? What if he tossed me away like a day-old fish? What if he tossed me away like Clay? I'd be crushed.

The doorbell rang, and I jumped off the sofa, mumbling something even I didn't understand to the girls as I waved goodbye to them. I grabbed my purse and skipped to the front door, slowing down to a walk the closer I got, trying to act natural. It was just Devin, after all. No big deal.

When I opened the door, I nearly laughed at my thoughts.

Devin? No big deal? In what universe?

"Hey, darlin'." His sexy Southern accent drawled out as he stood there, dripping hotness. His black T-shirt was just tight enough to emphasize his bulging arm muscles, and the faded dark jeans hanging low on his hips made my mouth water. He rocked from the back of his heels to his toes as he flashed me a lopsided grin. He was everything. "This is for you," he said smoothly as he handed me a single long-stem rose.

I took it eagerly, feeling like a *Bachelor* contestant. "Thank you, Devin. It's beautiful." I let the petals flutter across my cheek, and when I opened my eyes, Devin's hot gaze was on me. Hot and demanding. My panties dampened, and I rubbed my thighs, trying to ease the tension because we had to get through dinner before we could have dessert. "Am I dressed okay?" I asked, looking down at my black Converse and floaty dress. I didn't want to go overboard like I had with the accidental date with Adam. I tucked a piece of hair behind my ear, feeling nervous because I hadn't made the same effort as before. Would that offend him? When I finally looked back up, he was studying my outfit with a smile sprawled across his face.

"You look gorgeous, Reign."

He hardly ever called me by my name. Something about the way he rolled the R off his tongue sounded intimate. Like he wanted to take that R up to his room and spank it until it knew who was boss. I shook my head. I needed to focus.

"You always do. Although you have made it impossible to look at a bunny without thinking of you."

I swatted his chest, giggling at the memory. From now on, I'd keep my dress-ups to the bedroom. As angry as I felt about it the other day, the fact that Lyss and Laura got rid of most of the fallout had helped me feel better about it. Everyone did something stupid in college. That was just my mistake, and at least no one knew it was me. I'd heard rumors about different hazing rituals that happened at other campuses and how those events haunted girls for years after. Southern Collegiate seemed particularly brutal, so I guessed I could consider myself lucky for getting off so lightly.

"How long did you know it was me under there?" I asked, curious.

His eyebrow cocked. "Do you really want to know the answer to that?"

I nodded, and he wrapped his arms around me, forcing my hands to the back of his neck as he kissed me just behind the ear. A tickling sensation ran down my collarbone.

"The minute I saw that cute little birthmark on that tight little ass of yours, I knew it was you," he growled it out like he was annoyed I reminded him of it.

I turned my face to him, pecking at his soft lips, basking in their softness as we held each other close. Why did it feel so right just being in his arms like this? "Now, are you ready for this date because if we talk any more about you in that bunny costume, this will all end very quickly, and I don't just mean the date." He pulled out of our embrace, keeping one hand attached to my hip so that I could lean my body against his.

"You slicked your hair back," I pointed out as he walked me to his car in his driveway. He immediately touched it, laughing nervously.

"Thought I'd make an effort. This is the first date I've been on in three years."

I gave him a smile as he twiddled with the ends. My heart almost burst thinking that I was the only girl he'd taken out while he'd been at college.

"Is it okay?" His cheeks went a little pink, and it surprised me because he had nothing to be nervous of.

"I love it." I giggled as he opened his car door, helping me in.

He palmed the seat belt, dragging it over my body and taking his time as he leaned in to buckle it. His musky cologne filled my senses and reminded me of all kinds of naughty things we'd gotten up to. He had that kind of smell that made you want to jump in a pool and swim in it. Woody and all man. As he moved back and out of the car, he planted a slow, sensual kiss on my lips, holding me there as he slipped a little tongue in. When he backed away with a grin, he slid into his side of the car, knowing full well how hot he was making me with all the little light touches and strokes. I nearly considered calling off the date and dragging him to my room, but we needed to get out of there. For our own sake.

The ride was filled with idle chit-chat about our days and how Devin finally cleared the air with Adam. Thankfully, Devin hadn't held a grudge, and by the end of their discussion, they were laughing about how stupid the whole thing was. I was glad it worked out. The idea of getting in the middle of their friendship had me in knots, so I was relieved that Devin forgave his friend so quickly.

He stopped the car, and my brows furrowed as I looked at the building in front of me. Surely this wasn't where he was taking me? It made no sense. "We're going to a roller disco?" I wondered out loud.

I looked over at him, and he shrugged sheepishly. "I wanted to redo the first time we met, so I thought about what I would have done if we had arranged to go on an actual date instead of just hooking up."

My eyebrow cocked up. "You would have taken me to a roller disco?"

"Not quite, but I couldn't exactly take you out to a fancy dinner after you *just* went on a date with Adam the other night, could I?" he ground out with a hint of humor on his face as he watched my reaction.

I groaned and covered my eyes in shame, sinking further into the leather. "Why did you have to mention it like that?! It wasn't a date!"

He chuckled in amusement. "Are you sure? Adam's been talking about it all day like it was a date. *I got Reign a dozen roses. Oh, you only got her one. Reign loved the fancy French place I took her to. Oh, you didn't know that she loves French food?* I swear if I hadn't just made up with him, I would have punched that pretty-boy smirk off his face. Unless that was your plan all along?" He paused for a moment, with a wry smile and a mischievous glint in his eyes. "Tell me, darlin', were you looking for a ménage à trois? Is that how the French say it?"

I mumbled a response through my hands and shook my head, too mortified to meet his gaze.

"Sorry, darlin', you're going to have to speak up."

"I thought it was you," I finally admitted, throwing my hands onto my lap so I could stare at them.

His laugh was earthy and deep. "You thought Adam was me? I know you've been busy with your classes, but I think we might need to get you some glasses because the only thing Adam and I have in common is our height."

I slid to the side to face Devin, leaning on the brown leather seats as I started to explain. "He left a note and a rose on my bed about how he was going to take me out. No one else had access to my room, and how could I not think it was you after we watched *The Bachelor* together? That, and since *you* were the only one I've been with since I got here, I thought it could only be you. That's why I dressed up." His eyes lit up at that confession.

"If that's the case, then why did you go on the date, anyway?" He narrowed his eyes suspiciously.

"What was I supposed to do? I was all dressed up, and he brought me flowers. Laura was eavesdropping in the living room, anxiously waiting for my response. What I didn't realize was that she was in cahoots with Adam and put the note and roses on my bed. I was crushed inside when I found out it wasn't you, but I didn't want to hurt Adam's feelings. He's a nice guy." I left out the fact that I may have also thought Devin was sleeping with his sister, and in a desperate attempt to forget him, I believed going on a date with his best friend might help. Yeah, not my finest hour, but at least I learned something from the whole thing.

"Yet you don't mind hurting my feelings with your roller disco questions?"

"You've got thicker skin." I laughed, grabbing his arm and giving it a little pinch. That was a mistake. His muscles flexed underneath my palm, and it heated my skin. I tore my hand away, pretending he wasn't making me flustered. "You can handle it. Adam, on the other hand, I think the honesty that early on would have broken him, and we need him on the team next year." I shrugged. "Anyway, you were telling me why you thought I'd like to go to a roller disco." I waved my hand, hoping we'd be able to move off the topic of Adam.

He huffed out a breath. "Yeah, so you're going to have to forgive me. I didn't have time to watch the entire back catalog of *The Bachelor* to figure out the kind of date you might like. It was either this or take you to Vista Point. This won out."

"Vista Point is a make-out spot."

"Exactly. I didn't want you to think I only wanted you for your body." His eyes dropped, roaming my dress. "As much as I want your body, this means we can just hang out with no pressure." He turned the ignition off and leaned in close, like he was going to tell me a secret. "But if you want to take advantage of me, I'm all for it," he whispered with a wink. He leaned forward, resting his hand on the door to the entrance of the disco. "Now, are you ready to teach a huge football player how to skate?"

"Yes!" I squealed, more excited than I thought I would be for this.

When my skates hit the wooden floor, I was instantly reminded of the last time I did this as a kid. My dad used to take me, something Devin didn't know. He looked surprised when I spun on my heels, twirling perfectly in a spiral without falling. He just stood at the entrance to the rink, clutching the wall on either side of him as he tentatively took the first few steps onto the floor. I could tell he was cursing under his breath when little girls whizzed past him in their neon colors, singing and dancing to the music with little to no effort.

He took an unbalanced step, letting one hand go of the railing, but then fumbled, grabbing the side of the wall again. I tried to stifle a laugh, but I couldn't help it; watching this big, hot guy fumble around as children gracefully glide around him was too much. Finally, something he wasn't perfect at. He stood on the side, clutching the wall so hard I could see the whites of his knuckles from here. I figured I should take pity on him and help him out.

I skated over and leaned my back against the railing, looking at Devin with a coy smile. It was dark. The flickering light of the disco ball was the only thing showing his face, but I swore I could see his cheeks had ruddied in the ruckus. I leaned in closer, my lips just by his ear, wanting to tease him the way he teased me back at the house. "Do you know how to skate, D?" I asked, nipping his earlobe as I backed away.

He turned his face, eyes boring into mine. We were nose to nose, and he shook his head instead of kissing me like I'd hoped. "If you didn't know how to skate, why did you bring me here?"

Devin's smile shone brightly under the neon lights. "Because I thought we could learn together. You know, I was expecting you to fall and I would be able to catch you. I'd somehow maneuver us, so I was on my back with you on top. Then maybe you'd kiss me as a thank you." As he outlined his fantasies, he looked back down at me with mock disgust. "Turns out I brought a pro."

I took his hand. "Alright, D, let me teach you." I skated backward, holding his hands while he watched his skates, almost tripping himself up. "Eyes up, watch me, and trust your feet," I explained. He stood up taller, towering over me and taking my direction as we skated around the circle. He didn't take his eyes off me; I felt like the only person in the room as we skated around, never once letting go of each other.

When he got comfortable, I took it up a notch. Moving his hands to my hips, I turned around so I was facing forward. His fingers gripped me tighter as I skated faster around the rink, letting my skirt flow in the wind. Devin seemed to get tired of this position, following my lead for a short time until he wrapped his arms around me, guiding me to lean back on his chest, and I let him confidently lead us around the rink with ease.

"You picked that up fast," I said, surprised. He lifted me up a few inches, just enough to make me squeal as he skated faster around the rink.

"Did you expect anything less from an elite athlete?" he asked as his skates glided against the wood, and he nipped my collarbone from behind, pushing himself against me. I was getting hot and flustered in front of children. This was not good. Every time I pushed forward, he pulled me back, refusing to let me get away, and I loved every second of it. The longer we skated, the quieter the rink got. We were there so long that eventually, it was just the two of us and a few other couples spinning around on the floor.

Devin sang along to the country music, singing in my ear without a care in the world. He made me smile without even trying, and it was crazy to think he was the same guy as the one I'd met in the bar the first night. I can't believe how much I misjudged him. I assumed he was a lothario and just some hot guy to get Clay and Ally off my mind for the night. But somehow, he crept into the crevices of my heart, filling those spaces up, making me feel whole again. Mending old wounds that I didn't know needed healing. He made me feel things that I wasn't comfortable even thinking, let alone saying out loud. How could someone I'd only known a couple of months change my world so drastically?

"Do you want some ice cream?" he asked, his hands rubbing against my hips, reminding me of yesterday and how he spent the better part of two hours holding me in place, watching me have multiple orgasms. I gave him a small nod, skating us over to the exit because I needed something to help cool me down.

As I sat on the sticky seats, Devin sat across from me, handing over a giant green ice cream cone. "I hope you like mint chocolate chip. It's all they had left. Apparently, they were raided by a twelve-year-old's birthday party before I got there."

"I'm in luck then." I smiled, grabbing the cone and taking a few tentative licks. I stopped when I noticed Devin was watching me. "This is delicious," I purred, taking a long, suggestive lick. I smiled wickedly when his eyes tracked my tongue, and he stared at me with a dazed look. "Thanks for bringing me here. I've had a really great time."

It took a moment for him to respond because I purposely licked the ice cream again. "The pleasure was all mine. Do you think we could do this again?" he asked with a sly smile, and he pushed his tongue out, licking his own lips.

He wanted to play dirty. Fine.

This time, I took my time licking around the ice cream, flicking it across the top, much like I did to him yesterday. "I'd really like that."

Just as he was about to respond, his phone buzzed on the table. Instinctively, he snatched it and started reading the message. "Sorry, it's my sister. She's gained email privileges, and she won't stop sending me messages. I keep worrying it's the facility telling me she's escaped again."

"How's she doing?" I asked.

He nodded with a smile. "She's doing great, thanks. I haven't seen her this happy in a long time. It's only been a few weeks, but I can really see a difference in her."

My heart ached seeing how much he cared for her. Devin was a good guy; he would make an awesome brother. Chloe was lucky to have him to help her through this. Hearing how he talked about her made me wish I had someone to share the good and bad times with. Maybe things would have been easier if I weren't so alone if I had a brother or sister around for support. This was the first time I'd really thought about how alone I was in the world now. What with no parents. My aunt had tried to call me a couple of times, asking me about what happened and why I left in such a hurry, but I didn't have the heart to tell her about how her daughter betrayed me. Surely that was something Ally should have to deal with, not me.

In a way, I should be thankful that Ally pushed me away and forced me back home. Back to where I belong, because coming back here was the best decision I'd ever made. Starting a new life with friends who didn't know me as the girl whose parents died meant I went out. I did things I wouldn't have done otherwise. I wasn't treated with kid gloves, and Devin brought out things in me that Clay was never capable of. He built my confidence, was my friend, and supported me when I needed it. I wouldn't admit this to him, but he was starting to feel like home. Like my safe space.

"My mom's a lot more relaxed, too. She's just worried about when I…" He trailed off, looking at me like he just spilled the beans on a secret. His eyes darted down to the napkin he was playing with.

"What's she worried about?" I encouraged.

He threw the napkin down, leaning back into the leather seat. His eyes still refused to meet mine. "Just, uh, I'm entering the draft next month, and we don't know where I'll be after that."

My heart dropped. It wasn't like that was a secret or that he lied to me. I knew his plan all along was to enter the draft early to help his family. I guess I kind of thought it would be further down the line in the summer or something. Not right now. Not when we'd just started. Suddenly, the stark realization that we were on borrowed time had become all too real for me, and this conversation had become more serious than I thought either of us intended. Was I too attached to Devin already? How would I cope with him being gone?

He grabbed my hand, forcing me back into the room and into this conversation. "Just because I'm leaving doesn't mean I want to leave you behind." His hazel eyes were heavy as he tried to reassure me with a smile. I had to stop and think for a minute. Was this something I wanted to get myself into? Did I really want a long-distance relationship? "I really like you, Reign. I haven't pursued anyone except you since I came here because my end goal was always the draft," he said, like that alone would solve everything.

"What do you think is going to happen to us when you're gone?" I asked calmly, hoping I wasn't showing all of my cards. I may not have known him long, but this was the closest I'd been to caring about someone since my parents. The idea of him leaving me now made me queasy.

"Well, I'll be back here a lot to visit Chloe until I can move her to a facility closer to my team," he stated. "And to visit you if you'd let me?" I nodded, hiding the coy smile from hearing him say that. "Who knows, I could end up on a California team."

"Don't you already know where you're going? Teams have surely talked to you?" My brows furrowed in confusion. I didn't really have any idea how any of this worked, and that made me nervous. I didn't know the implications of the draft process or how it would affect his free time. It was all the things I'd have to find out later.

He nodded. "They have expressed interest, but no one can make commitments because it's all very strategic and depends on what the other teams do ahead of them. I know a couple of California teams are interested, but so are a couple of teams in Las Vegas and North Carolina."

North Carolina? But that is on the other side of the country. I was no expert, but I was guessing they got little free time. It would be nearly impossible to make this work in different states and time zones.

"Reign, it doesn't matter where I go or what time zone I'm in. My feelings for you are the same. I want you." My mouth hung open. Did I say that out loud?

I backed my hands away. "This is crazy, though. We've only known each other for a little over two months. This is our first date. We shouldn't be talking about things like this. We're getting ourselves too invested, too soon." I thought that more for my benefit than his. If we get any deeper, Devin would be able to move on from this. Me, I wasn't so sure.

"Be my girlfriend," he blurted out with wide eyes. Almost as though he was as shocked saying it as I was hearing it. He went with it, though. He grabbed my hand, leaning closer to me over the table. "I don't want another girl, Reign. Since the moment I laid eyes on you in that app, on Covey Connections, it's only been you. This may be our first date, but it's not what it feels like to me. You know me. I know you. We need each other." He was pleading with his eyes; I remained silent, still not fully convinced. "I just want you to at least try with me."

His eyes flitted back and forth, and when I didn't respond, he continued, "I'll be spending the next few months just sorting out my new living arrangements, and then I start preseason training in August. What are your plans for this summer?" My mouth moved, but no words came out. "If you wanted to, you could come and live with me. Just for the summer, of course," he clarified, noting my wide-eyed, shocked face. "You'll need to come back here to finish up your degree, obviously. But once you've qualified, maybe we could revisit that moving-in thought. Who knows, I might move to another team, too."

He was rambling, thinking up a future for us before I'd even answered his first question. It was kind of cute, but I wasn't there just yet. "Can I think about it?"

His face deflated hearing those words out of my mouth, but he tried to hide it. "The summer thing? or the girlfriend thing?"

I shook my head. "The summer thing. I hadn't planned anything further than transferring here, and I've only just adjusted to that huge change. Throwing another potential move, even if it's only for the summer, seems like a lot. I just need a minute to adjust to all the changes in my life before I agree to another huge one."

"Sure, makes sense." He nodded but then paused. "What about the girlfriend thing?" He narrowed his eyes, scrutinizing me with a shy smile on his face.

I bit my bottom lip. I knew what I wanted to say, but was it too soon? His eager eyes searched mine, and I didn't want to let him down. "Yes."

"Yes?"

"Yes, I'd love to be your girlfriend." He pushed out of the booth, crowding into my side, reminding me of the first time we met. He clasped my cheeks in his big paws, bringing me in for one of the most mind-blowing kisses I'd ever had. It was the perfect way to end our first real date.

✚✚✚✚✚✚✚

"How did it go?" Lyss asked, smiling from the sofa as I opened the door and leaned against it with a smile. I went to a dinky roller disco with kids everywhere, but the only thing I could focus on was Devin and how he made me feel. When we got back to our houses, we made out in his car for the better part of an hour. I loved every second of it.

After taking a moment, I opened my eyes and walked into the living room. "It was magical." I couldn't get the grin off my face. "It was everything I could have asked for and more."

Laura whistled out, adjusting to sit cross-legged on the couch. They were both in plaid pajamas, watching something on Netflix. "Oh, Reign's got a crush," Laura teased. She clasped her hands together. "Can you take a picture of his abs or something? Just as a memento for me?"

I shook my head. "Nope, they're all mine now." I giggled, thinking about all the things I wanted to lick off them and if Devin would let me. "Besides, don't you have your own set of abs?" I raised a brow, and her eyes widened.

"I have no idea what you're talking about."

"Oh, okay." I nodded with a smirk. "Guess all those rumors about you and Scotty from the hockey team are just that. Rumors, right?"

"I have no idea what you're talking about." She sank farther into her seat, her face flaming from embarrassment. Lyss gave me a knowing smile. I don't know what she was so smug about. We all knew she had some weird obsession with Aiden.

"Sure," I drawled. "Anyway, I'm going to head up to bed. I'm exhausted."

"I bet you are," Lyss teased.

I took the steps two at a time, racing to my room. When I got there, my head instinctively swung to the window, and I grinned. Devin was already there, leaning on the railing and waiting for me with just his T-shirt and boxers on. He bit his lip, taking me in as though I hadn't just spent the whole afternoon with him.

I met him at the window. "Hey, darlin'." His hand reached over the barrier to hold mine. "Where have you been?" His lip quirked as he waited for my answer.

I folded my arms, leaning across the railing, knowing full well I was giving Devin a great view of my cleavage. His gaze flicked down, and I heard a low rumble come from his chest. I looked up at the sky, acting innocent. "Oh, you know. I just went on a date with this really sweet and hot guy."

His head tilted, watching my every move. "Oh, yeah?" I nodded silently. "What'd you think?"

My hand trailed the top of the railing; I watched that instead of his reaction when I said, "I think the date was awesome, and I can't wait to see him again."

When I finally looked up, the heat behind his eyes was enough to melt my panties then and there. "I'm sure he's looking forward to taking you out again, too. In fact, I'm sure he'd love to show you just how much he enjoyed tonight."

I couldn't hide the smile now. He held his hand out to me as an invitation, and I took it without a second thought. That night, I stayed in his room, and we spent our night making out like teenagers. It was magical and everything I could ask for.

Twenty-Seven

Reign

I gasped out a breath; I could barely open my eyes or speak. "Right there." It was all I managed to whisper as Devin's hand held my stomach down. His other hand squeezed my thigh as he licked and nipped me in ways that were driving me insane. I only came upstairs to get my purse. I hadn't noticed Devin following me until he pushed me onto the bed, forcing me back to the mattress. With one quick flick, he'd lifted my dress up, pulled my panties to the side, and started feasting on me like I was his last meal.

He didn't answer me, just teased my opening with his thick finger. His mouth was all over me, making me cry out in frustration and pleasure. I needed more. His tongue lapped at my clit, and I pulled his hair, holding him in place as he hit all the right spots. If he moved, I was worried this would all be for nothing. He knew I was close; I was sure he could feel my body tense. Devin moaned into my center as two of his fingers entered me, filling me up while he ate me out. All it took was a few more strokes, and I was done for.

"Devin. I…I…" I couldn't hold back. My fingers dug into his scalp, and I scrunched my eyes shut as the wave of pleasure took over. It didn't stop him. Lick after lick sent me into a wave of pleasure as I climaxed against his fingers and mouth.

I wasn't sure if it was because it was unexpected, but it was so intense I could feel myself dripping.

What the hell just happened?

I had no time to be embarrassed or think it through because Devin pulled my panties over my soaked core and flipped my dress back into place. He glanced up, giving me a devilish smile as he propped himself on his elbow beside me, watching as I came down from my high. I couldn't focus on him; I was too busy regaining my composure. When I finally opened my eyes, he had this smug smile on his face. "Did you enjoy that?"

Before I could playfully slap him on the chest, he grabbed my hand, dragging me on top of him into his warm embrace. Not one to miss an opportunity, I snuggled down into his chest, loving how perfect it felt between us. "What do you think?" I asked sarcastically, nuzzling into his neck and fully prepared to return the favor. My hand hovered over his crotch, clutching at the rough fabric of his jeans. I could feel his growing hard-on, and it only made me want him more.

He chuckled, letting my hand linger there for a few more seconds while I massaged his dick into a semi-hard state. "Well, I'm guessing that's a yes." He checked his watch, lacing his hands with mine, and brought my attention to his face. "Now, come on. If we don't go in the next five minutes, we're going to be late." He jumped up, leaving just the warm sheets behind him as he walked over to my bathroom to wash his face and hands.

All I could do was gape at him with my hair mussed and panties a little wet from his adventures. "Why did you do that to me if you knew I couldn't take a shower?" I pouted, forcing myself up toward my drawers, desperately trying to pat down my sex hair. If I couldn't take a shower, the least I could do was change my panties.

Devin shrugged as he walked out of the bathroom, smelling minty fresh. I was glad I brought him that extra toothbrush since he practically lived in my room now. "It's payback for last night when we were watching the game, and you decided to brush your hand across my dick in front of the guys, knowing full well I couldn't do a damn thing about it." He pulled me into a hug and planted a gentle kiss on my forehead.

"You're acting like I didn't return the favor last night."

He smiled goofily, looking up at the sky. "Oh yeah, you've got a point. The things your tongue can do, make me lose sense."

"Ditto."

The last month had been a whirlwind; we'd been spending every free minute we had wrapped up in each other, knowing that we had a time limit on being this close together. It was perfect. Devin was everything I could have asked for in a boyfriend. I couldn't explain it, but we just fit.

"We've gotta go. We only get an hour with her, and I don't want to waste that time on the road." Devin took my hand, leading me out to his car. There was always an extra hop in his step on the days we went to visit his sister. Today was no different. It would be one of the visits he could do before the draft, so it wasn't a surprise he wanted to make it count. "In her last email, she mentioned she wants to talk to you about *The Bachelorette* choice. Something about the girl hooking up with Shawn in the ocean or something." He waved it off, acting as though he had no idea what Chloe was talking about. As though he didn't sit on my bed every Monday, eagerly waiting with wine and cheesy popcorn. Well, I should say the alcohol-free wine, because after my last attempt at seducing him, I switched.

"Sounds good. I also want to talk to her about a few bands she recommended."

Devin asked me if I wanted to meet Chloe a few days after making it official with him, and although it was a little daunting at first, I was happy that he'd introduced me to another part of his life. It was easy to see why he loved her so much. I didn't know her at her worst, but she seemed happy now and so full of life. Something Devin said he was worried he'd never see again. Her bright smile and light attitude made it hard not to be anything but happy around her.

When we arrived at the facility, the spongy grass clung to my shoes as we walked into the palatial gardens. Spring in California was gorgeous, with barely a hint of rain. "Chuck!" Devin yelled to his sister as she came bounding out into the yard. The clouds were clear, with the bright blue sky bearing down on us. Devin placed the wooden picnic basket on the ground as Chloe leaped into his arms, her smile emanating from ear to ear. You wouldn't think these two saw each other just a few days ago.

"I missed you, D." She trembled, and her hazel eyes watered as she took him in. As they smiled at each other, I couldn't believe I ever thought they were anything but siblings. They were almost identical, save for the hair color.

"Reign!" she exclaimed as though she had just noticed I was by Devin's side. She jumped out of her brother's embrace and hugged me tightly as I held the checkered blanket. "We have so much to talk about."

"That we do."

Sitting in the sun, having a picnic, we let Chloe talk about *The Bachelorette* and what a bad choice Claire was. We discussed in detail who would have been a better choice, with Devin occasionally chiming in to ask a question, which I already knew he knew the answer to. He just wanted to be part of the conversation. I found it hard to believe that Chloe was anything but a vivacious young girl with a healthy appetite for trash TV when she talked. There was no darkness that Devin spoke of before, and I could tell the change in her wasn't just because of the program she was in, but because she loved her big brother and she wanted to make him proud. He was sacrificing a lot for her, and she knew it.

With his sunglasses on, Devin was lying on his side with one leg over the other, and he popped a strawberry in his mouth. He was listening to Chloe talk about last night's episode as though he wasn't watching it with me last night. It was so nice to see him so relaxed and carefree. He'd mellowed out so much in the last month. Heck, Adam even told me he laughed at some stupid prank Aiden pulled on him the other day. I knew it was because things were coming together for him. His mom was happier, his place in the draft was more secure, but there was a teeny tiny part of me that hoped his happiness had a little something to do with me since he held such a big part in mine.

"I can't wait to watch you in the draft!" Chloe squealed. "I've told everyone here about it. We're going to have a watch party."

"I can't either, Chlo." He laughed, but I could hear a hint of hesitancy there. He was nervous about leaving her behind, knowing it would be at least a month before he'd be able to come back. He was also nervous about leaving Covey U without a degree. His eyes flicked to me, then back down to his hands. I'd also like to think he was nervous about leaving me, too. I knew I was. He'd become such an integral part of my life that I was worried about how I'd cope without him. He sat up with an air of seriousness. "Are you going to be okay with not seeing me until I can get you transferred to a facility closer to my new home?"

Her eyes flitted from me to Devin, finally choosing to rest them on him. "I really like it here, Dev. I've got friends now, and I feel better. I feel like this program is working. I'm afraid it won't be the same in a new place. I don't want to move and have to start over." She spoke quickly, trying to get it out before Devin could interrupt.

His smile fell, morphing into something like a frown. I knew he and his mom had talked about this before. Neither one of them wanted to dilute her progress, and the facility had also recommended she stay for at least another two months. He squeezed her knee. "But you'll be here on your own, Chlo. Mom and I will be in Texas until I move. That's hours away from here. Wouldn't you rather be closer to one of us in case something happens?"

She threw her hand in the air. "I'm nearly eighteen, D. Soon, I won't need parental permission to discharge myself," she said with a glint in her eye, and I could see the terror in Devin's eyes. She just smiled, pushing him on the shoulder. "Plus, Reign's here. I'll be fine." She pointed to me, and Devin's head shot up straight in shock. "She's like family now." Her voice was relaxed, and her smile was eager for me to reciprocate. I wrapped my arms around her, silently hugging her close. It'd only been a month, but I'd grown just as attached to her. Something I wouldn't admit to Devin in fear of freaking him out.

"You'll be there if I need something, won't you?" she asked.

"Of course," I replied without thinking, because I already knew I would. She and her brother were the closest thing I'd felt to a family in a long time, and I liked the idea of being relied on again. Her grin grew wider, and she hugged me tightly.

"See, Dev, it's all going to work out," she cooed. "You've got nothing to worry about." I glanced over at Devin, who was stuffing his hands in his pocket, looking hesitant.

"My sister and my girlfriend are in cahoots. Yeah, I've got nothing to worry about," he mumbled before sinking his teeth into another strawberry.

"Sorry about that whole thing with Chloe," Devin said, kicking some dust as we stood by his car. He was quiet the whole way back to college, deep in thought. I didn't bother to question it because I figured he would tell me what was upsetting him when he was ready. "You're the first girlfriend of mine she's ever met, and I think she's a little infatuated with you." He scratched the back of his head, a look of unease etched across his face.

I tilted my head, studying the gorgeous man before me as he stuffed his hands in his pocket and rocked from side to side, looking more like an awkward teenager than the soon-to-be pro-NFL player. "You didn't have a high school girlfriend?"

He gave me an easy smile. "I mean, there were girls," he choked out. "None that I would ever bring home to my mom or sister." He shrugged it off like what he said was no big deal, like bringing me into his life was nothing. I knew better than that, though.

I hid my grin. "You know, D, I'm more than happy to be put down as an emergency contact for Chloe if that would make you feel better while you're setting up in your new town." The words hurt to say because, in reality, we didn't know where that new town would be or what the future would look like in a few weeks, but I was doing my best to live in the present.

He shook his head vehemently. "No. I couldn't ask you to do that. This is my responsibility. I couldn't put you in that position." His eyes darted from side to side; I knew him well enough to know he was trying to think of a solution for Chloe, to make her happy while keeping himself calm, too.

I moved to stand in front of him, holding his shoulder and begging him to look at me instead of keeping it all to himself. His eyes met mine, and I could feel his shoulders relax as his smile eased. "Why don't you let me take some of the burden off your shoulders? It's not like I would be the sole emergency contact, and it means you won't have to rush over if something happens."

It made sense; he knew it did, but there was still the question of what would happen to us once he was gone. I knew that was playing on his mind because it'd been playing on mine, too. It was like a terrible movie on repeat in my brain. I didn't want to watch it, but it was the only thing on. "I just couldn't ask you to do that," he spurted out.

My smile softened. "You didn't ask, I offered. It's not like I would go over there all the time; I'm just here if she needs anything. Your sister is a sweet girl. She wants to stay here, and it's not like I'm going anywhere for the time being. I'm happy to help," I stressed, and when Devin didn't answer, I continued. "If something major happens and you aren't around, I could always get Adam to come and help me. Chloe mentioned they hit it off when she met him." I smiled, knowing that would rile him up.

He grumbled, looking back at me and forcing me into a hug. "Will you stop trying to make Adam and Chloe a thing? I have enough things to worry about. My best friend getting with my sister will not be one of them."

I waved off his concern, waggling my eyebrows. "You've got nothing to worry about. I've got plans for him and Britt."

"Britt?" The name sounded familiar, but I still couldn't place her.

"Matty's friend. Hot, blonde girl."

"The only hot blonde I know wears this Playboy bunny costume at night. Sometimes she even lets me handcuff her to the bedpost." He smiled into my hair as he planted a small kiss on my forehead. I just rolled my eyes.

"I do know there are other people on this campus, you know? You don't have to pretend you don't see them."

"Oh, but darlin', I don't because all I see is you." I smacked him on the chest but rested my cheek against it no less. "You know you're perfect, right?" he whispered, as though he didn't want me to hear it.

"And you know you don't have to do everything yourself, right? Just because you're a big, burly man doesn't mean you can take everything on."

He smirked. "Big, burly man?"

"Yeah? What's so funny?"

"Nothing." He chuckled, shaking his head. "Will you let me think about the emergency contact thing? I'm already having heart palpitations, wondering what my sister and girlfriend will talk about while I'm away. The idea that she can call you in at any moment might give me a heart attack before I even step onto the field." He seemingly chose to forget that she already had my number and messaged me on the regular in that moment.

His hand threaded through my hair, tipping my face up and leading me to him. He kissed me so hard I could feel the passion behind it in my toes. "Just think about it, okay?" I husked out as his lips parted mine.

"I will."

"Now, will you come upstairs with me and let me show you just how much I'm going to miss you?"

"Sure."

TWENTY-EIGHT
Devin

"Good luck, man." Adam clasped my shoulder, throwing one arm around me in a hug. I mumbled out a thank you because my nerves were shot, trying to hold it all together. This was my last day as a Covey U student. Tomorrow, hopefully, someone would pick me in the draft, and I'd officially be an NFL player. Hopefully, being the keyword there. "We'll be watching from here." Adam gestured back to half of the team sitting on our sofa. Well, Aiden's sofa now. I'd officially moved out. All my boxes, not that I had many, were sitting in Reign's room waiting to be shipped to my new home, wherever that may be. If I were lucky, maybe Reign would ship herself along with the boxes. She'd already agreed to spend the summer with me. Why not start early?

As I looked across the room, all of my friends smiled encouragingly. They were going to go on and do great things with the team; I just knew it. I couldn't help but let my mind drift, wondering which one of these guys would make it to the NFL. They were all sitting there, excitedly lounging on the sofa as if the draft was airing tonight. My only assumption was they were pre-gaming for the next twenty-four hours since it was like Christmas for them.

"You're gonna kill it," Jackson hollered from the sofa, lifting his beer toward me.

There were only four of us from Covey U entering the draft this year with a real prospect of making it. It was wild seeing my face on ESPN the other day. They spoke about me for all of five seconds, but that didn't matter. What mattered was they talked about *me*, and there was a very real chance I'd get drafted. The pressure was on my shoulders now. Since we won the championship game, Covey wanted to compete with the likes of St. Michaels and Clayton University for quality high school players to try to win the whole thing. If they wanted that prestigious image, they'd need to show a good production of elite players making it in the draft. With me entering this year, Adam next, and potentially Aiden the year after, they'd have set a solid example of what they could do, but they would need to keep it up.

"Thanks, guys," I shouted across the room and shucked the bag, my last possession in this house, over my shoulder. Turning back to Adam, I rested my hand on his shoulder, mimicking his move. Despite all the confusion that happened this year, he really was one of my best friends, and I would miss him. I tilted my head toward the door. "I should get going. Reign's already waiting in the car for me."

A silent acknowledgment passed between us. After he found out about Reign and me, he demanded the full story from the beginning, then proceeded to whack me on her head for being an idiot and not telling him in the first place. Bros before hoes and all that crap. Not that I would call Reign a hoe. Not in this lifetime. Love of my life was more like it.

"Does Reign need someone to warm her bed now that you're not around?" Aiden asked, clearly ignoring said bro code. "Maybe I should leave your room vacant and make it our own little sex room."

The whole team groaned. "Shut up, dude," Matty said as one of the new recruits, Tanner, expertly threw a pillow and hit Aiden in the head. "That room's already taken."

Aiden dragged his gaze lazily to Tanner with a small snarl. Aiden knew his position was in trouble. Tanner was a phenom in high school, and he was getting better and better each day. There was a very real possibility that he could take his starting quarterback position if he wasn't careful.

I shook my head, feeling a pang of sadness in my chest. As annoying as living in a house full of jocks had been, I was going to miss them. Nothing in my life would be like this again, and it was bittersweet cutting it short, but I had to do what was right for me. For my family. Even if it meant I didn't even get a degree to show for it.

Adam leaned in, laughing. "Don't worry, D. Aiden won't get anywhere near Reign. I'll protect her from that idiot."

I snorted in response. "Who's going to protect her from you?" I knew Adam wasn't interested in Reign anymore, but I still liked to rib him about it. From what Reign had been telling me, I had little to worry about with Adam anyway, considering he was still in love with that chick back home.

I said one final goodbye and got a round of hugs from the guys. When I shut the door, listening to the laughter inside, I let the sadness of it being over wash over me for just a second. Then I took a deep breath and walked toward my future. To the girl sitting in my car, singing along to some song while she waited for me and my new career, playing the game I love.

She was almost too busy jamming to the new band Chloe recommended to notice me open the car door. As I relaxed down into the seat next to her and clutched the leather of the steering wheel, she smiled, squeezing my thigh reassuringly. "Are you ready for this?" she asked. What a question.

Was I ready for the draft? *Yes.*

Was I ready to leave her behind? *Never.*

Instead of answering, I kissed her hard on the lips, hoping it showed her just how much she meant to me. "Let's get going. It's a nine-hour drive to Vegas with no stops, and I want to be able to shower before we see my mom for dinner," I whispered into her lips. We could have taken a flight, but since I didn't know when I'd be able to see her after this, I wanted to spend as much time with her alone as possible.

She reached up, clasping one hand in mine. "I hope your mom likes me," she said nervously, playing with the hem of her shirt.

I lifted her hand to my mouth, planting soft kisses across her knuckles. "I have no doubt she'll love you."

Because I already do.

She giggled as I put the car in drive, and we started the epic journey. But I was content and happy because there was no one else I wanted to take this journey with other than her.

The clinking of glasses and the loud chatter filled the large hall. All the drafted players were still here, celebrating with their new teams. "We're lucky to have you, Devin. I thought for sure the Texas Cavaliers would have taken you as their first-round pick," the general manager for the Charlotte Crossbills, Larry Hilt, said as he shook my hand.

Yes, you heard that correctly. *First round.* I was picked in the first round. It was something I wasn't expecting, and I still hadn't fully comprehended it. Admittedly, since the Crossbills made it to the conference championship, their pick was low in the first round, but I didn't care. First round pick was a FIRST ROUND PICK.

"Thank you. I'm beyond excited to be playing for you next year," I said, still in disbelief that this was happening.

Forty-eight hours ago, I left college, introduced my girlfriend to my mom, and I was just drafted by an NFL team. When we got back to the hotel room tonight, I was going to need to crash with Reign, hopefully on top of me. Naked.

Larry nodded back. "Don't thank me. Your performance at the Combine was impressive. We needed to improve our defense, and you'll be able to compliment Jacob Miller's offense." Another plus about being drafted there. Since Jacob Miller became their franchise quarterback a few years back, they've been building a team around him. Now he's leading a strong offense, they need a leader for their defense, and I hoped that was me. Larry glanced at another player. "Now, if you excuse me, I've got to go speak to Declan over there." He slapped me on the shoulder. "Looking forward to seeing you at training in July."

I said my goodbyes and adjusted the lapels on my suit. I had to buy one that was two sizes too big to fit my arms and couldn't afford to get it tailored. None of that mattered now, though, because if I wanted to, I could afford to buy another ten of these suits and get them all tailored to my exact measurements. Getting drafted in the first round meant I'd have more than enough money to pay for a house and Chloe's treatment. She could even stay in California if she wanted because I'd be able to fly out whenever I had a free weekend, which I would be doing anyway to see Reign.

As if my mouth couldn't get any wider, it did when I saw Reign standing next to my mom, smiling as they made small talk with other players and their family members. They were so comfortable in each other's presence already. No one would know they just met yesterday. My mom immediately loved her; I could tell just by the way she looked at her. And also the fact she kept talking about how cute her grandbabies would be. Way to be chill, Ma. I wasn't mad, though; who wouldn't fall for her? She was strong, determined, and compassionate. I could continue, but there was a real possibility I wouldn't stop. And besides, she was right. Our children would be gorgeous if they took after her mother.

They still hadn't noticed me yet, too engrossed in their conversation with one of the other players' moms to be looking at me. I got a tight feeling in my stomach just watching her. I loved her. The minute she met Chloe, I knew my feelings were stronger than just a mild obsession. She was my missing piece.

I was too busy staring at Reign to notice my mom had already excused herself from the conversation. "Devin. I'm so proud of you." She wrapped her arms around me, hugging me tightly. When she pulled away, her eyes were glossy; she was on the brink of tears, brimming with pride. She started crying when they announced the first overall draft pick and hadn't stopped since. I should add that she didn't know the guy who got drafted first. I thought it was because watching the other parents cry got her going. I was worried she was going to faint when they called my name and whisked me off on some boat to the stage in the middle of the venue. It was indulgent and insane, but I loved every minute.

"Thanks, Mom," I said, too overcome with emotion to say anything else. I'd finally freed our family from debt. From that town. And hopefully, from alcohol abuse.

"I don't know anyone more deserving than you," she continued. "You've always been so selfless, taking care of your sister and me when your father left. You deserve this and everything good that comes your way. Don't forget it."

I rolled my eyes. "Alright, Mom. Don't get too gushy on me."

I couldn't help but look back at Reign. She was wearing a black velvety cocktail dress which hugged her in all the right places. She was gorgeous and all mine.

My mom must have followed my gaze because she said, "You need to do whatever you can to keep Reign. That girl is special." She winked. The ease and happiness of her demeanor was something I hadn't seen since before my dad left. When we thought things were good and right.

"Don't I know it." I looked back at my mom, my eyes dazed and heady, cloudy from the excitement and celebrations of today.

"Chloe told me a lot about her. She was so glowing about her that I thought she was exaggerating to make sure I didn't give her a rough time. She wasn't. Reign is so sweet, and the way she looks at you with such care and admiration." Her hand was on her chest, beating it gently. She paused, blinking quickly, ridding herself of any errant tears. "You're perfect for each other."

"Thanks, Ma."

I could only hope she was right.

My gaze flicked up automatically, looking for Reign again. She smiled when I spotted her staring at me, hanging back to give me some time with my mom. It was the first time I could get back to them since my draft place was announced because I had to speak to the owner, do an interview, and take a few pictures with the other players drafted to the Crossbills. I nodded my head to her, silently asking for her to come over. She smiled, politely excusing herself, and made her way toward me. I unabashedly watched her thighs as her dress snuck up as she walked. That black velvet was all too reminiscent of that bunny outfit she wore a couple of months ago. And the other night when I begged to see it again. She told me I would get an extra special surprise if I got picked in the first round. My mind raced, wondering what she meant by that. I wondered if she'd let me choose.

"Congratulations, D," Reign said, wrapping her arms around me. I dropped my hands to her waist, holding her against me. I had no idea she was everything I needed until I got her, and now that I have her, I wasn't planning on letting her go. She softly kissed my neck, just below my earlobe, and then pulled back, linking her arm around my waist. Nothing could prepare me for how complete I felt with her by my side.

The click of the door shutting was enough to push me into action. I'd been waiting all day for this. Reign was still holding the doorknob when I turned her in my arms, gruffly grabbing her by the thighs and forcing her to wrap her legs around me. I swallowed her gasp with a dirty kiss full of want and need, letting her feel the hardness in my slacks. She had to know she made me feel like a starved animal by now.

I rocked myself against her body as I frantically kissed her, nipping her lips at every opportunity, swallowing her moans with my tongue. I knew she liked the feeling because she scratched her nails against the back of my shirt hard enough for it to hurt. The harder my hips jerked into her, the higher her dress rose, revealing her smooth, milky thighs. I will never stop wanting her. Needing her. Her head tilted back, knocking against the door as I trailed kisses down her neck and worked my way back up. When I reached her ear, I nipped her lobe and did something that I knew would change everything forever between us.

"I love you, Reign." I had to say it. I'd wanted to say it for so long, and I couldn't think of a better day to remind her of that. I was all in.

She paused. Even in her lust-filled haze, she heard that. She pushed me gently off her so she could look into my eyes. Her legs stayed wrapped around me as her eyebrows piqued. She didn't say anything for the longest time. She just stared at me in disbelief.

"I love you," I said again, more confidently in case she didn't hear it the first time, enjoying the way it sounded rolling off my tongue.

It was like I was frozen in time for a second. She didn't move, didn't speak, didn't acknowledge anything. There was no way she didn't feel the same way. The fact that she was here with me right now and offered to be my sister's emergency contact said more than the words themselves, but I couldn't deny that standing here waiting for her to react was a little awkward. My fingers relaxed against her thighs, not sure what to do. Do I keep kissing her, pretending I didn't just drop a bomb on the mood, or do I back off, giving her time to think?

Her head dropped to my shoulder, and I could feel her eyelashes fluttering against my skin as she muffled something out. I couldn't hear it, though. "What did you say?" I whispered.

It took her a minute to raise her head, lowering her forehead onto mine. Her eyes were closed, and I still had no idea what she was actually thinking. The longer time went on, the more I was growing concerned that I had upset her. Her lips parted. "I said no one except my family has ever said that to me." Her eyes were still closed, and I guessed that meant she'd never said it to anyone else either.

"Is that a bad thing?" I asked with a lilt in my voice, hoping it would lighten the mood.

She shook her head, her chocolate hair swaying against my cheeks with the movement. "No. it's just I never thought I'd hear it again." A small smile played across her lips, and my fingers tightened around her, holding her in place.

"I love you with all my heart, Reign," I reiterated, and her smile broadened. "You are everything I have ever wanted. I love you." I kept saying it as I peppered kisses across her face. This girl deserved to be loved, and I was the lucky guy who would show it to her. She giggled as the kisses got sloppier. She finally pushed me off when she'd had enough.

"Devin." She opened her eyes, staring into mine. "I've never felt this way about anyone but you. Thank you for showing me what true love means. I love you too." I crashed my lips against hers, hoping she could feel the love I had for her through it. I poured everything into that kiss. All my intentions and wants for the future were in it.

She squealed as I carried her over to the bed, depositing her onto the silky white sheets. "I love you, Reign," I husked out one more time as my hands ventured up her skirt. "I always will."

Her back arched as her hands gripped my shoulders, forcing me to relax back on my heels. "I love you too, D." Her eyes were hazy with need, and she gripped at my belt with a sexy ass grin. "Now, will you let me show you what you get for being drafted in the first round?" I leaned back onto the headboard of the bed, watching as she removed my pants and climbed on top of me with a playful glint in her eyes.

"Bring it on, darlin'."

EPILOGUE
Reign

Two years later

"Are you nearly ready, darlin'?" Devin called from downstairs.

I took one final look at my dress in the mirror and patted down the red sequins. With a slit all the way to the top of my thigh, I knew Devin would freak out when he saw me in this, and I was excited to see his reaction.

"Reign, are you going to make me come up there?" he threatened. "Because you know if I do, that we won't be leaving anytime soon."

"I'll be right there," I replied, grabbing a matching red satin purse and making my way down the stairs in my brand-new heels slowly. My feet clicked with each step, drawing Devin's attention to me. As I looked up, he took a sharp breath, and his smile made me falter.

As my heel slipped, he rushed over to me, holding me up. "Are you trying to give me a heart attack, darlin'?" With his hands resting on my hips, his gaze cut to my dress, then to me.

Placing my hands above his, I said, "I could ask you the same."

His impeccably tailored Armani suit fit him perfectly, emphasizing his wide shoulders and narrow waist. Whether he was in a suit, uniform, or sweats, I always loved the way he looked.

He let my hands roam his chest until I grasped his tie, smirking. "How did you know I was going to wear red?" I asked as I played with the fabric by threading it through my fingers.

A slow smirk grew on his face. "Would you believe me if I said I guessed?" I shook my head, pouting my lips. "I may have peeked."

Using his tie to bring him to me, I planted a quick kiss on his lips. "Good to know that you go snooping." He kissed me again, but this time he wanted to deepen it. I pushed back, all too aware that my bright red lipstick might not be a good look smeared across his face before dinner. After dinner, all bets were off on where my lipstick would end up. "Remind me to hide your presents at your mom's for Christmas. I didn't realize I was living with a child," I teased.

He shrugged. "You should probably just keep them out of our closet. I go in there a lot."

"Our closet."

"Yes. Our closet. I'm sorry this place didn't come with two, and I'd more than happily convert the small bedroom next door to one for you, but." He paused, his gaze flicking from my lips to my eyes.

"But?" I drawled out.

"But I might have some other plans for that room."

I rolled my eyes and dropped his tie. "Please don't tell me you're going to make that into a gaming room?"

"We'll see. Until then, you've got at least three-quarters of our closet anyway, so that should surely be enough room for now. You only had two tiny suitcases of stuff when you moved in here."

I smiled, remembering the day he wheeled them in for me. It'd been six months, but I still smiled when he said *our* closet. It was *our* closet, in *our* house, as we started *our* lives together. I moved in the day after I graduated, and I didn't look back. Building a home with Devin was the only decision for me. He'd bought the place for us, and it was the first time since my parents passed that I'd lived somewhere that felt like home. To be honest, Devin could have bought us a tiny shack instead of this palatial mansion and I'd be just as happy because it's him I want to be with. He had this innate ability to make me feel happy, settled, and safe just by being in the room. I realized that when I spent the summer with him after he was drafted. He was the only person I wanted to be with.

There was a point when I nearly cracked and transferred halfway through my senior year to Charlotte U just so I could be closer to Devin, but he convinced me to stay. To ride out the end of my college experience, at least for his sake, because he didn't get to do it either.

Not that leaving for the NFL was a wasted opportunity for Devin. He was now considered one of the best defensive linemen in the league. The Crossbills got to the conference championship for the last two years in a row. Next year, they were hoping for Super Bowl success, and I was sure they'd get it. They worked so hard; it felt like there was no other option.

Devin leaned his forehead against mine, pecking me gently on the lips this time and lacing his fingers through mine. "Are you ready?" he whispered, even though we were the only two people in the house.

"Of course I am, handsome."

He chuckled as he brought me to his side as he led me out to the front porch. Devin's car and driver, Flynn, were waiting for us at the bottom of the driveway. After greeting him, Devin ushered me into the car, insistent that we get going because we needed to be somewhere at a specific time. I stopped asking where he was taking me on dates a long time ago, preferring the surprise and also knowing he wouldn't tell me anyway.

When Flynn informed us we'd arrived, Devin kissed my hand and gazed into my eyes. "I just wanted to let you know I've been planning this date since the day I was drafted two years ago." A slow smirk grew on his face, and he gave my hand another kiss, sending sparks of electricity through my arm. "Just remember that."

I nodded with a smile, letting him help me out of the car, and that was when I registered where we were. There was a helicopter just in front, with its pilot standing outside. My mouth gaped open in shock.

"Are we going in that?" When Devin opened the door, I could barely hear him with all the people around, so he nodded. As he helped me out of the car, he stuck me on his side again.

Kissing the skin right next to my ear, he said, "You weren't expecting this?"

I looked down at my long evening gown. "I'm not dressed for this."

He smiled, following my gaze. "Yes, you are. Come on." He opened his hand out to me, and I immediately took it, trusting him. Devin led me to the helicopter, helping me into my seat, adjusting my dress so I was comfortable, and fixing the earphones over my head so it didn't affect my curled hair. He gave me the once-over, biting his bottom lip. "You look hot tonight, darlin'."

I swatted his chest away, letting him have a chat with the pilot before sitting next to me. Like always, his hand instinctively searched for mine, a habit he picked up shortly after we officially started dating.

The doors slammed shut, and my heart started beating faster when the blades moved. Devin squeezed my hand, leaning closer. "I'm scared," I said through the mic.

His smile warmed my soul as his thumb rubbed my palm. "What have you got to be scared about, darlin'? I'm right here." In that instant, the chopper took flight, and I squealed. "Remember when we went rollerblading on our first date?"

I nodded.

"You told me to keep my head up and watch you. You do the same right now. Keep your eyes on me."

I did as he said. The green and gold of his eyes glistened under the flickering lights surrounding us. I got so lost in just looking at the man I loved; I hardly noticed we'd made it out of takeoff and were flying smoothly in the sky.

"Do you trust me?"

"With my life."

His grin grew wide at my remark. "Great. Then look down." When I turned my body, Devin joined me, leaning his back against mine so he could look out my window. Down below were the twinkling lights of the city of Charlotte.

"It's so beautiful," I said.

"Yeah, it is." I looked back at Devin, and he wasn't looking at the city. He was looking at me. His hand was on my thigh, his thumb rubbing against my skin, and I knew that glare well. I knew what he was thinking, and I wanted to do that too. My body grew hot as I placed my hand on his, giving it a squeeze with a promise.

With his other hand, he pointed out my window, drawing my attention to the city again. "Look, you can see the baseball stadium from here." He pointed down, and the bright lights glared into the reflection.

The Carolina Catfish's stadium was just next door to the Crossbills, with the stadium light illuminating them both. I could see the baseball players running around the field and I smiled.

"They look so tiny from here."

I rested my hand against the glass and noticed the Crossbills stadium. "Why are the lights on at your stadium?"

He didn't answer. He just smirked, and I knew he was up to something. Just then, the helicopter started to descend, and my stomach rolled. Devin placed his hand over mine, concern marring his perfect features. "Are you okay?"

"I'm fine," I said, focusing on not throwing up. What a way to ruin a wonderful evening. Clutching his hand tighter, I closed my eyes until I felt the ground below us and the blades slowed.

"We're here, darlin'." His deep, melodic voice penetrated through my worries, and when I opened my eyes, I was surprised to see we'd landed on the Crossbills stadium helipad. I was surprised that it even had a helipad.

Devin gently removed my ear protectors, his eyes tracking my expression. "Are you sure you're okay?" I pursed my lips and nodded. He gave me a small smile before stepping out of the helicopter and then offered his hand to me.

Leading me off the helicopter, he kept hold of me until we ended up in a private room overlooking the stadium below. The bright lights illuminated an empty field, emphasizing the perfectly green turf and sharp white lines.

My breath caught when I saw the table with a single rose sitting on it. I couldn't help but smile when I asked, "Have you based this date on *The Bachelor?*"

"Will you do that thing with your tongue again if I say yes?"

I rolled my eyes, pushing him slightly, but he didn't move. I wasn't exactly threatening when compared to his teammates. When I narrowed my eyes at him, he chuckled.

"After two years of watching that show with you, I figured I couldn't go wrong. I may have also gotten Chloe's input."

"When did she have time?"

Attending Charlotte U and waitressing in her extra hours didn't leave her a lot of time to socialize, but I think that was how she liked it. She and her mom made the move to Charlotte a year and a half ago when she finished her treatment. It was definitely the best move for her, and the family only solidified when Devin signed a new five-year contract with the Crossbills.

Devin pulled back my chair, and as I sat down, I noticed he had a light sheen of sweat across his forehead. Was he nervous that this wouldn't live up to my *Bachelor* fantasies? "This is perfect, D," I said, and he offered me a half-smile as his gaze twitched around the room, ignoring the single rose sitting between us.

The door creaked open, and in came the waitstaff with towers of food for the two of us. "Thank goodness I couldn't eat all day." I laughed as a large chicken meal was placed in front of me.

"What about your lunch break?"

I raised my brows. "I didn't have one. There was an emergency at the hospital that we all needed to attend to."

"Me either," Devin muttered. His voice was uneven, and he ran a shaky hand through his hair.

"Everything okay, D?" I asked, stuffing a mini meatball in my mouth.

His lips pursed for a moment before he said, "Everything's fine. Have you tried the mac n' cheese? It's delicious."

We didn't speak much through the rest of the dinner, not that I didn't try. Devin answered my questions in grunts and groans because he was piling the food in his mouth like he was a man starved. I couldn't blame him; the food was delicious.

As I ate the final chocolate strawberry on my plate, Devin twiddled with the rose in his hand, glancing at me and then back down to the rose. "I've watched enough episodes of that show now to know how important the final rose is," he said, his voice still having a shaky hesitancy to it.

"It's not really that important. I swear most of the couples are broken up before the airing of *After the Final Rose.*" I chuckled, fully expecting to see him laughing with me. He wasn't. His shoulders dropped, and he adjusted his jaw. Looked like I had the wrong strategy. "Good thing we've already lasted longer than that, huh?"

"Reign, did I ever tell you how much I liked you before I even met you?"

I nodded. "Yes. Several times a day, babe." I ended with a giggle.

He wasn't deterred by my joking; he was going to get whatever he wanted to say out. "Good. Then I'm doing my job as your boyfriend, right? I'm telling you how much you mean to me every day."

"That you are."

"When I met you, it was like the first time I threw a ball on the football field and the first time I sacked a guy all at once."

"How romantic."

He waved off my sarcasm. "Let me finish. When those two things happened, I knew that was what I was supposed to be doing, where my life would take me. So, I focused everything I could to get that goal, and here we are," he said, gesturing around the football stadium in front of us. "When I met you, I had that same feeling. You were who I was supposed to be with, who I *wanted* to be with. You were where my life was taking me, and I knew that. Even through those tough days while you were still completing your last year of college and I was in my first year of the NFL, we made it work." His smile and confidence grew with his speech. He plucked the rose from the table, twirling it in his hands.

I wanted to say something. To tell him how much he meant to me, how he gave me a home when I never thought I'd find one again. How he was the only man I'd ever truly loved, but I didn't get that far because he grabbed my hand. "Even through my toughest defeats and my worst moments, you've been there to offer me a smile and make it better. Life won't always be roses." I looked down at the rose in hand as he offered it to me. "Even though roses are all you deserve." I took it from him, giving it a sniff, and smiled. "And when the times aren't so good, I promise I'll at least get you sunflowers in the hopes they brighten up your day as much as your smile brightens mine."

When his chair dragged across the floor and he got up, I watched him, assuming he was coming over to kiss me and tell me he loved me again. He did neither. He kneeled on one knee and pulled a black velvety box from his pocket. "Will you do me the honor of making me smile for the rest of my life?" When he opened the box, a giant diamond ring was winking back at me.

It was like the world stopped for a moment, and I couldn't breathe. When I didn't speak, his voice brought me back to the room. "Reign?" he asked, not bothering to hide the shakiness in his voice now.

I shook my head. "I'm sorry."

His hand dropped, along with his shoulders and head. "I get it. I'm sorry. It's all too soon." *Crap*. He thought I was rejecting his proposal.

The screech of my chair surprised him as I dropped to my knees, cupping his cheeks in my hands. "Devin, I was saying sorry for taking too long to answer. Nothing would bring me more happiness than being your wife," I whispered, mainly because I could barely speak after such a wonderful proposal.

His smile grew wider than I'd ever seen it, and without warning, he scooped me up in his arms and kissed me with fiery passion. I felt his hand lift but didn't let his lips leave mine. I didn't bother seeing why he was lifting his hand because I was kissing my fiancée, and that was all I wanted to do.

The moment was too perfect.

BANG! BANG! BANG!

I pulled away from Devin and looked out the window to see what the noise was. Down below, the entire marching band had filled the field and were playing music. Then, all of a sudden, fireworks painted the sky in beautiful golds, greens, and reds.

"Oh, Devin. Did you do this?"

"Yeah. Although there is a possibility that the Catfish just scored a homer. Fireworks come out for that too." He smiled smugly, squeezing me again. "How did I do?"

"On what? The proposal?" He nodded. "I couldn't ask for anything more.

"Screw you, Bachelor Shawn. I just one-upped you," Devin mumbled as he brought me in for another kiss.

"You're so competitive, D," I joked against his lips.

Pulling away from me, he took his ring and placed it around my finger, where it would stay for the rest of my life.

"And I've just won the best prize of them all," he said with a satisfied smirk before leaning down and placing another kiss on my lips as we let the music play behind us.

We stayed like that for the rest of the night, neither one of us ready to move, but both so excited for the rest of our lives. After my parents' deaths, I never thought I'd be the girl to find a happy ending, but looking into my fiancée's eyes now, I'm so happy I found it with him.

THE END

Other Titles by Ana Shay

Covey U Series

Swipe Me (Devin's Book)

Miss Me (Adam's Book)

Hate Me (Aiden's Book)

Teach Me (Tanner's Story)

Carolina Catfish Series

The Mascot (Tate's Story)

The Balk (Grayson's Story)

The Rookie (Austin's Story)

Standalones

The Quarterback Sneak (Zach's Story)

A Quarterback For Christmas (Drew's Story)

Before you leave, here's a sample of Adam's story, the next book in series.

Prologue

Adam

4 years ago

Senior Prom

"Hayden?" I whispered under my breath as I walked out of the hotel. The chilly night air hit me as my eyes darted in every direction, looking for her.

I was always looking for her.

Stuffing my hands in my pockets, I glanced around, hoping to see the glint of her crown or the flicker of her dress billowing in the wind because I was desperate for any hint of her whereabouts. God, this was pathetic. I was so attuned to her every move, and yet she didn't even notice me. But I couldn't help myself; the minute I saw her smile falter, I knew she was going to bolt, and I just had to be the one to comfort her. She was my puppet master, and I was hanging by the strings waiting for her to finally cut me loose.

I adjusted the lapels of my tux as the cold air slipped through my jacket; the champagne-themed boutonniere caught my attention. *Ivy.* My stomach lurched. I left my gorgeous date and on-again-off-again girlfriend in the middle of the dance floor, clutching her arms tightly and watching me go. Without a word, I walked out on her because I was too tied up with another girl. It wasn't like she didn't know the deal or that we hadn't talked about Hayden extensively, but that didn't make me feel any better about ditching her.

As I walked around to the back of the hotel, there was still no sign of Hayden. I waved at my friends as I passed. Thankfully, they were too caught up in their own drama to notice mine. The less people that knew about this, the better. As I turned the corner, the lights were dimmer, the road was quieter, and there was nothing to suggest that a senior prom was currently in full flow inside.

That was when I noticed something shimmering against the streetlights. *Hayden.* I knew it. I could feel her in my bones. She was perched on a ledge by the street, and I could just about make out her silk spun golden hair cascading down her back and the memories of how beautiful she looked when she walked up to accept her crown. My breath caught, and everyone else in the hall disappeared because even though she may have been their Prom Queen, she was the Queen of my Heart without even trying.

To say I had it bad would be an understatement.

I stopped as I watched her shoulders shake and heard her soft sobs. My chest tightened at her tears. She was upset. I already knew that much when I saw her run out of the banquet hall. Why she let herself get used by that idiot, I'd never know. *Didn't she know how perfect she was? Didn't she see that there was a guy waiting to treat her like the queen she was?* My feet moved without my mind's consent. I shouldn't have come out here. Ivy's inside waiting for me, and Hayden had made it clear countless times how she felt. She wasn't interested. I was her *friend.* That was it. But something about her always drew me back in. It didn't matter how many times I got stung; I'd keep going back until I died of anaphylactic shock if it meant she'd notice me.

Her quiet sobs echoed across the dark night; the only light came from the twinkling stars above and the reflection of her dress. The blue tulle reminded me so much of Cinderella when she ran out of the ball like her life depended on it. Albeit, Hayden's exit was a little less dramatic because she would die if anyone saw her as the less than perfect girl she portrayed in class. The one that Jared trained her to be, so she was good enough to hang out with him.

As her sobs grew louder. She needed saving, and the only person who was going to save her this time was me. The Knight on the sidelines, not her apparent Prince Charming - AKA Jared who hadn't even noticed she'd left because he was too busy flirting with a couple of cheerleaders. I was pretty sure he'd had a threesome with them a couple of months ago and wanted another round. Judging by the look on Hayden's face, she'd heard that rumor too.

Her face faltered as she tried her best to look like a Miss America contestant that hadn't just come third. Her brilliant white smile still beamed but curved down just the slightest at the ends. I wasn't surprised. It wasn't like Jared had ever treated her with an ounce of respect or shown more than a mild passing interest in her. One that only intensified when *I* happened to be around.

Jared was bathed in attention. The stereotypical high school quarterback with brilliant blue eyes and a panty-dropping smirk. At least, that was what the girls told me while they drilled me for information. I could have sworn on some days they'd form an orderly queue outside of the locker room just to get a glimpse of him.

I was jealous. Not because of the amount of female attention Jared got. I couldn't care less about that. If they wanted to be used and talked about like an order from a fast-food joint, that was on them. I was jealous because he got so much of Hayden's attention and she didn't seem to care that he was a horndog, prone to sticking his sausage in any patty he could find. Any tiny morsel of attention he threw her way, she lapped up like a greedy dog, waiting patiently for her next fix. That was what killed me. She was so infatuated with him; she couldn't see anyone else.

Infatuation could make you do stupid things.

I should know.

Jared's behavior tonight wasn't even the worst thing I'd seen or heard him do in the last week, let alone tonight. They'd finally made it official. That was what I assumed she was going to tell me a few months ago. I never let her get it out because hearing it would have been too painful. Not after what happened between us in Bethany's room.

I shouldn't have been surprised that she said yes to him so quickly. It was something they'd been flirting with for a little over two years now, but Jared never really seemed keen on the commitment since it wasn't exactly his strong point.

But by finally making that decision and throwing herself at him on the bleachers, he agreed and almost certainly guaranteed that I was driven to an early grave with her choice. She was *so close* to being mine. It should have been us coming to the prom together tonight. Jared didn't deserve her. Listening to his vile locker room talk about her for the last couple of years had been hell. Taking orders from him on the field had been worse. He was a dick. An arrogant asshole that got everything he wanted without working for it. Including the girl I'd been in love with since I was ten.

Her weeping got louder the closer I stepped, and I couldn't wait to wrap her in my arms and make her feel better. This was my chance to talk to her about what happened that night and to tell her how I felt. It was my chance to be the one to finally make her happy. Now that she'd seen that idiot's true colors, maybe she could get over him and see me as more than the friend she used for practice. The way *I'd* seen her since the first day I met her.

I reached out my hand, close enough to touch her shoulder, "Hay-." The loud screeching of a car drowned out my voice as it halted in front of her. She raised her arm to shield herself from the splashing water as her blue dress fluttered in the wind.

"What are you doing here?" She asked between sniffles and sobs as she approached the car. Jared was in the driver's seat, barely looking at her. I stayed deathly still, assuming they couldn't see me lurking in the darkness. Going back into the hall would probably be the smart thing to do, but I wanted to see how they spoke to each other when no one was watching. Maybe it would give me some insight as to why Hayden was so infatuated with him.

The glow of his cigarette darkened as he tipped it outside his car, depositing the used ash beside her dress. "I came for you." He said as he looked up with cold, steely eyes. "You left in a hurry." He deadpanned. He didn't bother asking her why she left because he didn't care, and he knew if he did, she'd have the upper hand. That wasn't how Jared liked his women. He wanted them gorgeous, compliant, and fawning all over him. Hayden fitted that criteria nicely.

She swiped away her tears, straightening her back. "Why would you do that? You seemed busy with Chelsea and Carrie?" She spat out, and a smile danced across my lips.

Has my girl finally got a backbone?

Jared leaned his head back onto the seat, holding the steering wheel with one hand. "We were just talking, Hayden. It's no big deal. You know it's always been you." She shook her head, resolute in her decision. "Hayden, come on, let's talk about this. Let's ditch this party. I don't care about it anyway. I care about you. Let's go so we can talk." He stressed that last word as he gave her a wolfish grin; I dug my fingernails into my skin, trying to think about anything other than what he was implying.

"No, I'm through with this, Jared. You've never been invested in me. You told me you changed. You said you were looking for a girlfriend. You begged me to go on a date with you, yet you've ignored me the whole night and danced with every girl in there but me."

"That's not true."

She laughed bitterly, "No, you're right. You danced with me when you had to. When we won Prom King and Queen. Lucky me." She grabbed the crown, tossing it off her head and into his window.

Jared was speechless. He was stunned into silence which was something I didn't see happen often. "I'm done, Jared." My body nearly burst with happiness. I crouched down further because she'd turned around, ready to go back into the party.

"Hayden," His plea made her stop on her heels. I could see the pain splashed across her face, and I was willing her to ignore him. To go back into the hall and find me. "If I wasn't invested, do you really think I'd be going to Southern Collegiate with you in the Fall?" He relaxed his head back onto the seat with a sigh.

I staggered back. *Southern Collegiate? Together?* That was the first time I'd heard of it. Not that Hayden and I talked about those things. Not anymore. Not since the last time we were alone together, and I screwed it up so royally that I was surprised my parents hadn't changed my name to Prince Party Pooper. I waited for her response like it was my last breath, only she said nothing. "Come on, Hayden." His voice was softer now. "Get in the car. Let's talk." If I didn't know him, I'd think he cared.

It took her all of two seconds to pick up the tulle of her evening gown and walk to the other side of the car. I dipped back further into the darkness, convinced neither one of them noticed my presence. When she sat down in the passenger seat, Jared dropped the cigarette out the window and gave a pointed look in my direction. I wondered if he could see me. If he knew I was out here watching them. She pulled him in for a kiss, and I should have walked away then, but something kept my feet planted in place. He turned back to the window with a smug smile on his face, then winked into the darkness.

Winked.

At me.

That was when all the pieces fell into place. He only came after Hayden because he saw me chase her. He wanted me to see this. He wanted to make sure I knew he had what I could only dream of, and I fell right into the trap.

His engine roared to life; his eyes still focused on me in the darkness as he pulled away. I was left standing there as misty rain fell, easing the stinging pain in my heart. I bent forward, gasping in breath, so I didn't puke all over my shoes. I just watched the girl I was in love with walk away and out of my life. Like she always did. I was never the one she wanted; I was just a means to an end. She trampled all over my body with her spiked heels and didn't even notice the bleeding heart she left behind.

I wanted to kick something to numb the pain radiating through my chest. I was in the exact same place as I always was with her. Friend zoned. The guy who she comes to asking for help. The guy she'd do anything with, just for practice. I'd watched her life from the sidelines these last few years, hoping one day she'd realize I'd been waiting there all along. Turned out I left the field wide open, and Jared snuck right in. I was the sucker of this story. The one who should be embarrassed because she treated me like a piece of gum on the bottom of her shoe. No, actually, it was worse than that. I was that sticky residue left on the bottom of your shoe after you thought you'd cleaned it off. It seemed I didn't learn my lesson. It didn't matter how shitty she treated me; I was still drawn in. She could use me however she wanted, and I'd let her with a wide grin on my face.

Standing up straight, I adjusted my lapels again, noticing that the calla lily on my boutonniere was curling at the sides. "Adam? Are you okay?" Ivy, my supposed date for the evening, asked behind me. As if tonight couldn't get worse. *How long had she'd been standing there? How much had she seen?* By the time I worked up the courage to face her, the answer was sprawled across her face. She'd seen the whole thing.

She knew.

No words were passed. I assumed she would leave me to wallow in my own misery. Only she didn't. She walked right up to me and crushed me in a hug. I had no choice but to hug her back. "I'm sorry, Adam." Her voice was laced with pity and remorse. I didn't know what was worse; that she knew I was in love with someone else or that she let me use her over and over again.

"I am too."

9 781917 205009